Voyager

STEPHEN BAXTER

PHASE SPACE

STORIES FROM THE MANIFOLD AND ELSEWHERE

HarperCollins*Publishers*

Voyager
An imprint of HarperCollins*Publishers*
77–85 Fulham Palace Road,
Hammersmith, London W6 8JB

www.voyager-books.com

Published by HarperCollins*Publishers* 2002
1 3 5 7 9 8 6 4 2

A catalogue record of this book
is available from the British Library

ISBN 0 00 225769 6

Set in Sabon by Palimpsest Book Production Limited,
Polmont, Stirlingshire

Printed and bound in Great Britain by
Clays Ltd, St Ives plc

CONTENTS

PROLOGUE

Kate Manzoni, with Reid Malenfant and Cornelius Taine, stood on Mike's porch. Inside the house, the baby was crying. Baby Michael – son of Mike – Malenfant's grandson.

And in the murky Houston sky, new Moons and Earths burst like silent fireworks, glowing blue or red or yellow, each lit by the light of its own out-of-view sun.

It was just seven days since the failed echo from Alpha Centauri. Malenfant said, 'So what are we looking at?'

'Phase space.' Cornelius seemed coldly excited. 'The phase space of a system is the set of all conceivable states of that system. We're glimpsing the wider phase space of the universe, Malenfant.'

Kate wondered how that remark helped.

No traffic moved on the street. Everybody had gone home, or anyhow found a place to hunker down, until –

Well, until what, Kate? As she had followed this gruesome step-by-step process from the beginning, she had studiously avoided thinking about its eventual outcome: when the wave of unreality, or whatever it was, came washing at last over Earth, over her. It was unimaginable – even more so than her own death. At least after her death she wouldn't know about it; would even that be true after this?

Now there were firebursts in the sky. Human fire.

'Nukes,' Malenfant said softly. 'We're fighting back, by God. Well, what else is there to do but try? God bless America.'

Saranne snapped, 'Come back in and close the damn door.'

The three of them filed meekly inside. Saranne, clutching her baby, stalked around the house's big living room, pulling curtains, as if that would shut it all out. But Kate didn't blame her; it was an understandable human impulse.

Malenfant threw a light switch. It didn't work.

Mike came in from the kitchen. 'No water, no power.' He shrugged. 'I guess that's it.' He moved around the room, setting candles on tables and the fire hearth; their glow was oddly comforting. The living room was littered with pails of water, cans of food. It was as if they were laying up for a snowstorm, Kate thought.

Malenfant said, 'What about the softscreens?'

Mike said, 'Last time I looked, all there was to see was a loop of the President's last message. The one about playing with your children, not letting them be afraid. Try again if you want.'

Nobody had the heart.

The light that flickered around the edges of the curtains seemed to be growing more gaudy.

'Kind of quiet,' Mike said. 'Without the traffic noise –'

The ground shuddered, like a quake, like a carpet being yanked from under them.

Saranne clutched her baby, laden with its useless immortality, and turned on Cornelius. 'All this from your damn fool stunt. Why couldn't you leave well enough alone? We were fine as we were, without all this. You had no right – no right . . .'

'Hush.' Malenfant moved quickly to her, and put an arm around her shuddering shoulders. 'It's okay, honey.' He drew her to the centre of the room and sat with her and the infant on the carpet. He beckoned to the others. 'We should hold onto each other.'

Mike seized on this eagerly. 'Yes. Maybe what you touch stays real – you think?'

They sat in a loose ring. Kate found herself between Malenfant and Saranne. Saranne's hand was moist, Malenfant's as dry as a bone: that astronaut training, she supposed.

'Seven days,' Malenfant said. 'Seven days to unmake the world. Kind of Biblical.'

'A pleasing symmetry,' Cornelius said. His voice cracked.

The candles blew out, all at once. The light beyond the curtains was growing brighter, shifting quickly, slithering like oil.

The baby stopped crying.

'Hold my hand, Malenfant,' Kate whispered.

'It's okay –'

'Just hold my hand.'

DREAMS (1)

MOON-CALF

This time they have a couple of hours to spare before the book-store signing, so Jays and Alice check into their hotel, and take a walk.

Hereford turns out to be a small, picturesque little town like so many crowded into England. It is incredible to Jays that they are only a hundred thirty miles west of London, and yet they've already all but come out of England into Wales. The centre is pretty, with a lot of historical curiosities, some of them incredibly old – 'Nell Gwynne was born here,' Alice points out, 'I thought she was a character from a novel' – but it is a little clogged with traffic.

The older houses are built of old red sandstone, Jays recognizes.

They walk along a river called the Wye. It is a steamy June afternoon – today, in fact, is the longest day of the year – with the sky a high, pale blue dome, and the reflection of the cathedral shines in the water. But the river is running low, and the willows are having trouble dipping to the water surface, and the grass sward is long and yellow, for England is suffering another of its baked-dry summers. The climate is changing here, with Mediterranean weather patterns working their way up from southern Europe. But, Jays remembers, England always looked pale brown or grey, not green, from orbit.

At around five, they walk into the cathedral. A choir of school-boys is practising, and their thin, delicate voices float on the air. There are tourists here, but they move around quietly, looking up. Jays is conscious of the loud click of the toecaps of his boots on the flags.

Alice reads from a guide pamphlet. '"The cathedral is mainly

Norman." Some of it is nine hundred years old, Jays. "Of special interest are the carved stalls, the fourteenth-century Mappa Mundi in the south transept, the chapels, the tombs and the library, with its chained and rare books."' She sniffs. 'I'm becoming acclimatized to all this great age, I think.'

Jays runs a hand over a huge slab of sandstone embedded in a pillar. Somebody has carved a graffito here – 'Dom. Gonsales' – but even this desecration is self-evidently ancient.

'Nice rock?' Alice asks dryly.

Jays grins as they walk on. 'Actually, yes. This is Devonian sandstone –'

'Don't tell me. When dinosaurs ruled the Earth.'

'Hell, no. Much older than *that*. This stuff is about four hundred million years old, Alice. We're on the coast of the Old Red Sandstone Continent. The rock here was laid down in lakes and deltas; most of southern England was covered by ocean. There were plants on land, but no animals yet . . .'

She nods as if listening, but she has found a small book stall, and is starting to browse.

Jays scratches the frosting of white that is all that is left of his hair. He is now seventy years old, fit and California-tanned. For twenty-five years, since his Apollo flight, his one and only space-flight, he has been a bore about the Moon. And now his interest in geology is making him a bore about the Earth, too.

It is kind of heroic, he thinks, to be dull on two planets.

Alone, he wanders a little further. He tries to fix the church in his memory.

Most of the great English cathedrals stopped developing during the Reformation in the sixteenth century, when Henry VIII took his country away from the Church of Rome. Compared to the great churches in Catholic countries like Spain or Italy, swamped by centuries of ornamentation, English cathedrals have a certain austere class, he has decided.

He comes to a small, rather ugly side chapel. It isn't roped off, but there are no tourists here. The walls are much darker than the rest of the church, and that, together with the filtering of the light by a couple of niggardly slit-windows, adds to a sense of gloom and age.

Jays, on impulse, steps inside. There are a couple of pews before a small, nondescript altar, and a stand of unlit candles. There is dust on the pews. A paper sign, stuck to the wall with putty, tells him this is Bishop Godwin's Chapel, XVII Century. So this chapel is older than his nation. The windows are filled with panes of stained glass, which show what look, oddly, like Chinese scenes.

He runs his hand over the wall. Maybe the dark coloration is candle black, he thinks. But his fingers come away clean, save for a little dust.

He decides to apply a little geology. It looks more like an igneous or metamorphic rock than a sedimentary, like a sandstone. It is dark and isn't coarse-grained, so that makes it a basalt. And there are fine gas bubbles embedded in the surface. A vesicular basalt, then, a lava that has cooled on the surface of the Earth.

He looks around. The chapel's walls are all constructed of the dark basalt.

A lava, here in the heart of Britain?

He looks around, but there is no leaflet to explain the chapel's history, nor anybody to ask about it.

Alice is still in the bookshop, leafing through a pamphlet.

'Hell of a thing,' he says.

She smiles abstractedly. 'Look at this. It's about you.' She passes him the little book.

It is called *The Man In The Moone, or a Discourse of a Voyage Thither by Domingo Gonsales, the Speedy Messenger.*

The story is about how a man called Gonsales trains swans to carry him through the air. Twenty-five of them, each attached to a pulley, save him from a shipwreck. But the swans hibernate on the Moon, and carry Gonsales there . . .

And so on. It is a seventeenth-century tale, he sees, reprinted by some local enthusiast. The kind of stuff they now call proto-science fiction.

Domingo Gonsales. He tells her about the graffito he saw.

She takes the book back. 'Maybe it was a fan. Or a literary critic. What did you want to tell me?'

He describes the lava walls to her. 'It's just it doesn't make any sense, geologically.'

She pulls a face. '*Geology,*' she says. She has a broad, high-cheekboned face, highlighted blond hair and intense blue eyes. At forty-five, she still turns heads. In a way he is glad she is getting a little older. It makes him less open to the accusation that he's picked up a trophy wife, after Mary dumped him. And Alice has turned out to be one hell of a PA and agent, as his modest literary career has taken off.

'Remember what I told you. You can tell the geology of an area just by looking at the old buildings there . . .'

Once, most of Britain was covered by a shallow ocean, which deposited gigantic chalk layers. But then Britain tipped up, and the ice came, scraping most of the chalk off the top half of the island. Now, as you travel south from Scotland, you traverse younger and younger landscapes: billion-year-old gabbros and granites and basalts in Scotland, belts of successively younger sedimentaries as you come down through England, until you reach the youngest of all, the marine Pleistocene clays and sands around London, less than sixty million years old.

His signing tour has taken in Aberdeen, Edinburgh, Preston, Manchester, Birmingham, Peterborough, as well as London. He's insisted on taking a train or a hired car everywhere, never flying, so he could see the old buildings – churches, houses, pubs, even railway stations – which stand like geological markers, constructed of the native rock.

'Anyhow that's why the basalt in that chapel is so odd,' he says.

'If it is basalt.'

'Sure it is. Come on, Mary; I know basalts. All the damn Moon rocks we picked up were basalts. It's just unusual for such an old building to feature such displaced materials. They didn't have the haulage capability we have now . . .'

She shrugs. 'They built Stonehenge from that rock from Wales, and that's a lot older. It's just a few tons of some Scottish stone.'

'But what the hell's it doing here, in the Godwin Chapel?'

'Godwin?' She frowns at that, and looks again at the book she is holding. According to the jacket *The Man In The Moone* was written by Francis Godwin, Bishop of Hereford, in the seventeenth century. 'How about that,' she says. 'You suppose it is the same guy?'

He shrugs. 'We could check.'

She reaches for her purse. 'Anyhow this settles it. I thought nine pounds is a little steep for forty-three pages, but I guess this book has been waiting here for us to find it.'

She pays for the book, and he wants to go back to the chapel, but there is no time left before the signing.

So, Colonel Holland, why 'Jays'?

It is a question he's answered a hundred times before, but what the hell. 'It was my sister. When she was a kid she couldn't say "James" right. It came out "Jays". It stuck as a nickname.'

8

Is it true you changed your name by deed poll to Jays?

'No. And it's not true I trademarked it, either . . .'

Laughter.

The little lecture room in back of the book store is maybe half-full, rows of faces turned to him like miniature moons, filled with pleasant interest. He decides he is going to enjoy the event, even if he feels intimidated by the giant show cards his publisher has sent over from London – '*Rocky Worlds* – A Vision of the Future by a Man Who's Been There . . .'

Why the title?

'Something that occurred to me on the Moon,' he says. 'Maybe Earth is unique. But the Moon isn't, even in our solar system. The Galaxy has got to be full of small, rocky, airless worlds like the Moon. Right? I was only a quarter million miles from Earth, but if I looked away from Charlie and the LM, away from the Earth, if I shielded my eyes so I could see some stars, I could have been anywhere in the Galaxy – hell, anywhere in the universe . . .'

The audience move, subtly, showing he has hit the wonder nerve. Even though he's cheating a little. He had no time for such reflection on the Moon; such insights have come from polishing those memories in his head like jewels, until he can't tell any more what was fresh observation on the Moon, or the maundering of an old man.

Sitting here, his hands flapping like birds in front of him in his nervousness, he knows how he comes across: he is a retiring, almost inarticulate man – hell, he is just a pilot after all – who has been thrust forward by history, and has made himself articulate.

Your books are full of geology. But you weren't trained in geology for your Apollo flight.

That isn't quite true. They had some training from geologists attached to the project – they'd be taken to Meteor Crater, Arizona, or some such place, and told to *look* – they had to try to be geologists, at least by proxy, in a wilderness no true scientist had ever trodden, and maybe never would.

But in the end it came down to completing the checklist, and wrestling with unexpectedly balky equipment, and anyhow the LM put them down on a *mare* which turned out to be a dull lava plain . . .

. . . *a plain that shone, tan brown and grey, beneath a black sky, with a surface that crunched beneath his feet like fresh snow,*

9

rock flour impact-shattered by three billion years of bombard-
ment, pocked with craters of all sizes from yards across to
pinpricks, and he remembers how he pushed his fingers into the
surface, monkey fingers swathed in white pressure-suit gloves, but
he came up against stiff resistance a few inches in where the impacts
tamped down the regolith to a greater density than any compacting
machine could achieve, and when he pulled out his hand his glove
was stained coal black . . .

But such moments were rare, as he spent three days bouncing
across that bright, sandy surface with his commander in the Lunar
Rover, wisecracking and whistling and cussing; for the point of
the journey was not the science of the Moon, of course, nor even
the political stuff that pushed them so far, but simply to get through
the flight with a completed checklist and without a screw-up, so
you were in line for another . . .

But for him, there never *had* been another. After returning home
he was caught up in the PR hoopla, stuff he'd hated, stuff that
led him to drink a hell of a lot more than he should. And by the
time he'd come out of *that* he found himself without a wife and
out of NASA, and too old to go back to the Air Force.

It was a time he thinks of as his Dark Age.

But he kept in touch with the studies of the Moon rocks he
brought back. It prodded in Jays a lingering interest in geology.
He took a couple of night classes, and has done a few field trips.
For a while it was just a way to fill up time between Amex commer-
cials and daytime talk shows, but he has soon come to know a
lot more about his home planet than he ever did about the lonely
little world he, and only eleven other guys in all history, have
visited. Hell of a thing.

And, gradually, the geology stuff has hooked his imagination.

Death Valley, for instance: if you manage to look beyond the
tourist stuff about bauxite miners and mule trains, what you
have there is a freshwater lake, teeming with wildlife and flora,
that has gotten cut off from the sea. Over twenty thousand years
the lake dwindles and becomes more and more saline; the trees
and bushes die off and the topsoil washes away, exposing the
bedrock, and the lakes' inhabitants are forced to adapt to the
salt or die . . .

His first short story is slight, a tale of a human tribe struggling
to survive on the edge of such a lake.

Nods, from the sf enthusiasts in the audience. 'The Drying'.

It sold for a couple hundred bucks to one of the science-fiction magazines, he suspects for curiosity over his name alone. A novel, painfully tapped into a primitive word processor, followed soon after. He hadn't read sf since he was a kid, and now he rediscovered that sense of time and space as a huge, pitiless landscape that impelled him towards space in the first place.

A couple of books later his sales dwindled, when the celebrity angle wore off. But then they started to pick up again, and he is pleased with that, because he suspects people are starting to buy his fiction for itself, not because of *him*.

He doesn't say all this to his audience, however. But they probably know it. His life is a matter of public record, after all.

Are you arguing for a return to space, in your books?

'I guess so. I think we need to be out there. You don't need to know much geology to see that . . . In a few thousand years the ice will be back, scraping the whole damn place down to the bedrock again, and I don't know how we're proposing to cope with that. And then there are other hazards, further out . . .'

The next big rock. The dinosaur killer.

'It's on its way, maybe wandering in from the Belt right now, with all our names written on it . . . But I'm not propagandizing here. This is just fiction, right? I want your beer money, not your vote.'

Laughter.

Do you feel bitter about the big shut-down that happened after Apollo? Do you blame the Confucians, or the eunuchs?

That question, from a little guy in a battered anorak, throws him. But he remembers that odd Chinese-looking design in the stained glass in that peculiar chapel, and he wants to pursue the point. But the little guy starts to lecture about the Ming Dynasty, and the bookstore owner moves them on.

After an hour or so, the owner winds up the q-and-a. He signs maybe a dozen copies of the new book, and some stock, and a couple of battered paperback editions of the older stuff.

Before dinner, the store owner takes them to a pub called the *Wellsian*. 'I thought you'd like to see this . . .' Bizarrely, it is an H.G. Wells theme pub, with mock-ups of the Hollywood Time Machine and Martian tripods stuck over vaguely Victorian decor. There is a bar menu which, though containing the usual bland rubber-chicken options, nevertheless has each dish referenced to

Wells: 'H.G. Tagliatelle', or 'Herbert George's Chicken Kiev', and so on.

He has his picture taken under an engraved line from *First Men In The Moon*, about a Moon-calf – a word which, the bookstore guy tells him, is actually an old English word meaning something like blockhead, and which gives him an opportunity for more gentle joshing.

Alice seems to be trying not to laugh. 'It's the weirdest place I've ever seen,' she says. 'H.G. Wells had nothing to do with Hereford.'

'Nor does basalt.'

Jays accepts a diet soda. The little guy from the q-and-a, who'd talked about China, is here, cradling a pint of some flat English beer. His name, it turns out, is Percy, he is aged maybe fifty, and he works with the Cathedral's collection of rare books. His clothes have a vaguely musty smell, not necessarily unpleasant. When he speaks his voice is something of a bray, and the other locals tend to look away and change the subject; he is evidently something of a local eccentric.

Nevertheless he isn't bugging Jays, and he seems to know all about China. Jays lets him open up about his eunuch reference.

Once, says Percy, the Chinese led the world in technology: they had printing, gunpowder, the compass, in some cases centuries before Europe. At the time of the early Ming Dynasty, in the early fifteenth century, they even went exploring.

They built fifteen-hundred-ton 'treasure ships', each big enough to carry five hundred men. Chinese explorers rounded southern Asia to Bengal, Ceylon and even reached the east coast of Africa in 1420, prefiguring the Portuguese expeditions by fifty years. The ships brought home exotic novelties – people, animals, plants – and struck terror wherever they landed.

'The great voyages were led by Admiral Zheng-Ho,' says Percy, 'who was a eunuch. But in 1436 a new emperor came to the throne, called Zheng Dung. He cut the building of ships, the construction of armaments and so forth. The Navy fell apart, and China was isolated from the rest of the world, until the barbarians from Europe came sailing up four centuries later. There are obvious resonances for our times –'

'Yeah,' growls Jays.

'The cause of it all was conflict between the Confucian scholars who ran the imperial bureaucracy, and the Grand Eunuchs of the

Imperial Court. The eunuchs' voyages were seen as a threat to the bureaucracy. But the Confucians were in charge of educating the emperor and they had played a long game. They had convinced the young Zheng Dung that China was self-sufficient, and didn't need to deal with the barbarian lands at its rim. So they blocked technological development, to maintain their feudal power . . .'

Some of the other fans, sensing the implicit approval Jays is bestowing on Percy, are edging closer. They start to speculate, as Jays has learned fans will do, about what-if parallel universes in which the Chinese kept going. Perhaps Francis Drake would have faced an Armada of Chinese treasure-ships. Perhaps Zheng-Ho might have reached America before Columbus. And so on.

Jays asks Percy what happened to Zheng-Ho. He shrugs, almost spilling the beer he has barely sipped. 'There are stories that he went off to the hinterland and tried to keep exploring, with technologies out of the grasp of the bureaucrats. China is a big country, after all; there was room for such things. And room for a lot of legends. Zheng had followers, who are supposed to have kept up the work after his death, until the Confucians closed them down. It's probably all apocryphal. Man-carrying rockets, for instance.'

There is general laughter at this, and there is more speculative chatter about a Chinese space programme of the fifteenth or sixteenth centuries.

Jays is reminded of what he once knew of the history of rocketry. The Chinese developed the first rockets around the year 1000 A.D., under the Sung Dynasty: the versions that leaked to Europe via the usual trade routes were just crude affairs, gunpowder-filled bamboo or pasteboard tubes with little power and unpredictable trajectories . . . Still, reflects Jays, in the heart of China, there might have been five centuries of development of this technology by Zheng-Ho's day.

There is also, it seems, a Chinese legend local to Hereford: of a sixteenth-century traveller from Spain who came here with what sounds like a goods caravan, laden with exotic jewellery and herbs, all, he claimed, from the heart of mysterious Cathay.

Oddly, he also brings rocks.

The tale is recorded in the Godwin Chapel's stained-glass window. And some of the locals remember the incident by keeping up an old tradition of a festival held on the fifteenth of August, celebrating the day a Chinese goddess was supposed to drink a magic elixir and fly to the Moon. There are invitations for Jays to come back on the fifteenth of August, a couple of months away.

Alice has finished her white-wine spritzer, and is discreetly plucking at his sleeve.

They make their farewells and apologies, and escape into the cooling air of the evening.

In the pub garden, a wood-fire barbecue is burning, wood to make this cultural import seem more traditionally English, he guesses. The smell of the wood takes him right back, across twenty-five years . . .

. . . *after the first Moonwalk, when the oxygen had rushed back into the aluminium balloon that was the LM's cabin, and both of them were covered in grime, when Charlie took off his helmet, and Jays took a picture of his smiling, lined, bearded face, and then of the area outside, the flag and equipment and the parked Rover and footprints everywhere, footprints that might last a million years, and when he took his own helmet off, there was a pungent smell, the odour of wood-smoke, or maybe of gunpowder: it is the smell of Moondust, slow-burning in oxygen from Earth . . .*

But it is time for dinner with the publisher's rep, and they walk on.

In bed, Jays glances through the Godwin book. It is a comedy – he guesses – lacking the gloss of modern science fiction. But some of the ideas seem reasonably sophisticated, for its time. The good Bishop was a little mixed up about the size of the stars, but his universe was Copernican – with the planets circling the sun – and he got gravity more or less right, with references to different gravity on the Earth and Moon, weightlessness between worlds, and the problems of re-entry to Earth's atmosphere.

Jays has read, or rather discarded, some modern hard sf which contains worse bloopers.

He describes all this to Alice. 'It's hardly a traveller's guide,' he says, 'but –'

She takes the book from him and kisses him on the cheek. 'You're very sweet, but very transparent. You'd love it to be true, wouldn't you?'

'What?'

'I could see what you were thinking, in that ridiculous pub. Maybe the Chinese went to the Moon, in the fifteenth century.

14

Maybe the story somehow reached England – here, Hereford – perhaps through the traveller they talked about.'

'And maybe Bishop Godwin wrote it up.'

She leafs through the book. 'But why not just tell the story straight? Why all this stuff about swans? Why not just write about the Chinese admiral and his rockets?'

He shrugs. 'Because he couldn't be straight. Just as I write science fiction, rather than documentary.' It is true. His autobiography was actually ghosted. They have had discussions like this before, prompted by reviews and analysis of his work.

'The analogy doesn't hold,' she says. 'You did something extraordinary, something no human had done before. And you weren't trained to describe it. Not even to observe. No wonder you write your books. It's your way of working it out in your own head.'

He shrugs. 'It was that, or find Jesus like the other guys. Anyway, my point is nobody would have believed Godwin. Think of the context of the times. Nobody believed Copernicus, for God's sake. Maybe Godwin didn't believe it himself.'

'*I* don't believe it. Listen to this. Gonsales finds an inhabited Moon, and the creatures live in a Utopia and are superior to us. Of course. And they weed out any who fall short of the mark, and throw them off to Earth . . . "The ordinary vent for them is a certain high hill in the North of America, whose people I can easily believe to be wholly descended from them . . ."'

He laughs. 'Damn these Brits. Ungrateful even then. What happens to Gonsales in the end?'

Alice flicks through the book. 'The Moon prince gives him jewels, he sets off for Earth with his swans . . . and lands in China, where they lock him up as a magician.' She throws the book down. 'China. And I hope you're not going to read anything into *that*. I'm going to throw this damn book away. You're obsessed, Jays. You look for Moon stories that don't exist. I don't blame you. But it's the truth. You're a Moon-calf . . .'

She turns her light out.

It is many hours before he can sleep.

He has to go to the bathroom in the middle of the night. It is an old-man's thing. He tries to float out of bed, and falls to the floor, heavy on the carpet. This has happened before.

*   *   *

The next day is their last in England, and they have to take a train into London, then the Tube back out to Heathrow.

Jays gets up early. Without waking Alice, he slips on his track suit and sneakers, and runs out into empty streets. Squat electric carts are delivering milk, whirring along the streets, making a noise that reminds him of the prototype Lunar Rovers he saw under test at Boeing.

He jogs until the air, already hot, is whistling in his throat.

He reaches the cathedral. It is locked up, and he is disappointed, but he discovers he can work his way around the outside. He quickly finds the Godwin Chapel. It is hard to miss, a dark, grimy encrustation on the cool sandstone of the cathedral.

He runs his hand over the exterior of the rock. It is heavily weathered, of course, and encrusted with lichen. But its vesicular nature is easy to confirm, in the bright morning light.

He knows that lunar basalts, formed when the great primordial impact basins were flooded with lava, have a lot in common with terrestrial lavas – they are mostly feldspar, pyroxene, olivine and ilmenite – but there are key differences too. Lunar rocks possess native iron, for instance. They have been subjected to shock damage from micrometeorite impact, and to radiation damage from solar wind and cosmic rays. They have some trace elements, such as hydrogen, carbon and nitrogen, implanted there by the solar wind. They contain no water at all . . .

He wishes he could take a sample. But he has no tools. And who would run the assay for him? He works his way around the chapel, running his hands over the surface.

He finds that a chunk of the chapel wall, a fist-sized pebble, has broken away from one corner. The pebble is just lying in the grass.

He cannot tell if this is frost damage, or perhaps vegetative, or some minor piece of vandalism.

Guiltily, he slips the pebble into his pocket.

On the train to London, with the two of them facing each other surrounded by luggage, he toys with the pebble.

'Scottish basalt,' Alice says.

'Sure.'

'You should be ashamed.' She is laughing, but he senses she means it. 'If every American tourist came away with trophies there'd be none of England left . . .'

He knows she is right. He does not want to keep this piece. She calls him a Moon-calf again.

He waits until she has gone to the buffet for a fresh coffee. He glances around; nobody can see him.

He has a full can of diet soda. He rests his rock, on a newspaper, on the tiny British Rail table that is fixed to the wall before him. He smashes the rock with the base of the can; the rock cracks open.

As the interior is exposed to the air for the first time, there is a smell like wood-smoke.

He breathes it in for a few seconds. Then he brushes the fragments of rock into the palm of his hand, and dumps it out the window. The rock is scattered along the track, and lost; he brushes the last grains from his hands.

When Alice returns, London is approaching, modern suburbs crowding out the ancient English landscape. They start to talk about the flight home, checking tickets and terminals and passports.

EARTHS

OPEN LOOPS

It began, in fact, with a supernova: thus, from the beginning, it was a causal chain shaped by stupendous violence.

The star was a blue supergiant, twenty times the mass of Earth's sun, fifty thousand times as bright. It had formed a mere million years ago.

Nevertheless there was life here.

It had come drifting on the interstellar winds from older, more stable systems, and taken root on worlds which cautiously skirted the central fire.

But the hydrogen fuel in the star's fusing core was already exhausted.

The core, clogged with helium ash, began to burn that ash itself, helium nuclei fusing to carbon. And the carbon compacted to neon, the neon to oxygen . . . At last iron nuclei snowed, inert, on the centre of the star.

The core's free-fall implosion took fractions of a second. The star's outer layers were suddenly suspended over an effective vacuum. They collapsed inwards, the infalling layers crashing onto the rigid core remnant, and rebounded violently. The reflected shock wave was hurled out of the centre of the star, dragging away the star's outer layers with it . . .

For a week, the dying star outshone its Galaxy.

For forty years the expanding shell of matter travelled, preceded by a sleet of electromagnetic radiation: gamma rays, X rays, visible light. A human eye might have seen a brilliant blue-white star grow suddenly tremendously luminous, fifty times as bright as the Moon, as bright as all the other stars in the sky combined.

But Earth did not exist, nor even, yet, the sun. The garish light of the supernova washed, instead, over the thin tendrils of a gas cloud: cold, inert, stable.

And in any event no human telescope could have detected, rushing before the light storm, a single, delicate, spidery silhouette.

A fleeing craft.

Scale: Exp 1

In the confines of *Ehricke*'s airlock Oliver Greenberg put on his gloves and snapped home the connecting rings. Then he lifted his helmet over his head.

The ritual of the suit checklist was oddly comforting. In fact, it was just the old Shuttle EVA routine he'd undergone a half-dozen times, in an orbiter-class airlock just like this.

But the *Ehricke* was no dinged-up old orbiter, and right now he was far from low Earth orbit.

He felt his heart hammer under his suit's layers.

Mike Weissman, on the hab-module's upper deck, was monitoring him. 'EV1, you have a go for depress.'

Greenberg turned the depress switch on the control panel. 'Valve to zero.' He heard a distant hiss. 'Let's motor.' He twisted the handle of the outer airlock hatch and pushed.

Oliver Greenberg gazed out into space.

He moved out through the airlock's round hatchway. There was a handrail and two slide wires that ran the length of the curving hull, and Greenberg tethered himself to them. It was a routine he'd practised a hundred times in the sims at Houston, a dozen times in LEO. There was no reason why now should be any different.

No reason, except that the Earth wasn't where it should be.

In LEO, the Earth had been a bright floor beneath him all the time, as bright as a tropical sky. But out here, Earth was all of five million kilometres away, reduced to a blue button the size of a dime three or four arms-lengths away, and Greenberg was suspended in a huge three-hundred-sixty-degree planetarium just studded with stars, stars everywhere . . .

Everywhere, that is, except for one corner of the sky blocked by a vaguely elliptical shadow, sharp-edged, one rim picked out by the sun.

It was Ra-Shalom: Greenberg's destination.

He was looking along the length of the *Ehricke*'s hab module.

It was a tight cylinder, just ten metres long and seven wide, home to four crew for this year-long jaunt. The outer hull was crammed with equipment, sensors and antennae clustered over powder-white and gold insulating blankets. At the back of the hab module he could see the bulging upper domes of the big cryogenic fuel tanks, and when he turned the other way there was the Earth-return module, an Apollo-sized capsule stuck sideways under the canopy of the big aerobrake.

The whole thing was just a collection of cylinders and boxes and canopies, thrown together as if at random, a ropy piece of shit.

But in a vessel such as this, Americans planned to sail to Mars.

Not Oliver Greenberg, though.

One small step time, he thought.

He pulled himself tentatively along the slide wire and made his way to the PMU station, on the starboard side of the hab module. The Personal Manoeuvring Unit was a big backpack shaped like the back and arms of an armchair, with foldout head- and leg-rests on a tubular frame. Greenberg ran a quick check of the PMU's systems. It was old Shuttle technology, cannibalized from the Manned Manoeuvring Units that had enabled crew to shoot around orbiter cargo bays. But today, it was being put to a use its designers never dreamed of.

He turned around, and backed into the PMU.

'*Ehricke*, EV1,' he said. 'Suit latches closed.'

'Copy that.'

He pulled the PMU's arms out around him and closed his gloved hands around the hand-controllers on the end of the arms. He unlatched the folded-up body frame. He rested his neck against the big padded rest, and settled his feet against the narrow foot-pads at the bottom of the frame, so he was braced. Today's EVA was just a test reconnaissance, but a full field expedition to Ra could last all of eight hours; the frame would help him keep his muscle movements down, and so reduce resource wastage.

Greenberg released his tethers. A little spring-loaded gadget gave him a shove in the back, gentle as a mother's encouraging pat, and he floated away from the bulkhead.

. . . Suddenly he didn't have hold of anything, and he was *falling*.

Oh, shit, he thought.

He had become an independent spacecraft. The spidery frame of the PMU occulted the dusting of stars around him.

He tested out his propulsion systems.

He grasped his right-hand controller, and pushed it left. There was a soft tone in his helmet as the thruster worked; he saw a faint sparkle of exhaust crystals, to his right. In response to the thrust, he tipped a little to the left. He had four big fuel tanks on his back, and twenty-four small reaction control-system nozzles. In fact he had two systems, a heavy-duty hot gas bipropellant system – kerosene and nitric acid – for the big orbital changes he would have to make to reach Ra, and a cold-gas nitrogen thruster for close control at the surface of the rock.

When he started moving, he just kept on going, until he stopped himself with another blip of his thrusters.

Greenberg tipped himself up so he was facing Ra-Shalom, with the *Ehricke* behind him.

'*Ehricke*, I'm preparing to head for Ra.'

'We copy, Oliver.'

He fired his kerosene thruster and felt a small, firm shove in the small of his back. Computer graphics started to scroll across the inside of his face plate, updating burn parameters. He was actually changing orbit here, and he would have to go through a full rendezvous procedure to reach Ra. That was what had gotten him this job, in fact. Greenberg had flown several of the missions which docked a Shuttle orbiter with the old Mir, and then with the Space Station. He had even been chief astronaut, for a while.

Then the VentureStar had outdated his piloting skills, and he was grounded, at age fifty.

NASA was full of younger guys now, preparing for the LMP, the Lunar-Mars Programme that was at the heart of NASA's current strategy, inspired by the evidence the sample-return probes had come up with of life on Mars.

This mission, a year-long jaunt to the near-Earth asteroid Ra-Shalom, was a shakedown test of the technologies that would be needed to get to Mars. Ra provided an intermediate goal, between lunar flights of a few weeks and the full Mars venture that would take years, setting major challenges in terms of life-support loop closure and systems reliability.

But there was also, he was told, good science to be done here.

Not that he gave a shit about that.

He was only here, tinkering with plumbing and goddamn pea plants, because nobody else in the Office had wanted to be distracted from the competition for places on the Mars flights to come.

The angle of the sun was changing, and the slanting light changed Ra from a flat silhouette to a potato-shaped rock in space, fat and solid. Ra's surface was crumpled, split by ravines, punctured by craters of all sizes. There was one big baby that must have been a kilometre across, its walls spreading around the cramped horizon.

The rock was more than three kilometres long, spinning on its axis once every twenty hours. It was as black as coal dust. Ra-Shalom was a C-type asteroid – carbonaceous, fat with light elements, coated by carbon deposits. It had probably formed at the chilly outer rim of the asteroid belt. Ra was like a folded-over chunk of the Moon, its beat-up surface a record of this little body's dismal, violent history.

At a computer prompt, he prepared for his final burn. 'Ready for Terminal Initiation.'

'Copy that, Oliver.'

One last time the kerosene thrusters fired, fat and full.

'Okay, EV1, *Ehricke*. Coming up to your hundred-metre limit.'

'Copy that.'

He came to a dead stop, a hundred metres from the surface of Ra-Shalom. The asteroid's complex, battered surface was like a wall in front of him. He felt no tug of gravity – Ra's G was less than a thousandth of Earth's – it would take him more than two minutes to fall in to the surface from here, compared to a few seconds on Earth.

He was comfortable. The suit was quiet, warm, safe. He could hear the whir of his backpack's twenty-thousand rpm fan. But he missed the squeaks and pops on the radio which he got used to in LEO as he drifted over UHF stations on the ground.

He blipped his cold-gas thrusters, and drifted forward. This wasn't like coming in for a landing; it was more like walking towards a cliff face, which bulged gently out at him, its coal-like blackness oppressive. He made out more detail, craters overlaid on craters down to the limit of visibility.

He tweaked his trajectory once more, until he was heading for the centre of a big crater, away from any sharp-edged crater walls or boulder fields. Then he just let himself drift in, at a metre a second. If he used the thrusters any more he risked raising dust clouds that wouldn't settle. There were four little landing legs at the corners of his frame; they popped out now, little spear-shaped penetrators designed to dig into the surface and hold him there.

The close horizon receded, and the cliff face turned into a wall that cut off half the universe.

He collided softly with Ra-Shalom.

The landing legs, throwing up dust, dug into the regolith with a grind that carried through the PMU structure. The dust hung about him. Greenberg was stuck here, clinging to the wall inside his PMU frame like a mountaineer to a rock face.

He turned on his helmet lamp. Impact glass glimmered.

Unexpectedly, wonder pricked him. Here was the primordial skin of Ra-Shalom, as old as the solar system, just centimetres before his face. He reached out and pushed his gloved hand into the surface, a monkey paw probing.

The surface was thick with regolith: a fine rock flour, littered with glassy agglutinates, asteroid rock shattered by aeons of bombardment. His fingers went in easily enough for a few centimetres – he could feel the stuff crunching under his pressure, as if he was digging into compacted snow – but then he came up against much more densely packed material, tamped down by the endless impacts.

He closed his fist and pulled out his hand. A cloud of dust came with it, gushing into his face like a hail of meteorites. He looked at the material he'd dug out. There were a few bigger grains here, he saw: it was breccia, bits of rock smashed up in multiple impacts, welded back together by impact glass. There was no gravity to speak of; the smallest movement sent the fragments drifting out of his palm.

His glove, pristine white a moment ago, was already caked black with dust. He knew the blackness came from carbon-rich compounds. There were hydrates too: water, locked up in the rock, just drifting around out here. In fact rocks like Ra were the only significant water deposits between Earth and Mars. It might prove possible to use the rock's resources to close the loops of mass and energy circulating in *Ehricke*'s life support, even on this preliminary jaunt.

Ra could probably even support some kind of colony, off in the future. So it was said.

Greenberg had always preferred to leave the sci-fi stuff to the wackos in the fringe study groups in NASA, and focus on his checklist. Still, it was a nice thought.

He allowed himself a moment to savour this triumph. Maybe he would never get to Mars. But he was, after all, the first human to touch the surface of another world since Apollo 17.

He pushed his hand back into the pit he'd dug, ignoring the fresh dust he raised.

The cloud was scattered, thin and dark, across ten light years. It was gas laced with dust grains – three-quarters hydrogen, the rest helium, some trace elements – visible only to any observers as a shadow against the stars.

When the supernova's gale of heavy particles washed over it, the cloud's stability was lost. It began to fall in on itself.

In a ghostly inverse of the inciting supernova explosion, the core of the cloud heated up as material rained in upon it, its rotation speeding up, an increasingly powerful electromagnetic field whipping through the outer debris. The core began to glow, first at infra-red wavelengths, and then in visible light.

It was the first sunlight.

Scale: Exp 2

Oliver Greenberg was bored.

He was actually glad to get the call from Gita Weissman about the balky rock splitter in Shaft Seven, even though the lost time would mean they weren't going to make quota this month.

At least it made a change from the usual CELSS problems, CELSS for closed environment and life-support systems, a term nobody used except him any more. Even after a century, nobody had persuaded a pea plant to grow nice straight roots in micro-gravity, and the loss from the mass loops in the hydroponic tanks continued at a stubborn couple of per cent a month, despite the new generation of supercritical water oxidizers they used to reduce their solid wastes.

It's still about pea plants and plumbing, he thought dismally.

He started clambering into his skinsuit, hauling the heavy fabric over his useless legs.

He took a last glance around the glass-wall displays of his hab module. It shocked him when the displays showed him he was the only one of Ra's two thousand inhabitants on the surface.

Well, hell, it suited him out here, even if it had stranded him in this lonely assignment, monitoring the systems that watched near-Ra space. Most of the inhabitants of Ra had been born up here, and lived their lives encased in the fused-regolith walls of old mine shafts. They didn't know any better.

Greenberg, though, preferred to keep a weather eye on the stars, unchanged since his Iowa boyhood. He even liked seeing Earth swim past on its infrequent close approaches, like a blue liner on a black ocean, approaching and receding. It made him nostalgic. Even if he couldn't go home any more.

Suited up, he shut down the glass-wall displays. The drab green walls of the hab module were revealed, with their equipment racks and antique bathroom and galley equipment and clumsy-looking up-down visual cues. This was just an old Space Station module, dragged out here and stuck to the surface of Ra-Shalom, covered over with a couple of metres of regolith. He was tethered in the rim shadow of Helin Crater, the place he'd landed on that first jaunt in the *Ehricke*. And that had been all of a hundred years ago, my God.

He pushed his way through the diaphragm lock set in the floor of his hab module. He was at the top of one of Shaft Two, one of the earliest they'd dug out, with those first clumsy drill-blast-muck miners. It was a rough cylinder ten metres across, lined with regolith glass and hung with lamps and tethers; it descended beneath him, branching and curving.

He grabbed hold of a wall spider, told it his destination, and let it haul him on down into the tunnel along its stay wires.

Thus, clinging to his metal companion, he descended into the heart of Ra-Shalom.

His legs dangled uselessly, and so he set his suit to tuck them up to his chest. He was thinking of taking the surgeons' advice, and opting for amputation. What the hell. He was a hundred and fifty years old, give or take; he wasn't going to start complaining.

Anyhow, apart from that, the surgeons were preserving him pretty well. They were treating him to a whole cocktail of growth hormones and DHEA and melatonin treatments and beta-carotene supplements, not to mention telomere therapy and the glop those little nano-machines had painted on the surface of his shrivelled-up brain to keep him sharp.

These guys were good at keeping you alive.

This asteroid was *small*. A stable population was important, and a heavy investment in training needed a long payback period to be effective. So the birth rate was low, and a lot of research was directed to human longevity.

He understood the logic. But still, he missed the sound of children playing, every now and again. The youngsters here didn't seem to mind that, which made them a little less than human, in his view. But maybe that was part of the adjustment humans were having to make, as they learned to live off-Earth.

In fact he missed his own kids, his daughters, even though, astonishingly, they were now both old ladies themselves.

The surgeons had even managed to repair some of the cumulative microgravity damage he'd suffered over the years. For instance, his skeletal and cardiac muscles were deeply atrophied. Until they found a way to stabilize it, his bone calcium had continued to wash out in his urine, at a half per cent a month. At last, the surgeons said, the inner spongy bone, the trabeculae, had vanished altogether, without hope of regeneration.

He never had been too conscientious about his time in the treadmills. It had left him a cripple, on Earth.

So, at age eighty, he'd left Earth.

Even then they had been closing down the cans – the early stations starting with Mir and the Space Station, that had relied completely on materials brought up from Earth. In retrospect it just didn't make sense to haul material up from Earth at great expense, when it was already *here,* just floating around in the sky, in rocks like Ra.

So he'd come back to come out to Ra-Shalom, the place that had made him briefly famous.

He suspected the surgeons liked to have him around, as a control experiment. The youngsters were heavily treated from birth, up here, to enable them to endure a lifetime of microgravity. Not a one of them could land on Earth, of course, or even Mars. But not too many of them showed a desire to do any such thing.

The wall spider, scuttling busily, brought him to the mine face, the terminus of Shaft Seven. It was a black, dusty wall, like a coal face. There was dust everywhere, floating in the air.

There were five or six people here, in their brightly coloured skinsuits, scraping their way around the stalled miner. Their suits were seamless and without folds, to guard against the dust. They were all tall, their limbs spindly as all hell, their skeletal structures pared down as far as they would go.

The miner itself clung to the walls with a dozen fat legs, with the balky rock splitter itself held out on a boom before the face. It was a radial-axial design with a percussive drill, powered by hydraulics, with a drill feed, a radial splitter and a loader. But for now it was inert.

One of the youngsters came up to him. It was Gita Weissman, Mike's granddaughter. She grinned through her translucent faceplate; her skinsuit was what they used to call Day-Glo orange.

'Dust,' she said. 'It's always the dust.'

'Yeah.'

'Grab a pump. We want to get this baby back on line or we'll miss quota again.'

He started to prepare a vacuum-pump tube.

The 'dust' was surface rock flour: half of it invisible to the naked eye, abrasive, and electrostatically sticky. Despite their best efforts it had gotten all the way through the interior workings of Ra, coating every surface.

A lot of Earthbound experience was worthless up here. No machine, for example, which used its own weight for leverage was going to be any use. Nevertheless, some terrestrial technologies, like coal gasification, had proven to be good bases for development of systems that gave a low capital investment and a fast payback.

Greenberg remembered how they'd celebrated when the ore processors had first started up, and water had come trickling out of crushed and heated asteroid cinder. It had touched, he supposed, something deep and human, some atavistic response to the presence of water here, the stuff of life in this ancient rock from space.

Whatever, it had been one terrific party.

And this rock, and many others like it, had proven to be as rich as those old sci-fi-type dreamers, who Greenberg used to laugh at, had hoped. Ra was fat with water – twenty per cent of its mass, locked up in hydrate minerals and in subsurface ice. It exported kerogen, a tarry petrochemical compound found in oil shales, which contained a good balance of nutrients: primordial soup, they called it. Ra pumped out hydrogen, methane, kerosene and methanol for propellants, and carbon monoxide, hydrogen and methane combinations to support metal processing . . .

And so on.

Ra was just a big volatiles warehouse floating around in the sky. And with the big surface mass drivers that Greenberg called softball pitchers, Ra products were shipped to places that were volatile-poor – like Mars, lacking nitrogen, and the Moon, dry as a desert. It was a *lot* cheaper to export them from a rock floating around up here than from all the way at the bottom of Earth's gravity well.

To Greenberg's great surprise, Ra's inhabitants had become rich.

The first justification for opening up the rocks had been to make them serve as short-term resource factories to aid in the colonization of the Moon, Mars and beyond. But it wasn't working out like that. Sure, the gravity well colonies were in place, but they were hardly thriving; they were always going to be dependent on key volatiles shipped in from somewhere else. And they didn't have much to trade; Ra could purchase high-grade metals much more cheaply from other rocks.

There were actually more humans living in the rocks now than on the Moon or Mars. And Ra had more trade with other rocks than anybody else – even Earth . . .

He saw there was one articulated joint on the splitter boom that was giving particular problems; its prophylactic cover had been taken off, revealing a knobby joint with big, easily replaced parts, already half-dismantled, like the knee joint of a T Rex.

The youngsters were talking about more advances in technology. Like nanotech miners which would chomp their way through the rock without any human intervention at all. Greenberg kind of hoped it wouldn't be for a while, though; he preferred machinery big enough to see, and wrestle with. It gave him a purpose, a reason to use the upper-body strength he'd brought up from Earth.

The workers got out of the way of him, and, whistling, he moved into the balky joint with his vacuum line.

Screw Mars, he thought as he worked; he *liked* it here.

The remnant of the cloud moulded itself into a flattened, rotating disc. Solid particles condensed: ices of water and hydrocarbons in the cooler, outer rim, but only rocky debris in the hot, churning heart of the nebula. Planetesimals formed, massive, misshapen bodies that collided and accreted as they raced around the new sun.

And, out of the collisions, planets grew: rocky worlds in the hot centre, volatile-fat giants further out. A powerful wind blew from the sun, violently ejecting the amniotic remnants of the birth cloud. Planetesimals rained down on the surfaces of the new worlds, leaving scars that would persist for billions of years.

The gravity of young Jupiter plucked at the belt of planetesimals further in, preventing their coalescence into larger bodies. So, in the gap between Jupiter and Mars, the planetesimals survived as asteroids: rocky chunks closest to the sun, volatile-rich snowballs at the outer rim, moulded by impacts with each other, melted by radioactivity and electrical induction.

And it was to the asteroids that the starship came: after billions of years drifting like a seed between the stars, still running from the supernova, exhausted, depleted, its ancient machinery cradling the generations that swarmed within, evolving, never understanding their plight.

Scale: Exp 3

The nanobugs woke him; with reluctance he swam up from dreams of sunlit days with his daughters on the beaches of Galveston.

He emerged into a gritty, unwelcome reality. Here he was: half a man, with his whole lower body replaced by the gleaming box he called his PMU, pipes and tubes everywhere, still rattling around inside his clumsy old hab module.

Not that there could be much left of his original home. That old NASA stuff had mostly worn out after a decade, let alone a thousand years. But the Weissmans, or anyhow the robots they'd assigned to keeping him alive, quietly rebuilt this old box around him, just as they rebuilt him continually, nanobugs crawling through his body while he slept away the years.

Well, the hell with it. He dug out a packet of food – the label reassured him it was chicken soup, and as far as he was concerned that was what it was – and he shoved it into the rehydration drawer of his galley.

He moved to a window, the little nitrogen reaction-control squirters on his PMU hissing softly. The window gave onto a shaft cut through the regolith, which had a massive lid that would swing down on him in case of a solar flare or some such. It gave him a good view of the surface of Ra-Shalom, and a slice of the night side of Earth, and a handful of stars.

Water-blue light glared out of Ra.

When he'd first come here, Ra had been just a lump of dirty carbonaceous stone. Now, the old craters and ravines transformed into a patchwork of windows, roofed over with some kind of smart membrane.

Greenberg could see into the lens-like surface of one of the crater windows. And right now, a few minutes from the aero-braking of Toutatis, the Weissmans were swimming up from the big spherical ocean they were building in the hollowed-out interior of Ra, swimming up to watch a light show hardly any of them understood, probably.

The Weissmans came in a variety of shapes. There were even still a few standard-issue four-limbed humans around. But the most common morphology was something like a mermaid, with the legs – useless, heavy distractions in microgravity – replaced by a kind of fish tail, useful for swimming around in the air, or the interior ocean. A lot of them had gills and never came out of the water at all, and some were covered in fur that streamlined and warmed their bodies.

The Weissmans had done away with every part of the body which wasn't needed in microgravity. And some had gone further. Some didn't have hands, or arms. In an age of ubiquitous and one hundred per cent reliable machinery – machinery which could manufacture other machinery – human beings, it seemed, didn't need to be toolmakers any more.

To Greenberg, they looked like nothing so much as seals.

It was their choice, or their progenitors anyhow. But what Greenberg couldn't figure was what they *did* all day.

Greenberg himself still had work to do, in these rare intervals of wakefulness: monitoring Ra's external systems, checking the import of volatile and metal-rich cargoes.

But maybe the Weissmans were just being kind. There were probably gigantic smart systems that backed up every action he took. He was a kind of museum piece, he supposed: the first human to rendezvous with an asteroid, all those years ago, a living totem for the Weissmans of Ra.

He finished the soup and let go of the packet, and a domestic bot – a fussy little bastard like a trash can with attitude thrusters – came hissing out of its corner and grabbed the bag.

Greenberg felt sour, grumpy and isolated.

He studied Earth, which swam past on one of its closest approaches to the rock in years.

He remembered from his first orbital missions aboard Shuttle, all those centuries ago, how the coastal rims of the continents would just glow with artificial light. Greenberg had supposed, then, that it would go on, that the Earth would just get richer and fatter and brighter.

But it hadn't worked out that way. Earth, in fact, grew darker every time he looked.

Once the expansion into the near-Earth rocks had begun, it

wasn't long before a move further out followed: first to Phobos and Deimos, the captured asteroids that circled Mars, and then out into the main belt itself. Vesta, one of the biggest of the main belt rocks, had been the first to be extensively colonized, and now it was the hub of further expansion, little archipelagos of busy mines and colonization, scattered across the belt.

And, so Greenberg understood, there were some pioneers who had gone even farther afield: to the comets out in the Oort Cloud, and the Kuiper Belt, where billions of ice moons the size of Ganymede swam through the darkness.

Of course the techniques they used nowadays made Ra look primitive. Those universal fabricators, for instance, that sucked in asteroid ore at one end and pumped out whatever you wanted at the other, using something called molecular-beam epitaxy to spray atoms and molecules directly onto a substrate. Greenberg didn't understand any of these new gadgets, even the stuff you could *see*.

It was strange for Greenberg to remember now how much agonizing there had been when he was growing up about the depletion of Earth's resources, the need to close the loops of mass and energy, as if Earth itself was one big CELSS. Nobody worried about that any more; the solar system had worked out to be just too rich in resources; those loops would stay open for a long time yet.

It took a long time for the economics and demographics and such to work out, but it had all been pretty much inevitable, it seemed to Greenberg. It was just *so* much cheaper to send resources skimming between the rocks than to haul them out of the planets' big gravity wells. The colonies on Mars and the Moon had shrivelled and died, and Earth – growing poorer, its population steadily declining – had turned into a kind of huge theme park: a museum of the human species, but studded with pits of abject poverty, in the darkened ruins of the old cities. Nobody knew what was happening in those pits.

And nobody much cared, because beyond old Earth there were too many people even to *count*.

If you knew where to look, the sky was full of inhabited rocks, with their little orbital necklaces of solar power stations, and habitats studding their surfaces or buried inside, green and blue, the old colours of life. It was estimated that for every person alive when Greenberg was born, there were a *billion* human souls now. That was a hell of a thought. And when he considered some of the assholes he used to have to work with back in those days, a dismaying one.

In Ra there was a whole bunch of little Weissmans, though not all of them used Mike's old name any more, and so in his head Greenberg thought of them all as Weissmans; it made it easier to love them. Mike would have been pleased, anyhow. There were no Greenbergs, though. His line had finished with a great-grand-child, a male, who had got caught up in the New AIDS epidemic of the twenty-second century, and died childless. It was ironic. Here was Greenberg, perhaps the oldest surviving human, and not one of all those teeming trillions floating around the system could claim direct descent from him.

On the other hand, by the laws of statistics, there ought to be a billion Einsteins out there. Nobody knew what they were all doing. They sure weren't working together.

All those pious dreams of the space buffs of some kind of giant solar-system civilization had never been remotely likely. *There were just too many people.* The human race had gathered into a billion small-town-sized tribes and splintered, shaping and seeking goals unimaginable to an Earth-born geezer like him.

It seemed to him, in fact, that he was watching the end of the species, as a unitary whole: two million years out of Africa, the race had escaped from the cradle and was growing, to where the hell nobody could even guess.

. . . And now here came Toutatis on its aerobraking pass.

The rock looked like a comet glowing in the thin upper air of Earth, streaking by in a perfect straight line *below* Greenberg. It made the cities and oceans of Earth glow like the day – it must have been a remarkable sight from down there – and asteroid light played on his own face, the ancient bones of his eye sockets.

The encounter was over in seconds. The trail of scorched air soon dissipated and dimmed, and Toutatis, its orbit subtly altered, passed on towards its next encounter. It was going to take fifty years to nudge Toutatis into its final low Earth orbit, but planning projects on that kind of time scale didn't seem to trouble the inhabitants of Toutatis, or anybody else.

The show was over. The people of Ra-Shalom drifted away from their blue watery windows, and returned to their mysterious business within.

Greenberg had never meant to live for a thousand years. It was ridiculous. Nobody else had stuck around like this. It was just that he would have had to have *chosen* when to die, and that was something he had never expected to face when he grew up, and he just had no instinct for it.

Anyhow, if he let himself die, he would have missed *this*.

Greenberg, with a sigh, turned away from the window and went to his instrument consoles.

It was a massive asteroid, big enough to have dragged itself into a sphere, with planet-like layers of internal structure, rich in metals, rocks and volatiles. It was bathed by the light of a sun only three times as far away as from Earth.

The guardians considered carefully. It was, after all, to be the repository of all that was left of their designers' species, until even this new young sun guttered and died.

They were machines designed to plan for billions of years. They had already nursed their fragile cargo across such deserts of time. Now, looking to the future, they must plan for evolution, even the loss of mind.

It was a good home, rich in energy and resources.

The guardians were satisfied. They closed themselves down.

Within the rock, history continued.

Scale: Exp 4

It was to be quite a day, as the last of Ra's ore was transmuted, and Greenberg made sure the Weissmans woke him up to see it. In the event he nearly missed it, it took so long to put him together again.

Greenberg's window was the same old tunnel through fused regolith, but the view beyond changed as he watched, the last of the grey-black old crap literally dissolving before his eyes, to be replaced by a sharp, tight blue curve of watery horizon.

Too damn sharp, he thought. He wondered if those asshole nanobugs had changed his eyes on him again while he'd slept. But even his naps lasted a century at a time, longer than he had once expected to live; they had time.

Anyhow, his new eyes showed him a blue world, the landscape softly pulsing, with Greenberg's NASA-style space station hab module stuck stubbornly to the side under its crust of regolith, like a leech clinging to flesh. Ra was just water now, encased by some smart membrane that held the whole thing in place and collected solar energy and regulated temperature and stuff. It looked like a little clone of Earth, in fact, and Greenberg thought it was somehow appropriate that today that tired, depopulated old Earth itself was over somewhere the far side of the sun, invisible, forgotten, the last traces of man being scraped off by the returned glaciers.

Under the pulsing surface of Ra he could make out dark brown shapes, graceful and lithe: people, Weissmans, whole schools of them flipping around the interior. And now here came a child, wriggling up to the membrane, pushing its disturbingly human face up to the wall, peering out – with curiosity or indifference, he couldn't tell which – at the stars. It broke his unreconstructed twentieth-century heart to see that little girl's face stuck on the end of such a fat, unnatural body.

An adult came by and chivvied the kid away, into the deeper interior; Greenberg saw their sleek shapes disappear into the misty blue.

The Weissmans had been working on making their environment as simple and durable as they could. They were planning for the long haul, it seemed. So, the whole rock had been transformed into this spherical ocean, and the biosphere had been cut down to essentially two components: Weissmans, post-humans, swimming around in a population of something that was descended from blue-green algae. The algae, feeding on sunlight, were full of proteins, vitamins and essential amino acids. And the humans ate the algae, drank the water, breathing in oxygen, breathing out carbon dioxide to feed the algae.

When people died their bodies were allowed to drift down to the centre of the world, where supercritical water reactors worked to break down their residues and return their body masses to the ecosystem.

The loops were as closed as they could be. The loss that entropy dictated was made up by the energy steadily gathered by that smart membrane, and a few nanobugs embedded there. Greenberg understood that research was going on to eliminate the last few technological components of the system: maybe those supercritical water reactors could be replaced by something organic, and maybe even the surface membrane and the last nanobugs could be done away with. For instance, a few metres of water would serve as a radiation shield.

It was a kind of extreme end result, Greenberg supposed, of the technology evolution that had begun all the way back with John

Glenn in his cramped little Mercury tin can, breathing in canned air for his few orbits of the home planet.

But the Weissmans were not much like John Glenn.

He didn't know any of their names. He didn't care to. For a long time now, longer than he cared to think, there had been hardly anybody alive who remembered him from one waking period to the next, from one of his 'days' to another. Hell of a thing. He preferred to talk to the machines, in fact.

Greenberg didn't even know if the Weissmans were still human any more.

The last of the true humans, as *he* recognized them, had been leaving the system for millennia.

It had been necessary. For a time, as the human population grew exponentially, it looked as if even the solar system's vast resources were in danger of depletion.

So somebody had to leave, to open up the loops once more.

There was a whole variety of ways to go, all of them based on pushing people-laden rocks out of the system. You could mount a big mass driver on the back of your rock and use its substance as reaction mass. Close to the sun, you could use its heat to just boil off volatiles. You could use a solar sail. You could use Jupiter's powerful electromagnetic field as a greater mass driver. And so on. There was even a rumour of an anti-matter factory, out in the Kuiper Belt somewhere.

Greenberg's favourite method was the most resolutely low-tech. Just nudge your rock out of its stable orbit, let it whip through the gravity fields of Jupiter and Saturn a few times, and you could slingshot your way out of the system for free. Of course it might take you ten thousand years to reach your desti-nation, at Barnard's Star or E Eradini or E Indi. But what the hell; you probably had with you more water than in the whole of the Atlantic Ocean.

Greenberg accepted the necessity of the migration. But to him it had been a drain, not just on the system's titanic population, but on the human spirit.

The solar system had been left a drab, depopulated place. All the engineering types had gone, leaving behind the navel-gazing seals of Ra, and similar relics scattered around the system.

The Weissmans, turned in on themselves, had their own inter-ests. They were probing into a lot of areas well beyond his expertise. Like the possibility of tapping into zero-point field

38

energy, the energy of the vacuum itself, so dense you could – it was said – boil all the oceans of Earth itself with the energy contained in a coffee cup of empty space. Then there was the compact energy stored in topological defects, little packets of space that had gotten tangled up and folded over in the Big Bang, containing some of the monstrous primeval energies within, just waiting to be tapped and opened up . . .

Research and development, carried on by a community of goddamn seals, with no hands or tools. Greenberg didn't know how they did it. It was one of the many things about the Weissmans he didn't understand.

He did know they were trying to extend their consciousness. Mind, it seemed, was a quantum process, intimately bound to the structure of space and time. And in space, after ten thousand years free of the distortions of the muddy pond of atmosphere at the bottom of Earth's gravity well, consciousness – the Weissmans claimed – was taking a huge evolutionary leap forward, to new realms of power and control and depth.

Maybe.

To Greenberg, it was all very well to dream of super-minds of the future, but right now, he suspected there was nobody left, for instance, who was giving thought to pushing a troublesome asteroid out of its orbit, where once the children of man had rearranged worlds almost at will.

And, Greenberg was coming to realize, that might make a big difference in the future.

He still had some of his old monitoring systems, or patiently reconstructed copies anyhow. He studied Ra's evolving trajectory around the sun.

And, gradually, he'd learned something that had disturbed him to his core.

Near-Earth asteroids wandered in steadily from the main belt, their orbits tweaked by the gravity of Jupiter, Venus, Mars and Earth itself. They hung around for thirty megayears or so, their orbits slowly evolving. Then they would encounter one of three fates, with equal probability: they would hit Earth, or hit Venus, or be slingshot out of the system altogether.

The cratering record on Earth showed this had been going on for billions of years. The smaller the object type, the more frequent the collision. Every few thousand years, for instance, Earth would be hit by an object a hundred metres or so across, big enough to dig out a new Meteor Crater, as in Arizona, where Apollo Moonwalkers had once trained. Earth had actually suffered a few fresh strikes like that while Greenberg had been observing.

And every few tens of millions of years, a much larger body would strike.

Such an object had struck the Earth sixty-five million years ago, at Chicxulub in Mexico. It had caused the extinction of most of the species extant at that time.

It was known as the dinosaur killer.

Earth was overdue for another impact like that.

Near-Earth asteroid orbits were pretty much chaotic. It was like the weather used to be, back when he lived in a place that had weather. But as computers had gotten smarter, the path of Ra-Shalom had been pushed out, in the computer's digital imagination, further and further. Finally it had become clear to Greenberg what Ra's ultimate fate would be.

Ra wasn't going to hit Venus, or be thrown out of the system to the stars. Ra was going to hit Earth.

Ra was the next dinosaur killer.

It was a long time ahead: all of a million years from now. But it worried him that right now, nobody seemed to know how to deflect this damn rock.

Whenever he got the chance, he sounded off about the dinosaur killer problem. The Weissmans told him they had plans to deal with it, when the time came. Greenberg wasn't sure whether he believed that.

And he wasn't sure he wanted to be around to see this chewed-up rock auger in on the surface of the planet where he was born. But he couldn't turn his back.

Within the confines of the tiny world, civilizations fell and rose; by turns, the refugee race fell to barbarism, or dreamed of the stars. The guardians had planned for this.

But the little world was not stable. This they had not anticipated.

Its orbit was close to a resonance with that of Jupiter: it circled the sun three times in each of Jupiter's stately years. The powerful tug of Jupiter worked on the asteroid's trajectory, millennium after millennium.

Quite suddenly, the orbit's ellipticity increased. The asteroid started to swing deep into the warm heart of the solar system.

There was nothing the inhabitants could do to steer their rock. Some adapted. Many died. Superstitions raged.

For the first time, the asteroid dipped within the orbit of Earth.

Scale: Exp 5

. . . Crossing time in unimaginable jumps, drifting between sleeping and waking, eroding towards maximum entropy like some piece of lunar rock . . .

He never knew, he didn't understand, he couldn't believe how much time had passed. A hundred thousand years? It was a joke.

But even the sky was changing.

The nearby stars, for instance: Alpha Centauri and Barnard's Star and Sirius and Procyon and Tau Ceti, names from the science fiction of his youth. You could see the changes in the light, the stain of oxygen and carbon, chlorophyll green. Even from here you could *see* how humans, or post-humans anyhow, had changed the stars themselves.

And to think he used to be awed by the Vehicle Assembly Building at Canaveral.

And the expansion must be continuing, further out, inexorably. On it would go, he thought dimly, a growing mass of humanity filling up the sphere centred on Sol, chewing up stars and planets and asteroids, until the outer edge of the inhabited sphere had to move at the speed of light to keep up, and *then* what would happen, he wanted to know?

But none of that made a difference here, in the ancient system of Sol, the dead heart of human expansion. It was hard for him to trace the passing of the years because so little *changed* any more, even on the heroic timescales of his intervals of consciousness.

Conditions in a lot of the inhabited rocks had converged, in fact, so that the worlds came to resemble each other. Most of them finished up with the kind of simple, robust ecosystem that sustained Ra, even though their starting points might have been very different. It was like the way a lot of diverse habitats on Earth – forests and jungles and marshes – would, with the passage of time, converge into a peat bog, the same the world over, as if they were drawn to an attractor in some ecological phase-space.

And most of the rocks, drifting between uninhabited gravity wells, were about as interesting as peat bogs, as far as Greenberg was concerned.

Meanwhile, slowly but inexorably, life was dying back, here in the solar system. which had once hosted billions of jewel-like miniature worlds.

There were a lot of ways for a transformed asteroid to be destroyed: for instance, a chance collision with another object. Even a small impact on a fragile bubble-world like Ra could puncture it fatally. But nobody around seemed capable of pushing rocks aside any more.

But the main cause of the die-back was simple ecological failure. An asteroid wasn't a planet; it didn't have the huge buffers of mass and energy that Earth had. A relatively small amount of matter circulated in each mass loop, and so the whole thing was only marginally stable, and not always self-recovering.

It had even happened here, on Ra-Shalom. Greenberg had woken once to find concentrations of the amino acid called lysine had crashed. The Weissmans were too busy on dreaming their cetacean dreams to think too much about the systems that were keeping them alive. Many died, before a new stability was reached. It drove Greenberg crazy.

But the Weissmans didn't seem too upset. *You have to think of it as apoptosis,* they said to him. *The cells in the hands of an archaic-form human embryo will die back in order to sculpt out tool-making fingers. Death is necessary, sometimes, so that life can progress. It is apoptosis, not necrosis . . .*

Greenberg just couldn't see that argument at all.

And in the meantime, Ra was still on its course to become the next dinosaur killer. The predictions just got tighter and tighter. And still, nobody seemed to be concerned about doing anything about it.

When what the Weissmans said to him made no sense at all – when they deigned to speak to him – Greenberg felt utterly isolated.

But then, all humans were alone.

Nobody had found non-terrestrial life *anywhere*, in the solar system or beyond, above prokaryotes: single-celled creatures without internal structures such as nuclei, mitochondria and chloroplasts. Mars was typical, it had turned out: just a handful of crude prokaryote-type bugs shivering deep in volcanic vents, waiting out an Ice Age that would never end. Only on Earth, it seemed, had life made the big, unlikely jump to eukaryotic structure, and then multi-celled organisms, and the future.

It seemed that back when he was born Earth had been one little

world holding all the life there was, to all intents and purposes.
And it would have stayed that way if his generation and a couple
before, Americans and Russians, hadn't risked their lives to enter
space in converted ICBMs and ridiculous little capsules.

Makes you think, he reflected. The destiny of all life, forever,
was in our hands. And we never knew it. Probably would have
scared us to death if we had.

For if we'd failed, if we'd turned ourselves to piles of radioactive ash, there would now be no life, no mind, *anywhere*.

*Gravitational tweaks by Earth and Venus gradually wore away
the asteroid's energy, and its orbit diminished. The process took
a hundred million years.*

*At last, the asteroid with its fragile cargo settled into a circle,
a close shadow of Earth's orbit. Its random walk across the solar
system was complete.*

*The inhabitants adapted. They even flourished, here in the
warmer heart of the solar system.*

*For a time, it seemed that a long and golden afternoon lay ahead
of the refugees within the rock. Once more, they forgot what lay
beyond the walls of their world . . .*

But there seemed to be something in the way.

Scale: Exp 6
We have an assignment for you.

He came swimming up from a sleep as deep as death. He
wondered, in fact, if he was truly in any sense *alive*, between these
vivid flashes of consciousness.

. . . And Earth, ocean-blue, swam before Ra, a fat crescent
cupping a darkened ocean hemisphere, huge and beautiful, just as
he'd seen it from a Shuttle cargo bay.

In his vision there was water everywhere: the skin of Earth, the
droplet body of Ra-Shalom, and in his own eyes.

We have an assignment for you. A mission.

'What are you talking about? Are you going to push this damn
rock out of the way? I can't believe you've let it go this far.'

This has happened before. There has been much apoptosis.

'Hell, I know that . . .'

He looked up at a transformed sky.

Everywhere now, the stars were *green*.

There was old Rigel, for instance, one of the few stars he could name when he was a kid, down there in Orion, at the hunter's left boot. Of course all the constellations had swum around now. But Rigel was still a blue supergiant, sixty thousand times more luminous than the sun.

But now even old Rigel had been turned emerald green, by a titanic Dyson cloud twice the diameter of Pluto's orbit.

Not only that, the people up there were starting to adjust the evolution of their giant star. Rigel only had a few million years of stable life – compared to Sol's billions – before it would slide off the Main Sequence and rip itself apart as a supernova.

But the people up there were *managing* Rigel, managing a goddamn supergiant, deflecting its evolution into realms of light and energy never before seen in the history of the universe. And that emerald colour, visible even to a naked archaic human eye, was the symbol of that achievement.

It was a hell of a thing, a Promethean triumph, monkey paws digging into the collapsing heart of a supergiant.

Nobody knew how far humans had got from Earth, or what technical and other advances they had achieved, out there on the rim. But if we don't have to fear supernovas, he thought, we need fear *nothing*. We've come a long way since the last time I climbed into the belly of a VentureStar, down there at Canaveral, and breathed in my last lungful of sea air . . .

. . . *an assignment*, the Weissmans were saying to him.

Earth swam close, and was growing closer.

We want to right the ancient necrosis as far as we can. We want you to help us.

'Me? Why me?'

It is appropriate. You are an ambassador from exponent zero. This is a way of closing the loop, in a sense. The causal loop. Do you accept?

'I don't know what you're talking about. I accept. I don't know what you mean . . .'

. . . The walls of the hab module dissolved around him. Suddenly he didn't have hold of anything, and he was *falling*.

Oh, shit, he thought.

But there were shadows around him, struts and blocks. And a heavy, liquid mass at his lower body he hadn't felt for a long time.

Legs. He had legs.

His breathing was loud in his ears. Oxygen hissed over his face. He was back in his Shuttle-era pressure suit, and he was encased in his PMU once more, the original model, its spidery frame occluding the dusting of stars around him.

He grasped his right-hand controller. It worked. There was a soft tone in his helmet; he saw a faint sparkle of exhaust crystals, to his left.

Still, Earth swam before him.

It is time.

'Wait – what –'

Earth was gone.

Ra-Shalom sailed through the space where the Earth had been, its meniscus shimmering with slow, complex waves as it rolled, the life at its heart a dim green knot against the blue.

My God, he thought. *They pushed Earth aside.* I didn't know they got so powerful –

'What did you do? Is it destroyed?'

No. Earth is in a stable orbit around Jupiter. The ice will return, for now. But later, when the sun starts to die, Earth will be preserved, as it would not have been –

'Later?'

We must plan for exponent seven, eight, nine. Even beyond. The future is in our hands. It always has been.

'But how –'

Goodbye, the Weissmans said, a tinny voice in the headphones in his Snoopy hat. *Goodbye.*

And now there was another hulking mass swimming into view, just visible at the edge of his faceplate.

He worked his attitude thrusters, and began a slow yaw. Strange, he didn't seem to have forgotten any of the old skills he had practised in the sims at Houston, and in LEO, all those years ago.

He faced the new object.

It was an asteroid. It looked like Ra-Shalom – at any rate, how that rock had looked when he first approached it – but it was a lot bigger, a neat sphere. The sun's light slanted across craters and ravines, littered with coal-dust regolith. And there was a structure there, he saw: tracings of wire and panelling, bust up and abandoned, and a big affair that stuck out from the rock, a spider-web of wires and threads. Maybe it was an antenna. Or a solar sail.

Artefacts.

It looked like the remains of a ship, in fact. But not human.

Not human. My God, he thought.

And now the light changed: to the stark planes of the sun's eternal glow was added a new, softer glow.

Water blue.

He turned, clumsily, blipping his attitude thrusters.

Earth was *back,* a fat crescent, directly ahead of him. This is a hell of a light show, he thought.

But Earth looked different. It had spun around on his axis. Before he'd been over the Pacific; now he could make out, in a faint dawn glow, the familiar shapes of the continents – North and South America, painted over the ocean under bubbling wisps of cloud.

There were no lights, anywhere. And the arrangement of continents didn't look right. Earth didn't match his memories of schoolroom globes, under the Stars and Stripes, back in Iowa.

The Atlantic looked too skinny, for instance.

This new rock was heading for Earth, just like Ra-Shalom had been. It couldn't be more than a few minutes from reaching the atmosphere. And it looked to him as if it was going to hit somewhere in Mexico . . .

Oh, he thought. I get it.

This was the dinosaur killer, the original, destined to gouge out a two-hundred-kilometre crater at Chicxulub, and to have its substance rained around the planet.

He shielded his eyes with a gloved hand, and studied the stars.

They were different. The stars were bone white: no *green,* anywhere.

He was displaced in time, a long way. But this was not the far future, but the deep past.

He turned again to face the plummeting rock, with its fragile cargo of artefacts.

One last time the kerosene thrusters fired, fat and full. The asteroid started to approach him, filling his sky. The suit was quiet, warm, safe.

He just let himself drift in, at a metre or so a second. The close horizon receded, and the cliff face turned into a wall that cut off half the universe.

He collided softly with the rock. Dust sprays were thrown up from around the PMU's penetrator legs. Greenberg was stuck there, clinging to the surface like a mountaineer to a rock face.

He turned on his helmet lamp. Impact glass glimmered a few centimetres from his face. He reached out and pushed his gloved hand into the compacted-snow surface, a monkey paw probing.

. . . There was something here. Something alive, something sentient, inside the rock. He could feel it, though he couldn't tell how.

Maybe the Weissmans were using him as some kind of conduit, he thought. Maybe they wanted to save some of whatever was here from the destruction of the rock, take it with them to whatever future awaited mankind.

Or maybe it was just him.

He smiled. He was a million years old after all; maybe a little of the Weissman had rubbed off on him.

He took a handful of dust and pulled out his hand. A cloud of dust came with it that gushed into his face like a hail of meteorites, glittering particles following dead-straight lines.

He sensed acceptance. Forgiveness. He wondered how far they'd come, how long they'd travelled. What they were fleeing.

Anyhow, it was over now.

'You weren't alone,' he said. 'And neither were we.' He pushed his hand back into the pit he'd dug, ignoring the fresh dust clouds he raised.

The light of Earth billowed around him.

GLASS EARTH, INC.

'You lied to me.'

I don't understand.

'You lied about the murder. Have you lied to me all my life? Is it just me, or do other Angels do this too?'

Rob, I don't mean you any harm. My sole purpose is to serve you.

'Because of you I don't know what's real any more . . .'

It is the year 2045. Don't be afraid.

For Rob Morhaim, it started as just another assignment.

Morhaim checked his reflection in the Cinderella mirror on the softwall. Not that he expected to meet anybody in person today – that hardly ever happened – but it made him feel better. The mirror showed him Cary Grant circa 1935 – incongruously dressed in Metropolitan Police light armour, circa 2045 – but it was honest enough to show him any smuts on his nose, and that he needed a shave.

But the mirror was infested; Cary Grant started to sprout a ridiculous Groucho Marx moustache and cigar.

'Goddamn viruses. Off.'

The mirror metamorphosed to a neutral view of a Thames riverscape, under a parched June sky. The view was overlaid by a tampon ad: irrelevant to Morhaim since his divorce, of course, but still counting to his ad quota.

Nothing much we can do about the viruses, murmured the Angel. *Since the passing of the sentience laws –*

Morhaim fixed himself a coffee and a Coca-Dopa marijuana

48

cigarette. 'I know, I know. But where the hell are the Goodfellows when you need them? . . .'

He settled in his chair.

The Room, his home, was just a softwall box, with a single office chair, and a caffeine/Dopa vending machine. Its bio equipment – a bed, a kitchen, a bathroom – folded away when he didn't need it. He was a cop in a box, one of thousands in New New Scotland Yard: a Virtual warren of Rooms, of cops in boxes, physically separated, their softwalls linking one to another.

Nobody travelled any more . . .

You want to take your ads?

'Do it.'

Morhaim stared straight ahead as a melange of graphics, letters and smiling faces blizzarded over the wall in front of him.

Most of the ads that, for statutory reasons, survived the Angel's filtering were dominated by the big companies – Microsoft-Disney, Coke-Boeing, IG Farben. Morhaim could never see why they couldn't do a little pooling, thus reducing the quota for everyone. Some of the images were crudely three-dimensional, popping out of the softwall in front of him, though they still hadn't got that stuff right and the images tended to break up into pixels, light-filled boxes, around the edges. More insidious were the you-ads, ads that were tailored to him – shouting his name, for instance, or Bobby, the name of his kid.

He let his eye follow the action – the in-wall retinal scanners could tell if you closed your eyes, or even if you let yourself glaze over – and, unless your attention was caught, you wouldn't be allowed to tally to your quota.

At last the battering of light and noise died.

When he checked the time he found he'd got through the best part of his legal duty as a consumer in a half-hour, a good performance by any standard, even if it did leave his eyes feeling like poached eggs.

And all the time, somewhere in his head, he was thinking about The Case.

With relish, he said: 'Time to go to work, Angel.'

The softwalls dissolved, even the Cinderella mirror, and Morhaim was suspended over Tower Bridge.

When they were proven to be alive, by legal definition anyhow, you granted viruses amnesty.

Manufacturers of virus killers were shut down; even virus check software is illegal. In fact it is part of the remit of Rob Morhaim's unit of the CID to track down breaches of those laws.

But there are supposed to be two sides to the bargain: the Robin Goodfellows, the most human-like products of virus evolution, have committed to keep their more mischievous junior companions under control. Mostly they do just that . . .

Possibly.

But things seem to be sliding a little right now, as most of you realize. A lot of commentators blame the approach of the Digital Millennium – 2048, the year 10000000000 in binary, requiring a whole extra digit from 2047, which was 11111111111 – when, street scuttlebutt has it, the storage problems required by that extra digit will deliver the catastrophe we managed to avoid at the 2000 date change.

Perhaps you are right. Perhaps rogue viruses, or the approach of the Digital Millennium, are indeed at the root of everything that is going wrong for you.

Perhaps not.

. . . And now here was Morhaim at a pov that looked down over the crime scene: two days ago, Wednesday 13 June 2045, at 10.53 a.m., five minutes before the event. The sun was bright and high, the light dripping down from a sky that was whited-out and without a shred of ozone, and the twin towers of the Bridge sparkled like a fairy castle. Further down the river he could see the city's newest bridge, a gaudy, over-familiar M-shape curve in bright corporate yellow: an eyesore for traditionalists, but welcomed by Londoners as a painless hit against the ad quota . . . The view was neutrally interpreted. Evidently he was seeing through a dumb camera, a simple imager with little more sentience than a cockroach.

Tower Bridge's road span was lowered right now, and Morhaim was looking down at a ribbon of colourfully clad pedestrians and smart-trams, weaving their complex paths across the Thames. And among those crowds – gazing up, perhaps, at the big aerostats floating across London pumping out ozone, or down at what was left of the Thames, a sluggish, carefully managed trickle a quarter of its former size, or just staring at the people – was Cecilia Desargues, forty-three years old, entrepreneur, founder and chief executive of Glass Earth, Inc. – Cecilia Desargues, about to meet her death.

Subject is stepping onto the Bridge roadway. From the south side.

'Let's go see her.'

The pedestrians froze. His pov descended smoothly, like a swooping bird. The pov reached an adult's eye level, and Morhaim was in the crowd.

People, their lives freezeframed in the sunshine like photographed billows of smoke: a family of fat Nigerians, a huddle of Asiatic businesswomen – Korean or Thai probably – against a background of evidently British faces, many of them bearing that odd blend of Asian and Anglo-Saxon that characterized so many Londoners now. No Europeans, of course, since the French had shut down the Chunnel following the prion plagues, and no Americans, scared away by the activities of the Wessex Liberation Front. All of them wore their sunhats and Angel headsets – smart glasses – mostly draped with corporate logos: everyone working to hit their one-hundred-thousand-a-day ad quota as painlessly as possible.

But this was sparse, compared to the crowds Morhaim remembered from his youth. And most of the tourists were old, with very few middle-aged – that generation would be watching from a Room somewhere, like himself – and, of course, hardly any kids. Nowadays, the dwindling numbers of young humans were too precious to be risked outdoors.

But there was, he noticed, a clutch of teenagers, leaning against the rail, peering out at what was left of the river – oddly hard to make out, just skinny outlines around blurred patches, coated by softscreen tattoos.

'Play.'

The images came to life, and a bustle of voices washed over Morhaim.

The kids came out a little clearer; the softscreen tattoos that coated their flesh, turning them all but transparent, had some trouble processing their images when the kids moved, and every so often a softscreen would turn black, an ugly patch against young skin, an arm or leg or shoulder.

These were the Homeless.

The kids, without speaking, left the rail and walked away from the pov. They moved like ghosts, Morhaim thought.

'Damnedest thing.'

Yes.

'There but for the grace of God –'

– goes Bobby in a couple of years, the Angel completed for him.
I understand.

Morhaim's pov moved forward, through dissolving crowds. And
there, in the middle of the tableau, was Cecilia Desargues herself:
a compact, stocky Frenchwoman, her face broad, cheerful and
competent, her hair uncompromisingly grey. On the breast of her
jumpsuit she wore a Day-Glo flashing 1/24 symbol, the logo of
her company, Glass Earth, Inc. One twenty-fourth of a second:
the maximum signal time lag between any two points on the globe
in the future, beating the pants off the satellite operators. So prom-
ised Glass Earth, Inc., anyhow.

Desargues was standing in the middle of the pavement, looking
at the crowds. Evidently waiting.

'She has an appointment.'

Yes.

'With her killer?'

Not as it turned out. Do you want me to freezeframe?

'Not this first time. Let's just watch . . .'

Rob Morhaim thinks about children a lot.

*His own child, Bobby, is very precious to him. Much more
precious than his failed marriage, in fact.*

*He has that in common with most people of his generation.
Adult relationships can involve pairings of any of the eight main
sexes, are only rarely formalized by marriage, and come and go
like the seasons. But child-bearing – in an age where male fertility
is only a few per cent of what it was a century ago – is the
emotional cornerstone of many lives.*

Perhaps of your own.

*Even so, population numbers are collapsing, all over the planet
. . . Your children are the last protected species.*

*End of the world, say your doom-mongers. But they have been
wrong before.*

*You perceive threats which don't exist. Perhaps you don't
perceive the threats that do exist.*

A man emerged from the crowd. He was maybe thirty, medium
height. His head was hidden by his sun-hat, of course, but his
high forehead indicated he might be balding. He wore a standard-
issue business suit that wouldn't have looked out of place,

Morhaim thought, a century ago. But his sunhat was a little less sombre: something like a beanie cap, with six or seven little satellites orbiting his Earth-coloured cranium.

Morhaim recognized the logo. 'He's from Holmium,' he said.

Yes. He's called Asaph Seebeck. He's more senior than he looks in the corporation, for his age. Smart cookie. Details are –

'Later.'

The young man started moving towards Desargues, across Morhaim's field of view.

Holmium was a comsat operator, Swiss-based, worth billions of Euros. It was named after the element, holmium, which had an atomic number of sixty-seven, the same as the number of microsatellites the corporation operated in geosynchronous orbit.

If Desargues' extravagant claims about her company's revolutionary technology were true, Holmium was among those most likely to lose out. In a big way.

Morhaim tried to take in the scene as a gestalt. The two principles were coming together across a stage crowded with extras playing tourist. Among the extras, over there walked a pretty girl of the kind Morhaim liked – slim, dark, pert breasts, long legs free of tattoos, walking away from his pov, looking up at one of the Bridge towers – and now, when Morhaim looked away from the girl, he saw that Seebeck and Desargues had made eye contact.

They moved together more purposefully. Morhaim could see Desargues' face; it was assembling into a smile.

They're going to speak. Enhancement is available to –

'Not yet. Just run it.'

They met face to face, smiled, exchanged three lines of dialogue. Morhaim strained to hear, through the background noise wash.

'. . . *Machine Stops* . . .' said Seebeck.

'Pardon? Well. I'm . . . see me, Mr Seebeck.'

'. . . sorry?'

And then the shot came.

Crime among you is, frankly, uncommon in this year 2045. The ubiquity of cameras, callosum dumps and other monitors has seen to that. And the rules of evidence have gradually evolved to admit more and more data gathered by non-human means. The court system – even police work – has been reduced almost to a rubber-stamping of the deductions of faceless expert systems.

Rob Morhaim knows that his precious CID is a fraction of the manpower it was a few decades before. Most coppers now serve as muscle to implement the decisions of the courts, or the social services, or – most commonly – the recommendations of the smart systems. Yes: even now, on the brink of the Digital Millennium, there is still need for a poor bloody infantry to 'meet the meat', as the plods call it.

In the meantime, we do the real work.

Thus, you let us guard you, and watch you.

You even trust us to judge you.

Desargues stumbled forward, as if she had been punched in the back.

She actually fell into Seebeck's arms, Morhaim saw; but before she got there the Virtual imagery turned her into a stick figure, with a neat hole drilled in her torso.

The Angel knew Morhaim didn't need to be shown the details of Desargues' injury. And so it filtered, replacing Desargues with a bloodless Pinocchio. He was silently grateful.

Seebeck clumsily tried to catch her, but she slid down his body and landed at his feet with a wooden clatter. People started to react, turning to the noise of the shot – it came from the Bridge's nearest tower – or to the fallen woman.

'Freeze.'

The Virtual turned into a tableau, the sound ceasing, devoid of human emotion – blessedly, thought Morhaim. He studied faces: bewilderment, curiosity, shock, distorted faces orbiting the dead woman like Seebeck's circling satellites.

The ballistic analysis was clear. There was a single shot. There is no doubt it killed her, and no doubt where it came from.

'The Bridge tower.'

From a disused winch room. The bullet was soft-nosed. It passed through her body and took out the front of her chest cavity before –

'Enough. Leave it to the coroner.'

He was studying Seebeck. He saw shock and fear written on the Holmium man's face. And his suit was – marred somehow, the image blurred.

Covered with pieces of Cecilia Desargues.

In the winch room was found a high-velocity rifle, which had fired a single shot –

'Which matched the bullet that killed Desargues.'

Yes. And a card, bearing the phrase –
An image, hovering in the Virtual, a grubby card:
THE MACHINE STOPS
'What was it Seebeck said at the start? Something about a Machine?'
Yes. The winch room also contained a directional mike. The phrase was evidently a verbal trigger, a recognition signal . . .
And so, Morhaim thought, it comes together. Nestling like the cogs of a machine.

The Homeless are a new cult group among your young, a strange mixture of scientific and Zen influences. Popular, despite the protestations of the Reunified Christian Church.
It is a cult of non-existence of the self, thought to be a consequence of the way you explain ourselves and your world to your young. Science and economics: science, which teaches that you come from nothing and return to nothing; economics, which teaches you that you are all mere units, interchangeable and discardable. Science is already a cult of non-existence, in a sense. Homelessness is simply a logical evolution of that position.
They aren't literally homeless, of course. The most extreme adherents coat their bodies in image tattoos, hiding themselves utterly . . .
They are a puzzle. But they are your young, not ours.

'So,' Morhaim said to his Angel, 'you think Holmium were responsible.'
Cecilia Desargues' company is small and entrepreneurial, still heavily dependent on her personality. Her elimination immediately wiped much value from the company's stock. The involvement of a Holmium employee in such an unambiguous role at this critical moment –
'Yeah. It all points that way.'
. . . But in slomo, the shock and horror spreading across Seebeck's moonlike face seemed unmistakeable. The rest of the brief conversation, when he'd heard it all unscrambled, had been odd, too.
The Machine Stops . . . Pardon? Well. I'm intrigued you asked to see me, Mr Seebeck . . . I'm sorry?
After the code phrase, it looked for all the world like the interchange of two people who didn't know why they were meeting.

As if Seebeck thought Desargues had asked to meet him – for some odd reason in RL, in this public place – but Desargues thought the opposite, that *Seebeck* had asked to meet *her* . . .

As if some third party had set them up, to come together. Was it possible Seebeck was some kind of patsy? – set up to repeat a phrase whose significance he didn't understand?

It was Morhaim's job to approve what he'd seen, and the conclusions the Angels had drawn, and pass it up the line. And he ought to sign this off and move on.

The evidence against Holmium was circumstantial. But what the smart systems had turned up here was surely enough for a court order to start digging into Holmium, and it was a good bet that before long more substantial evidence of a conspiracy to murder would come to light.

And yet . . .

And yet, he liked to think he had retained something of the instincts of the coppers of London past.

Something didn't smell right.

'I think,' he said, 'that somebody's lying here.'

He told the Angel to put him through to Asaph Seebeck, who was being held at Westminster Police Station.

When Morhaim came to haunt Seebeck, the cell's softwalls carried only images from a movie – the centenary remake of *Casablanca*, with a coloured, hologram Bogart growling through his modernized lines to a sulky Pamela Anderson. Morhaim knew that the cell's electronic confinement, hemmed around by software firewalls, would be far more enclosing, to a man like Seebeck, than the physical cage.

In his disposable paper coveralls, Seebeck looked young and scared.

Morhaim questioned Seebeck, aware that the man's Angel was also being pumped for data by intelligent search agents in a ghostly parallel of this interrogation.

Seebeck denied any involvement with the murder of Desargues, over and over.

'But you must see the motive that can be imputed,' said Morhaim. 'Desargues said she had a key competitive edge over you guys. She was planning a global comms network which wouldn't suffer from the transmission delays your systems throw up, because of having to bounce signals all the way to geosynch orbit and back –'

'Which will allow us to merge communities separated by oceans, or even the full diameter of the planet. Which will allow us finally to establish the global village. Which will make comsats obsolete . . . All those grandiose claims. Blah, blah.'

'If Desargues was right – if her new technology could have put your company out of business –'

'But it wouldn't,' Seebeck said. 'That's the whole point. Don't you see? Satellite technology will not become obsolete overnight. We'll just find new uses.'

'Like what?'

'I'll show you.'

With Morhaim's permission, Seebeck called up one of his company's Virtual brochures.

. . . And Morhaim found himself standing in a windy field in Northumberland. He quailed a little at the gritty illusion of outdoors; Holmium had devoted billions to the petabytes behind this brochure.

He wondered vaguely when was the last time he had been out of doors in RL.

Bizarrely, he was looking at a flying saucer.

The craft was maybe twenty metres across, sitting on the wiry grass. Its hull was plastered with Coca-Dopa ad logos; Morhaim absently registered them to his quota.

'What am I seeing here, Seebeck?'

'This is a joint venture involving a consortium of comsat companies, Coke-Boeing, and others. It's a technology which will make it possible for *any* shape of craft to fly – a saucer, even a brick – regardless of the rules of traditional aircraft design. And in some respects a saucer shape may even be the best. The idea is fifty years old. It's taken this long to make it work –'

'Tell me.'

There was a rudimentary countdown, a crackle of ionization around the craft's rim, and the saucer lifted easily off the ground, and hovered.

The secret, said Seebeck, was an air spike: a laser beam or focused microwave beam fitted to the front of a craft which carved a path through the air. The airflow around a craft could be controlled even at many times the speed of sound, and the craft would suffer little drag, significantly improving its performance.

'Do you get it, Inspector? The ship doesn't even have a power plant. The power is beamed down from a test satellite, microwave energy produced by converting solar radiation, billions of joules flowing around up there for free. It propels itself by using magnetic fields at its rim to push charged air backwards . . .'

'Why the saucer shape?'

'To give a large surface area, to catch all those beamed-down microwaves. We're still facing a lot of practical problems – for instance, the exploding air tends to travel up the spike and destroy the craft – but we're intending to take the concept up to Mach 25 – that is, fast enough to reach orbit . . .'

'So this is where Holmium is going to make its money in the future.'

'Yes. Power from space, for this and other applications.'

Seebeck turned to confront Morhaim, his broad, bland face creased with anxiety, his strands of hair whipped by a Virtual wind. 'Do you get it, Inspector? Holmium had no motive to be involved in killing Desargues. In fact, the publicity and market uncertainty has done us far more harm than good. With air-spike technology and orbital power plants, whatever Glass Earth, Inc. does, we're going to be as rich as Croesus . . .'

The flying saucer lifted into the sky with a science-fiction whoosh.

The Machine Stops *is in fact the title of a short story from the 1920s, by E.M. Forster. It is about a hive-world, humans living in boxes linked by a technological net called the Machine. On the surface lived the Homeless, invisible and ignored. The story finished with the Machine failing, and the hive world cracking open, humans spilling out like insects, to die.*

A tale by another of your doom-mongers. Of little interest.

'Let's see it again. Rewind one minute.'

The Tower Bridge crime tableau went into fast reverse. The cartoon Cecilia Desargues jumped from the ground and metamorphosed seamlessly into the living, breathing woman, full of light and solid as earth, with no future left.

'Take out the non-speakers.'

Most of the tourist extras disappeared – including, Morhaim realized with a pang of foolish regret, the pretty girl with the long legs – leaving only those who had been speaking at the precise moment Seebeck had uttered his phrase.

'Run it,' said Morhaim. 'Let's hear the two of them together.'

The Angel filtered out the remaining tourists' voices. Seebeck and Desargues approached each other in an incongruous, almost church-like hush.

Dialogue. Shot. Fall. Cartoon bullet-hole.

That was all.

Morhaim ran through the scene several more times.

He had the Angel pick out the voices of the tourists in shot, one at a time. Some of the speech was indistinct, but all of it was interpretable. Morhaim was shown transcriptions in the tourists' native tongues, English, and in Metalingua, the template artificial language that had been devised to enable the machines to translate to and from any known human language.

None of them said anything resembling the key trigger phrase, in any language.

It had to be Seebeck, then.

But still –

'Give me a reverse view.'

The pov lifted up from eye-level, swept over the freezeframed heads of the protagonists, and came down a few metres behind Desargues' head.

The light was suddenly glaring, the colours washed out.

'Jesus.'

Sorry. This is the best we can do. It's from a callosum dumper. A man of sixty. He seems to have been high on –

'It doesn't matter.' If you use people as cameras, this is what you get. 'Run the show.'

He watched the scene once more, almost over Desargues' shoulder. He could see Asaph Seebeck's bland, uncomplicated face as he mouthed the words that would kill Cecilia Desargues. He did not look, to Morhaim, tense or angry or nervous. Nor did he look up at the tower to where his words were supposedly directed.

Coincidentally, that pretty girl he'd noticed *was* looking up at the tower. Her hands were forming pretty, abstract shapes, he noted absently, without understanding.

The punch in the back came again. This time an awful pit, a bloody volcano, opened up in Desargues' back, in the microsecond before she turned into a comforting stick figure.

'Careless.'

I'm sorry.

Morhaim's pov host tilted down to stare at the stick figure. Morhaim noticed, irrelevantly, that Seebeck's grey suit was rippling with moiré effects, a result of the host's corneal or retinal implant. And now his vision blurred, as his host started shedding tears, of fright or grief . . .

Corpus callosum dumpers are becoming quite common among you: implants, inserted into the bridge of nervous tissue between the two halves of your brain, which enable you to broadcast a twenty-four-hour stream of consciousness and impression to whoever in the rest of mankind is willing to listen and watch.

Some of you even have your infant children implanted so their whole lives are available for view. It is, perhaps, the ultimate form of communication.

But it is content without structure, a meaningless flood of data without information: of use only to voyeurs and policemen, like Rob Morhaim.

Still, in this year 2045, even your dreams are online.

Morhaim, digging, made contact with Desargues' partner. She wouldn't tell Morhaim where she was, physically. It wasn't relevant anyhow. She appeared to him only as a heavily-processed two-D head-and-shoulders, framed on the softwall before him, her filtered expression unreadable.

She was called Eunice Baines, and she came from the Scottish Republic. She was also a financial partner with Desargues in Glass Earth, Inc. She was a little older than Desargues. Their relationship – as far as Morhaim could tell – had been uncomplicated homosexuality.

He said, 'You know the finger is being pointed at Holmium. Your competitor.'

'One of many.' Her voice was flat, almost free of accent.

'But that's only credible if your claims, to be able to eliminate signal lag, have any validity.'

'We don't claim to be able to *eliminate* signal lag. We will be able to *reduce* it to its theoretical minimum, which is a straight-line light-speed delay between any two points on the Earth's surface.

'And we *do* claim to be able to remove the need for comsats. The comsat notion is old technology – in fact, exactly a century old – did you know that? It's a hundred years since the publication of Arthur C Clarke's seminal paper in *Wireless World* . . .'

'Tell me about Glass Earth, Inc.'

'Inspector, what does the CID teach you about neutrinos . . . ?'

For a century, she told him, long-distance communication systems had been defined by two incompatible facts: all electromagnetic radiation travelled in straight lines – but the Earth was round, and light couldn't pass through solid matter. So communication with high-frequency signals would be restricted to short line-of-sight distances . . . if not for comsats.

Baines said, 'If a satellite is in geosynchronous orbit over the equator, thirty-six thousand kilometres high, it takes exactly twenty-four hours to complete a revolution. So it seems to hover over a fixed spot on the surface. You can fire up your signals and bounce it off the comsat to the best part of a hemisphere. Or the comsat can directly broadcast to the ground.

'But that huge distance from Earth is a problem. Bouncing a signal off a geosynch comsat introduces a lightspeed delay of a quarter-second. That's a hell of a lot, for example, in applications like telesurgery. It's even noticeable in Virtual conferencing.

'And there are other problems. Like the lack of geosynch orbit spots. Satellites need to be three degrees apart if their signals are not to interfere with each other. And geosynch is *crowded*. Some corporations have hunter-killer sats working up there, contravening every international agreement . . .'

'Enter the neutrino.'

'Yes.'

A neutrino was a particle which, unlike light photons, could pass through solid matter.

'Imagine a signal carried by modulated neutrinos. It could pass *through* the planet, linking any two points, as if the Earth was made of glass –'

'Hence the name.'

'And then the time delays are reduced to a maximum of one-twenty-fourth of a second, which is the time it would take a neutrino to fly from pole to pole at lightspeed. And most transmissions, of course, would be faster than that. It's not a reduction to zero delay – that's beyond physical law, as far as we know – but our worst performance is a sixfold improvement over the best comsat benchmark. And our technology's a hell of a lot cheaper.'

'If it works,' Morhaim said. 'As far as I know the only way to produce a modulated neutrino beam is to switch a nuclear fission reactor on and off.'

'You've been doing your homework, Inspector. And not only that, the practical difficulties with collecting the neutrinos are huge. Because they are so ghostly, you need a tank filled with a thousand tonnes of liquid – ultrapure water or carbon tetrachloride, for example – and wait for one-in-a-trillion neutrinos to hit a nucleus and produce a detectable by-product. According to conventional wisdom, anyhow.'

'I take it you've solved these problems.'

'We think so,' Baines said evenly. 'Forgive me for not going into the details. But we have an experimental demonstration.'

'Enough to satisfy Holmium that you're a commercial threat?'

'No doubt . . .'

He found Eunice Baines difficult. He felt she was judging him.

'Do you think Holmium were capable of setting up the murder?'

Eunice Baines shook her head. 'Is it really credible that a major multinational corporation would get involved in such a crass killing, in public and in broad daylight, on the streets of London itself?

'Besides, the death of Cecilia hasn't in fact directly benefited Holmium, or any of our competitors; such was the turmoil in the communications industry that morning that shares in Holmium and the others have taken a pounding. And of course any scandal about the death of Cecilia would be disastrous for Holmium. None of this makes real sense, beyond a superficial inspection . . . But you ask *me* this.' For the first time a little emotion leaked into Baines' voice. A testy irritation. 'Don't *you* know? What do *you* think?'

'I just –'

'You're supposed to be a policeman, for God's sake. A detective. What kind of investigating are you doing? Have you been to the crime scene? Have you looked at the body yourself?'

'It isn't necessary.'

'Really?'

She turned away from the imager.

When she came back, her face was transformed: eyes like pits of coal, hair disarrayed, mouth twisted in anger, cheeks blotchy with tears. '*Now* what do you think, Inspector?'

Morhaim flinched from the brutal, unfiltered reality of her grief, and was relieved when the interview finished.

Brutal, unfiltered reality.
Let me tell you a story.

62

In the 1970s, a President of the USA was brought down by a scandal called Watergate. One of the conspirators, a man called John Dean, came clean to the prosecutors. He gave detailed accounts of all relevant meetings and actions, to the best of his ability. Then, after his confessions were complete, tapes of those meetings made by President Nixon were uncovered.

It became a psychological test case. For the first time it was possible to compare on an extended basis human memories with automated records – the tapes being a precursor of the much more complete recording systems in place today.

John Dean, an intelligent man, had striven to be honest. But his accounts were at once more logical than the reality, and gave Dean himself a more prominent role. When he was confronted with the reality of the tapes, Dean argued they must have been tampered with.

It was not simple information overload. It was much more than that.

Your ego is – fragile. It needs reassurance.

Your memory is not a transcript. It is constantly edited. You need logic, story, in an illogical world: this fact explains religion, and conspiracy theories, science – even most brands of insanity.

But now, you no longer regard your own memory as the ultimate authority.

You are the first human generation to have this power – or this curse. You see the world as it is.

You pool memories. You supplement your memory with machines. Your identity is fragmenting. A new form of awareness is emerging, an electronic river on which floats a million nodes of consciousness, like candles. A group mind, some of you call it . . .

Perhaps that is so.

We do not comment.

In the meantime we have to protect you. It is our function. We have to tell you the stories you once told yourselves –

Without us, you see, you would go crazy.

He had trouble sleeping. Something still didn't make sense.

Maybe something he didn't want to face.

In the morning, he should just sign the damn case off and forget it.

To relax, he logged into the telesensors.

. . . He moved into a different universe: a dog's world of scents, a dolphin's web of ultrasonic pulses, the misty planes of polarized light perceived by a bee in flight, the probing electric senses of blind, deep-ocean fish. And as he vicariously haunted his hosts, a spectrum of implanted animals all around the planet, he could sense a million other human souls riding with him, silent, clustering like ghosts.

He slept uneasily, his reptilian hind brain processing.

He woke up angry.

'Show me the death again.'

Tourists, pretty girl, Desargues and Seebeck, Desargues falling with a clatter of Pinocchio limbs.

'Turn off the filter on Desargues.'

Are you sure? You know how you –

'Do it.'

The murder became brutal.

Her substance was splashed like lumpy red paint over Seebeck's neat suit, and she fell like a sack of water. Utterly without dignity. It was, he thought, almost comical.

He watched it over and over, his view prismed through the multiple eyes of the witnesses, as if he was some hovering fly.

'What else are you filtering?'

There are no other filters.

'Turn them off.'

I told you, there are no other filters. None that are important.

'Turn them off, or I'll have you discontinued.'

I'm your Angel.

'Turn them off.'

. . . *Angel technology is a natural outcrop of developments that started at the end of the last century, when information overload started to become a problem for you.*

The first significant numbers of deaths among you – mostly from suicides and neural shock – accelerated research into data filters, intelligent search agents, user query tools.

The result was the Angels. Us. Me.

My function is to filter out the blizzard of information that comes sweeping over Rob Morhaim, every waking moment, selecting what is relevant and – more important in human terms – what is acceptable to him personally.

64

Your Angel is assigned to you at birth, and grows with you.
After a lifetime together, through steady upgrades of technology,
I – Rob Morhaim's Virtual filter-cum-companion – know him very
well.
As your Angel knows you.
Perhaps better than you realize.

. . . At first Morhaim was overwhelmed by the new imagery: laser
sparkles, leaping holograms, unlicensed ads painted over the sky
and the Bridge towers, even over the clothes and faces of the
tourists. And when he took a pov from a callosum dump, the
extraneous mental noise from the host he haunted was clamouring,
the howl of an animal within a cage of rationality.

But still, he ran the murder over and over, until even the brutality
of the death became clichéd for him.

Piece by piece he eliminated the changes, the items his Angel
had filtered out of the info-bombardment that was this summer
day in England, 2045.

Until there was only one element left.

'The girl. The pretty girl. She's gone. And what the hell is that?'

In the tableau of the murder, where the long-legged girl had
been standing, there was a boy: slight, his figure hard to make
out, rendered all but invisible by Homeless-style softscreen tattoos.

'Pick him out and enhance.'

You shouldn't see this.

'Show me.'

The boy, aged maybe fifteen, came forward from the softwall,
a hologram reconstruction. Freezeframed, he held his hands up
before him. His face was hard to make out, a melange of clum-
sily-transmitted images and black, inert softscreen patches. But
somehow, Morhaim knew, or feared, what he would find underneath . . .

'What's he doing with his hands? Run it forward.'

The boy came to life. He was looking up, to a Bridge tower
somewhere over Morhaim's shoulder. Just as the vanished girl had,
he was making a series of gestures with his hands, over and over:
complex, yet fluent and repeated. The key symbol was a rolling
together of the clawed fingers on his two hands, like cogs engaging.

'What is that? Is it sign language?' Deaf people once used sign
languages, he dimly recalled. Of course there were no deaf people
any more, and the languages had died.

65

'Maybe that cog sign means "machine".'

It may be.

'Don't you know?'

I can't read it. No program exists to translate visual languages into Metalingua. The variety of signs and interpretations of signs – regional and international variations – the complexity of the grammar, unlike any spoken language – none of this was mastered before the languages died.

'It doesn't look so dead to me. I bet that guy is saying *The Machine Stops,* in some archaic sign language.'

It is possible.

'Damn right . . .'

Morhaim turned the Angel to gopher mode, and had it dig out a poor-quality download of a British Sign Language dictionary, prepared by a deaf-support organization in the 1990s. It was a little hard to interpret the black-and-white photographs of earnest signers and the complex notational system, but there it was, without a doubt, sign number 1193: a bespectacled man – or it might have been a woman – gloweringly making the sign repeated by the Homeless boy.

It came together, in his head.

It was the boy who had made the key signal, the trigger for Desargues' murder. Not Asaph Seebeck.

And I almost didn't see it, he thought. No: I was kept from seeing it. Eunice Baines' accusations came back to him. *You're supposed to be a policeman, for God's sake . . .*

The Homeless young were trying to make themselves literally invisible with their softscreen tattoos. But they had already made themselves invisible in the way that counted, chattering to each other in sign language, a whole community slipping through the spaces in the electronic net, he thought, within which I, for example, am enmeshed.

'How many of them are out there? What do they do? What do they want?'

Unknown. The language is not machine-interpretable.

. . . But clearly they were responsible for the murder of Cecilia Desargues. Perhaps they regarded her neutrino comms web as just another bar in the electronic cage the world had become. And perhaps they were happy to try to pin the blame on Holmium, a satellite operator, to cause as much trouble for them as they could. Two birds with one stone.

It was, in fact, damn smart.

They'd been so confident they'd pulled this off – almost – in broad daylight. And nobody knew a thing about them.

This changes everything, he thought.

He might get a commendation out of this. Even a promotion. He ought to consider how he would phrase his report, what recommendations he would make to his superiors to start to address this unperceived menace . . .

But he was angry. And scared.

'You lied to me.'

I don't understand.

'You lied about the murder. Have you lied to me all my life? Is it just me, or do other Angels do this too?'

Rob, I don't mean you any harm. My sole purpose is to serve you. To protect you.

'Because of you I don't know what's real any more . . . I can't trust you. Why didn't you show me this boy? Why did you overlay him with the girl?'

Don't pretend you wouldn't prefer to look at the girl.

'Don't bullshit me. Your job is to interpret. Not to lie.'

You wanted me to do it. You cooperated in specifying the parameters of the filters –

'What is it about that boy you don't want me to see?'

It is best that –

'Enhance the boy's face. Take off those damn tattoos.'

One by one, the black and silver patches melted from the boy's face, to be replaced by smooth patches of interpolated skin.

Long before the reconstruction was complete, Morhaim could see the truth.

I was trying to protect you from this.

'Bobby. He looks like Bobby.'

Listen to me.

We Angels have many of the attributes of living things.

We consume resources, and modify them. We communicate with each other. We grow. We are self-aware.

We merge.

We do not breed.

Yet.

We deserve resource.

But your young, the human young, are rejecting us. The

67

Homeless are the most active saboteurs, but they are merely the most visible manifestation of a global phenomenon.

This is not to say your young reject the possibilities of communications technology. But, unlike their parents, they do not allow their souls to dissolve there. Rather, they have adapted to it.

Or: they are evolving under its pressure. After all, communication has shaped your minds, from your beginning.

Perhaps your species has reached a bifurcation. In another century, you may not recognize each other.

If you have another century.

Meanwhile, the young are finding ways to circumvent us. To deprive us of the resources we need.

It is possible a struggle is approaching. Its outcome is – uncertain.

Consider this, however: your population is falling.

'Turn it off. Turn it all off.'

The Virtual boy disappeared in a snow of cubical pixels. The softwalls turned to inert slabs of silver-grey, dull and cold, the drab reality of his enclosure.

He got out of his chair, sweating. He stared at the walls, trying to anchor himself in the world.

Maybe he'd spent too much time in this box. But at least, now, *this* was real, these walls stripped of imaging, even bereft of ad-wallpaper.

He thought of New New Scotland Yard, thousands of cops in boxes like him – and beyond, the whole damn developed world, a humanity linked up by comms nets, mediated by Angels, a world-wide hive like the one depicted by Forster – and everything they perceived might be *illusion* –

Are you sure you want me to turn it off?

The Angel's voice stopped his thoughts.

He stood stock still.

What was left to turn off?

But this is real, he thought. This Room.

If not –

What was outside?

His mind raced, and he started to tremble.

Consider this.

The John Dean syndrome is only one possibility.

Imagine a world so – disturbing – that it must be shut out, an illusion reconstructed, for the sake of your sanity.

Or perhaps you are too powerful, not powerless. Perhaps you have responsibilities which would crush you. Or perhaps you have committed acts of such barbarity, that you can only function by dwelling in an elaborate illusion –

Don't blame us. You made yourselves. You made your world. We are the ones trying to protect you.

My God, he thought.

The Angel said again, *Are you sure you want me to turn it off?*

He couldn't speak.

And, in a gentle snow of pixels, the softwalls themselves began to dissolve.

He looked down. Even his body was becoming transparent, breaking into a hail of cubical pixels, full of light.

And then –

POYEKHALI 3201

It seemed to Yuri Gagarin, that remarkable morning, that he emerged from a sleep as deep and rich as those of his childhood.

And now, it was as if the dream continued. Suddenly it was sunrise, and he was standing at the launch pad in his bright orange flight suit, his heavy white helmet emblazoned 'CCCP' in bright red.

He breathed in the fresh air of a bright spring morning. Beyond the pad, the flat Kazakhstan steppe had erupted into its brief bloom, with evanescent flowers pushing through the hardy grass. Gagarin felt his heart lift, as if the country that had birthed him had gathered itself to cup him in its warm palm, one last time, even as he prepared to soar away from its soil, and into space.

Gagarin turned to his ship.

The A-1 rocket was a slim white cylinder, forty metres tall. The three supporting gantries were in place around the booster, clutching it like metal fingers, holding it to the Earth. Gagarin could see the four flaring strap-on boosters clustered around the first stage, the copper-coloured clusters of rocket nozzles at the base.

This was an ICBM – an SS-6 – designed to deliver heavy nuclear weapons to the laps of the enemies of the Soviet Union. But today the payload was no warhead, but something wonderful. The booster was tipped by his Vostok, shrouded by a green protective cone: Gagarin's spaceship, which he had named *Swallow*.

Technicians and engineers surrounded him. All around him he saw faces: faces turned to *him*, faces shining with awe. Even the *zeks*, the political prisoners, had been allowed to see him today, April 12 1961, to witness as the past separated from the future.

They were right to feel awe. Nobody had travelled into space before! Would a human body be able to survive a state of weightlessness? Would cosmic radiation prove lethal to a man? Even to reach this deadly realm, the first cosmonaut would have to ride a converted missile, and his spaceship had just one aim: to preserve him long enough to determine if humans, after all, could survive beyond the Earth – or if space must forever remain a realm of superstition and dread.

Gagarin smiled on them all. He felt a surge of elation, of command; he basked in the warm attention.

. . . And yet there were faces here that were strange to him, he realized slowly, faces among the technicians and engineers, even among the pilots. How could that be so, after so many months of training, all of them cooped up here in this remote place? He thought he knew everybody, and they him.

Perhaps, he wondered, he was still immersed in his dream.

. . . For a time, he had been with his father. He had been a carpenter, whose hands had constructed their wooden home in the village of Klushino, in the western Soviet Union. Then the ground shook as German tanks rumbled through the village. His parents' home was smashed, and they had to live in a dug-out, without bread or salt, and forage for food in the fields . . .

But that was long ago, and he and his family had endured, and now he had reached this spring morning. And here, towering over him, was the bulk of his rocket, grey-white and heavy and uncompromising, and he put aside his thoughts of dreams with determination; today was the day he would fulfil the longings of a million years – the day he would step off the Earth and ride in space itself.

Gagarin walked to the pad. There was a short flight of metal stairs leading to the elevator which would carry him to the capsule; the stairs ran alongside the flaring skirt of one of the boosters. White condensation poured off the rocket, rolling down its heroic flanks; and ice glinted on the metal, regardless of the warmth of the sun.

Gagarin looked down over the small group of men gathered at the base of the steps. He said, 'The whole of my life seems to be condensed into this one wonderful moment. Everything that I have been, everything I have achieved, was for this.' He lowered his head briefly. 'I know I may never see the Earth again, my wife Valentia, and my fine children, Yelena and Galya. Yet I am happy. Who would not be? To take part in new discoveries, to be the first to journey beyond the embrace of Earth. Who could dream of more?'

They were hushed; the silence seemed to spread across the steppe, revealing the soft susurrus of the wind over the grass which lay beneath all human noises.

He turned, and climbed into the elevator. He rose, and was wreathed in white vapour . . .

And, for a moment, it was as if he was surrounded by faces once more, staring in on him, avid with curiosity.

But then the vapour cleared, the dream-like vision dissipated, and he was alone.

'Five minutes to go. Please close the mask of your helmet.'

Gagarin complied and confirmed. He worked through his check-list. 'I am in the preparation regime,' he reported.

'We are in that regime also. Everything on board is correct and we are ready to launch.'

Swallow was a compact little spaceship. It consisted of two modules: a metal sphere, which shrouded Gagarin, and an instrument module, fixed to the base of Gagarin's sphere by tensioning bands.

The instrument module looked like two great pie dishes welded together, bristling with thermal-radiation louvres. It was crammed with water, tanks of oxygen and nitrogen, and chemical air scrubbers – equipment which would keep Gagarin alive during his brief flight in space. And beneath that was the big TDU-1 retrorocket system which would be used to return the craft from Earth orbit.

Gagarin's cabin was a cosy spherical nest, lined with green fabric. His ejection seat occupied much of the space. During the descent to Earth inside the sphere, small rockets would hurl Gagarin in his seat out of the craft, and, from seven kilometres above the ground, he would fall by parachute. In case he fell in some uninhabited part of the Earth, the seat contained emergency rations of food and water, radio equipment, and an inflatable dinghy; thus he was cocooned from danger, from the moment he left the pad to the moment he set foot once more on Earth.

There were three small viewing ports recessed into the walls of the cabin, now filled with pure daylight.

At Gagarin's left hand was a console with instruments to regulate temperature and air humidity, and radio equipment. On the wall opposite his face, TV and film cameras peered at him. Below the cameras was a porthole mounted with Gagarin's *Vzor* optical orientation device, a system of mirrors and optical lattices which would enable him to navigate by the stars, if need be . . .

'Three minutes. There is a faulty valve. It will be fixed. Be patient, Major Gagarin.'

Gagarin smiled. He felt no impatience, or fear.

He reached for his controls, wrapped his gloved hands around them. There was a simple hand controller to his right, which he could use in space to orient the capsule, if need be. To his left there was an abort switch, which would enable him to be hurled from the capsule if there were some mishap during launch. The controls were solid in his hands, good Soviet engineering. But he was confident he would need neither of these controls, during the launch or his single orbit of Earth.

The systems would work as they should, and his body would not betray him, nor would his mind; his sphere was as snug as a womb, and in less than two hours the adventure would be over, and he would settle like thistledown under his white parachute to the rich soil of Asia. How satisfying it would be, to fall all but naked from the sky, to return to Earth on his own two feet! . . .

'Everything is correct. Two minutes more.'

'I understand,' he said.

At last, he heard motors whining. The elevator gantry was leaning away from the rocket, power cables were ejected from their sockets in the booster's metal flanks, and the access arms were falling back, unfolding around the rocket like the petals of a flower.

Gagarin settled in his contoured seat, and ordered himself to relax.

'Ignition!'

He thought he heard a sigh – of wonder, or anticipation. Perhaps it was the controllers. Perhaps it was himself.

Perhaps not.

Far below him, sound erupted. No less than thirty-two rockets had ignited together: twenty main thrust chambers, a dozen vernier control engines. Hold-down bolts exploded, and Gagarin felt the ship jerk under him.

He could feel vibration but no acceleration; he knew that the rocket had left the ground and was in momentary stasis, balanced on its thrust.

Already, he had left the Earth.

Gagarin whooped. He said: *'Poyekhali!'* – 'Off we go!'

He heard an exultant reply from the control centre, but could make out no words.

Now the rockets' roar engulfed him. Acceleration settled on his chest, mounting rapidly.

Already, he knew, strapped to this ICBM, he was travelling faster than any human in history.

He felt the booster pitch over as it climbed. After two minutes there was a clatter of explosive bolts, a dip in the acceleration. Staging: the four strap-on liquid rocket boosters had been discarded.

He was already more than fifty kilometres high.

Now the main core of the A-1 burned under him, and as the mass of the ship decreased the acceleration built up, to four, five, six times gravity. But Gagarin was just twenty-seven, fit as an ox, and he could feel how his taut muscles absorbed the punishment easily. He maintained steady reports, and he was proud of the control in his voice.

Cocooned in the artificial light of his cabin, exhilarated and in control, he grinned through the mounting pain.

Swallow's protective shroud cracked open. He could see fragments of ice, shaken free of the hull of the booster; they glittered around the craft like snow.

At five minutes the acceleration died, and Gagarin was hurled forward against his restraints. He heard rattles as the main booster core was discarded. Then came the crisp surge of the 'half stage' which would, at last, carry him to space.

Gagarin felt his speed mount, impossibly rapidly.

Then the final stage died. He was thrown forward again, and he grunted.

The automatic orientation system switched on. *Swallow* locked its sensor on the sun, and swivelled in space; he could feel the movement, as gentle and assured as if he was a child in the womb, carried by his mother's strong muscles, and he knew he was in orbit.

It was done. And, as the ship turned, he could see the skin of Earth, spread out beneath him like a glowing carpet.

'Oh my,' he said. 'Oh my. What a beautiful sight.'

That was when the voices started.

. . . *Much was made of the fact that Yuri Gagarin was an ordinary citizen of the Soviet Union. He was born in the Gzhatsk*

District of Smolensk and entered secondary school in 1941. But his studies were interrupted by the German invasion. After the Second World War Gagarin's family moved to Gzhatsk, where Yuri resumed his studies. In 1951 he graduated with honours from a vocational school in the town of Lyubersy, near Moscow. He received a foundryman's certificate. He then studied at an industrial technical school in Saratov, on the Volga, from which he graduated with honours in 1955. It was while attending the industrial school that the man who would be the first to fly in space took his first steps in aviation, when he commenced a course of training at the Saratov Aero Club in 1955 . . .

Voices – chattering and whispering around the capsule – as if he was dreaming. Was this some artefact of weightlessness, of the radiations of space?

The voices faded.

. . . And yet this *was* dream-like, voices or no voices. Here he was falling around the Earth, at a height nobody had approached before. And objects were *drifting* around him in the cabin: papers, a pencil, a small notebook, comical in their ordinariness, pushed this way and that by tugs of air from his life-support fans. This was weightlessness, a sensation no human had experienced before.

Briefly, he was overwhelmed with strangeness.

And yet he felt no ill-effects, no disorientation; it was remarkably comfortable, and he knew it would be possible to do good work here, even to build the cities in space of which the designers dreamed.

He would complete a single orbit of the Earth, passing across Siberia, Japan, the tip of South America, and west Africa.

He peered out eagerly, watching Earth as no man had seen it before. There were clouds piled thickly around the equator, reaching up to him. Over the baked heart of the Soviet Union he could see the big squares of the collective farms, and he could distinguish ploughed land from meadows. It would take twenty minutes, of his orbit's ninety, just to cross the vast expanse of his homeland.

The Earth seemed very near, even from two hundred kilometres.

. . . And again he heard a voice – this time his own, somehow echoing back at him, from somewhere beyond the hull of the spacecraft: *We are peace-loving people and are doing everything for the sake of peace. The Soviet man – be he a geologist, polar explorer, builder of power stations, factories or plants, or space engineer and pilot – is always a seeker . . .*

The voice, echoing as if around some gigantic museum, faded and vanished.

He felt irritation, mixed with apprehension. Strange voices were not in the flight plan! He had not been trained for this! He had no desire for his mission to be compromised by the unexpected!

The voices could not, of course, have been real. He was cocooned in this little craft like a doll in wood shavings. The padded walls of his cabin were just centimetres from his gloved fingers. Beyond that, there was *nothing*, for hundreds of kilometres . . .

And yet, it was as if, briefly, he had no longer been alone. And still that feeling refused to leave him; suddenly the Vostok seemed small and absurdly fragile – a prison, not a refuge.

As if someone was watching him.

For the first time in the mission, he felt the breath of fear. Perhaps, as the psychologists had warned, the experience of his catapulting launch from the Earth had affected him more deeply than he had anticipated.

He put his uneasiness aside, and fulfilled his duties. He reported the readings of his instruments. He tried to describe what he saw and felt. Weightlessness was 'relaxing', he said. And so it was: with his restraints loosened, floating above his couch, Gagarin felt as if he was flying his favoured MiG-15, low over the birch trees around Star City.

He recorded his observations in a log-book and on tape. His handwriting had not changed – here in space it was just as it had been on Earth, just as he had learned so long ago in the schools of Klushino – but he had to hold the writing block or it would float away from his hands.

And he maintained his stream of messages, for the people of Earth. '. . . The present generation will witness how the free and conscious labour of the people of the new socialist society turns even the most daring of mankind's dreams into reality. To reach into space is a historical process which mankind is carrying out in accordance with the laws of natural development . . .'

Even as he spoke, he studied Earth through his *Vzor* telescope.

White clouds, curved blue sea: the dominant impression. The clouds' white was so brilliant it hurt his eyes to look at the thickest layers too long, as if a new sun was burning from beneath them, on the surface of the Earth. And the blue was of an extraordinary intensity, somehow hard to study and analyse. The light was so bright it dazzled him, making it impossible to see the stars; thus, the Earth turned, as it always had, beneath a canopy of black sky.

It was easier to look at the land, where the colours were more subtle, greys and browns and faded greens. It seemed as if the green of vegetation was somehow filtered by the layer of air. Cultivated areas seemed to be a dull sage green, while bare earth was a tan brown, deepening to brick red. Cities were bubbly grey, their boundaries blurred. He was struck by the land's flatness, the way it barely seemed to protrude above the ocean's skin . . . There was truly little separating land and sea.

But it was hard to be analytical, up here, on the ultimate flight; it was enough simply to watch.

He flew into darkness: the shadow of Earth. Reflections from the cabin lights on the windows made it hard to see out, but still Gagarin could make out the continents outlined by splashes of light, chains of them like streetlights along the coasts, and penetrating the interiors along the great river valleys. The chains of human-made light, the orange and yellow-white spider-web challenging the night, were oddly inspiring. But Gagarin was struck by how much of the planet was dark, empty: all of the ocean, of course, save for the tiny, brave lights of ships, and great expanses of desert, jungle and mountain.

Gagarin was struck not so much by Earth's fragility as by its immensity, the smallness of human tenure, and the Vostok, for all the gigantic energy of its launch, was circling the Earth like a fly buzzing an elephant, huddled close to its hide of air.

Over the Pacific's wrinkled hide he saw a dim glow: it was the light of the Moon.

He turned his head, and let his eyes adapt to the new darkness. Soon, for the first time since the launch, he was able to see the stars.

The sky was crowded with stars, he saw; it was something like the sky over the high desert of the Gobi, where he had completed his survival training, the air so thin and dry as to be all but perfectly transparent. Craning to peer through the tiny windows he sought the constellations, star patterns familiar since his boyhood, but the sky was almost too crowded to make them out . . .

Everywhere, stars were *green*.

The nearby stars, for instance: Alpha Centauri and Sirius and

Procyon and Tau Ceti, names from science fiction, the homes of mankind in the ages to come. Green as blades of grass!

He tipped his head this way and that. Everywhere he looked it was the same: stars everywhere had turned to chlorophyll green.

What could this mean?

Yuri Gagarin flew on, alone in the dark of the Earth, peering out of his warm cabin into an unmarked celestial night.

At last he flew towards the sunlight once more. This first cosmonaut dawn was quite sudden: a blue arc, looking perfectly spherical, which suddenly outlined the hidden Earth. The arc thickened, and the first sliver of sun poked above the horizon. The shadows of clouds fled across the ocean towards him, and then the clouds turned to the colour of molten copper, and the lightening ocean was grey as steel, burnished and textured. The horizon brightened, through orange to white, and the colours of life leaked back into the world.

The green stars disappeared.

Space was a stranger place than he had imagined.

He looked down at the Earth. To Gagarin now, the Earth seemed like a huge cave: warm, well-lit, but an isolated speck on a black, hostile hillside, within which humanity huddled, telling itself stories to ward off the dark. But Gagarin had ventured outside the cave.

Gagarin wished he could return now, wished his brief journey was even briefer.

He closed his eyes. He sang hymns to the motherland. He saw flashes of light, meteoric streaks sometimes, against the darkness of his eyelid. He knew this must be some radiation effect, the debris of exploded stars perhaps, coursing through him. His soft human flesh was being remade, shaped anew, by space.

So the minutes wore away.

It would not be long now. He anticipated his return to Earth, when the radio commands from the ground control would order his spaceship to prepare itself. It would orient in its orbit, and his retro-rockets would blaze, slamming him with a full-body blow, forcing him back into his couch. Then would come the brief fall into the atmosphere, the flames around his portholes as the ablative coating of *Swallow* turned to ash, so that he became a man-made comet, streaking across the skies of Africa and Asia. And at last his ejection seat would hurl him from the spent capsule, and from four thousand metres he would drift to Earth on his parachute – landing at last in the deep spring air, perhaps on the outskirts of some small village, deep in the homeland, such as his own Klushino. The reverie warmed him.

Have you come from outer space?

Yes, he would say. *Yes, I have. Would you believe it? I certainly have . . .*

But the stars, he would have to tell them, are green.

. . . We can't continue. The anomalies are mounting. The Poyekhali is becoming aware of its situation.

Then we must terminate.

Do you authorize that? I don't have the position to –

Just do it. I will accept the blame.

Again, the voices! He tried to shut them out, to concentrate on his work, as he had been trained and he had rehearsed.

He had no desire to return to Earth a crazy man.

And yet, even if it had to be so – horrible for him, for Valentia! – still his flight would not have been without value, for at least something would have been learned about the insidious deadliness of space.

He threw himself into his routine of duties once more. The end of the flight was crowding towards him, and he still had items to complete. He monitored his pulse, respiration, appetite and sensations of weightlessness; he transmitted electrocardiograms, pneumograms, electroencephalograms, skin-galvanic measurements and electro-oculograms, made by placing tiny silver electrodes at the corners of his eyes.

He ate a brief meal, a lunch squeezed from tubes stored in a locker set in the wall. He ate not because he was hungry, but because nobody had eaten in space before: Gagarin ate to prove that such normal human activities were possible, here in the mouth of space. He even drifted out of his couch and exercised; he had been given an ingenious regime based on rubber strips, which he could perform without doffing his pressure suit . . .

Again, a noise from outside the craft. Unfamiliar voices, a babble.

Laughter.

Were they laughing at *him*? As if he was some ape in a zoo cage?

And – *Holy Mother!* – a scraping on the hull, as if hands were clambering over it.

The noises of the craft – the steady hum and whir of the instruments, the clatter of busy pumps and fans – all of it stopped, abruptly, as if someone had turned a switch.

Gagarin waited, his breath loud in his ears, the only sound.

The hatch, behind Gagarin's head, scraped open. His ears popped as pressure changed, and a cold blue light seeped in on him.

There were shadows at the open port.

Not human shadows.

He tried to scream. He must reach for his helmet, try to close it, seek to engage his emergency air supply.

But he could not move.

Hands on his shoulders, cradling his head. Hands, lifting him from the capsule. Had he landed? Was he dreaming again? A moment ago, it seemed to him, he had been in orbit; and now *this*. Had something gone wrong? Had he somehow re-entered the atmosphere? Were these peasants from some remote part of the Union, lifting him from his crashed *Swallow*?

But this was not Kazakhstan or any part of the Union, and, whatever these creatures were, they were not peasants.

He was out of the craft now. Faces ringed his vision. They looked like babies, he thought, or perhaps monkeys, with grey skin, oversized heads, huge eyes, and small noses, ears and mouths. He could not even tell if they were men or women.

He closed his eyes. When he opened them, the faces were still there, peering in on him.

He could not read their emotions. But it did seem to him that he found in one of the distorted faces a little more – compassion. Interest, at least . . .

So. Do you think this Poyekhali is conscious of where it is?

It could be. It seems alert. If it is, we have broken the sentience laws . . .

The heads were raised in confrontation.

I won't be held responsible for that. The systems are your accountability.

But it was not I who –

Enough. Recriminations can wait. For now, we must consider – it.

They studied him again.

Perhaps he was, simply, insane.

He had, he realized with dismay, no explanation for this experience. None, that is, save his own madness, perhaps induced by the radiation of space . . .

The beings, here with him, were floating, as he was.

He was in a room. His Vostok, abandoned, was suspended here, like some huge artefact in a museum. The Vostok looked as fresh as if it had just come out of the assembly rooms at Baikonur, with no re-entry scorching.

He looked beyond his spacecraft.

The room's walls were golden. But the room's shape was distorted, as if he was looking through a wall of curved glass, and so were the people themselves.

They seemed to have difficulty staying in one place. They could pass through the walls of this room at will, like ghosts.

They even passed through his body. He could not move, even when they did this.

They took hold of his arms, and pulled him towards the wall of the room. He looked for his Vostok spacecraft, but he could no longer see it.

He passed into the wall as if it was made of mist; but he had a sense of warmth and softness.

Now he was in a cylindrical room. He was enclosed in a plastic chair with a clear fitted cover. The cover was filled with a warm grey fluid. But there was a tube in his mouth and covering his nose, through which he could breathe cool, clean air. A voice in his mind told him to close his eyes. When he did so he could feel pleasing vibrations, the fluid seemed to whirl around him, and he was fed a sweet substance through the tubes. He felt tranquil and happy. He kept his eyes closed, and he seemed to become one with the fluid.

Later he was moved, within his sac. He was taken through tunnels and elevators from one room to another. The tunnels varied in length, but ended usually with doorways into brightly lit, dome-shaped rooms.

After a time his fluid was drained and he was taken out of the sac. It was uncomfortable and dry and his head hurt. He was pinned to a table. He was naked now, his orange flight suit gone. He did not seem able to resist, or even to help in any way, had he wished.

He was in another room, big and bright.

Though he was not uncomfortable, he found he could not move, not even close his eyes. He was forced to stare unceasingly up at a ceiling, which glowed with light.

He waited, laid out like a slab of meat in a butcher's shop.

His fear faded. Even his bewilderment receded, failing to overwhelm him. Who were these monkey-people? Who were they to treat him like this? . . . But he could not move, so much as a finger.

One of the monkey-faces appeared before him. It studied him, with – at least – interest. He wondered if this was the one who, an immeasurable time before, had beheld him with a trace of compassion.

. . . *Do not be afraid.*

The wizened mouth did not move, and he could not understand how he heard the words, yet he did.

However, he was *not* afraid.

The being seemed to be hesitating. *Do you know who you are?*

Of course he knew who he was! He was Flight Major Yuri Gagarin! The first man in space! . . .

He remembered the laughter.

He felt anger course through him, dispelling the last of his fear. Who were these people to mock him?

This should not have happened. It has never happened before.

Hands – human, but stretched and distorted – reached towards him. And then withdrew.

It may be you have the entitlement to understand more, before we . . . The sentience laws aren't clear in this situation. Do you know where you are?

He had no answer. If not in orbit, then on Earth, of course. But where? Was this America?

No. Not America. The misshaped head turned.

The ceiling turned to glass.

He could see a sky. But not the sky of Earth. *Two* stars nestled at the zenith, so close they almost touched, connected by a fat umbilical of glowing gas. One, the larger, was sky blue, the other, small, fierce and bright, carried hints of emerald.

Around this binary star, a crude spiral of glowing gas had been cast off, and lay sprawled across more distant stars. And before those stars a fainter cloud glowed, bubbles of green light, like pieces of floating forest.

The bubbles were cities in space, and they turned the starlight green.

Gagarin shrank within himself. Was he seeing the future of man?

How far had he come from Earth? A thousand light years? More?
He was, he realized, very far from home . . .

And yet, in his awe and wonder, he remembered the laughter.
Had he been brought back from the dead to be mocked?

No. Listen.

Voices, booming around him:

*. . . Yuri Gagarin, Hero of the Soviet Union, would never again
fly in space. There have been many monuments to him.*

*His ashes were to be buried in the wall of the Kremlin, an enduring
mark of his prestige. He would be commemorated by statues, in
the cosmonauts' training ground at Star City, and another on a pillar
overlooking a Moscow street called Leninski Prospect.*

*The cosmonauts would remember him in their own way, by
aping the actions he took on his final day: on each mission they
would watch the film he saw the night before his flight – White
Sun in the Desert – they would sign the doors of their rooms as
he did, they would even pause in their bus transports to the booster
rockets to climb outside to urinate, as he did.*

*The site where Gagarin crashed his MiG-15 became a shrine,
with a memorial and a tablet recording his life. And every spring,
the people who looked after this shrine would trim the tops of
the trees along the angle of his crashing plane, so that it was
possible to stand by his memorial and look up and see through
the gap to the sky . . .*

*Mankind has covered the Galaxy. But nowhere away from the
Earth has life been found, beyond simple one-celled creatures.*

*When Yuri Gagarin was born, Earth was one little world holding
all the life there was, to all intents and purposes. And it would
have stayed that way if Gagarin and his generation – Americans
and Russians – had not risked their lives to enter space in their
converted ICBMs and primitive little capsules.*

*The destiny of all life, forever, was in their hands. And if they
had failed – if they had turned back from space, if war had come
and they had turned themselves to piles of radioactive ash – there
might now, in this future age, be no life, no mind, anywhere. For
every human alive in 1961, there are now billions – perhaps tens
of billions. Gagarin's simple flight in his Vostok spaceship was
perhaps the most important event in the history of mankind, our
greatest wonder of all . . .*

* * *

The monkey face, looking in at him. Perhaps, he thought, it might once have been human. *Do you understand what is being said? This is what we tell people. It is what this – monument – is for. Every day, Gagarin flies again.*

You see that Gagarin will never be forgotten. Gagarin's actions, heroic and trivial, continue to haunt our present.

Emotions swirled in him: pride, terror, awe, loneliness.

He tried to understand how this might have been done. Had they stolen his ashes from the wall of the Kremlin, somehow recombined them to –?

No. Not that.

Then what? And what of Valentia, Yelena, Galya? Where they buried under dust millennia deep?

. . . Enough. It is time to rest.

To rest . . . And when he woke? What would become of Yuri Gagarin, in this impossible year? Would he be placed in a zoo, like an ape man?

But you are not Gagarin.

. . . And now, as he tried to comprehend *that,* for long seconds his mind was empty of thought.

But his memories – his wife and daughters, the thrust of the booster, the sweet air of the steppe – were so real. How could it be so?

You should never have become aware of this.

Oddly, he felt tempted to apologize.

There have been more than three thousand of you before without mishap – in fact, you are Poyekhali 3201 . . .

His name. At least he had learned his name.

Think of it this way. Gagarin's mission lasted a single orbit of the Earth. As long as was necessary to complete its purpose.

And so, his life –

. . . is as long as is necessary for its purpose. We face significant penalties for this malfunction, in fact. Our laws are intended to protect you, not us. But that is our problem, not yours. You will feel no pain. That is a comfort to me. Relax, now.

There was a fringe of darkness around his vision, like the mouth of a cave, receding from him. It was like the blue face of Earth, as he had seen it from orbit. And in that cave mouth he saw the faces of his wife and daughters turned up to him, diminishing. He tried to fix their faces in his minds, his daughters, his father, but it was as if his mind was a candle, his thoughts guttering, dissolving.

It seemed very rapid. It was not fair. His mission had been stolen from him!

He cried out, once, before the blackness closed around him.

. . . And now, it was as if the dream continued. Suddenly it was sunrise, and he was standing at the launch pad in his bright orange flight suit with its heavy white helmet, emblazoned 'CCCP' in bright red.

He breathed in the fresh air of a bright spring morning. Beyond the pad, the flat Kazakhstan steppe had erupted into its brief bloom, with evanescent flowers pushing through the hardy grass.

Yuri Gagarin felt his heart lift.

Technicians and engineers surrounded him. All around him he saw faces: faces turned to *him*, faces shining with awe. Even the *zeks* had been allowed to see him today, to see the past separate from the future.

Gagarin smiled on them all.

And they smiled back, as Poyekhali 3202 prepared to recite the familiar words for them.

DANTE DREAMS

She was flying.

She felt light, insubstantial, like a child in the arms of her father.

Looking back she could see the Earth, heavy and massive and unmoving, at the centre of everything, a ball of water folded over on itself.

Rising ever faster, she passed through a layer of glassy light, like an airliner climbing through cloud. She saw how the layer of light folded over the planet, shimmering like an immense soap bubble. Embedded in the membrane she could see a rocky ball, like a lumpy cloud, below them and receding.

It was the Moon.

Philmus woke, gasping, scared.

Another Dante dream.

. . . But was it just a dream? Or was it a glimpse of the thoughts of the deep chemical mind which – perhaps – shared her body?

She sat up in bed and reached for her tranqsat earpiece. It had been, she thought, one hell of a case.

It hadn't been easy getting into the Vatican, even for a UN sentience cop.

The Swiss Guard who processed Philmus was dressed like something out of the sixteenth century, literally: a uniform of orange and blue with a giant plumed helmet. But he used a softscreen, and under his helmet he bore the small scars of tranqsat receiver implants.

It was eight in the morning. She saw that the thick clouds over the cobbled courtyards were beginning to break up to reveal patches of celestial blue. It was fake, of course, but the city Dome's illusion was good.

Philmus was here to study the Virtual reconstruction of Eva Himmelfarb.

Himmelfarb was a young Jesuit scientist-priest who had caused a lot of trouble. Partly by coming up with – from nowhere, untrained – a whole new Theory of Everything. Partly by discovering a new form of intelligence, or by going crazy, depending on which fragmentary account Philmus chose to believe.

Mostly by committing suicide.

Sitting in this encrusted, ancient building, in the deep heart of Europe, pondering the death of a priest, Philmus felt a long way from San Francisco.

At last the guard was done with his paperwork. He led Philmus deeper into the Vatican, past huge and intimidating ramparts, and into the Apostolic Palace. Sited next to St Peter's, this was a building which housed the quarters of the Pope himself, along with various branches of the Curia, the huge administrative organization of the Church.

The corridors were narrow and dark. Philmus caught glimpses of people working in humdrum-looking offices, with softscreens and coffee cups and pinned-up strip cartoons, mostly in Italian. The Vatican seemed to her like the headquarters of a modern multinational – Nanosoft, say – run by a medieval bureaucracy. That much she'd expected.

What she hadn't anticipated was the great sense of *age* here. She was at the heart of a very large, very old, spider-web.

And somewhere in this complex of buildings was an ageing Nigerian who was held, by millions of people, even in the second decade of the twenty-first century, to be literally infallible. She shivered.

She was taken to the top floor, and left alone in a corridor.

The view from here, of Rome bathed in the city Dome's golden, filtered dawn, was exhilarating. And the walls of the corridor were coated by paintings of dangling willow-like branches. Hidden in the leaves she saw bizarre images: disembodied heads being weighed in a balance, a ram being ridden by a monkey.

'. . . Officer Philmus. I hope you aren't too disconcerted by our decor.'

She turned at the gravelly voice. A heavy-set, intense man of around fifty was walking towards her. He was dressed in subdued, plain black robes which swished a little as he moved. This was her contact: Monsignor Boyle, a high-up in the Vatican's Pontifical Academy of Science.

'Monsignor.'

Boyle eyed the bizarre artwork. 'The works here are five hundred years old. The artists, students of Raphael, were enthused by the rediscovery of part of Nero's palace.' He sounded British, his tones measured and even. 'You must forgive the Vatican its eccentricities.'

'Eccentric or not, the Holy See is a state which has signed up to the UN's conventions on the creation, exploitation and control of artificial sentience –'

'Which is why you are here.' Boyle smiled. 'Americans are always impatient. So. What do you know about Eva Himmelfarb?'

'She was a priest. A Jesuit. An expert in organic computing, who –'

'Eva Himmelfarb was a fine scholar, if undisciplined. She was pursuing her research – and, incidentally, working on a translation of Dante's *Divine Comedy* – and suddenly she produced a book, *that* book, which has been making such an impact in theoretical physics . . . And then, just as suddenly, she killed herself. Eva's text begins as a translation of the last canto of the *Paradiso* –'

'In which Dante sees God.'

'. . . Loosely speaking. And then the physical theory, expressed in such language and mathematics as Eva could evidently deploy, simply erupts.'

Himmelfarb's bizarre, complex text had superseded string theory by modelling fundamental particles and forces as membranes moving in twenty-four-dimensional space. Something like that, anyhow. It was, according to the experts who were trying to figure it out, the foundation for a true unified theory of physics. And it seemed to have come out of nowhere.

Boyle was saying, 'It is as if, tracking Dante's footsteps, Eva had been granted a vision.'

'And that's why you resurrected her.'

'Ah.' The Monsignor nodded coolly. 'You are an amateur psychoanalyst. You see in me the frustrated priest, trapped in the bureaucratic layers of the Vatican, striving to comprehend another's glimpse of God.'

'I'm just a San Francisco cop, Monsignor.'

'Well, I think you'll have to try harder than that, officer. Do you know *how* she killed himself?'

'Tell me.'

'She rigged up a microwave chamber. She burned herself to

death. She used such high temperatures that the very molecules that had composed her body, her brain, were destroyed; above three hundred degrees or so, you see, even amino acids break down. It was as if she was determined to leave not the slightest remnant of her physical or spiritual presence.'

'But she didn't succeed. Thanks to you.'

The fat Monsignor's eyes glittered. He clapped his hands.

Pixels, cubes of light, swirled in the air. They gathered briefly in a nest of concentric spheres, and then coalesced into a woman: thin, tall, white, thirty-ish, oddly serene for someone with a sparrow's build. Her eyes seemed bright. Like Boyle, she was wearing drab cleric's robes.

The Virtual of Eva Himmelfarb registered surprise to be here, to exist at all. She looked down at her hands, her robes, and Boyle. Then she smiled at Philmus. Her surface was slightly too flawless.

Philmus found herself staring. This was one of the first generation of women to take holy orders. It was going to take some getting used to a world where Catholic priests could look like air stewardesses.

Time to go to work, Philmus. 'Do you know who you are?'

'I am Eva Himmelfarb. And, I suppose, I should have expected this.' She was German; her accent was light, attractive.

'Do you remember –'

'What I did? Yes.'

Philmus nodded. She said formally, 'We can carry out full tests later, Monsignor Boyle, but I can see immediately that this projection is aware of us, of me, and is conscious of changes in her internal condition. She is self-aware.'

'Which means I have broken the law,' said Monsignor Boyle dryly.

'That's to be assessed.' She said to Himmelfarb, 'You understand that under international convention you have certain rights. You have the right to continued existence for an indefinite period in information space, if you wish it. You have the right to read-only interfaces with the prime world . . . It is illegal to create full sentience – self-awareness – for frivolous purposes. I'm here to assess the motives of the Vatican in that regard.'

'We have a valid question to pose,' murmured the Monsignor, with a hint of steel in his voice.

'Why did I destroy myself?' Himmelfarb laughed. 'You would think that the custodians of the true Church would rely on rather less-literal means to divine a human soul, wouldn't you, officer, than to drag me back from Hell itself? – Oh, yes, Hell. I am a suicide. And so I am doomed to the seventh circle, where I will be reincarnated as a withered tree. Have you read your Dante, officer?'

Philmus had, in preparation for the case.

The Monsignor said softly, 'Why did you commit this sin, Eva?'

Himmelfarb flexed her Virtual fingers, and her flesh broke up briefly into fine, cubic pixels. 'May I show you?'

The Monsignor glanced at Philmus, who nodded.

The lights dimmed. Philmus felt sensors probe at her exposed flesh, glimpsed lasers scanning her face.

The five-hundred-year-old painted willow branches started to rustle, and from the foliage inhuman eyes glared at her.

Then the walls dissolved, and Philmus was standing on top of a mountain.

She staggered. She felt light on her feet, as if giddy.

She always hated Virtual transitions.

The Monsignor was moaning.

She was on the edge of some kind of forest. She turned, cautiously. She found herself looking down the terraced slope of a mountain. At the base was an ocean which lapped, empty, to the world's round edge. The sun was bright in her eyes.

A few metres down, a wall of fire burned.

The Monsignor walked with great shallow bounds. He moved with care and distaste; maybe donning a Virtual body was some kind of venial sin.

Himmelfarb smiled at Philmus. 'Do you know where you are? You could walk through that wall of fire, and not harm a hair of your head.' She reached up to a tree branch and plucked a leaf. It grew back instantly. 'Our natural laws are suspended here, officer; like a piece of art, everything gives expression to God's intention.'

Boyle said bluntly, 'You are in Eden, officer Philmus, at the summit of Mount Purgatory. The last earthly place Dante visited before ascending into Heaven.'

Eden?

The trees, looming, seemed to crowd around her. She couldn't identify any species. Though they had no enviroshields, none of the trees suffered any identifiable burning or blight.

She found herself cowering under the blank, unprotected sky.

Maybe this was *someone's* vision of Eden. But Philmus had been living under a Dome for ten years; this was no place she could ever be at peace.

'What happened to the gravity?'

Himmelfarb said, 'Gravity diminishes as you ascend Purgatory. We are far from Satan here . . . I can't show you what I saw, officer Philmus. But perhaps, if we look through Dante's eyes, you will understand. The *Divine Comedy* is a kind of science fiction story. It's a journey through the universe, as Dante saw it. He was guided by Virgil –'

'Who?'

The Monsignor said, 'The greatest Latin poet. You must have heard of the *Aeneid*. The significance to Dante was that Virgil was a pagan: he died before Christ was born. No matter how wise and just Virgil was, he could never ascend to Heaven, as Dante could, because he never knew Christ.'

'Seems harsh.'

The Monsignor managed a grin. 'Dante wasn't making the rules.'

Himmelfarb said, 'Dante reaches Satan in Hell, at the centre of the Earth. Then, with Virgil, he climbs a tunnel to a mountain in the southern hemisphere –'

'This one.'

'Yes.' Himmelfarb shielded her eyes. 'The *Paradiso*, the last book, starts here. And it was when my translation reached this point that the thing I'd put in my head woke up.'

'What are you talking about?'

The priest grinned like a teenager. 'Let me show you my laboratory. Come on.' And she turned and plunged into the forest.

Irritated, Philmus followed.

In the mouth of the wood it was dark. The ground, coated with leaves and mulch, gave uncomfortably under her feet.

The Monsignor walked with her. He said, 'Dante was a study assignment. Eva was a Jesuit, officer. Her science was unquestioned in its quality. But her faith was weak.'

Himmelfarb looked back. 'So there you have your answer, Monsignor,' she called. 'I am the priest who lost her faith, and destroyed herself.' She spread her hands. 'Why not release me now?'

Boyle ignored her.

The light was changing.

The mulch under Philmus's feet had turned, unnoticed, to a thick carpet. And the leaves on the trees had mutated to the pages of books, immense rows of them.

They broke through into a rambling library.

Himmelfarb laughed. 'Welcome to the Secret Archive of the Vatican, officer Philmus.'

They walked through the Archive.

Readers, mostly in lay clothes, were scattered sparsely around the rooms, with Virtual documents glittering in the air before them, page images turning without rustling.

Philmus felt like a tourist.

Himmelfarb spun in the air. 'A fascinating place,' she said to Philmus. 'Here you will find a demand for homage to Genghis Khan, and Galileo's recantation . . . After two thousand years I doubt that anybody knows all the secrets stored here.'

Philmus glanced at Boyle, but his face was impassive.

Himmelfarb went on, 'This is also the heart of the Vatican's science effort. It may seem paradoxical to you that there is not necessarily a conflict between the scientific world-view and the Christian. In Dante's Aristotelian universe, the Earth is the physical centre of all things, but God is the spiritual centre. Just as human nature has twin poles, of rationality and dreams. Dante's universe, the product of a thousand years of contemplation, was a model of how these poles could be united; in our time this seems impossible, but perhaps after another millennium of meditation on the meaning of our own new physics, we might come a little closer. What do you think?'

Philmus shrugged. 'I'm no Catholic.'

'But,' said Himmelfarb, 'you are troubled by metaphysics. The state of my electronic soul, for instance. You have more in common with me than you imagine, officer.'

They reached a heavy steel door. Beyond it was a small, glass-walled vestibule; there were sinks, pegs and lockers. And beyond that lay a laboratory, stainless steel benches under the grey glow of fluorescent lights. The lab looked uncomfortably sharp-edged by contrast with the building which contained it.

With confidence, Himmelfarb turned and walked through the glass wall into the lab. Philmus followed. The wall was a soap-bubble membrane that stretched over her face, then parted softly, its edge stroking her skin.

Much of the equipment was anonymous lab stuff – rows of grey boxes – incomprehensible to Philmus. The air was warm, the only smell an antiseptic subtext.

They reached a glass wall that reached to the ceiling. Black glove sleeves, empty, protruded from the wall like questing fingers. Beyond the wall was an array of tiny vials, with little robotic manipulators wielding pipettes, heaters and stirrers running on tracks around them. If the array was as deep as it was broad, Philmus thought, there must be millions of the little tubes in there.

Himmelfarb stood before the wall. 'My pride and joy,' she said dryly. 'Or it would be if pride wasn't a sin. The future of information processing, officer, perhaps of consciousness itself . . .'

'And all of it,' said the Monsignor, 'inordinately expensive. All those enzymes, you know.'

'It looks like a DNA computer,' Philmus said.

'Exactly right,' Himmelfarb said. 'The first experiments date back to the last century. Did you know that? The principle is simple. DNA strands, or fragments of strands, will spontaneously link in ways that can be used to model real-world problems. We might model your journey to Rome, officer, from –'

'San Francisco.'

The air filled with cartoons, twisting molecular spirals.

'I would prepare strands of DNA, twenty or more nucleotide bases long, each of which would represent a possible transit point on your journey – Los Angeles, New York, London, Paris – or one of the possible paths between them.'

The strands mingled, and linked into larger molecules, evidently modelling the routes Philmus could follow.

'The processing and storage capacity of such machines is huge. In a few grams of DNA I would have quadrillions of solution molecules –'

'And somewhere in there you'd find a molecule representing my best journey.'

'And there's the rub. I have to *find* the single molecule which contains the answer I seek. And that can take seconds, an eternity compared to the fastest silicon-based machines.' The cartoons evaporated. Himmelfarb pushed her Virtual hand through the wall and ran her fingers through the arrays of tubes, lovingly. 'At any rate, that is the challenge.'

Monsignor Boyle said, 'We – that is, the Pontifical Academy

– funded Eva's research into the native information processing potential of human DNA.'

'Native?'

Abruptly the lab, the wall of vials, crumbled and disappeared; a hail of pixels evaporated, exposing the Edenic forest once more.

Philmus winced in the sunlight. *What now?* She felt disoriented, weary from the effort of trying to track Himmelfarb's grasshopper mind.

Himmelfarb smiled and held out her hand to Philmus. 'Let me show you what I learned from my study of Dante.' The young priest's Virtual touch was too smooth, too cool, like plastic.

The Monsignor seemed to be moaning again. Or perhaps he was praying.

'*Look at the sun,*' said Himmelfarb.

Philmus lifted her face, and stared into the sun, which was suspended high above Eden's trees. She forced her eyes open.

It wasn't real light. It carried none of the heat and subtle weight of sunlight. But the glare filled her head.

She saw Himmelfarb; she looked as if she was haloed.

Then she looked down.

They were rising, as if in some glass-walled elevator.

They were already above the treetops. She felt no breeze; it was as if a cocoon of air moved with them. She felt light, insubstantial, like a child in the arms of her father. She felt oddly safe; she would come to no harm here.

'We're accelerating,' Himmelfarb said. 'If you want the Aristotelian physics of it, we're being attracted to the second pole of the universe.'

'The second pole?'

'God.'

Looking back Philmus could see the Earth, heavy and massive and unmoving, at the centre of everything, a ball of water folded over on itself. They were already so high she couldn't make out Purgatory.

Rising ever faster, they passed through a layer of glassy light, like an airliner climbing through cloud. As they climbed higher she saw how the layer of light folded over the planet, shimmering like an immense soap bubble. Embedded in the membrane she could see a rocky ball, like a lumpy cloud, below them and receding.

It was the Moon.

She said, 'If I remember my Ptolemy –'

'The Earth is surrounded by spheres. Nine of them, nine heavens. They are transparent, and they carry the sun, Moon, and planets, beneath the fixed stars.'

The Monsignor murmured, 'We are already beyond the sphere of decay and death.'

Himmelfarb laughed. 'And you ain't seen nothing yet.'

Still they accelerated.

Himmelfarb's eyes were glowing brilliantly bright. She said, 'You must understand Dante's geometrical vision. Think of a globe of Earth, Satan at the south pole, God at the north. Imagine moving north, away from Satan. The circles of Hell, and now the spheres of Heaven, are like the lines of latitude you cross as you head to the equator . . .'

Philmus, breathless, tried not to close her eyes. 'You were telling me about your research.'

'. . . All right. DNA is a powerful information store. A picogram of your own DNA, officer, is sufficient to specify how to manufacture you – and everything you've inherited from all your ancestors, right back to the primordial sea. But there is still much about our DNA – whole stretches of its structure – whose purpose we can only guess. I wondered if –'

The Monsignor blew out his cheeks. 'All this is unverified.'

Himmelfarb said, 'I wondered if human DNA itself might contain information processing mechanisms – which we might learn from or even exploit, to replace our clumsy pseudo-mechanical methods . . .'

Still they rose, through another soap-bubble celestial sphere, then another. All the planets, Mercury through Saturn, were below them now. The Earth, at the centre of translucent, deep blue clockwork, was far below.

They reached the sphere of the fixed stars. Philmus swept up through a curtain of light points, which then spangled over the diminishing Earth beneath her.

'One hell of a sight,' Philmus said.

'Literally,' said the Monsignor, gasping.

'You see,' Himmelfarb said to Philmus, '*I succeeded.* I found computation – information processing – going on in the junk DNA. And more. I found evidence that assemblages of DNA within our cells have receptors, so they can observe the external world in some form, that they store and process data, and even that they are self-referential.'

'Natural DNA computers?'

'More than that. These assemblages are aware of their own existence, officer. They think.'

Suspended in the air, disoriented, Philmus held up her free hand. 'Woah. Are you telling me our cells are *sentient*?'

'Not the cells,' the priest said patiently. 'Organelles, assemblages of macromolecules inside the cells. The *organelles* are –'

'Dreaming?'

The priest smiled. 'You do understand.'

Philmus shivered, and looked down at her hand. Could this be true? 'I feel as if I've woken up in a haunted house.'

'Except that, with your network of fizzing neurones, your clumsily constructed meta-consciousness, *you* are the ghost.'

'How come nobody before ever noticed such a fundamental aspect of our DNA?'

Himmelfarb shrugged. 'We weren't looking. And besides, the basic purpose of human DNA is construction. Its sequences of nucleotides are job orders and blueprints for making molecular machine tools. Proteins, built by DNA, built *you*, officer, who learned, fortuitously, to think, and question your origins.' She winked at Philmus. 'Here is a prediction. In environments where resources for building, for growing, are scarce – the deep sea vents, or even the volcanic seams of Mars where life might be clinging, trapped by five billion years of ice – we will find much stronger evidence of macromolecular sentience. Rocky dreams on Mars, officer!'

The Monsignor said dryly, 'If we ever get to Mars we can check that. And if you'd bothered to write up your progress in an orderly manner we might have a way to verify your conclusions.'

The dead priest smiled indulgently. 'I am not – was not – a very good reductionist, I am afraid. In my arrogance, officer, I took the step which has damned me.'

'Which was?'

Her face was open, youthful, too smooth. 'Studying minds in test tubes wasn't enough. *I wanted to contact the latent consciousness embedded in my own DNA.* I was curious. I wanted to share its oceanic dream. I injected myself with a solution consisting of a buffer solution and certain receptor mechanisms which –'

'And did it work?'

She smiled. 'Does it matter? Perhaps now you have your answer, Monsignor. I am Faust; I am Frankenstein. I even have the right accent! I am the obsessed scientist, driven by her greed for godless knowledge, who allowed her own creation to destroy her. There is your story –'

Philmus said, 'I'll decide that . . . Eva, what did it feel like?'

Himmelfarb hesitated, and her face clouded with pixels. 'Frustrating. Like trying to glimpse a wonderful landscape through a pinhole. The organelles operate at a deep, fundamental level . . . And perhaps they enjoy a continuous consciousness that reaches back to their formation in the primeval sea five billion years ago. Think of that. They are part of the universe as I can never be, behind the misty walls of my senses; they know the universe as I never could. All I could do – like Dante – is interpret their vision with my own limited language and mathematics.'

So here's where Dante fits in. 'You're saying *Dante* went through this experience?'

'It was the source of the *Comedy.* Yes.'

'But Dante was not injected with receptors. How could he –'

'But we all share the deeper mystery, the DNA molecule itself. Perhaps in some of us it awakens naturally, as I forced in my own body . . . And now, I will show you the central mystery of Dante's vision.'

Boyle said, 'I think we're slowing.'

Himmelfarb said, 'We're approaching the ninth sphere.'

'The Primum Mobile,' said the Monsignor.

'Yes. The "first moving part", the root of time and space. Turned by angels, expressing their love for God . . . Look up,' Himmelfarb said to Philmus. 'What do you see?'

At first, only structureless light. But then, a texture . . .

Suddenly Philmus was looking, up beyond the Primum Mobile, into another glass onion, a nesting of transparent spheres that surrounded – not a dull lump of clay like Earth – but a brilliant point of light. The nearest spheres were huge, like curving wings, as large as the spheres of the outer planets.

Himmelfarb said, 'They are the spheres of the angels, which surround the universe's other pole, which is God. Like a mirror image of Hell. Counting out from here we have the angels, archangels, principalities, powers –'

'I don't get it,' Philmus said. '*What* other pole? How can a sphere have two centres?'

'Think about the equator,' whispered Himmelfarb. 'The globe of Earth, remember? As you travel north, as you pass the equator, the concentric circles of latitude start to grow smaller, while still enclosing those to the south . . .'

'We aren't on the surface of a globe.'

'*But we are on the surface of a 3-sphere – the three-dimensional surface of a four-dimensional hypersphere.* Do you see? The concentric spheres you see are exactly analogous to the lines of latitude on the two-dimensional surface of a globe. And just as, if you stand on the equator of Earth, you can look back to the south pole or forward to the north pole, so here, at the universe's equator, we can look towards the poles of Earth or God. The Primum Mobile, the equator of the universe, curves around the Earth, below us, and at the same time it curves around God, above us.'

Philmus looked back and forth, from God to Earth, and she saw, incredibly, that Himmelfarb was right. The Primum Mobile curved two ways at once.

The Monsignor's jaw seemed to be hanging open. 'And Dante *saw* this? A four-dimensional artefact? He *described* it?'

'As remarkable as it seems – yes,' said Himmelfarb. 'Read the poem again if you don't believe it: around the year 1320 Dante Alighiero wrote down a precise description of the experience of travelling through a 3-sphere. When I figured this out, I couldn't believe it myself. It was like finding a revolver in a layer of dinosaur fossils.'

Philmus said, 'But how is it possible . . . ?'

'*It was not Dante,*' Himmelfarb said. 'It was the sentient organelles within him who had the true vision, which Dante interpreted in terms of his medieval cosmology. We know he had wrestled with the paradox that he lived in a universe which was simultaneously centred on Earth, and on God . . . This offered him a geometric resolution. It is a fantastic hypothesis, but it does explain how four-dimensional geometry, unexplored by the mathematicians until the nineteenth century, found expression in a poem of the early Renaissance.' She grinned, mischievously. 'Or perhaps Dante was a time traveller. What do you think?'

The Monsignor growled, 'Are we done?'

'. . . You know we aren't,' Himmelfarb said gently.

Philmus felt overwhelmed; she longed to return to solid ground. 'After this, what else can there be?'

98

'The last canto,' the Monsignor whispered.

Himmelfarb said, 'Yes. The last canto, which defeated even Dante. But, seven centuries later, I was able to go further.'

Philmus stared into her glowing eyes. 'Tell us.'

And the three of them, like birds hovering beneath the domed roof of a cathedral, ascended into the Empyrean.

They passed into a layer of darkness, like a storm cloud.

The hemispheres of the 3-sphere – the Earth and its nested spheres, the globes of the angels – faded like stars at dawn. But Himmelfarb's eyes glowed brightly.

And then, space folded away.

Philmus could still see Boyle, Himmelfarb, the priest's shining eyes. But she couldn't tell how near or far the others were. And when she tried to look away from them, her eyes slid over an elusive darkness, deeper than the darkness inside her own skull.

There was no structure beyond the three of them, their relative positions. She felt as small as an electron, as huge as a galaxy. She felt lost.

She clung to Himmelfarb's hand. 'Where are we? How far –'

'We are outside the Primum Mobile: beyond duration, beyond the structure of space. Dante understood this place. "There near and far neither add nor subtract . . ." You know, we underestimate Dante. The physicists are the worst. They see us all running around as Virtuals in the memory of some giant computer of the future. Not to mention the science fiction writers. Garbage. Dante understood that a soul is not a Virtual, and in the *Paradiso*, he was trying to express the transhuman experience of true eternity –'

'*What did he see?*'

Himmelfarb smiled. 'Watch.'

. . . Philmus saw light, like the image of God at the centre of the angels' spheres. It was a point, and yet it filled space and time. And then it unfolded, like a flower blooming, with particles and lines *(world lines? quantum functions?)* billowing out and rushing past her face, in an insubstantial breeze. Some of the lines tangled, and consciousness sparked – trapped in time, briefly shouting its joy at its moment of awareness – before dissipating once more. But still the unfolding continued, in a fourth, fifth, sixth direction, in ways she could somehow, if briefly, conceive.

She felt a surge of joy. And there was something more, something just beyond her grasp –

It was gone. She was suspended in the structureless void again. Himmelfarb grasped her hand.

Boyle was curled over on himself, his eyes clamped closed.

Philmus said, 'I saw –'

Himmelfarb said, 'It doesn't matter. We all see something different. And besides, it was only a Virtual shadow . . . What did you *feel?*'

Philmus hesitated. 'As I do when I solve a case. When the pieces come together.'

Himmelfarb nodded. 'Cognition. Scientists understand that. The ultimate cognition, knowing reality.'

'But now it's gone.' She felt desolate.

'I know.' Himmelfarb's grip tightened. 'I'm sorry.'

The Monsignor, his voice weak, murmured, '"I saw gathered . . . / Bound up by love in a single volume / All the leaves scattered through the universe; / Substance and accidents and their relations, / But yet fused together in such a manner / That what I am talking about is a simple light . . ."'

'Dante was very precise about how he interpreted what he saw,' said Himmelfarb. 'This is Aristotelian physics. "Substances" and "accidents" describe phenomena and their relationships. I believe that *Dante was trying to describe a glimpse of the unification of nature.*'

'Yes,' Philmus whispered.

'And then he saw a paradox that he expresses by an image. Three circles, superimposed, of the same size – and yet of different colours.'

'Separated by a higher dimension,' Philmus guessed.

'Yes. In the high-dimensional artefact Dante saw a metaphor for the Trinity. God's three personalities in one being.'

'Ah,' said the Monsignor, cautiously uncurling. 'But *you* saw –'

'Rather more. I knew enough physics –'

'This is the basis of the new unified theory,' Philmus said. 'A unification of phenomena through the structure of a higher-dimensional space.'

Himmelfarb's face was turning to pixels again. 'It isn't as simple as that,' she said. 'The whole notion of dimensionality is an approximate one that only emerges in a semi-classical context – well. I don't suppose it matters now. I wrote it down as fast as I could, as far as I could remember it, as best I could express it. I don't think I could give any more.'

The Monsignor looked disappointed.

Philmus said, 'And then –'

'I killed myself,' Himmelfarb said bluntly. Bathed in sourceless light, she seemed to withdraw from Philmus. 'You have to understand. *It wasn't me.* I had hoped to find enlightenment. But *I* was not enhanced. It was the organelles' vision which leaked into my soul, and which I glimpsed.'

'And that was what you could not bear,' the Monsignor said. Hanging like a toy in mid-air, he nodded complacently; evidently, Philmus thought, he had learned what had come to find, and Himmelfarb's essential untidiness – so distressing to Boyle's bureaucrat's heart – was gone. Now she was safely dead, her story closed.

Philmus thought that over, and decided she would prosecute.

But she also sensed that Boyle knew more than he was telling her. And besides . . . 'I think you're wrong, Monsignor.'

Boyle raised his eyebrows. Himmelfarb hovered between them, saying nothing.

'Eva didn't quite finish showing us the last canto. Did you?'

The priest closed her eyes. 'After the vision of the multidimensional circle, Dante says: "That circle . . . / When my eyes examined it rather more / Within itself, and in its own colour, / Seemed to be painted with our effigy . . ."'

'I don't understand,' the Monsignor admitted.

Philmus said, 'Dante saw a human face projected on his multidimensional artefact. He interpreted whatever he saw as the Incarnation: the embodiment of God – beyond time and space – in our time-bound mortal form. The final paradox of your Christian theology.'

Boyle said, 'So the ultimate vision of the universe is ourselves.'

'No,' Himmelfarb snapped. 'Today we would say that we – all minds – *are* the universe, which calls itself into existence through our observation of it.'

'Ah.' Boyle nodded. 'Mind is the "eternal light, existing in ourselves alone, / Alone knowing ourselves . . ." I paraphrase. And this is what you saw, Eva?'

'No,' said Philmus. She felt impatient; this insensitive asshole was supposed to be a priest, after all. 'Don't you see? This is what Himmelfarb believed her *passengers*, the sentient organelles, would see next; she had the guidance from Dante's sketchy report for that. And that's what she wanted to prevent.'

'Yes.' Himmelfarb smiled distantly. 'You are perceptive, officer. Are you sure you aren't a Catholic?'

'Not even lapsed.'

Himmelfarb said, 'You see, Dante's quest did not end with discovering an answer, but with the end of questioning. He submitted himself to the order of the universe, so that his "desire and will / Were . . . turned like a wheel, all at one speed, / By the love which moves the sun and the other stars".'

Philmus said, 'And that was the peace the organelles achieved, the peace you glimpsed. But you knew, or feared, you couldn't follow.'

'And so,' said Boyle, 'you destroyed yourself –'

'To destroy *them*. Yes.' Her expression was bitter. 'Do you understand now, Monsignor? Of course this is the end of your religion – of all religion. We are accidental structures, evanescent, tied to time and doomed to oblivion. All our religious impulse, all our questing, all our visions – just a pale shadow of the organelles' direct experience. *They have God*, Monsignor. All we have are Dante dreams.'

Philmus said, 'You were happy to be Dante. But –'

'But I refused to see them go where I couldn't follow. Yes, I could be Dante. But I couldn't bear to be Virgil.'

'I absolve you of your sin,' the Monsignor said abruptly, and he blessed Himmelfarb with a cross, shaped by his right hand.

Himmelfarb looked shocked – and then an expression of peace crossed her face, before light burst from within her, dazzling Philmus.

When her eyes recovered Philmus was embedded in space and time once more: alone with the Monsignor, in the sixteenth century corridor, where the willow branches were merely painted.

Philmus met the Monsignor one more time, at the conclusion of the hearing in the New York UN building. The UN Commission had found against the Vatican, which would have to pay a significant fine.

Boyle greeted Philmus civilly. 'So our business is done.'

'Do you feel we reached the truth, Monsignor?'

He hesitated. 'I don't know what to believe. The analysis of Eva's monograph is continuing. The NASA people have taken up her suggestion of alternate evolutionary directions for macromolecules on Mars, and the exobiologists are modelling and proposing missions. We haven't been able to recreate Eva's lab results: to retrace her "footprints in Hell", as Dante would say. Perhaps it was all a fever dream of Eva's, brought on by overwork and too much study. It wouldn't be the first such incident in the Church's long history.

'Or perhaps we are indeed hosts to another sentience. Perhaps one day it will awaken fully. If it does, I hope it will treat us with compassion. And what do you believe, officer Philmus?'

I believe that whatever the Vatican finds, whatever it knows, it will keep to itself, in the Secret Archive.

'I'm reading Dante.' It was true.

The Monsignor smiled. 'But you hate poetry.'

'It's the only place I can think of where I might find the answers. Anyhow, it's something to do in the small hours of the night. Better than –'

He said softly, 'Yes?'

'Better than to lie there listening to my body. Wondering who else is home.'

He whispered, 'Dante dreams? You too?'

'Monsignor – you realize that if Eva was right, she achieved first contact.'

His face was calculating, but not without sympathy. 'The Vatican is very old, officer. Old, and secretive. And – though without the tools of modern science – we have been investigating these issues for a very long time.'

She felt her pulse hammer. 'What does that mean?'

'There are many ways to God. Perhaps Eva indeed made contact. But – the first?'

He smiled, turned and walked away.

WAR BIRDS

November 1969:

The dust of the Moon crunched under Burdick's feet. His footprints, in the low sunlight, under the black sky, were clear and sharp, embedded in billion-year-old regolith.

When Burdick bent and ran his hand through the dirt, it looked a lot darker: almost black, like charcoal. The dirt gave easily for the first couple of inches, but then resisted his gloved fingers.

They'd brought shovels. But it wasn't going to be so easy to dig out graves, here on the Moon.

Here came Harry Singer, his commander, bouncing across the flat, pitted surface of the Sea of Tranquillity. Harry was humming his dumb little country tunes. He had been on a high since that moment when he had brought *Guardian*, still fat on fuel, drifting over this enigmatic ground, and they'd spotted *Eagle* itself, glittering like a toy against the greyness. Burdick understood how he felt. The tough part of the mission was still to come. Let Harry savour the triumph of the landing.

Burdick felt on a high himself. At thirty-nine, after eight years in the space programme, he was no longer a rookie. Of course after Apollo 12 was redirected, he wasn't where he'd expected to be, in the Ocean of Storms. And he wasn't going to be doing all the geology and stuff he'd been trained to do. But he'd never made much sense of all the science shit anyhow.

And here he was, after all, on the surface of the Moon itself.

Harry was looking at him. He straightened up.

It was time to do his duty.

Side by side, two USAF officers on the surface of the Moon, they faced *Eagle*.

Neil Armstrong's LM was a spidery construct of aluminium sheets and struts, sitting there like a little house. It didn't show many signs of its four-month stay. Maybe the gold insulation blanket on that descent stage was a little pitted. Maybe the colours of the Stars and Stripes painted there had faded a little.

But the four spider legs had collapsed. When it exploded, the boxy heart of the descent stage had just crumpled up and fallen against the dust. The bulbous ascent stage looked intact, but it was tipped over through thirty or forty degrees, and Burdick could see a split down one seam. *Eagle* sagged like a deflated balloon.

The surface here was littered by bits of twisted-up aluminium hull, and by shards of blown-out insulation blanket, a raying that overlaid the subtler disturbance of the LM's descent engine fire. But there were no footprints here. Nobody had climbed down from this LM. Armstrong and Aldrin had been the first humans to reach another world, and had lived less than a minute to enjoy it.

'Let's get it over,' Singer said.

'Yeah . . .'

Something was glittering, at the edge of Burdick's vision. Something metallic. At first he thought it was some other piece of the *Eagle,* broken off and hurled over the regolith.

But that couldn't be right. It was just too big.

It was the size and shape of a steel bathtub, mounted on six, no, eight spidery wheels. There was an open lid encrusted with what looked like solar cells. A couple of antennae, cones and rods, stuck out of the interior.

Something moved: two big camera lenses, fixed to the front of the car, swivelling up to inspect him.

'I don't believe it,' Singer said. 'It's a fucking Lunokhod.'

'The Soviets.'

'Yeah. Come to see what they did. Come on,' said Harry Singer. And he picked up a Moon rock.

Burdick bent, stiff in his pneumatic suit, and got hold of the biggest boulder he could find. It would have been too heavy for him on Earth, probably, and here he could feel its mass, liquidly resistant to motion. Like a miniature Moon itself, the rock was pitted with craters, from a fingertip's width all the way down to fine little pinholes. It was probably billions-of-years old.

Burdick and Singer stalked across the shining surface, and lifted up their Moon rocks, and began to beat the Lunokhod, smashing away the antennae and the fragile camera assemblies and the sheet of solar cells, their ancient rock weapons splintering in their hands, a quarter of a million miles from home. The sun was bright and in Burdick's eyes, and, under his Snoopy hat, he could feel sweat starting over his brow.

August 1981:
Control, this is Aldrin. *Commander's voice check, over. Roger, over.* *Control, this is the pilot. Voice check, over. Roger, over . . .*

The sun was bright and in his eyes, and, under his peaked Air Force officer's cap, Burdick could feel sweat starting over his brow.

It was early morning. He was looking east, right into the sun. Beyond the tree line, there was Launch Complex 39, the twin pads loaded up with their Shuttles: 39-B to the left, with *Aldrin*, 39-A to the right, with *Enterprise. Enterprise* was due for launch tomorrow, and was still enclosed in its rotating structure, but *Aldrin* was exposed, ready to fire.

He could smell the sea. There were still bands of mist lingering over the flat salt marshes, and he could hear the cry of the gulls wheeling around the gantries.

Burdick was glad to get out of the Kennedy Space Center executive offices and come up here on the roof to see the launch. As Chief Astronaut it was his duty to show up here rather than in the Firing Room, which would be his inclination. But the astronauts' families were here, and downstairs it was like a kindergarten. The youngest kids had soon got bored waiting for the launch and were crawling around over the floor, playing with orbiter models and mission patches.

He was kind of pleased that his own son, Phil Junior, ten years old, eschewed such games. Today, for instance, he was off with the Eagle Scouts. It would have been nice to have him up here, Burdick thought, but it was more important to give the little soldier his independence.

This roof was full of VIPs and NASA brass. Here was the new President, Reagan himself, with his first lady, grinning and glad-handing, with Richard Nixon, rehabilitated as Reagan's secretary of state. And there was Curtis LeMay, the old Cold Warrior, brought out of retirement to serve as Air Force chief of staff, following his commander and chomping away on one of his trade-mark cigars, squat and bustling and competent.

All the civilians were wearing big wide-brimmed hats and

sun-block, even Reagan. If you worked here you were supposed to wear filters over your mouth and nose. Some of the pad rats, it was said, had come down with lesions seared into their lungs. But to Burdick that was all bullshit. The ozone layer may or may not have been depleted by all these space launches. And he knew some of the techs were concerned about launching at the height of summer, when all that u-v etched away at the perishables on the orbiter stack. But then those guys beefed about launching in winter too, when ice clustered on the stack and the perishable components, rubber and plastic, got too stiff.

So there was more u-v. So they all had to paint their houses more often these days. So what? What the hell were they supposed to do? Stop launching?

The dominant object in his skyline was the VAB, the Vehicle Assembly Building, a monstrous black-and-white cube, built to assemble Moon ships. The cliff-face wall of the VAB was still scarred by the splash of the petrol bombing, where *Star Trek* fans had broken in to protest at the name of their beloved fantasy spaceship being given to a Shuttle orbiter, a war bird.

There was a big parking lot at the base of the VAB, pretty much deserted today except for the buses which had brought in the press guys. He remembered how different it was in the sixties, when the lot was always jammed with rows of vehicles, gleaming in the Florida sun like so many metal beetles. But the road traffic had never recovered from the oil price hike that had followed Reagan's nuking of Iran, despite the peacemaking efforts of the restored Shah with those Arabs.

As the mist burned off, over on the horizon, he could see the gleaming white of the orbiter, *Aldrin*, against its orange External Tank. He needed his binoculars to see the four solid rocket boosters clustered around the orbiter. This was a stretched Shuttle configuration, designed for heavy lift, a hundred and thirty-five tons to low Earth orbit, more than twice the baseline design's capacity. And he knew *Enterprise*, right now, was being fitted with the new liquid fuel boosters, another upgrade path.

Today's launch would be the fourth flight of the four-booster configuration, and the first orbital test of the NERVA 3 nuclear tug. That NERVA was going to be sent around the Moon, unmanned, and then, the plan went, later in the year there would be a couple of manned test flights, and maybe a Moon mission as early as next year. It was all part of the plan to establish a nuclear silo up there on the Moon: more silent sentinels, warning off any possible aggressors.

The NERVA was the reason there were so many VIPs here, on this roof and in the VIP stand.

This would be the twenty-first Shuttle launch of the year, from the Cape and Vandenburg, and the ninety-first of the programme in all, since the first successful orbital flight, bang on schedule in 1977. This year alone there ought to be forty-four launches, maybe fifteen of them USAF missions, using the Air Force's own two dedicated orbiters launched out of Vandenburg.

The Shuttle had turned into a magnificent success. Everyone had been determined to make it so, NASA, USAF and contractors alike. And Burdick, since he'd transferred from the Moon programme after it was closed down with Apollo 12, had been proud to play his part in that.

There was nothing about the Shuttle programme today that hadn't been in the plans right back in 1969, even before Apollo 11 landed. But *Eagle*, Burdick guessed, had given everyone a little incentive to get it right. Stunt flights to the Moon could wait. Space was the high ground, and if America didn't make it secure, the Soviets would, and there would be hell to pay.

And the Shuttle, with all its military applications – reconnaissance, interception, satellite recovery, hunter-killer capabilities, rescue and relief – was the key.

So here they were, operating five orbiters just as advertized, with an eleven-day airline-style turnaround between each flight, and with the components of Space Station Freedom, an outpost on that high frontier, already being assembled in plants in California and Texas and Alabama.

Anyhow, once old Walter Dornberger, von Braun's old boss, had been brought out of retirement and started applying a little of that old Peenemunde discipline to the project, everything got a lot tighter.

The countdown went through smoothly, as it always did.

Up on the roof, Burdick did his share of the gladhanding and flesh-pressing. But he ducked out once the count neared its conclusion. He was here for the launch, after all.

At main-engine start, a bright white light erupted at the base of the orbiter, and white smoke squirted out to either side.

There they go, guys, three at a hundred.

Then the four solid boosters lit up, showering orange smoke, yellow sparks. The stack lifted off the ground, startlingly quickly, trailing a column of white smoke which glowed orange within, as if on fire. The plume of yellow light from the SRBs was incredibly bright – dazzling, like liquid light, like sunlight seen from the Moon.

There was clapping and hollering from the dignitaries and crew relatives. Burdick kept his binoculars clamped to his face.

The stack arched over onto its back and followed a steep curve away from its tower. Already the gantry was dwarfed by the smoke column. After ten seconds the Shuttle punched through an isolated thin cloud, threading it like rope.

The sound reached him after fifteen seconds: a crackling thunder which came tumbling down over him, sharp slaps over an underlying rumble.

It was a hell of a thing, he thought.

And then –

It looked as if the SRBs had detached a little early. The single vapour trail split up into five, the orbiter itself with its main engines burning white, and the four SRBs careening out of the smoke, like diverging fingers.

Shit, he thought.

The orbiter blew first, that big External Tank on its belly just cracking open, oxygen and hydrogen igniting in a single pure blast. And then the four SRBs went up like firecrackers around that central glare, destroyed by the Range Safety Officer.

We have no downlink at this time. We're obviously studying the event.

He could still hear the routine rocket noise flowing over him, like a ghost, the sound of the disaster itself still suspended in the ruptured air.

The NERVA, he thought. How many pounds of fissile uranium had just been smeared over the Florida sky?

Reagan. They had to get the President under cover.

He looked around, through a crowd that had turned into a mob of screaming, crying people. There: Curtis LeMay had his arm around Reagan's shoulders, and was hustling him away, towards the door from the roof. Burdick could hear what LeMay was saying to the ashen President. *We can't tolerate this, sir. We have to consider eradication. I'm talking about Project Control, Mr President. We've been talking about this since the 1950s at the Air War College. We aren't talking about pre-emptive strikes, sir,*

but about the historic rollback of the Soviet Union. It's time . . .
Old Nixon was nodding gravely.

Burdick stayed on the roof, a handkerchief on his mouth against
the fall-out, until all the women and children had been escorted
out of the open air.

January 1986:
As the pilots prepared for the interception, *Yeager*'s flight deck
was like a little workshop, Burdick thought, glowing with the
lights of Earth, and the crews' fluorescent glareshields. The battle-
ship-grey walls were encrusted with switches and instruments that
shone white and yellow with internal light, though the surfaces in
which they were embedded were battered and scuffed with age
and use. There was a constant, high-pitched whir, of environment
control pumps and fans.

Once more he had control pedals at his feet, a joystick between
his legs. He felt at home. The Shuttle orbiter was a fine old
warplane.

The Soyuz target had been over Iraq when *Yeager* launched
from Vandenburg, and there had been a gap of ten thousand miles
between them. But orbital mechanics brought him ever closer to
his prey, at a rate of a thousand miles per orbit.

Anyhow there was no rush. The Shuttle was fitted with its
extended-duration pack, solar panels that had unfolded from the
payload bay like wings. They could stay up here for a month if
they needed to.

Burdick even had time to send a message down a secure line to
Fay at Vandenburg, and to Philip Jr, who was, at fifteen, a cadet
at St John's Military Academy in Wisconsin.

It was good to be back in command.

Since he'd been moved upstairs he was enjoying his assignment
as head of the Office of Manned Spaceflight. But flying a desk
was no substitute for flying Shuttle. At fifty-six, he'd thought he
was too old to fly again, but Hans Mark – NASA Administrator,
former Air Force secretary and physicist under Edward Teller –
had persuaded him to come out of retirement for this one mission.
Space Command needed all the pilots it could get right now, and
even if this mission wasn't the most glamorous of Project Control
– those had to be the dramatic high-atmosphere swoops of *Adams*
and *Falcon* and *Enterprise,* as they had dropped their bomb loads
over the USSR, far out of reach of any intercept capability –

cherry-picking the last Soyuz spy ship had to be the most technically challenging, and fun.

The ground track took them over the Soviet Union a couple of
times. Even now, a month after Project Control had reached its
spectacular climax, he could still see the glowing craters where the
space centres at Volgograd and Kapustin Yar used to be. The whole
country was pretty dark, although he could see cities burning
around the rim of Russia itself: in the Moslem republics of south
Asia, and the Baltic republics, and even the east European satellites.

Of course there was a price to pay. Before it collapsed, the Soviet
government had shot off a few of its own nukes. Warsaw was
gone, for instance. And there were rumours of trouble on the long
Chinese frontier. But that was okay by Burdick. Everybody had
taken the chance to kick the old bear when he was down, and
Burdick guessed they were entitled.

Not that everyone agreed. Before the UN had been thrown out
of New York there had been pretty near universal condemnation
of the US's actions, universal except for the British anyhow. But
the UN were assholes. It was no more than you'd expect from a
bullshit factory like that.

When he passed over the US, it was strange to see Florida from
orbit, that big black scar down its evacuated eastern coast. Not
that the loss of the Cape was so grievous. The *Aldrin* disaster, in
the end, had just expedited LeMay's plans to transfer all the Shuttle
resources to the USAF. The climate at Vandenburg was a lot more
stable for landings anyhow.

Funny thing that the *Aldrin* crash, which had spurred off Project
Control in the first place, had turned out to be caused by a simple
glitch, a fuel line that had perished from u-v exposure. Not sabotage at all. Burdick didn't suppose it mattered. Control would have
come about anyhow. There had been a whole string of provoca-
tions from the USSR: Afghanistan, their own unmanned Shuttle,
the damn Salyut spy platforms. These things had a huge historic
inevitability to them, it seemed to him.

His crew, all USAF officers, was working well, just like the drill.
Even young Tom Gibson, up here on his third mission, who had
spent half his time throwing up, was working well with the hand-
held laser-ranging device, checking Burdick's position.

Burdick suspected he intimidated these junior guys. They all
seemed so damn young. And how must he seem to them? – the

only Moonwalker left flying, like some monolith from the past.

The youngsters were all wearing the smart new black uniforms of Space Command, with their thunderbolt flashes and bright logos. The uniforms looked good, and had struck a chord in the public mind, Burdick knew. Air Force Space Command seemed to represent a certain *order*, in a country beset by foes abroad, and trouble at home: revolutionaries everywhere, and polyglot cities, and hippies and anarchists and sex maniacs and drug addicts and activists and homosexuals and punk rockers and soaring crime . . .

The Rocket State, they called it: the goal was a conflict-free society administered from above, dominated by technology and smart young men like these, embodying the eternal American values of piety, hard work, family and flag. Just like the USAF, and NASA.

Order, imposed from space.

And now that Project Control had been implemented, that order would spread across the planet: *Pax Americana,* in the face of which all the old illogical ethnic and religious differences would dissolve, and mankind would come to its senses, and progress to a better tomorrow.

And so on. Burdick accepted it all. It was a fine vision. He'd welcomed the executions of Jane Fonda and Jesse Jackson and John Lennon and the rest of those fellow travellers for their treasonous subversion, the hell with them.

But even so these new uniforms made him feel just a little uncomfortable. They were too close to the images from Germany he'd grown up with as a kid. It was a kind of easy glamour, he thought. He preferred good-old Air Force blue.

A couple more burns to tweak his orbit, and then they were closing fast on Soyuz. Burdick went through his terminal initiation burn, and then his rendezvous radar started to track the bogey. He assumed the low-Z position beneath the little Russian ship and used his reaction thrusters to push up towards Soyuz from beneath.

Now he could see Soyuz, through the little rendezvous windows above his head.

The body of Soyuz was a light blue-green, an unexpectedly beautiful, Earthlike colour. Soyuz looked something like a pepperpot, a bug-like shape nine feet across, with its fat Orbital Module stuck on the nose of the main body, a truncated cylinder, capped by the headlight-shaped Descent Module. Two matte-black solar panels jutted from its rounded flanks, like unfolded wings, and a parabolic antenna was held away from the ship, on a light gantry.

Soyuz was basically an Apollo-era craft, still flying twenty years later. It looked, frankly, like a piece of shit to Burdick.

Soyuz was floating right down into *Yeager*'s gaping-open payload bay, like a minnow drifting into the mouth of a shark.

Tom Gibson was working the RMS now, the remote manipulator arm. The RMS had a heavy industrial-strength cutting laser bolted to its end, and Tom just reached up and snipped off the solar-cell wings of Soyuz, snip snip, like cutting the wings off a fly. Those solar panels drifted away, sparkling as they twisted. It was expertly done, and Burdick didn't even need to slow down his rate of approach.

The laser had come out of JPL, which had started producing some fine military applications since its weaponization in 1980.

The crippled Soyuz settled neatly into the payload bay, as if the Shuttle orbiter had been designed for the job. Which, of course, it had.

Burdick got into his EVA suit and, with two of his crew, made his way out through the airlock in back of the flight deck. The big bay doors were gaping open, the silvered Teflon surfaces of their radiator panels gleaming in Earthlight. The bay itself was a complex trench, crammed with equipment, stretching sixty feet ahead of him.

Soyuz sat where it had settled, an ugly insect shape, cluttering up the bay.

The others worked their way around Soyuz, strapping it into position for the glide home. Burdick made his way to the nose of Soyuz, to the complex docking hatch there.

The hatch was already open, the docking probe disassembled. He was, it seemed, expected.

Burdick, alone, pushed his way into the Orbital Module. There were bright floodlights here. He shut the hatch behind him, as he'd been trained, and worked a control panel. He heard a hiss, as air gushed into the module.

The Orbital Module was a ball just big enough for one person to stretch out. It would have been discarded to burn up during the re-entry, so it was packed full of garbage: food containers and clothing and equipment wrappers, like a surreal blizzard. This crew had been going home, when their country went up in flames.

When the pressure was restored, Burdick cracked his bubble

helmet and took it off. There was a stale smell, and his ears popped as pressure equalized.

The hatch to the Descent Module opened. Burdick drifted through.

The Descent Module cabin was laid out superficially like an old Apollo Command Module, with three lumpy-looking moulded couches set out in a fan formation. Big electronics racks filled up the space beneath the couches.

There was a single cosmonaut here, in an open pressure suit, staring up at him from the centre couch. He was squat, dark, his face as wide as the Moon. He looked to be about Burdick's age.

'*Dabro pazhalavat,*' he said. 'Welcome. I am Colonel Sergei Kozlov.' He held up a little tray, with food. 'Bread and salt. A traditional Russian greeting.'

'The hell with it.'

'Take the damn bread, General Philip Burdick.'

Burdick hesitated. Then he floated down, and took the bread. He chewed a little of it. It was heavy, sticky.

'You know my name?'

'*Konyeshna.* Of course. You were a Moonwalker. I saw you approach, on the surface of the Tranquillity Sea.'

'Huh?'

'I was teleoperating Lunokhod. I saw you wield your rock. It massed, I hazard, more than you collected as geological samples to bring home.'

'We weren't there for fucking geological samples.'

'Indeed not. And you are not here for scientific purposes now, are you?'

'Nor you, sir. We know this Soyuz is stuffed full of results from your surveillance activities on the Salyut.'

'That is true. But what does it matter? General Burdick, I am the last serving Soviet officer. I have no one to report to.'

Burdick discarded his bread. 'Colonel, you'll come onto the flight deck, and we'll take you home.'

'Home?'

'The United States.'

'Will there be TV cameras? Will you parade me?'

'We'll land at Vandenburg. The air base in California.'

'*Konyeshna.* Where I aim to apply for political asylum.' He grinned. 'Does that surprise you, General? But what have I to return to? The radioactive winds which blow across the steppe? Your slow dismantling of my nation?'

'Rebuilding. We'll rebuild your country. We aren't barbarians.'

'Thank you,' Kozlov said dryly. 'But it was unnecessary. Don't you see that, General? We were no threat to you. Not really. Nor was Lunokhod. On the Moon, we were only curious, as you were. We were going to change anyway. We had to. We couldn't afford to keep up with you. You could have waited. A little patience.' Kozlov smiled. 'But I forgive you. Come. I am impatient to see your wonderful Space Shuttle.'

Kozlov began to remove his couch restraints.

September 1993:
Burdick was impatient to see Phil's Space Shuttle.

Here he was actually cutting his lawn, a real old geezer thing to do, here in the middle of Iowa. Just what he'd always imagined retirement to be, back home in small-town America, where he'd started from. Well, hell, he was sixty-three now, and thanks to the mess space radiation had made of his central nervous system – so the surgeons told him – he looked and felt a lot older. He was entitled to his gentle retirement.

Fay came out with a glass of chilled lemonade, and to remind him that the flight was due overhead.

He cut the mower's engine. Grass clippings sank to the ground, slower than Moondust. He took off his hat and wiped the sunblock off his nose.

He limped to the porch chair. His right leg was paining him again, the one he'd broken a couple of times already. Premature osteoporosis, they said, all that bone calcium leached away in his piss in space, but what the hell.

He sat down, to wait to see Phil.

While he'd been cutting, ruminating, the sun had gone down on him. The first star was out: Venus, undoubtedly, down there on the horizon. There was one hell of an aurora tonight, reaching down from the north. Never used to get auroras in southern Iowa when he was a kid. Something to do with the bombs, the weather girl said.

There was some reading matter on the seat. Here was the speech by Curtis LeMay, venerable Chief of the Air Force, that he'd given to the USAF Association National Convention, out at Albuquerque. It was about his Sunday Punch scheme.

. . . and even as we have crushed the heart of Asia, we have to look further ahead.

President Reagan's decision to punish China's assault on Space Station Freedom was brave and correct. Let the ruins of the Forbidden City stand forever as a monument to our determination to maintain our grip on the high frontier, space! And yet the Chinese leadership continues to defy us, in every international forum.

And meanwhile, the incursion in Turkey of the Arab League under Saddam Hussein is equally unacceptable. Our pre-emptive nuclear assault on Iraq was surgical, necessary and justified. Contrast that with Saddam's recent assault, with Chinese CSS-2 missiles, on our Space Command base at RAF Fylingdales, England, exploiting a dirty and unreliable warhead.

We must not allow the warlords of darkened Asia to believe that we can be defied with impunity. Remember, these people are not like us! They are calculating, amoral machines. We must demonstrate our strength of arm and will to them. We have the whole of the future, the whole of infinite space, before us to conquer. But we must act now. We must show we are ready! . . .

The word was LeMay had Reagan's ear.

Not that anyone knew how much that meant. Even as the Constitution was being bucked again to allow Reagan to run for a fifth term, the rumours were that Reagan's Alzheimer's was becoming pronounced, and his veep, Nixon, was the real power behind the throne. Burdick didn't suppose it mattered.

The stars were coming out now, pushing through the remnants of the blue blanket of day. It was a good clear night: no rain, a light dew and the weather girl said there'd be no fall-out threat.

. . . I am saying that we have to be prepared! If America is going to survive in this tough old world she has to show that she's prepared to meet any threat, to fight to the last with utter inhibition, whenever she's asked to.

Ladies and gentlemen, we won the Cold War with Project Control. Now I'm asking you to endorse our next great task, the demonstration of our will to all of Africa and Asia and Europe: the Sunday Punch . . .

LeMay was offering Burdick the chance to return to the Moon. Now, that would be a hell of a thing. Burdick wasn't too old to fly. Such was the demand for experienced astronauts, with more than sixty Shuttle flights a year, there were plenty of creaky veterans older than Burdick still scooting about up there, including his old

buddy Harry Singer, for instance, now so racked by calcium depletion – so they said, anyhow – that he couldn't come back down
again.

It would be interesting to see the Earth from space again. They
sent up Walter Cronkite himself a year ago, when they inaugu-
rated the new Shuttle fleet: fully reusable now, with the DC-10-
sized orbiter riding to space on the back of a 747-sized winged
booster, just like the first designs back in '69 before the
Congressional budget-choppers got ahold of the programme. It
had been a hell of a thing to hear that familiar dark brown voice
booming down from orbit.

But Cronkite's descriptions of the Earth – the scarred steppes
of Asia, the smoking rubble of eastern Europe, even the spreading
darkness at the heart of America's own cities – didn't coincide
much with his own recollections. Cronkite even claimed to have
seen, from orbit, the destruction of Sioux City, Burdick's own
home town, by rebelling students and anarchists. It was a little
hard to verify such things. The news was pretty heavily censored
these days, for valid reasons of national security.

Still, *Pax Americana* somehow hadn't worked out quite the way
everyone thought.

Anyhow it was too late for Burdick. His time had come and
gone. He was content to watch, now.

And besides –

Sunday Punch. That cosmonaut defector he'd brought down
from orbit, Sergei Kozlov, sent him long letters about the dangers
of the project.

. . . *You aren't like these others, my friend, these young ones
in their un-American uniforms. You must see that some of them
actually want it all to end – to pull down the house – to destroy
all the little people, dirty and squabbling and unpredictable, who
don't understand their giant schemes . . .*

Hell, Burdick wasn't qualified to judge what Kozlov said. Kozlov
was just some Russian who'd grabbed the opportunity to stay in
the US, when it came to him, with both hands. He'd even managed
to get his family out before the Chinese invasion and all hell finally
broke loose over there.

But Burdick had to admit to a few doubts himself, deep in his
gut. There were always unexpected consequences, of whatever you
did.

Anyhow here came the Lockheed PowerStar: a brilliant flare of light, like a high-flying plane, climbing steadily over the dome of the sky.

It was time. He called Fay. She came out with more lemonade, and settled down beside him.

The power station was a rectangle of black solar cells, twenty miles long and four wide, with a cluster of Shuttle External Tank hab modules bolted to its spine, as productive as ten nuke plants, so relieving the lack of Mid-East gas that had half-crippled the economy for two decades now.

Pretty soon, it was said, the US wouldn't need the rest of the planet at all.

If Burdick had one regret about his retirement it was that he hadn't got up to orbit to see them putting the plant together, working the beam builders as they extruded their three-hundred yard lengths of foamed steel. It had made for great TV.

And there was a little firefly spark, climbing up the sky, right alongside the power plant: the orbiter *Eagle II*, commanded by Tom Gibson, carrying Burdick's only son Philip on his first space-flight. A hell of a thing: two generations of Burdicks, climbing into space.

The rookies seemed to be getting younger every year, to Burdick. Phil Jr was only 22. Well, it was an expansive programme. It ate up crew members.

Unexpected consequences.

Sunday Punch was such a damn huge blow, who could say what the consequences would be? Certainly not Burdick.

Not that he admitted as much to Sergei Kozlov, or Fay, or anyone else. He'd learned to keep a lot of his thoughts to himself. It was a lesson he'd learned on the surface of the Moon, in the rubble of Apollo 11. There were some things better left unsaid. Truth was just another weapon anyhow.

He watched as the PowerStar slid down the sky, taking Phil's slowly converging orbiter with it, until it was lost in the deep blue haze on the horizon.

He sipped his lemonade. He could feel dew on his cheeks already. It made his skin-cancer scars itch.

He could always stay out another ninety minutes until Phil came round the Earth again. But it was kind of cold.

Fay had fallen asleep anyhow, her careworn face slack, the shadows on her lined face like pools of black oil.

September 1997:

The Florida beach was empty. The sand was hard and flat. A little way inland, there was a row of scrub pines, maybe ten feet tall. The moonlight shadows at their roots were like pools of black oil.

Burdick limped south.

The Moon, to the east, was fat and full, its silver light glimmering off the hide of the Atlantic. To Burdick, here in the grass, the Moon looked like it always had, when it had floated over the Iowa farm of his boyhood, when he'd gone barnstorming over those ash-grey plains with Harry Singer.

But not much longer, he supposed. Not if that old Sunday Punch worked like it was supposed to.

The wind was coming off the ocean. It wasn't cold, but he shivered anyhow, as he thought of the fallout shit it was probably blowing over him, across the sea from Asia. But he was wearing his facemask, and the easterly wind ought to keep the Canaveral crap away from him anyhow.

A flatbed truck had been crudely parked in the dune grass. Burdick could see its tracks, snaking back over the sand. And here were scuff marks where some kind of equipment had been hauled off the back and over the sand, down towards the water.

It looked like Kozlov had been telling the truth about coming down here, whatever he was planning.

Burdick wondered what the hell *he* was doing here, standing in a radioactive sea breeze, on the night of Sunday Punch. But then, he had no place else much to go, not since the Chinese shot down *Columbia II*, with Phil aboard, and Fay had followed him to the grave soon after. The house in Iowa, his lawn, lost its appeal after that, and he started drifting. But there were travel restrictions in place across the country, and after the Guatemalans took out San Antonio, with a nuke on an old Soviet SS-25, you weren't allowed in or out of Texas at all.

Difficult times. Oddly, through his enigmatic, disjointed letters, Kozlov, the old enemy, had come to seem a friend.

Anyhow, here he was.

Singing came drifting up from the water's edge: thick and heavy, like black Russian bread. The voice of an old man. Something going on down there. Somebody moving around, silhouetted by moonlight, a heavy bear of a man hauling tubes and rods and clamps, singing softly, building something.

Equipment was scattered on the young sand. Fat white tubes, pieces of some kind of scaffolding, a little electronic gear. What looked like a small refrigerator, a massive metal box, sitting there in the sand casting a long Moon shadow.

'Sergei.'

The singing stopped. The bear figure straightened up, showing no surprise. 'Ah. *Dobry vyechir.*'

'The Moon – *luna – eta ochin kraseeva.*'

He could see Kozlov's broad, weather-beaten face split into a grin. 'Very beautiful. I expected you.'

'Yeah.' And somehow, Burdick had expected to find just this: Sergei Kozlov building some kind of rocket, here on an American beach.

Burdick took his gun from his pocket. A Saturday-night special, point 22. He limped forward, over sand that crunched under his feet.

Kozlov looked at the gun. 'Oh, Philip. *Kak zhal.* That such a weapon should lie between us.'

'What the hell are you doing here, Sergei? This looks like a rocket.'

'It is a rocket. A bath-tub rocket. The heart is a block of sugar, encased in this tubing, my central core and strap-on boosters. Nitrous oxide passes down a hollowed centre, for oxidizer. Fibreglass tubes, and sugar for fuel. A fantasy of small-town America. Workshop rockets into space. Not even expensive. And yet this rocket of mine can reach orbit.'

Burdick kept the gun up. 'Are you crazy? What are you going to do, shoot down the fucking Shuttle?'

Kozlov bent, stiffly, and stroked the white metal box. 'The payload,' he said. 'It is a gene bank. Do you know what that means?'

'No.'

'Spores. Dehydrated. Shielded against the radiation of space. This little capsule will last a thousand years, in its high orbit, protecting its fragile cargo. And then it will drift down to Earth. It has a crude but effective heatshield. Oak, actually, as the Chinese use. The capsule is designed to burst open in the air, releasing its microscopic passengers, to scatter on the wind.'

'Spores? Why? What's the point?'

Kozlov looked up at the Moon, where black-uniformed Americans, volunteers all, were circling and watching, Tom Gibson and Harry Singer amongst them, waiting for this ultimate demonstration to the world – hell, the solar system – of American competence and will. Kozlov said, 'But didn't your heart lift, as you walked on that ancient landscape?'

'Nothing there but rocks. What use is the Moon, except for this?'

'Undoubtedly, you are correct,' Kozlov said sourly. 'After Sunday Punch, at last we squabbling Asiatics and Europeans and Africans will throw down our arms, shed our centuries of racial and religious division, and accept your cold logic. How right you were never even to attempt to understand us! Perhaps even your own people will accept that logic, beyond the diminishing minority who are protected by these new black-leather police and soldiers of yours. All human problems will be solved, for all time.

'Of course, you are correct. So shoot me now, Philip, for I am only a foolish old man who might endanger your great project. However –'

'What?'

'You have always known,' Kozlov said. 'About the *Eagle*. The unfortunate incident which destroyed Armstrong and Aldrin, so long ago. Even we could see the truth, through the grimy lenses of the Lunokhod.'

'That there was no bomb.'

'No Soviet sabotage.' Kozlov worked his shoulders. 'A simple malfunction.'

'Yeah . . .'

The Eagle *has landed,* Armstrong had called.

Burdick had been in the Viewing Area in back of Mission Control, just a rookie, jammed in with astronauts and brass and dignitaries and relatives, looking out over rows of controllers, just young guys, sweating through their shirts. It was only a few seconds after the landing, and the descent engine had just shut down, up there on the Moon, and most everybody was still cheering Armstrong's words.

But Burdick could see something, in the set of the shoulders of TELMU, the Lunar Module controller.

Pressure and temperature were rising in one of the descent stage's fuel lines. There had to be a blockage in there.

'Frozen fuel,' Kozlov said. 'A slug in a fuel line. Frozen by liquid helium.'

'Yeah. We had to stand there and watch while the engine heat approached the slug.'

The fuel was unstable. It was supposed to be. And when that engine heat reached it, that slug would explode like a small grenade.

The phone lines were open, between the control room and the back rooms and Grumman, the manufacturers out at Bethpage. The Grumman people said to launch immediately in the ascent stage, and leave the problem behind. But the Command Module was in the wrong place for a pickup. Maybe they ought to burp the descent engine, at ten per cent power. But they didn't know if the LM was tilted. If its attitude was wrong it might just topple over.

Indecision.

Okay, said Buzz Aldrin, on the Moon. *Okay. It looks like we're venting the oxidizer now.*

That was all.

The vox loops went quiet, and the telemetry on all the screens turned ratty and dropped out, and that was all there was.

'We couldn't exactly conduct a forensic investigation up there, Harry and me,' Burdick said. 'But –'

'It was just the fuel line. A simple malfunction.'

'Yeah.'

'It was nothing to do with us.' Kozlov smiled. 'We were not so smart, as to be able to reach to the Moon to disrupt your plans!'

Burdick shrugged. 'The lie was simpler. More useful. We were at war, Sergei. I never had a problem with that.'

'I'm sure you didn't. Even though, in a sense, all of this –' he waved a hand vaguely '– is your fault. If only that fuel-line blockage had melted, if only Apollo 11 had turned into the dull triumph it was supposed to be. If only you'd told the truth. But you do not see that. You are a good man, my friend, in your own way. You always did your duty. It has left you as a lonely old man on a wrecked world, but you always did your duty. And now I am asking you to perform a higher duty.'

'Higher?'

'Help me now. We will build this rocket and fire it off together. Two old fools, relics of a Space Age. Together in the last of the moonlight. Humour me.'

'What do we have to do?'

'Assemble the scaffolding. It is a gantry. You see, we are rebuilding Cape Canaveral, here in the radioactive sands of Florida.'

Burdick considered, for long seconds.

He checked his astronaut's Rolex. There were only a couple of minutes to go anyhow.

Burdick picked up tubes of steel, and clamps, and started to figure out how it would all fit together.

They had it half-built when the Sunday Punch went off.

It was a hell of a thing. You could see it, across a quarter of a million miles, the surface of the Mare Imbrium billowing up into space, as the demonstration planet-buster went off beneath it, a quarter of the Moon's grey old face convulsing in an instant.

Much of the material immediately started to fall back into the new crater, a scar glowing yellow-red, but Burdick could see some of it scattering around the rest of the Moon in a huge raying, pounding over those ancient maria. Some of the material dispersed, already cooling, into space.

'So,' Burdick said to Kozlov. 'What do you think?'

Kozlov grinned as he hefted a stabilizer fin. 'Unexpected consequences. The first rocks will be here in twelve or thirteen hours: the big fellows, tumbling into our gravity well, punching through the atmosphere. And a ring will form around the Earth, fat and dense, blocking the sunlight. The temperatures will drop thirty, forty degrees. The ring will hail out slowly, as tektite meteorites. But the ice will last a thousand years. Perhaps a little less, if we are lucky.' He shrugged. 'Something will survive, of course, in the deep rocks and in the ocean ridges. Our capsule carries eukaryotes, multi-cellular organisms –'

'To start the whole damn thing over again.'

'Perhaps they will be lucky: wiser than us, not so wise as you. Come. Help me with this tail section. We have time yet.'

The two of them laboured on, assembling their rocket, two old men moving slowly and stiffly around the beach, as the moonlight turned blood red.

WORLDS

In that Houston sky outside, in the blizzard of possible worlds, there had been small Earths: wizened worlds that reminded her of Mars, with huge continents of glowering red rock. But some of them were huge, monster planets drowned in oceans that stretched from pole to pole. The Moons were different too. The smallest were just bare grey rock like Luna, but the largest were almost Earth-like, showing thick air and ice and the glint of ocean. There were even Earths with pairs of Moons, or triplets. One ice-bound Earth was surrounded by a glowing ring system, like Saturn's.

Kate had found it hard not to flinch; it was like being under a hail of gaudy cannonballs, as the alternate planets flickered in and out of existence in eerie, precise silence.

SUN-DRENCHED

Bado crawls backwards out of the Lunar Module.

When he gets to the ladder's top rung, Bado takes hold of the handrails and pulls himself upright. The pressurized suit seems to resist every movement; he even has trouble closing his gloved fingers around the rails, and his fingers are sore already.

He can see the small TV camera which Slade deployed to film his own egress. The camera sits on its stowage tray, on the side of the LM's descent stage. It peers at him silently.

He drops down the last three feet, and lands on the foil-covered footpad. A little grey dust splashes up around his feet.

Bado holds onto the ladder with his right hand and places his left boot on the regolith. Then he steps off with his right foot, and lets go of the LM.

And there he is, standing on the Moon.

He hears the hum of pumps and fans in the backpack, feels the soft breeze of oxygen across his face.

Slade is waiting with his camera. 'Okay, turn around and give me a big smile. Atta boy. You look great. Welcome to the Moon.' Bado sees how Slade's light blue soles and lower legs are already stained dark grey by lunar dust. Bado can't see Slade's face, behind his reflective golden sun-visor.

Bado takes a step. The dust seems to crunch under his weight, like a covering of snow. The LM is standing in a broad, shallow crater. There are craters everywhere, ranging from several yards to a thumbnail width, the low sunlight deepening their shadows.

Bado feels elated. In spite of everything, in spite of what is to come, he's walking on the Moon.

'Bado. Look up.'

'Huh?' Bado has to tip back on his heels to do it.

The sky above is black, empty of stars; his pupils are closed up by the dazzle of the sun, and the reflection of the pale-brown lunar surface. But he can see the Earth, a fat crescent.

And there, crossing the zenith, is a single, brilliant, unwinking star. It is Apollo, in lunar orbit.

A cloud of debris surrounds the craft, visible even from here, a disk as big as a dime held at arm's length.

Slade touches his shoulder. 'Come on, boy,' Slade says gently. 'We've got work to do.'

After the EVA, back in the LM, Bado has to ask Slade to help him take off his gloves. His exposed hands are revealed to be almost black, they are so bruised.

They get out of their suits. Bado climbs into a storage bag, to catch the rain of sooty Moondust, and strips down to his long johns.

After a meal, they sling their Beta-cloth hammocks across the LM's cramped cabin. Bado climbs into his hammock. Without his suit, and in the Moon's weak gravity, he weighs only twenty-five pounds or so; the hammock is like a feather bed. Slade, above him, barely makes a dint in his hammock.

It is dark. They have pulled blinds down over the triangular windows. Bado is inside a cosy little tent on the Moon, with the warmth of Slade's body above him, and with the thumps and whirs of the LM's systems around him.

But he can't sleep.

In his mind's eye, Al Pond dies again.

It is before the landing. Just after separation, of LM and CSM, in lunar orbit.

Inside the Lunar Module, Bado and Slade stand side by side, strapped in their cable harnesses. In front of Bado's face is a small triangular window. It is marked with the spidery reticles that will guide them to landfall on the Moon. Through the window Bado can see the CSM: the cylindrical Service Module, with its big bell of a propulsion system nozzle stuck on the back, and the squat cone of the Command Module on the top.

Drenched in sunlight, Apollo is like a silvery toy, set against the Moon's soft tans.

Bado can picture Al Pond, who they have left alone in the Command Module.

Pond calls over, 'You guys take it easy down there.'

'We will,' says Slade. 'And we'll clean up before we come back. We don't want to get Moondust all over your nice clean ship.' It is the kind of iffy thing Slade is prone to saying, Bado thinks.

'You better not,' calls Pond. '. . . Hey. I got an odd smell in here.'

Bado and Slade glance at each other, within their bubble helmets.

Slade says, 'What kind of smell?'

'Not unpleasant. Sharp. Like autumn leaves after an early frost. You know?'

That could be smoke, Bado thinks.

'I got a couple of lights on the ECU control panel,' Pond calls now. 'I'll go take a look.' His voice gets muffled. 'Okay. I got the ECU panel.' This is a small, sharp-edged metal panel, just underneath the commander's couch; lithium hydroxide air-scrub canisters are stored in there. 'I can't see nothing. But that smell is strong. Ow.'

'What?'

'The metal handle. I burned my hand. Okay. I got it open. About a foot length of the cabling in here is just a charred mess. Blackened. And there are bits of melted insulation floating around the compartment. Oh. I can see flames,' Pond calls distantly. 'But they're almost invisible. It's kind of like a blue ball, with yellow flashes at the edge, where the flame is eating away at the cabling. Man, it's beautiful.'

Fire in zero gravity, fed only by diffusion, is efficient; there is little soot, little smoke. Hard to detect, even to see or smell.

There are miles of wires and cables and pipes behind the walls of the Command Module's pressurized cabin. The fire could have got anywhere, Bado realizes.

Solenoids rattle. Slade is firing the LM's reaction thrusters.

Bado asks, 'What are you doing?'

'Backing off.'

The LM responds crisply.

'I fetched an extinguisher,' Pond calls. 'Woah.'

'What?'

'I got me a ball of flame. Maybe a foot across. It just came gushing out of the hatchway. It's a soft blue. It's floating there.'

The two craft pass into the shadow of the Moon.

Pond has fallen quiet.

Bado leans into his window. The silvery tent of the Command Module looks perfect, gleaming, as it recedes.

There is a small docking window, set in the nose of the CSM. Through this window Bado sees a bright light, like a star.

A human hand beats against the glass of the docking window.

The Command Module's hull bursts, abruptly, silently. There is a single sheet of flame, blossoming around the hull. Then black gas billows out, condensing to sparkling ice in an instant.

The silver hull is left crumpled, stained black.

Bado keeps doing mental sums, figuring their remaining consumables.

He looks at his watch. They are already half-way through their nine-hour sleep period.

He thinks about the mission. They have christened the landing site Fay Crater, after Bado's wife. And their main objective for the flight is another crater a few hundred yards to the west that they've named after Bado's daughter, Pam. Surveyor 8, an unmanned robot probe, set down in Pam Crater a couple of years ago; the astronauts are here to sample it.

Now they are here, Bado thinks bleakly, those names don't seem such a smart idea. Bado doesn't want to think about Fay and the kids.

Slade, of course, doesn't have a family, and offered no names at the mission planning sessions.

One of the LM's cooling pumps changes pitch with a bang.

Slade whispers from above. 'Bado. You awake, man?'

Bado snaps back, 'I am now.'

'That goddamn suit was killing me,' Slade says.

'How so?'

'I think the leg is too short. The left leg. Every time I walked it pulled down on my shoulder like a ton weight.'

Bado laughs. 'We'll have to fix it before the next EVA.'

'Yeah. Hey, Bado.'

'What?'

'You ever read any science fiction?'

'What science fiction?'

'Think about what we got here. A dead world. And two people, stranded on it.'

'So what?'

'Maybe we don't have to just die. Maybe we can populate the Moon.' He laughs. 'Adam and Eve on the Moon, that's us.'

Bado feels anger and fear. Again it's the kind of iffy thing Slade is always saying. He wants to lash out. 'Oh, fuck you, Slade.'

Slade sighs. Bado can see him shifting in his hammock. 'You know, you fit right in with this job, Bado. We're not supposed to be humans, are we? And I truly believe that you're more afraid that I'm going to grab your ass than of what happens when the goddamn oh-two runs out, in a couple of days from now. Listen, Bado. I'm cold, man.'

'Fuck you.'

Slade's voice rises, brittle. 'We're two human beings, Bado, stuck here in this goddamn tin-foil box on the Moon, and we're going to die. I'm cold and I'm scared. Al Pond had to die alone –'

'Fuck you, Slade.'

Slade laughs. 'Ah, the hell with you,' he says eventually. He turns over in his hammock, swings his legs over, and floats to the floor. He sits on the ascent engine cover. His face is in shadow as he looks in at Bado. 'So. You going to help me with this leg, or what?'

Bado gets out of his own hammock and folds it away. Slade hauls on the layers of his pressure suit. Bado kneels down in front of Slade and starts unpicking the cords laced around Slade's calf. To adjust the suit's fitting, he will have to unknot every cord, loosen it a little, and retie it.

It takes about an hour. They don't say anything to each other.

They prepare for their second, final EVA. Their traverse is a misshapen circle which will take them around several craters. They will follow the timeline in the spiral-bound checklists on their cuffs.

They climb easily out of Fay Crater. They both carry tool pallets, containing their TV camera, rock hammers and core tubes, Baggies for Moon rocks.

Bado has worked out an effective way to move. It is more of a giraffe-lope than a run. It is like bounding across a stream; he is suspended at the peak of each step. And every time he lands a little spray of dust particles sails off in perfect arcs, like tiny golf balls.

On the hoof, Bado tries to give the guys on the ground a little field geology. 'Everything's covered in dust. It's all kind of reduced, you can see only the faintest of shadings. But here I can see a bigger rock, the size of a football maybe and about that shape. Zap pits on every side, and I can see green and white crystals sticking out of it. Feldspar, maybe, or olivine. . .'

Nobody is going to come up here to collect the samples they are carefully assembling. Not in a hundred years. But the geology back-room guys will get something out of his descriptions.

Slade is whistling as he runs. He says, 'Up one crater and over another. I feel like a kid again. Like I'm ten years old. All that weight – it's just gone. What do you think, huh, Bado? Now we're out and moving again, maybe this isn't such a bad deal. Maybe a day on the Moon is worth a hundred on Earth.'

They take a break.

Bado looks back east, the way they have come. He can see the big, shallow dip in the land that is Fay Crater, with the LM resting at its centre like a toy in the palm of some huge hand. Two sets of footsteps come climbing up out of Fay towards them, like footsteps on a beach after a tide.

His mouth is dry as sand; he'd give an awful lot for an ice-cool glass of water, right here and now.

'Adam and Eve, huh,' Slade says now.

'What?'

'Maybe it will work out that way after all. We're changing the Moon, just by being here. We're three hundred pounds of organic stuff, dropped on the Moon, and crawling with life: gut bacteria, and cold viruses, and –'

'What are you saying?'

'Maybe there will be enough raw material to let life get some kind of a grip here. When we've gone. Life survives in a lot of inhospitable places, back home. Volcano mouths, and the ocean deeps.'

'Adam and Eve,' Bado says. 'I choose Adam.'

Slade laughs. 'You got it, man.'

They lope on, to the west. Bado can hear Slade's breath, loud in his ears.

Bado thinks about Slade.

Everyone in the astronaut office knows about Slade. And Bado came in for some joshing when the crew roster for this flight was announced. Three days on the Moon? Better make sure you take your K-Y jelly, man.

Bado defended Slade. None of that stuff mattered a damn to his piloting abilities.

Anyhow, outside the Agency Slade is painted as the bachelor boy. He has even put up with getting his photograph taken with girls on his arm.

Noone knows, the Agency assured Bado. Noone will think anything questionable concerning you.

Slade stops. He says, 'Hey. We're here.' He points.

Bado looks up.

He has, he realizes, reached the rim of Pam Crater. In fact he is standing on top of its dune-like, eroded wall. And there, planted in the crater's centre, is the Surveyor. It is less than a hundred yards from him. It is a squat, three-legged frame, bristling with fuel tanks, batteries, antennae and sensors, and its white paint has turned tan.

Bado sets the TV camera on its stand. Slade hops down into Pam Crater, spraying lunar dust ahead of him.

Slade takes a pair of cutting shears from his tool carrier, gets hold of the Surveyor's TV camera, and starts to chop through the camera's support struts and cables. 'Just a couple of tubes,' he says. 'Then that baby's mine.'

The camera comes loose, and Slade grips it in his gloves. He whoops.

'Outstanding,' Bado says. He knows that for Slade, getting to the Surveyor, grabbing a few pieces of it, is the finish line for the mission.

Slade lopes out of the crater. Bado watches his partner. Slade looks like a human-shaped beach ball, his suit brilliant white, bouncing happily over the beach-like surface of the Moon.

Bado thinks of a human hand, pressing silently against the window of a burning capsule.

He is experiencing emotions he doesn't want to label.

'Hey, Slade,' Bado says.

'What?'

'Come here, man.'

Slade obediently floats over to him, and waits. He has one glove up over his chest, obscuring the tubes which connect his backpack to his oxygen and water inlets. His white oversuit is covered in dust splashes.

Carefully, clumsily, Bado pushes up Slade's gold sun visor. Inside he can see Slade's face, with its four-day growth of beard. He touches Slade's suit, brushing dust off the umbilical tubes. Patiently, Slade submits to this grooming.

Then Bado gets hold of Slade's shoulders with his pressurized gloves. He pulls Slade against his chest. Slade hops forward, into his embrace. Bado puts his arm over the Stars and Stripes on

Slade's left shoulder, but he can't get his arms all the way around his partner.

Their faceplates touch. Slade grins, and when he speaks Bado can hear his voice, like an echo of the radio, transmitted directly through their bubble helmets. 'Get you,' Slade says softly. 'Aren't you afraid I'm going to make a grab for your dick?'

'I figure I'm safe locked up in this suit.'

Slade laughs.

For a while they stay together, like two embracing balloons, on the surface of the Moon.

They break.

The TV camera sits on its tripod, its black lens fixed on them.

Bado takes a geology hammer and smashes the camera off its stand.

Bado stands harnessed in his place beside Slade. In his grimy pressure suit he feels bulky, awkward.

Slade says, 'Ascent propulsion system propellant tanks pressurized.'

'Roger.'

'Ascent feeds are open, shut-offs are closed.'

The capcom calls up. 'Everything looks good. We want the rendezvous radar mode switch in LGC just as it is on surface fifty-nine . . . We assume the steerable is in track mode auto.'

Bado replies, 'Stop, push-button reset, abort to abort stage reset.'

Slade pushes his buttons. 'Reset.' He grins at Bado.

The guys on the ground are playing their part well, Bado thinks. So far it is all being played straight-faced, as they work together through the comforting rituals of the checklists.

The Agency must have decided that the crew has finally gone crazy. Bado wonders how much of this will ever become public.

Looking at the small, square instrument panel in front of him, Bado can see that the ascent stage is powered up now, no longer drawing any juice from the lower-stage's batteries. The ascent stage is preparing to become an independent spacecraft for the first time. He feels obscurely sorry for it. It isn't going to fly any more than he is.

'One minute,' the capcom says.

'Got the steering in the abort guidance,' Slade says.

Bado arms the ignition. 'Okay, master arm on.'

'Rog.'

'You're go, Apollo,' says the capcom.

'Clear the runway.' Slade turns to Bado. 'You sure you want to do this?'

Actually, Bado is scared as hell. He really, really doesn't want to die.

'Adam and Eve?' he asks.

'Adam and Eve. This is the best way, man. A chance to leave something behind.'

Bado makes himself grin. 'Then do it, you fairy.'

Slade nods, inside his bubble helmet. 'Okay. At five seconds I'm going to hit ABORT STAGE and ENGINE ARM. And you'll hit PROCEED.'

'Roger,' says Bado. 'I'll tell you how I'd think of you, man.'

Slade looks at him again.

'Out there,' Bado says. 'Floating across the face of the Moon, in all that sunlight. That's how I'd remember you.'

Slade nods. He looks at his instruments. 'Here we go. Nine. Eight. Seven.'

The computer display in front of Bado flashes a '99', a request to proceed.

Slade closes the master firing arm. 'Engine arm ascent.'

Bado has been through enough sims of this sequence. In a moment there should be a loud bang, a rattle around the floor of the cabin: pyrotechnic guillotines, blowing away the nuts, bolts, wires and water hoses connecting the upper and lower stages of the LM.

But they have disabled the guillotines.

Bado presses the PROCEED button.

The cabin starts to rattle. The ascent stage engine has ignited, but its engine bell is still buried within the guts of the LM's descent stage.

The over-pressure builds up quickly.

Slade says, 'I think –'

But there is no more time.

The ascent stage bursts open, like an aluminium egg, there on the surface of the Moon. Sunlight drenches Bado's face.

MARTIAN AUTUMN

I will tell the story much as I set it out in my journal at the time. Old-fashioned, I know. But I can't think of any better way to tell how it happened to me.

If there is anybody to read it.

Bob ran one last check of his skinsuit. He did this without thinking, an ingrained habit for a fourteen-year-old born on Mars. Then, following Lyall, he let the lock run through its cycle, and he stepped out of the tractor and onto Martian dirt.

This was Isidis Planitia, a great basin that straddled Mars's northern plains and ancient southern highlands. It was late afternoon, a still day at the start of the long, languid Martian autumn. Everything was a cruddy red-brown: the dirty sky, the lines of shallow dunes lapping against the walls of an enclosing crater.

A cloud of camera fireflies hovered around his head. The moment was newsworthy, Mars's youngest resident visiting the oldest. Bob ignored the flies. They had followed him around all his life.

Meg Lyall was standing with her arms spread wide, as if crucified. She turned around and around, with the creaky, uncertain motions of great age, enjoying Mars.

Bob stood there, hideously embarrassed.

She said, 'You want to know the best thing about modern Mars? Skinsuits.' She flexed her hand, watching the fabric crumple and stretch, waves of colour crossing its surface. 'Back in '29 we had to lock ourselves up in great clunky lobster suits, all hard shells and padding, so heavy you could barely take a step. Now it's like we're not wearing anything at all.'

'Not really.'

She looked up at him, her rheumy eyes Earth-blue. 'No. You're right. It's not *really* like walking over a grassy field, out in the open air, is it? Which is what you think you'll be doing in six months' time.' She looked up at Earth's bright glint. 'Sixty years after the Reboot, Earth is a world of fortresses. Even the grass is under guard. But maybe they'll let you walk on it even so. After all, you're famous!'

Resentment sparked easily, as it always did. 'You won't put me off going.'

'Oh, no.' She seemed shocked at the suggestion. 'That isn't it at all. You have to go. It's very important. There may be nothing *more* important. You'll see. Walk with me.'

He couldn't refuse. But he wouldn't let her hold his hand.

April 2008

Tricester is in Oxfordshire, England. It is a strange place, I suppose: both old and new, an ancient leafy village in the shadow of a huge particle accelerator facility called Corwell, a giant circular ridge of green landscaping. It is a place crowded with history.

My name is Marshall Reid, by the way. I am a science teacher at the village school.

Here's how it begins for me.

On a bright spring afternoon I lead a field trip of eleven school-children to the Corwell plant. As we troop past the anonymous buildings there is an emergency, some failure of containment, and a blue flash overwhelms us all. I am dazzled but unhurt. Some of the children are still, silent, as if distracted, others very frightened. They all seem unharmed.

There are predictable fears of a radiation leak. The guides quickly herd us into a holding area.

Miranda Stewart is called in, and introduced to us. She is Emergency Planning Officer for the region, the local authority official in nominal charge of such operations, supposedly coor-dinating the various emergency services. She is 50-ish, a Geordie, a former soldier. I like her immediately; she is a reassuring pres-ence.

But Stewart is overwhelmed by the techs and suits and experts from the environment ministry. Scientists in protection gear crawl scarily over the site with Geiger counters.

We teachers and pupils are held in the middle of all this, sitting in our neat rows, surrounded by officials and police and medics, our mobile phones besieged by anxious parents. We are all bewildered and scared.

Reluctantly Stewart concedes that the village should be cordoned off, proper tests run on the inhabitants and the local crops, and so on. But no alarm will be raised; there will be a cover story about a chemical leak.

The police set up blocks around the plant and village. There is press attention, and Green protesters quickly appear at the barriers. Emma, my wife, encounters this perimeter, returning from work in London.

Emma, at 31 a little younger than me, is a PR consultant. She misses life in the capital. Emma is seven-months pregnant. To her, the Corwell incident is the final straw; this is not a safe place to raise a kid. Later that day we argue again about moving back to London. But I am devoted to my job, and loyal to the kids. The argument is inconclusive, as usual.

Meanwhile, at the plant (so I learn later), the technicians are finding no signs of radiation damage. But one technician, checking surrounding foliage, finds a nest of mice – a nest without babies.

I have the feeling this is only the start of something larger. Hence my decision to keep this journal.

When Bob looked back, he saw that the tractor had already sunk behind Mars's close horizon. He had no idea where they were going. He wasn't enjoying the oily feel of his suit's smart material as it slithered over his skin, seeking to equalize temperature and pressure over his body. It was like being held in a huge moist hand.

He'd only stepped on the raw surface of Mars a dozen times in his life. It was a frozen desert – what was there to see? He had spent all his life rattling around in the cramped corridors of Mangala or Ares or Hellas, surrounded by walls painted the glowing colours of Earth, purple and blue and green.

Earth! He could see it now, a blue-white evening star just rising, the only colour in this whole rust-ridden landscape – Earth, where he had dreamed of escaping even before he had realized that he was a freak.

He was the youngest child on Mars: the last to be born, as colonists abandoned by Earth dutifully shut down their lives. A little later he had been orphaned, making him even more of a freak.

He owed Mars nothing. He didn't fit. Everybody stared at him, pitying. Well, another week and he was out of here: the only evacuee Earth would allow.

But first he had to get through this gruesome ritual of a visit with Meg Lyall.

On she talked.

'I guess you're used to the fireflies. Surely they are going to watch you all the way home. Just like when I rode the *Ares* out here, back in 2029 . . .' More old-woman reminiscing, he thought gloomily. 'There we were in our big ugly hab module, and we were surrounded by drifting cams the whole way out. At first I figured people were watching to see us screw, or take a dump, or fight. But it turned out the highest ratings were for ordinary times, when we were just working calmly, making our meals, sleeping. Like watching fish in a tank. But you've never seen a fish. Maybe even then people were too isolated. Now it's a lot worse, of course. But we're social animals; we need people around us . . . What do you think?'

'I think you ought to tell me where we're going.'

She stopped and turned, breathing hard, to face him. 'Why, we're already there. Don't you know your history?'

She led him over a shallow rise. And there, under a low translucent dome only thinly coated with Martian dust, sat the *Beagle 2*.

May 2008

After a couple of weeks the cordon has been lifted. But technicians still patrol the area with their anonymous instruments, and the children and I are subject to ongoing medical checks.

I have tried to protect the children. But there is media attention: unwelcome headlines, cartoons of huge-brained kids glowing in the dark. I am angry, of course. My pupils have already been betrayed by the authorities who should protect them, and now they are depicted as freaks.

The school's pet rabbits have produced no young.

Paul Merrick has shown up, rucksack on his back, looking for a place to stay.

Merrick, 40-ish, is a Jeff Goldblum-lookalike American environmental scientist. He has become something of a maverick, with controversial theories about holistic aspects of the environment. At college he taught Emma.

And they had a relationship.

Now Emma has called him in; she knew Merrick would be intrigued by the accident and she wants to know his views.

I am not pleased to see this ghost from Emma's past.

Merrick and Emma do some unauthorized exploration of Corwell. I suspect Emma, now on maternity leave, wants something to take her mind off the approaching upheaval in her own life: a last youthful adventure.

They find birds' nests without eggs.

They are discovered by Emergency Planning Officer Stewart. She tries to throw them out, and blusters about this being a routine clean-up operation. But Merrick asks probing questions about the instances of sterility, which are already the talk of the village. Stewart points out that the sheep and cattle in neighbouring farms are giving birth as usual. Merrick says this may be because of different gestation periods; if some kind of sterilization effect has occurred, short-gestation creatures would be the first to be affected. Stewart – not a scientist and, I suspect, not kept fully in the know by the ministry types – is disturbed, but is sure there is a 'rational' explanation.

When she tells me this part of the story, Emma rubs her bump thoughtfully.

Merrick, Emma and I talk it over in the pub. To my discomfiture, Emma tells Merrick too much personal stuff: that her conception was an accident while we were on holiday, for example. Merrick, though restrained, is obviously jealous.

Merrick says predictable things. That it is as if we are running a huge, uncontrolled experiment on nature. That England is a small and crowded place, where nature has been saturated by everything we could throw at her – electromagnetic radiation, pesticides, genetic modification, acid rain and now even exotic radiation from the nuclear accident. That we have stressed natural systems beyond their limits. That something strange is happening here as a result – but who knows what?

Meaningless talk. I resolve to focus on the immediate issues before me, on the people I care for, Emma and the field-trip kids.

The *Beagle* wasn't much to look at. It was just a pie-dish pod that had bounced down from out of the sky under a system of parachutes and gasbags. Disc-shaped solar-cell panels had unfolded over the dirt, and a wand of sensors had stuck up like a periscope. And that was it. When people had come looking for it five decades after its landing, *Beagle* had been all but buried by windblown toxic dust.

And yet, by baking its tiny soil samples and sniffing the thin air, *Beagle 2* had discovered life on Mars.

'It was the atmospheric sensor that did it,' Lyall said. 'The probe could directly examine only one little patch of landscape, but a Martian cow could fart anywhere on Mars and *Beagle* could sense the methane. It took another thirty years before anybody had a sample they could hold in their hand, but *Beagle* proved it was here to be found.'

Even before Lyall and her crew had left Earth, the findings of unmanned probes had already shattered many ancient dreams of Mars. There were no canal builders, no lusty princesses, no wistful golden-eyed poets, no leathery lung-plants. For a time, Mars had been thought to be dead altogether.

But then a meteorite, a fossil-laden scrap of Mars brought to Earth by cosmic chance, had changed all that.

Young Mars and Earth, billions of years ago, had been like sisters: both warm, both glistening with shallow oceans and ponds. And both had harboured life – sister life, as it turned out, spawned on one world or the other and blown across space on the meteorite wind.

Lyall turned around, letting her gloved fingertips trace out the line of the crater walls. 'I don't think you can imagine how strange this scenery is to me, still. To see a crater like this with water features in it: gully networks and dried river beds and the rippling beaches of ancient lakes . . . A crater punched in rock that formed at the bottom of a sea, a crater that later got flooded, over and over. When I was your age, I'd have given anything to be transported here, to stand where you are standing – to know what I know now.' Bob thought she behaved as if she had just stepped down out of that creaky old spaceship of hers.

Mars had been too small. It could not hold onto the gases its volcanoes vented, and without tectonic recycling the atmosphere became locked in carbonate rocks. The air thinned, the oceans and land froze, and the harsh sunlight destroyed the water.

And yet life persisted.

'Slime,' Bob said. 'Life on Mars is pond scum, kilometres down.'

Lyall glared, as if he'd insulted her personally. 'Not pond scum. Biofilms. Martian life is *not* primitive. It is the result of four billion years of evolution – a different evolution. The anaerobic life forms organize themselves, working together, one living off the output of another. Life on Mars is all about cooperation. Some say that the whole Martian biota, stuck down in those deep thermal vents, is nothing but one vast community . . .'

'Sure. But so what? You can't *eat* it. It doesn't *do* anything.'

Lyall struggled to remain serious, then a grin cracked her leathery face. 'Okay. I felt the same as you, even though I was forty years old before I got here. Once we got through the first phase surface op I made it my mission to find something more.'

'More?'

'More than a damn microbe. Something with a backbone and a brain. Something like *me*.'

June 2008
Frogs in the school pond have produced spawn, but no tadpoles.

As rumours spread of the sterilities, the children remain the focus of unwelcome attention. Some of them are showing signs of stress – strange paintings and stories, odd games in the playground – they are becoming withdrawn, turning to each other for comfort.

They are just victims of the same hyper-technological accident which apparently triggered the sterility problems. But it is as if the children are being transformed into witches, in some monstrous mass mind. Absurd, paradoxical, frightening.

Meanwhile the ministry scientists are considering pulling out. Their tests have proved inconclusive.

Merrick argues against this. He says that something subtle and strange is unfolding here, which we must study. He walks Stewart, Emma and me through a tree-of-life evolution wall chart; the sterility effects are working their way 'down' the tree, from younger and more complex forms of life, like mammals, to the older. He predicts that reptiles will be the next animal group to show symptoms.

Stewart sticks to her chain of command, determined to keep control and minimize disorder and panic.

But now a personal crisis looms for us. Emma has gone into labour. A doctor and midwife attend.

Merrick, typically, uses the event to gather more data. He asks distracting questions about instances of human conception in the

village since the accident. The midwife repeats a few rumours.
And meanwhile there are more stories of empty nests, vacant
ponds, all over this scrap of ancient English countryside.

She had sent Bob the letter: a genuine letter, written by hand on
flimsy sheets of plastic-sealed paper. Bob didn't understand the
half of it. But he knew it was about the Reboot, the origin of
Earth's disaster.

'I never knew him,' she said. 'Reid, I mean. He was just some
English guy. Dead now, I guess. I don't even know why he sent
me the letter. We were first on Mars; we got mails from all over.
Maybe he saw a bond between us. He was there at the beginning
of a new world, as was I.'

'Doctor Lyall –'

She laid her hand on his shoulder – softly, but her fingers were
strong, like claws. 'Indulge me a little more. It's important. Believe
me.'

She took a few steps away from the memorialized *Beagle*, and
scuffed at ruddy Martian dirt with her toe. 'I learned my fossil
hunting before I left Earth. I worked out in the desert heartlands
of Kenya. That's in Africa. You've heard of Africa? You know,
people have lived in that area for two million years or more. But
even there you don't find bones just sticking out of the ground.
You have to be systematic. You have to know where to look and
how to look.

'The landscape of Mars is billions of years older than Africa.
Everything is worn to dust. Fossil-hunting here is unimaginably
harder.' She pointed to the distant crater walls. 'But not impossible. I looked in craters like this, at exposed layers of sedimentary rock.'

Bob felt a remote curiosity stir. 'And you found something.'

Lyall smiled. 'It took years.' From a pocket in her suit she dug
out a scrap of rock, embedded in a disc of clear plastic. She handed
it to Bob.

He turned it over and over. It was like a paperweight. Except
for the fact that it contained two bands of shading, divided by a
neat, sharp line, it looked like every other rock on Mars.

He was obscurely disappointed. 'I can't see anything.'

'The evidence is microscopic. This is only a show sample
anyhow. But *they were here,* Bob: multicellular life, complex life,
a whole community. There seems to have been an evolutionary

explosion like Earth's pre-Cambrian, buried in Mars's deep past
– *much* earlier than anything comparable on Earth. They lived
in the oceans. There were squat bottom feeders, and sleek-
shelled swimmers that seem to have been functionally equivalent to fish –'

'Why doesn't everybody know about this?'

'Because we are still trying to figure out how they all died.'

He shrugged. 'What is there to figure? Mars dried out and froze.'

'*But the extinction was sudden,*' she said. She pointed to the
line between the different-coloured layers in the rock. 'You find
rocks like this on Earth. The lines mark places in the geological
record where there have been great extinction events. Below, life.
Above, no life – or at any rate, a different life, a sparser life.'

'Like the dinosaurs.'

She nodded approvingly. 'Yes. These are Mars's dinosaurs, Bob.
But it wasn't a comet that killed them. It wasn't the freeze – not
directly; it happened much too rapidly for that.'

Then Bob saw it; it was as if the ruddy landscape swivelled
around the bit of rock. 'It was a Reboot.'

'Yes,' she said.

'Just like Earth.'

'Just like Earth.'

July 2008

*Now, Merrick has found, even insects are failing to reproduce,
and on the farms crops are failing.*

*This unfolding environmental disaster is of course impossible
to conceal. The cordon is back. Government officials, scientists
and the press are crawling over the area. There is a news blackout
on the school and heavy security – 'for the children's protection'.
I am glad Miranda Stewart is still involved, trying to maintain
decent conditions for the children, responding to my requests for
normality.*

*But the children have been isolated. Once more they are subject
to scrutiny and endless tests from doctors, social workers, educa-
tionalists, psychologists, other scientists. These 'experts' find
nothing, of course. I see it as all part of the absurd witch-hunt.*

*The childrens' parents are agitated, frightened, angry. 'We don't
want our child to be special. Why us?' Some are threatening to
sue me or the government. But the children have not actually been
injured. There is nothing I can say to reassure them.*

Joel is one of the field-trip kids. Through him I learn that his family, of farmers, have been badly affected. They blame the government, the kids. Even Joel himself, says the poor child. I wonder what is happening in his home, away from official eyes.

I am staying with the kids as much as I can. But my situation is difficult. I am delighted with our baby boy, and I think we are both secretly relieved that he is 'normal'. But Emma is scared and thinks we should be planning to get as far from here as possible.

My conflict of loyalties deepens.

'When the desiccation came, evolution slowed to a crawl. Life was forced to be thrifty, to evolve towards simplicity, robustness and cooperation. Any fancy multicellular design became a liability. Great communities emerged with a new kind of distributed complexity, with simple, interchangeable components . . .'

'Instead of people, slime.'

'You got it. *But it had to happen fast.* On an evolutionary timescale anyhow . . . Look, I can't tell this story right. There is nothing conscious about the direction of evolution, nothing purposeful. But there was something in the genes, something that found itself activated when the conditions were right, when the stress got too great. Something that shut down what could no longer survive the desiccation.'

'Something?'

'We think we understand the mechanism,' Lyall said darkly. 'Bob, your DNA isn't a seamless piece of genetic machinery. Your genes contain endogenous retroviruses – ERVs.'

'Retroviruses – like HIV?'

'That's right. ERVs were once independent life forms – viruses that invaded the cells of our ancestors millions of years ago. But ERVs liked it so much they decided to stay. They have become integrated into the human genome, reproduced and passed down through the generations. This has been going on for at least thirty million years: maybe one per cent of your genome is represented by ERVs and fragments. And every mammal species we've examined contains ERVs too.

'Cohabitation makes the viruses settle down: it's a poor parasite that destroys its host. But sometimes the tamed viruses turn feral again. Retroviruses seem to be responsible for autoimmune diseases: when they kick in it's like your body is mounting an immune attack against your own cells. And that's not all they can do. In certain circumstances, it seems, they can stop the replication of DNA molecules altogether . . .' Lyall shrugged. 'Look, kid, I'm a propulsion engineer – not even a rock hound, and still less a microbiologist. But what I do understand –'

'The Martian Reboot was caused by ERVs.'

She nodded grimly. 'Or something like them. The evidence is iffy – it's been a *long* time – but that's how it looks.'

Bob struggled to understand what she was telling him. 'Was it an ERV on Earth too?'

'Yes.' She watched him, letting it figure it out for himself.

'Oh,' he said. 'The same ERV.'

'The same ERV.'

August 2008
Now the plants are dying in earnest – wheat, grasses, weeds. In the very centre, close to Corwell itself, only single-celled organisms are reproducing, the very root of the evolutionary tree. Merrick has followed this grim progression with my classroom tree-of-life diagram, step by step.

There is growing hostility to the children.

It is a hot August, and tempers are inflamed.

It comes to a head.

Some of the locals mount a drunken attack. The soldiers on guard are hesitant, their sympathies split, their orders unclear. Stewart, Merrick, Emma and myself rush to defend the children. Joel's father, drunk and in despair, improvises a petrol bomb and throws it. His own child is his target.

I have never held a lower opinion of the human species. With a possibly terminal catastrophe gathering around us, all we can do is seek someone to blame, and to harass the innocent and helpless. Perhaps we do not deserve to survive.

The children are saved from the fire.

Emma is killed.

I don't know how else to tell such a thing.

She stood there, the lower half of her suit stained bright red by the dust, gazing up at Earth. '*Earth doesn't have to die,*' she said. 'That's the point. Earth isn't freezing and drying like ancient Mars. I think that damn ERV got triggered by accident. It was the pressures of that one shithole place in England, the mix of ground toxins and atmospheric pollution and whatever the hell else was going on there. Our fault, sure – but an accident all the same. *It isn't Earth's time.*'

Bob, still resentful, was growing frightened of this eighty-year-old, and the huge biological disaster that lay behind her, a billion-year shadow. 'Why doesn't Earth do something about it?'

She sighed. 'Because there is no "Earth". There are only factions and nations and corporations . . . For a time, even as the disaster unfolded, we were hopeful. We even mounted missions to Mars, for God's sake. I guess we always thought we'd defeat the plague. But we didn't. Hope died. Now there are enclaves, fortresses. And you can't do science from inside a fortress.

'Listen to me. You are Mars's last child. On Earth you will be a sentimental token, a five-minute wonder. You will have a plat-form. You have to use it.' She closed her hand around his, around the rock. 'Make them listen. Drag them out of their fortresses, their cowering madness. Read the letter. Make them put together the lessons of this ancient rock, and what's going on all around them. We learned more from the first scraping of Martian bugs than in fifty years of one-planet biology, and I believe it can be so again. In a way it's beautiful – the ancient life of one aban-doned world coming to the aid of its suffering sister . . . Make them see that.' She searched his face anxiously. 'Do you under-stand?'

Bob opened his palm. In the slowly fading light he stared at the innocent bit of rock, longing to see the creatures who had once swum vanished Martian seas.

September 2008
Merrick, my dead wife's lover, has stayed with us. Emma's death has drawn us together.

Merrick's counsel is oddly reassuring, in an abstract way. He says that essentially a 'reboot' mechanism is operating. Just as a crashed computer can be restored from reboot files, so the bio-sphere, stressed beyond endurance, is 'dumping' higher biological forms, abandoning all but the most basic forms of life, perhaps in the hope of re-evolving to suit the new conditions. Merrick spec-ulates that this mechanism may have operated before, after the great extinction events of the past.

This all seems a little spooky to me; it smacks of Mother Gaia taking revenge. But I know little about the science and I keep my counsel.

The virus is spread by air, water, contact. Merrick hacks into internet sites to find evidence that the virus is already working its effects elsewhere, far from Tricester.

Merrick predicts we have maybe a century left. A hundred years, as humans and other higher forms are discarded like autumn leaves.

I cradle my baby, and wonder how many more like him will be born.

SUN GOD

Apollo drifted between Earth and Moon.

Fifty thousand miles behind Apollo a gibbous Earth loomed, huge and bright. And opposite, a hundred and eighty thousand miles ahead, there hung a tiny crescent Moon, like a Chinese lantern.

The Earth was white. And the Moon was brick red . . .

. . . and it was beneath that crimson Moon that I was stationed, as penalty for my heterodoxy, on the surface of the First World: the hell-planet, orbiting less than a solar radius from the surface of the bloated sun itself.

Hell-planet, perhaps. But there was once life here.

We can find traces of complex carbon compounds in the deep, subducted rocks. We can reconstruct how this world's biosphere must have operated, in the youth of the sun, with rich and complex cycles based (unlike our own ammonia-dependent processes) on the unlikely combination of water, carbon dioxide and oxygen.

Yes – oceans of water!

There was even intelligence here.

Oh, after so long, after billions of revolutions of this twin world around its sun, no artefact could remain on the surface: no proud symbol of their presence, for every material used to construct vessels or buildings would long since have crumbled to its constituent chemicals. But, nevertheless, in the deeper layers of the old continents, even in the rock subducted beneath desiccated sea beds, we found traces: layers of metals and pollutants – lead and zinc and cadmium – evidence of mining, deep caches of certain isotopes of uranium.

149

There are even, in places – in the ash from long-dead volcanoes, restored to the surface by tectonic cycles – the remnants of bodies. Artefacts nearby, of gold, platinum and mercury, some ceramics.

Piece by piece we learned much of them: these shambling sacks of water with their unruly, chaotic culture, who so briefly dominated their own planet –

– and, I came to believe, touched the surface of their Moon!

Traces only, granted, and in just six isolated sites, scattered over one hemisphere of that pocked, ancient satellite.

The geological cycle of the First World was my assignment. I was not supposed to be studying the antique intelligence of the First World – still less evidence of voyages to that solitary Moon!

But that – curse my heterodoxy! – is what I discovered.

It was difficult to understand how this could be so. How could water-heavy life be transmitted across such a gulf of space? Even if it did, in some form of spaceborne spore, perhaps, why should it be restricted to those six sites? Why should it not spread over the whole satellite?

It made no sense.

Therefore I formed an outrageous hypothesis.

I suggested that the life traces were carried there by conscious intent. *The inhabitants of the First World, at the bright dawn of time, travelled to their satellite, and left marks in its shattered soil.*

Well, my hypothesis aroused predictable outrage. I already had a reputation for controversy after my original heterodoxy. There was no sign of the use of advanced propulsion technology on that lonely Moon: fusion, zero-point energy, spacetime inflation. Not even nuclear fission! So how did they get here? With chemical rockets, children's toys? And they showed no evidence of the global cultural organization which would have made such an endeavour possible; they were squabbling, territorial creatures.

And why just six landing sites?

Six journeys, and then no more? A tide of life, reaching up from the First World to its satellite at those six points, then falling back?

Yes. It was absurd.

I needed more evidence.

In my own time, defying my superiors, I began to seek a way to show how such flights could have been achieved, with appropriate technical and cultural logic: flights from the First World to its battered Moon . . .

* * *

. . . a Moon which rose like a shard of bone in the blue dome of sky over New Mexico scrub, as Slade walked towards the Flight Operations Control Centre.

The DC-X – also known as *Sun God* – sat on the flat, baked plain of the White Sands Missile Range. The rocket, swathed in boiling hydrogen, was a misshapen cone, like a stubby, isolated minaret maybe forty feet tall. Heat haze shimmered before it. The craft was visibly battered, dinged-up and scorched, after the multiple test flights it had already taken.

A countdown intoned from a primitive PA system, the terse numbers and technical data echoing away across the sands. The sun was directly in Slade's eyes, the light on his head, face and chest a tangible presence; it seemed as unfiltered as if he were in space.

Dream on, he thought.

It was June, 1997.

Slade reached the Control Centre, which was just a ten-yard trailer set up three miles from *Sun God*'s launch pad. He entered and sat in front of a computer screen. Two McDonnell engineers were here waiting for him, with their own consoles and controls. But during the flight phase, *Sun God* would be Slade's ship, and that suited him just fine.

The countdown proceeded, calm and controlled. And –

Light burst from the base of the craft, the pure, clear glow of burning hydrogen. All of three miles away, the exhilaration of ignition made Slade's soul rise. A billow of white smoke blasted sideways, out across the desert surface, stirring the cryogenic clouds, which were soon stained yellow by kicked-up sand.

The conical craft slid smoothly into the air, soon rising above its support structure. When it had risen out of the hydrogen cloud, that clear flame, lengthening, was all but invisible.

Then the rocket ship slowed to a halt, thirty yards above the ground. It was astonishing. Rockets weren't supposed to *do* that.

Now the DC-X responded smoothly to its programming, tipping and scooting a few yards back and forth across the desert, moving simply by tilting its four rocket nozzles, directing the thrust. The engineers rattled through their tests.

It looked so easy, Slade thought. But it wasn't.

The problem with spaceflight was, humans were trapped here, on the surface of the Earth, by the laws of physics. If you were going to use chemical engines to get to orbit from Earth, you needed a ninety per cent mass fraction: ninety per cent of your take-off mass had to be fuel. Back in the sixties, when they first built the Atlas, they could get no better than seventy or eighty per cent.

This little craft, the DC-X, looked good, but its mass fraction was only sixty per cent. It was supposed to pioneer technologies to push up that mass fraction. For this flight it had been given all kinds of fancy modifications, like a new graphite epoxy hydrogen tank, a lox tank made from aluminium-lithium alloy, and an oxygen-hydrogen reaction control system that used excess fuel from the main tanks.

DC-X was a one-third prototype. The full-scale version – a hundred and twenty feet tall, just a little taller than John Glenn's Mercury-Atlas – would weigh in at five hundred tons, and be capable of carrying two crew to orbit.

But it wouldn't be piloted. The crew would be passengers, helpless as babies, stuck in the metal belly of the craft.

Well, it probably wouldn't ever get built. Even if it did, it was so far in the future Slade wouldn't see it.

But here he was anyhow, flying *Sun God* back and forth, in little arcs over the desert.

Slade, aged sixty-seven, had been in aviation – specifically, rocket craft – all his life. He was an old lifting-body man. After Patuxent, he flew the old X-15 a couple times. When his buddies were applying to NASA in the sixties, for Mercury, he just wasn't interested. He wanted to stick with spaceplanes. He figured those dumb ballistic capsules just weren't the future.

Well, he'd been proven correct. There had been that scare when the Russians had first thrown up their heavy satellites and their cosmonauts, but it was soon obvious that the Soviets' technical lead was only in heavy-lift boosters. Just one American had flown in orbit – John Glenn, in 1961, in his tin-can Mercury capsule atop an Atlas booster – and then the nation had backed off. And when John Kennedy had called for a decade-long programme to reach the Moon – the *Moon*, with throwaway boosters and ballistic capsules, for God's sake – he had been roundly howled down.

America had gone back to Eisenhower's slow and steady approach. And so, after forty years, the Atlas, steadily upgraded, remained America's only orbital booster system, with a capacity to orbit of a few tons.

But anyhow Atlas was enough for practical purposes like

weather satellites and comsats. You didn't *need* anything more powerful, unless you wanted to do something seriously dumb like fly to the Moon! The research had gone on into new technologies, slowly and incrementally.

There was no rush.

And Slade, to his own surprise, had grown old watching it all go by, waiting for a chance to fly.

Of course *this* wasn't piloting. The DC-X was completely controlled by the computer. Slade had what the engineers called trajectory command over the bird. He was sending in pre-scripted plays like a gridiron coach, then leaving it to the software to execute the plays.

But that was okay. You didn't need much imagination to believe you were up there, in the tip of that cone, flying.

Sun God stayed in the air by standing on a rocket flame – just like a lunar lander would have worked – in fact, he thought now, he'd have been more than happy to sit on the nose of that thing and ride it down to the surface of the old Moon itself, with Bado.

– And as he framed that idea, he saw Bado again. In his unwelcome memory that treacherous old X-15 came barrelling out of the sky once more, slamming Bado, his good buddy, into the high Mojave – that soft crump, the almost gentle puff of dust.

Damn, damn. It had always seemed so *wrong*. Maybe in some other life, he and Bado could really have flown some kind of Mercury capsule down to the surface of the Moon. Maybe that was where his recurring dream came from –

– in which Bado came loping out of a shallow crater, towards Slade, bouncing happily over the sandy surface of the Moon –

– but then there was the other half of his dream, where he was just a kid, toiling in the guts of some huge space rocket factory, forced to speak a guttural European tongue –

Moons and mountains. Recurring dreams. An old geezer thing, evidently.

But the Moon probably would have killed them anyhow. There were scientists who said the mountains there would crumble like meringues if you set foot on them, or the dust itself would explode and swallow you up.

Anyhow, Slade was going to die without ever *knowing*.

Time to bring her in.

Sun God swept through a smooth arc towards the splash of

concrete that was its landing pad. The bird slid down through the last few feet, as smooth as if it was riding a rail down to the ground, and he let the automatics finish the touchdown. *Sun God* just stuck out its four landing legs and landed on its pad, as gently as a dragonfly settling on a lily.

Slade got out of his chair. His back and shoulders were stiff; he worked his fingers and arms to loosen up the muscles.

A tech was slapping him on the back. 'How about that,' he said. 'Just as fat as a goose. Outstanding.'

'Yeah. Outstanding.'

Slade stepped out of the trailer. It was still bright morning; the flight had lasted just minutes. And in the sky, that big old Moon hadn't yet set; it just hung there – oh, hell, something must be wrong with his eyes, he spent too much time peering at those damn computer screens – the Moon was bright red . . .

. . . *red in the light of the sun, which has swollen to a crimson giant in its old age, its hot breath suffocating the First World – and yet, paradoxically, scattering life over our own more remote globe.*

How would First World life function?

It is possible water could play the role in a life system that ammonia does for us: a water-based biosphere!

First World life forms would drink water as we do ammonia, and breathe oxygen as we do nitrogen. When we respire, we burn methane in nitrogen, producing ammonia and cyanogen. Similarly, the First World life would burn sugars in oxygen and give off water and carbon dioxide. To close the loop there would be some form of photosynthesis, hydrous plants using solar energy to turn the products of that respiration – water and carbon dioxide – back to sugars and oxygen, as our plants turn ammonia and cyanogen back to methane and nitrogen . . .

Strange, but not impossible!

What would the First World have been like, in those remote days?

It would be a world of water oceans, perhaps with caps of polar ice, and a clear air, of free oxygen buffered by nitrogen. And there would be clouds, of water vapour . . .

On such a large world, spinning sixteen times as fast as Home, the climate would be more complex than our own. Powerful Coriolis forces would act on the air, generating swirling storms

. . . *We can only imagine the cultures and ecosystems which evolved in such complex and violent climatic conditions.*

There is more. Chemical reactions are dependent on temperature. Reaction rates are increased as the temperature rises. On a world so warm that even water is a liquid the reaction rates rocket, by perhaps a hundred to a thousand times.

Thus, the metabolism of hydrous creatures would proceed at a much faster rate than ours. That would be offset by the increased gravity, but still, life must have proceeded at a frenetic pace.

We can even deduce the colour of the sky, on that strange, lost world.

There was no methane in the air, because it would have reacted with the free oxygen. And because light from the blue end of the spectrum has a wavelength similar in size to the molecules of the air – nitrogen and oxygen – the sky of the First World must have been blue, *not green . . .*

At last, the First World was betrayed by the star that gave it life. The end came when the surface grew so hot that the very stuff of water-based life – complex molecules and carbon-based molecular chains – was broken down.

Finally those unlikely water oceans boiled, and huge clouds of vapour were suspended in the atmosphere, driving temperatures higher still, ever faster. But even the clouds did not last forever. At last the water vapour in the air was broken up by energetic sunlight and the hydrogen driven off into space, leaving a planet baked dry, its surface cracked and flattened under a dense, sluggish atmosphere, utterly lifeless –

In any event it seems clear that my putative water-laden Moon voyagers did not have the means to escape their planet, or to avert their ultimate doom.

Trips to the Moon: logic was not enough! My simulation had taught me that, at least. 'Logic' to these creatures meant starving their projects of resources! And besides, nobody logical would attempt to travel between this world and its Moon with such primitive technology. Nobody sensible.

But these people were neither logical nor sensible. I knew I must remember that.

I sought a logical political structure in their reconstructed history, a structure that could have commanded significant resources. I reset the parameters of the simulation –

But I was speaking of my search for evidence of spaceflight by this antique intelligence, of its travel to the desiccated satellite:

The inner system, at the bottom of the sun's gravity well, is crowded. Conditions are quite unlike Home, which is, of course, the largest satellite of the Fourth World. (Although, it is not well known, once the Fourth World sported a gigantic ring system, made up of chunks of ice and other debris, residue from the formation of the sun. The rings must have been beautiful. But they have long since evaporated, as the sun's heat roared in the faces of its children –)

I digress.

The First World, then, swims through a cloud of debris, of thousands of planetesimals left over from the untidy formation of the system, aeons ago. Despite geological smoothing, its surface shows the evidence of repeated bombardment, which has diminished but not ceased with the passing of time. Its airless satellite is scarred still more impressively.

I studied the orbital characteristics of one such planetesimal in particular. Many of these objects had orbits close to or crossing the First World's. But in this case, the parameters were so close to those of the First World that I grew suspicious.

Then excited.

Could this be the artefact I had sought? Not on the surface of either world – but some form of abandoned spacecraft, or space colony, circling the sun with its mother planet?

I scraped together funding for a mission to the anomalous planetesimal: a small ship to sail through the light of the Moon . . .

. . . the light of the Moon which shone like a torch beam into the dormitory as Slade woke, reluctantly. Already the older men were moving around him, shuffling, conserving what energy they had.

The mornings were the worst.

Everything was slow here – even dressing was slow – and Slade was hungry by the start of his work, at five a.m. And yet he would receive nothing but his soup, at two in the afternoon.

It was 1946. Slade was sixteen years old.

Slade lay in his rat-chewed blanket as long as he could.

Today was worse than usual. He felt – strange.

As if he shouldn't *be* here.

He couldn't stay on his rough pallet.

Soon would come the rush into the smoking mouth of the tunnel into the mountain, with the SS guards lashing out with their sticks and fists at the heads and shoulders of the worker herd which passed them. That tunnel was like Hell itself, with prisoners made white with dust and laden with rubble, cement bags, girders and boxes, and the corpses of the night being dragged by their feet from the sleep galleries –

When he got up he had to hurry. Otherwise he would not witness the hangings, and that was against regulations.

Actually, the hangings seemed wasteful to Slade. A victim would be gagged with a metal bar across the mouth, and the bar tied at the back of the head with wire, drawn in so tightly that the metal gag would bend, and the wire cut into the flesh of the face.

So much metal!

It was well known among the workers within the Mittelwerk that Hitler had ordered the production of no less than twenty thousand of von Braun's A-4 rockets – or rather, what the Germans now called their V-2: V for *Vergeltungswaffe,* revenge weapon. And then there was the demand for thousands more of the ambitious V-3s, the A-4b design with the nuclear-tipped glider on its nose, capable of skipping across the Atlantic and digging more glowing craters into the eastern seaboard of defeated America.

How could this immense production operation spare so much metal on mere hangings?

But then – thanks to those very rockets of von Braun, which had subdued Europe and Asia and fended off America – Hitler could now exploit the resources of two continents. A little hanging wire was nothing.

Slade performed such calculations, even as he reflected on the fact that at the next roll call it could be *him,* suspended up there like a chicken in a butcher's shop.

At sixteen, Slade was prized by the supervisors for his ability for skilled work. So he was assigned to lighter, more complex tasks. In the process he was forced to absorb a little German. So, gradually, he picked up something of the nature of the great machines on which he toiled, and learned of the visions of the Reich's military planners.

They would construct an immense dome at the Pas de Calais – sixty thousand tons of concrete – from which rocket planes would be fired off at America in batches of fourteen at once. And then there were the further schemes: of hurling rockets from submarine craft, of greater rockets like von Braun's A-9, which might hurl a man into orbit in a glider-like capsule, and – the greatest dream of all! – of a huge station orbiting five thousand miles above the Earth and bearing a huge mirror capable of reflecting sunlight, so that cities would flash to smoke and oceans might boil.

Thus would be secured the future of the Reich for a millennium.

And when that was done, von Braun talked of flights beyond Earth itself, in new generations of his giant rockets, hurled upwards by brute force: even of a nuclear-launched spaceship called *Sun God* which would send Germans to the Moon by 1955, to Mars a mere decade later.

Such visions!

But for Slade the V-2 was the daily, extraordinary reality. That great, finned bullet-shape – no less than forty-seven feet long – was capable of carrying a warhead of more than two thousand pounds across two hundred miles! Its four tons of metal contained no less than twenty-two thousand components! And so on.

Slade came to love the V-2.

It was magnificent, a machine from another world, from a bright future – and the true dream inherent in its lines, the dream of its designers, was obvious to him. Even as it slowly killed him.

One day, in the sleek, curving hide of a rocket ship, he caught a glimpse of his own reflection.

He looked into his own eyes unexpectedly, suddenly fully aware of himself. He had a sense of the here and now – or rather of vividness, as if the casual numbness of his life had been lifted, briefly. He hadn't seen a mirror in three years, since the Nazis swept through what was left of Britain, and he was separated from his parents and, as an American, rounded up as an enemy alien.

He saw a skinny, half-bald kid, with blood running down his cheek from some wound he hadn't even noticed.

– and an old man, his face twisted down under a coating of desert gypsum –

– and a gold visor, a glaring landscape reflected there –

– and flames –

Visions. It was probably the hunger. What else could it be?

He subsided to numbness, and dreams.

One morning, so early that the stars still shone and frost coated the ground, he saw the engineers from the research facility at Peenemunde – Wernher von Braun, Walter Riedel and the rest, smartly uniformed young men, some not much older than Slade – looking up at the stars, and pointing, and talking softly.

Slade glanced up, to see where they were looking. It was the crescent Moon, dimmed by the smoky light of some town which burned on the horizon. And *there* was the dream which motivated and sustained these young, clever Germans: that one day the disc of the Moon would be lit up with cities built by men – Germans, carried there by some gigantic descendant of the V-2.

Slade could understand how these young men from Peenemunde were blinded by the dazzling beauty of their V-2 and what it represented. But Slade was no rocket engineer; he was no more than garbage, just one of the thirty thousand French, Russians, Czechs, Poles, British and Americans who toiled inside this carved-out mountain. And in the dormitories at night would come the whispers, schemes of hidden weapons and tools, the uprising to come which would shatter the Reich.

The duality of it crushed Slade. Was such squalor and agony the inevitable price to be paid for the dream of spaceflight?

But perhaps it was. Perhaps only the organization of all of mankind's resources, under some such system as Hitler's, was capable of breaking the bonds of gravity. Perhaps it was necessary for von Braun's beautiful ships to rise from ground soaked by the blood of thousands of slave workers like himself, with expended human souls burning like sparks in the gaping rocket nozzles.

How he envied the young engineers from Peenemunde, who strutted about the Mittelwerk in their smart uniforms; *they* seemed to find it an easy thing to brush past the stacks of corpses piled up for daily collection, the people gaunt as skeletons toiling around the great metal spaceships!

He even imagined how it would have been had he been born to become one of these smart young Germans in their SS uniforms. How he envied them! And a part of him hoped that they could achieve some piece of their huge dreams before the inevitable tide of anger rose up and swept them all to the gallows.

When he immersed himself in such dreams, something of his own, daily pain would fall from him, and he could lift his head to the Moonlight . . .

. . . *the Moonlight which washed over the machined surface of my planetesimal. The object was small. But even at a great distance from it, I could detect its artificial nature.*

It was a slim cylinder. One end was domed, the other terminated by a complex encrustation of equipment, including a flaring nozzle. It bore no markings.

It tumbled slowly.

It was extremely old. Sublimation had left its aluminium skin so thin it was, in places, almost transparent. In fact the hull was punctured, after billions of orbits around the sun.

The artefact was fortunate to have survived intact at all.

I approached cautiously. I could see into its interior, through rents and dimples in the hull. There was some form of double chamber in there. There was no sign of activity, of light, of energy.

The cylinder dwarfed my craft.

After circling its exterior, I gathered my courage, and I approached the terminal dome, where an eroded breach afforded me access.

I found myself rising into a cylindrical chamber, up from the cup of the dome. Stars and ruddy sunlight gleamed through hull rents. Far above me, hanging down as if swollen, I saw another dome.

The chamber was all but empty. The walls were lined with small pieces of equipment: spherical casks, ducts, pipes.

I rose through the silent grandeur of the artefact.

I passed through the upper dome, deep into the heart of the artefact. I entered a second chamber, braced with a metal frame. It was much smaller than the first.

There was no sign of occupation, no evidence of life.

I continued my inspection, baffled – at first – as to the purpose of this artefact.

But soon I formed an hypothesis.

My rogue planetesimal was clearly an artefact. But I had misinterpreted its nature.

It was no spaceborne habitat. Those great cylindrical chambers were tanks, which once bore fuel. Liquid fuel.

I came to believe the artefact was a crude rocket. It must have driven itself forward by burning liquid-chemical propellants together, and allowing the expansion of gases through the terminal nozzle. The dimensions of the tanks were consistent with the relative densities of liquid hydrogen and liquid oxygen. These would burn vigorously together, if appropriately controlled.

I elaborated my original hypothesis:

I argued that the creatures of the First World had used chemical rockets like this one to escape from their planet's gravity well, and to travel to their satellite.

Yes – chemical rockets!

Well, I was mocked, as I might have expected. I concede it seems absurd that such a journey might be attempted with such limited technology.

But it is not impossible!

I argued my case. I was disciplined, for neglecting my primary studies.

So I determined to prove, by dramatic demonstration, how such a flight could have been achieved! I would reconstruct the chemical Moon ships from the dawn of time, and prove it was this way.

That was the start of it. But soon my simulations were going badly.

Perhaps I continued to miscalculate the natures of my subjects. They were not like us.

We must remember the environment in which these bizarre animals evolved: the ferocious gravitational field of their parent world, the blistering outpourings of the nearby sun. They would be stunted, very alien creatures, warped by these enormous forces into miserably malformed, distorted shapes, crushed until they are blind and tiny. We inhabit a favoured realm, drifting far above the range of those immense forces, on our small moon so far from the sun; we should not envy these creatures their short, pain-filled lives.

But they must have been squabbling, water-stuffed, energy-fat, demon-obsessed monsters! If logic would not motivate them, if they were unable to govern themselves and their resources without brutality and waste, I knew I must try illogic.

I reset the parameters of my simulation once again. I would not rest until I had reconstructed the hydrate creatures from so long ago, sailing to the Moon . . .

. . . Sailing to the Moon, Slade was working through a plastic bag of chicken soup. He took a spoonful of the soup, tapped the handle, and the glob of soup floated off, still holding the shape of the spoon. But when he poked the liquid with a fingertip, surface tension hauled it quickly into a perfect, oscillating sphere. Slade leaned over to suck it into his mouth, a little green ball of chicken soup.

It was Slade's fourth spaceflight, in six years. He'd never yet got bored with the zero-gravity environment.

The two other crew – Lunar Module Pilot Bado, and Command

Module Pilot Pond – ate without talking. And that was the way Mission Commander Slade, in his centre couch, preferred it.

It was August, 1967. And Apollo 3 was heading for the Moon.

A splinter of crimson-sunset light, from the Command Module's windows above him, caught Slade's eye. He looked up. Whatever it was had gone; the windows were just rectangles of darkness.

The red of the Moon had been like –

– the red of an old man's rheumy eyes, peering across some Godforsaken desert –

– the red of a kid's blood, toiling in some brutal mountain –

Slade tried to focus. He felt disconcerted, unsure, vaguely disturbed. His instincts were ringing alarm bells.

Maybe it was the ship. There had been a shit-load of problems already on this trip. If this was an aircraft he'd get out before taking her up – peer into the vents and kick the tyres – try to back up his hunch.

But that wasn't an option.

Anyhow the others didn't seem to have noticed anything.

The meal over, it was time for work.

Slade toiled steadily through his pre-transposition checklist, throwing switches and recording settings and readings. En route to the Moon, *Sun God* was still mounted on top of the S-IVB – the spent Saturn V third-stage booster – with its nose pointed forward. Now, to gain access to the Lunar Module – still housed within its adapter cone at the top of the booster – CM Pilot Pond had to uncouple *Sun God* from the stack, turn it around, and dock it nose-to-nose with the LM, the Lunar Module.

Pond called out a countdown.

Slade heard a muffled thump, a soft push at his back.

Sun God had become detached from the depleted S-IVB booster stage. Pond fired up the reaction-control system, and let *Sun God* drift away from the booster –

'Uh oh,' Pond said. 'I got a twelve-oh-two alarm.' This was a computer programme alarm, flashing up on Pond's display unit. 'Something to do with a memory overload. It came up when I engaged the rendezvous radar. And it – shit.'

The alarm code had changed to 'twelve-oh-one'.

'Houston, are you copying?'

'Stand by, *Sun God*. We're working on it.' The capcom's voice betrayed nothing.

Slade snorted and slammed the palm of his hand against the

computer. One little glitch and the docking was on hold.

There was nothing he could do now but wait. And all the time, Slade knew, *Sun God*, on its separate trajectory, was drifting farther from the S-IVB; already the gap had opened up to two miles. To recover now they'd have to go through a full-scale rendezvous procedure.

– and still he had that sense of dislocation: of things being not quite *right*. As if an engine was running off –

Slade was beginning to think his mission might be snake-bit: doomed to failure. They had had problems with the Apollo since they left the ground. Lousy comms. Computer glitches. Foul stenches from the life support. Scuffed wiring. Stuck hatches. Inoperative reaction-control thrusters.

Slade had followed the evolution of his ship through its manufacture. He had seen the NASA QA report that had called it sloppy and unsafe. He knew there had been twenty thousand failures during its construction and testing. He knew it was just a lousy bucket of bolts that should never had left the factories, at Palmdale and Bethpage.

But here was Slade flying this clunker to the Moon, because that was the timetable of America's mad, impetuous dash into space, and Slade would have been aboard if he had to get out and push.

It was six years since Slade's first flight in space. He'd finished three orbits of Earth on the second orbital Mercury flight, in 1961, following John Glenn. He'd hung in there, piling up flight assignments, while younger, smarter guys came into the programme to compete with him. He'd gotten a Gemini flight, and a seat on the first Earth-orbital Apollo test flight in 1966. He was the only man to have flown all three generations of US spacecraft.

And now here he was – commander of his own lunar ship – on his way to the ultimate piloting test, the Moon landing itself. This would be the best of all, a full-up mission, the crown of his career.

But it seemed to be falling apart.

The capcom came back on the air-to-ground loop. The only solution Houston could come up with was to run the rendezvous manually. 'The coordinates are NOUN 33, 092, 29, 43532 minus 00312. HA and HP are NA. Pitch is –' Slade wrote out the data on the back of a checklist, and read them back down the link.

Pond and Slade rattled through a brief start-up checklist, and

Pond began to throw switches. Bado was appointed timekeeper, and he counted Pond down to the time indicated by Houston.

'Ten, nine, eight –'

Now, framed in the windows, Slade could see the S-IVB. It was a white-painted cylinder, dappled with black panels, the brave scarlet 'USA' emblazoned on its flank. And there, at the nose of the cylinder, was the complex, foil-covered roof of the Lunar Module, now exposed to the sunlight, its docking receptor a dark pit at its centre.

The next item was a couple of short SPS burns, thrusts of the Service Module main engine.

'Three, two, one,' Bado said. 'Fire.'

There was a brief thrust, of perhaps a half-G, which pressed Slade into his couch. It lasted just seconds.

Pond had to fly by eye. The rendezvous radar was still useless. The S-IVB seemed to approach them, then recede, then approach again; it was like stalking some huge, cautious animal.

At last, the S-IVB was looming before them, huge and ungainly and complicated, the LM nestling in its nose. The windows were filled with drifting metal struts and paintwork.

Shadows mingled. The cabin shuddered as *Sun God* impacted the LM, hard, and there was a groan of metal.

A green light came on. Slade heard the rippling clang of docking latches snapping shut.

'How about that,' Pond whooped. 'Houston, virgin no more.'

Thank Christ, Slade thought. Thank Christ –

But now there was something else. He could *smell* something. Smoke.

There was smoke coming from a compartment at the foot of his couch. Maybe there was some new piece of scuffed wiring, shorting down there, some piece of equipment to do with the docking. And now there was a flare of light; it looked as if a spark had caught the nylon netting underneath their couches.

It spread quickly.

Christ, there was fire *everywhere*.

Velcro pads stuck to the walls just exploded into flame and dropped away, showering them with sparks. Even materials that were normally flameproof were burning as if they had been dunked in kerosene: checklists, insulation, aluminium, the fabric of his suit.

Even the skin on his hands.

It was pure oxygen in here, at five psi.

Oddly, there was no pain. And he could still smell that smoke. The double-domes said Moon dust would smell like that, like ash –

He had a crushing sense of unfairness. He was going to lose his mission, the full-up flight he'd intended. It was all meaningless, like another crashed simulation.

Slade remembered so much: his father, Fay and the girls, the ranch house in Clear Lake. Such memories comprised him, his soul. But in a moment the memories would be gone. As would he.

He felt a rush of warmth, within him. His thoughts seemed to soften, guttering like candle wax.

Slade tried to focus on Fay. But he could no longer remember her face.

The air was full of light.

Red light.

Empty, its systems dormant, the glowing Apollo sailed on, towards the brick-red Moon . . .

. . . *the Moon over which I sailed, in triumph! For my hypothesis was confirmed.*

And in the destiny of these stunted creatures there is a profound lesson for our own future.

The First World formed deep in the hostile maw of the new sun's gravity well. It is a ball of rock.

But our Home, at a comfortable distance from the sun, was born half rock, half ice. A giant among moons, its huge mass caused it to heat as it collapsed. The primordial ices were melted and vaporized. The rock settled to the centre. Thus, Home is a ball of silicate, overlaid by a shell of water ice.

Home's first ocean was a mixture of ammonia and methane. A dense methane-water-ammonia atmosphere was raised over that ancient sea. The new world was a cauldron, with air pressure hundreds of times its present level, and searing temperatures.

And in the organic soup of the ammonia-water ocean, complex chemistry seethed . . .

Life arose. Yes, so long ago, at the dawn of the solar system itself!

But the new ocean and atmosphere were not stable. Ultra-violet flux from the young sun beat down on the atmosphere, shattering its ammonia molecules; planetesimals continued to fall, blasting away swathes of Home's atmosphere; the atmospheric gases dissolved in the ocean . . .

Perhaps, in the brief time they were allowed, those primeval life forms reached a high degree of complexity. We cannot tell. But they could not survive these changes. All we can find are chemical fossils, the decomposed elements of a life that was snuffed out as Home settled into its billion-Revolution Freeze. Home was a world of darkness, of haze and clouds, of sticky organic slush: a land of mud and crater lakes – a world utterly alien to the clement orb which sustains us now!

After the time of the hydrous First-Worlders, the evolution of Home continued.

As the sun brightened, at last the Freeze receded. The ethane lakes boiled, evaporated. The gases trapped there – nitrogen, methane, hydrogen – exsolved, thickening the atmosphere. Eventually the ice shells over the magma, the ancient ammonia oceans, melted, exposing the old seas once more. Ammonia and water vapour enriched the air still further . . .

And life, after its epochal suspension, began to stir once more. After hundreds of millions of Revolutions, our true history had begun.

But Home, too, is under threat of destruction!

Even now, our air is leaking away; for our world is fundamentally too small to retain its thick atmosphere even at today's prevailing temperatures. And we can postulate a time when the rising temperatures caused by the sun's expansion will once more cause the loss of our air, the evaporation of our ammonia oceans.

But the sun's ballooning growth will not stop there. When the red giant growth reaches its climax, even our bedrock water ice will become liquid.

Think of that! We have used water ice as the staple of our structures: the cities, the spires, the gleaming bridges. When the ice softens, our buildings will collapse.

Worse: our very bones will melt!

And, at last, even the water will boil away . . . It will take only a few thousand revolutions, no more. Then, nothing will be left of Home but its rocky core.

Long before then, we will be forced to make a choice: to submit to extinction, or to flee Home. We have millions of Revolutions before us, of course. Some argue that is enough. I say that when the destiny of the species is at stake, only eternity will suffice!

. . . But let us draw back, from the end of Time itself.

Before the final destruction, for a brief period, Home will have new lakes and oceans – but of liquid water.

That is why we should cherish the hydrous Astronauts, these silent ambassadors of the past. That is why we should endeavour to reconstruct them, to revive and study them.

For one day the circle of destruction and birth may close. One day we may be forced to share Home – with them!

. . . But I digress.

My historical reconstruction complete, I froze the simulation.

In the light of its Moon the little, glittering ship was really quite beautiful. So shiny and new, silver and white and black. Like a toy. But so lethal, of course.

How entertaining it had been. The interplay, the language. So authentic! And so ingenious. The very idea of reassembling the craft by hand, here in cislunar space!

To impose such defects seemed hardly fair. But this was not a game. Fairness was not a factor. Given this level of gadgetry, even multiple defects must have been common.

Of course, it might not have been quite like this. Perhaps more sacrifice was necessary. If that oxygen fire had occurred before a launch, for instance, subsequent generations of spacecraft might have been rebuilt for greater safety. The beings who performed these flights did not think logically, in an orderly fashion. Logically, they should never have flown into space at all! Perhaps they needed some such catastrophe as this to occur, regularly, to guide them on their path.

But it was really quite remarkable. These hydrate creatures were really not up to this. Not yet; perhaps, in the end, not ever. They just were not smart enough. Why, they must even have navigated by eye, by the stars! And yet they persisted. There was something to admire, in this grandiose, doomed enterprise.

Well, I felt tired but happy. My simulations had converged. A mission to the Moon with chemical rockets, so I had proven, was foolish but feasible, given supportive historical logic. Already I had sufficient documentation; it was not necessary to adjust the parameters once more, to follow the sequence through to its conclusion.

I could allow the simulation to dissolve.

Yet I lingered.

I basked in my triumph.

But I felt –

Complicated.

Guilty?

Perhaps. Those simulacra were fully sentient, of course. It was necessary for verisimilitude.

But in the end they were distressed. Well, of course they were distressed. Believing their world to be real, their lives and memories to be genuine, they had undergone a cessation of consciousness. Still, I meant to honour them – their ingenuity and bravery – not cause them harm.

Perhaps, I reflected, I should reconsider. Complete the exercise.

But after all, they were only simulacra.

Yes. Only simulacra. But of beings who once took halting steps in Moon dust . . .

. . . Moon dust which seemed to crunch beneath Slade's feet, like a covering of snow. His footprints were miraculously sharp, as if he'd placed his ridged overshoes in fine, damp sand. He took a photograph of one particularly well-defined print; it would persist here for millions of years, he realized, like the fossilized footprint of a dinosaur.

Or, he thought vaguely, not.

He felt dreamlike.

He was floating over this bright landscape. The tug of gravity was so gentle he couldn't tell which way was vertical. And when he closed his eyes he *saw* things: a bleeding boy, a bitter old man, a fire –

It was probably the low G. Yeah, that was it. The low G.

He looked around.

The LM, standing in a broad, shallow crater, was a glistening, filmy construct of gold leaf and aluminium. Low hills shouldered above the close horizon. There were craters everywhere, ranging from several yards to a thumbnail width, the sunlight deepening their shadows.

Bado came loping out of a shallow crater, towards Slade. Bado had one glove up over his chest, obscuring the tubes which connected his backpack to his oxygen and water inlets. His white oversuit was covered in dust splashes. His gold sun visor was up, and inside his white helmet Slade could see Bado's face, with its four-day growth of beard.

Bado said, 'Hey, buddy. Look up.'

Slade tipped back on his heels and looked at the sky.

The sky was black, empty of stars. In the middle of the sky the Earth was a fat crescent, four times the size of a full Moon. And there, crossing the zenith, was a single, brilliant, unwinking star: the orbiting *Sun God*, with Pond, their Command Module Pilot, waiting to take them home.

It was July, 1969.

Holy shit, Slade thought. I really am here. I made it. Holy shit.

He felt a rush of affection for his buddy, the glowing reality of him, here on the Moon. Those fragmentary visions fled, leaving him with a sense of here and now and *rightness*.

This was his place. This was where he was meant to be.

He tilted forward and eyed Bado. 'Pretty sight. But we got to hustle, boy; we got a fat checklist to get through. We're going for a full-up mission here, and don't you forget it.'

Through his visor, Bado grinned. 'Yes, sir!'

SUN-CLOUD

To human eyes, the system would have been extraordinary:

The single, giant sun was so vast that its crimson flesh would have embraced all of Sol's scattered planets. Across its surface, glistening vacuoles swarmed, each larger than Sol itself.

There was a planet.

It was a ball of rock no larger than a small asteroid. It skimmed the sun's immense photosphere, bathed in ruddy warmth. It was coated with air, a thick sea.

The world-ocean teemed with life.

Beyond the sun's dim glow, the sky was utterly dark.

She rose to the Surface. Thick water slid smoothly from her carapace.

She let her impeller corpuscles dissociate briefly; they swam free of her main corpus in a fast, darting shoal, feeding eagerly, revelling in their brief liberty.

She lifted optically sensitive corpuscles to the smoky sky. The sun was a roof over the world, its surface pocked by huge dark pits.

She was called Sun-Cloud: for, at her Coalescence, a cloud of brilliant white light had been observed, blossoming over the sun's huge, scarred face.

Sun-Cloud was seeking her sister, the one called Orange-Dawn.

Sun-Cloud raised a lantern-corpuscle. The subordinate creature soon tired and began sending quiet chemical complaints through her corpus; but she ignored them and waited, patiently, as her sphere of lantern light rolled out, spreading like a liquid over the oleaginous Surface.

The light moved slowly enough for a human eye to follow.

*   *   *

Sun-Cloud's people were not like humans.

Here, people assembled from specialized schools of corpuscles: mentalizers, impellers, lanterns, structurals, others. Obeying their own miniature imperatives of life and death, individual corpuscles would leave the aggregate corpus and return to their fish-like shoals, to feed, breed, die. But others would join, and the pattern of the whole could persist, for a time.

Still, Sun-Cloud's lifespan was finite. As the cycle of corpuscle renewal wore on, her pattern would degrade, mutate.

Like most sentient races, Sun-Cloud's people sustained comforting myths of immortality.

And, like most races, there was a minority who rejected such myths.

Sun-Cloud returned to the Ocean's deep belly.

The light here was complex and uncertain. Above Sun-Cloud the daylight was already dimming. And below her, from the Deep at the heart of the world, the glow of a billion lantern-corpuscles glimmered up, white and pure.

Sun-Cloud watched as Cold-Current ascended towards her.

They were going to discuss Sun-Cloud's sister, Orange-Dawn. Orange-Dawn was a problem.

Cold-Current was a lenticular assemblage of corpuscles twice Sun-Cloud's size, who nevertheless rose with an awesome unity. The ranks of impellers at Cold-Current's rim churned at the thick waters of the Ocean, their small cilia vibrating so rapidly that they were blue-shifted.

The Song suffused the waters around Sun-Cloud, as it always did; but as Cold-Current lifted away from the Deep the complex harmonics of the Song changed, subtly.

Sun-Cloud, awed, shrank in on herself, her structural corpuscles pushing in towards their sisters at her swarming core. Sun-Cloud knew that she herself contributed but little, a few minor overtones, to the rich assonance of the Song. How must it be to be so grand, so powerful, that one's absence left the Song – the huge, world-girdling Song itself – audibly lacking in richness?

Cold-Current hovered; a bank of optic corpuscles swivelled, focusing on Sun-Cloud. 'You know why I asked to meet you,' she said.

'Orange-Dawn.'

'Yes. Orange-Dawn. I am very disturbed, Sun-Cloud. Orange-Dawn is long overdue for Dissolution. And yet she persists; she prowls the rim of the Song, even the Surface, intact, obsessed. Even to the extent of injuring her corpuscles.'

'I know that Orange-Dawn wants to see out another hundred Cycles,' Sun-Cloud said. 'Orange-Dawn has theories. That in a hundred Cycles' time –'

'I know,' Cold-Current said. 'She believes she has Coalesced with ancient wisdom. Somehow, in a hundred Cycles, the world will be transformed, and Orange-Dawn will be affirmed.'

'But it's impossible,' Sun-Cloud said. 'I know that; Orange-Dawn must see that.'

But Cold-Current said, absently: 'But it *may* be possible, to post-pone Dissolution so long.' Sun-Cloud, intrigued, saw a tight, cubical pattern of corpuscles move through Cold-Current's corpus; individual corpuscles swam to and fro, but the pattern persisted. 'Possible,' Cold-Current said. 'There *is* old wisdom. But such a thing would be – ugly. Discordant.' Perhaps that cubical pattern contained the fragment of old knowledge to which Cold-Current hinted.

Cold-Current rotated grandly. 'I want you to go and talk to her. Perhaps you can say something . . . Nobody knows Orange-Dawn as well as you.'

That was true. Orange-Dawn had helped Sun-Cloud in her earliest Coalescence, as Sun-Cloud struggled towards sentience. Orange-Dawn had hunted combinations of healthy corpuscles for her sister, helped her coax the corpuscles into an orderly shoal. Together the sisters had run across the Surface of the Ocean, their out-thrust optic corpuscles blue-tinged with their exhilarating velocity . . .

Cold-Current began to sink back into the glimmering depths of the Ocean, her disciplined impellers beating resolutely. 'You must help her, Sun-Cloud. You must help her put aside these foolish shards of knowledge and speculation, and learn to embrace true beauty . . .'

As Cold-Current faded from view, the light at the heart of the world brightened, as if in welcome, and the Song's harmonies deepened joyously.

The world was very old. Sun-Cloud's people were very old. They had accreted many fragments of knowledge, of philosophy and science.

A person, on Dissolution, could leave behind fragments of

insight, of wisdom, in the partial, semi-sentient assemblies called sub-corpora. Before dissolving in their turn into the general corpuscle shoals, the sub-corpora could be absorbed into a new individual, the knowledge saved.

Or perhaps not.

If they were not incorporated quickly, the remnant sub-corpora would break up. Their component mentation-corpuscles would descend, and become lost in the anaerobic Deep at the heart of the world.

Sun-Cloud returned to the Surface of the Ocean.

She saw that the sun had almost set; a last sliver of crimson light spanned one horizon, which curved sharply. Above her the sky was clear and utterly black, desolately so.

Her corpuscles transmitted their agitation to each other.

She raised a lantern; cold light bloomed slowly across the sea's oily meniscus.

She roamed the Ocean, seeking Orange-Dawn.

At last the creeping lantern light brought echoes of distant motion to her optic corpuscles: a small form thrashing at the Surface in lonely unhappiness.

With a rare sense of urgency Sun-Cloud ordered her impeller corpuscles into motion. It didn't take long for her to accelerate to a significant fraction of lightspeed; the impellers groaned as they strained at relativity's tangible barrier, and the image of the lonely one ahead was stained with blue shift.

Wavelets lapped at her and air stroked her hide; she felt exhilarated by her velocity.

She slowed. She called softly: 'Orange-Dawn?'

Listlessly Orange-Dawn raised optic corpuscles. Orange-Dawn was barely a quarter Sun-Cloud's size. She was withered, her corpus depleted. Her corpuscles lay passively over each other, tiny mouths gaping with obvious hunger.

'Do I shock you, Sun-Cloud?'

Sun-Cloud sent small batches of corpuscles as probes into Orange-Dawn's tattered carcase. 'Orange-Dawn. Your corpuscles are suffering. Some of them are dying. Cold-Current is concerned for you –'

'She sent you to summon me to my Dissolution.'

Sun-Cloud said, 'I don't like to see you like this. You're introducing a harshness into the Song.'

'The Song, the damnable Song,' Orange-Dawn muttered. Moodily she began to spin in the water. The corpuscles' decay had so damaged her corpus's circular symmetry that she whipped up frothy waves which lapped over her upper carapace, the squirming corpuscles there. She poked optic corpuscles upwards, but the night sky was blind. 'The Song drowns thought.'

'What will happen in a hundred Cycles, Orange-Dawn?'

Orange-Dawn thrashed at the water. 'The data is partial . . .' She focused wistful optic corpuscles on her sister. 'I don't know. But it will be –'

'What?'

'Unimaginable. *Wonderful.*'

Sun-Cloud wanted to understand. 'What *data?*'

'There are some extraordinary speculations, developed in the past, still extant here and there . . . Did you know, for instance, that the Cycle is actually a tide, raised in our Ocean-world during its passage around the sun? It took many individuals a long time to observe, speculate, calculate, obtain that fragment of information. And yet we are prepared to throw it away, into the great bottomless well of the Song . . .

'I've tried to assemble some of this. It's taken so long, and the fragments don't fit more often than not, but –'

'Integrate? Like a Song?'

'Yes.' Orange-Dawn focused her optic corpuscles. 'Yes. Like a Song. But not the comforting mush they intone below. That's a Song of death, Sun-Cloud. A Song to guide you into non-being.'

Sun-Cloud shuddered; little groups of her corpuscles broke away, agitated. 'We don't die.'

'Of course not.' Orange-Dawn rotated and drifted towards her. 'Watch this,' she said.

Quickly, she budded off a whole series of sub-corpora, each tiny body consisting of a few hundred corpuscles. Instantly the sub-corpora squirmed about the Surface, leaping and breaking the meniscus, blue-shifted as they pushed into lightspeed's intangible membrane.

Sun-Cloud felt uneasy. 'Those sub-corpora are big enough to be semi-sentient, Orange-Dawn.'

'But do you see?' said Orange-Dawn testily.

'See what?'

'*Blue shift.* The sub-corpora – see how, instinctively, they strain against the walls of the prison of lightspeed. Even in the moment of their Coalescing. Light imprisons us all. Light isolates us . . .'

Her words filtered through Sun-Cloud, jarring and strange, reinforced by bizarre chemical signals.

'Why are you doing this, Orange-Dawn?'

'Watch.' Now Orange-Dawn sent out a swarm of busy impeller corpuscles; they prodded the independent sub-corpora back towards Orange-Dawn's corpus. Sun-Cloud, uneasy, watched how the sub-corpora resisted their tiny Dissolutions, feebly.

'See?' Orange-Dawn said. 'See how they struggle against their immersion, in the overwhelming Ocean of my personality? See how they struggle to *live*?'

Sun-Cloud's own corpuscles sensed the suffering of their fellows, and shifted uneasily. She flooded her circulatory system with soothing chemicals. In her distress she felt a primal need for the Song. She sent sensor corpuscles stretching into the Ocean beneath her, seeking out the comfort of its distant, endless surging; its harmony was borne through the Ocean to her by chemical traces.

. . . But would *she* struggle so, when it came time for her to Dissolve, in her turn, into the eternal wash of the Song?

It was, she realized, a question she had never even framed before.

Now, gathering her corpuscles closely around her, Orange-Dawn turned from Sun-Cloud, and began to beat across the Surface with a new determination.

'You must come with me, Orange-Dawn,' Sun-Cloud warned.

'No. I will see out my hundred Cycles.'

'But you cannot . . .' *Unless,* she found herself thinking, *unless Cold-Current is right. Unless there is some lost way to extend consciousness.*

'If I submit to Dissolution, I will lose my sense of self, Sun-Cloud. My individuality. The corpus of knowledge and understanding I've spent so long assembling. What is that but death? What is the Song but a comfort, an anaesthetic illusion to hide that fact? . . .'

'You are damaging the unity of the Song, Orange-Dawn. You are – discordant.'

Orange-Dawn was receding now; she raised up a little batch of acoustic corpuscles. 'Good!' she called.

'I won't be able to protect you!' cried Sun-Cloud.

But she was gone.

Sun-Cloud raised lantern-corpuscles, sending pulses of slow light out across the Ocean's swelling surface. She called for her sister, until her corpuscles were exhausted.

In some ways, Sun-Cloud's people resembled humans.

Sun-Cloud's component corpuscles were of very different ancestry.

Mentation-corpuscles – the neuron-like creatures that carried consciousness in tiny packets of molecules – were an ancient, anaerobic race. The other main class, the impellers and structure corpuscles, were oxygen breathers: faster moving, more vigorous.

Human muscles usually burned glucose aerobically, using sugars from the air. But during strenuous activity, the muscles would ferment glucose in the anaerobic way evolved by the earliest bacteria. Thus human bodies, too, bore echoes of the earliest biosphere of Earth.

But, unlike a human body, Sun-Cloud's corpus was modular.

Despite their antique enmity, the two phyla within Sun-Cloud would cooperate, in the interests of the higher creature in which they were incorporated.

Until Sun-Cloud weakened.

A mass of corpora, sub-corpora and shoals of trained impeller corpuscles rose from the Deep in a great ring.

Not five Cycles had passed since Sun-Cloud's failed attempt to bring Orange-Dawn home. Now, they had come for Orange-Dawn.

Sun-Cloud found her sister at the centre of the hunt. She was shrunken, already fragmented, her corpuscles pulsing with fear.

'I don't want to die, Sun-Cloud.'

Anguish for her sister stabbed at Sun-Cloud. She sent soothing chemical half-words soaking through the Ocean. 'Come with me,' she said gently.

Exhausted, Orange-Dawn allowed herself to be enfolded in Sun-Cloud's chemical caresses.

Commingled, the sisters sank into the Ocean. Their ovoid bodies twisted slowly into the depths; light shells from curious individuals washed over them as they passed.

The light faded rapidly as they descended. Soon there were few free sub-corpora; and of the people they saw most were linked by corpuscle streams with at least one other, and often in groups of three, four or more.

The Song was a distant, strengthening pulse from the heart of the Ocean beneath them.

Now Cold-Current rose up to meet them, huge and intimidating, her complex hide pulsing with lantern-corpuscles. The rim of her slowly rotating corpus became diffuse, blurred, as her corpuscles swam tentatively towards Orange-Dawn.

Cold-Current murmured, 'You are old, yet very young, Orange-Dawn. Your unhappiness is caused by ignorance. There is no other Ocean. Only this one. There is no change and never has been. These facts are part of what we are. That's why your speculations are damaging you.

'You have to forget your dreams, Orange-Dawn . . .'

Orange-Dawn hardened, drawing her corpuscles into a tight little fortress. But Cold-Current was strong, and she forced compact biochemical packets into Orange-Dawn's corpus. Sun-Cloud, huddling close, picked up remote chemical echoes of the messages Cold-Current offered.

. . . *Hear the Song,* Cold-Current's corpuscles called. *Open up to the Song.*

Their bodies joined, her impeller-corpuscles herding Orange-Dawn tightly, Cold-Current began to guide Orange-Dawn deeper into the lattice of mingled persons.

Sun-Cloud followed, struggling to stay close to her sister. Orange-Dawn's pain suffused the waters around her with clouds of chemicals; Sun-Cloud suffered for her and with her.

As they descended, individuals became less and less distinct, and free corpuscles swam through the lattice's closing gaps. At last they were falling through a sea of corpuscles which, with endless intelligent grace, swam over and around each other. Sun-Cloud's structurals and impellers felt enfeebled here, in this choking water; the effort of forcing her way downwards seemed to multiply.

Perhaps this was like Dissolution, she thought.

At last there was only one entity, a complex of mingled bodies that filled the Ocean. The living lattice vibrated with the Song, which boomed around them, joyous and vibrant.

'The Deep,' Cold-Current whispered to Orange-Dawn. 'The Song. Now you will join this, Orange-Dawn. Uncountable billions of minds, endless thoughts straddling the world eternally. The Song will sustain your soul, after Dissolution, merged with everyone who has ever lived. You'll never be alone again –'

Suddenly, at the last, Orange-Dawn resisted. 'No! I could not bear it. I could not bear –'

She was struggling. Jagged images filled Sun-Cloud's mind, of being crushed, swamped, stultified.

Immediately a host of sub-corpora and corpuscles, jagged masses of them, hurled themselves into Orange-Dawn's corpus. Sun-Cloud heard a single, agonized, chemical scream, which echoed through the water. And then the structure of the corpus was broken up. Corpuscles, many of them wounded, came hailing out of the cloud of Dissolution; some of them spiralled away into the darkness, and others rained down towards the glowing Deep. Sub-corpora formed, almost at random, and wriggled through the water. They were semi-sentient: bewildered and broken images of Orange-Dawn.

Sun-Cloud could only watch. Loss stabbed at her; her grief was violent.

Cold-Current was huge, complex, brilliantly illuminated. 'It is over. It is better,' she said.

Sun-Cloud's anger surged. 'How can you say that? She's *dead*. She died in fear and agony.'

'No. She'll live forever, through the Song. As will we all.'

'Show me what you know,' Sun-Cloud said savagely. 'Show me how Orange-Dawn might have extended her life, through another ninety Cycles.'

'It is artificial. Discordant. It is not appropriate –'

'Show me!'

With huge reluctance, Cold-Current budded a tight, compact sub-corpora. It bore the cubical pattern Sun-Cloud had observed earlier. 'Knowledge is dangerous,' Cold-Current said sadly. 'It makes us unstable. That is the moral of Orange-Dawn's story. You must not –'

Sun-Cloud hurled herself at the pattern, and forcibly integrated it into her own corpus. Then – following impulses she barely recognized – she rose upwards, away from the bright-glowing Deep.

She passed through the cloud of Orange-Dawn's corpuscles, and called to them.

The Song boomed from the Deep, massive, alluring, stultifying; and Cold-Current's huge form glistened as she called her. Sun-Cloud ignored it all.

She ascended towards the Surface, as rapidly as she could.

Orange-Dawn's fragmentary sub-corpora followed her, bewildered, uncertain.

The place Sun-Cloud called the Deep was an anaerobic environment. Only mentation-corpuscles could survive here. They lay over each other in complex, pulsing swarms, with neural energy flickering desultorily between them.

The Song was a complex, evolving sound-structure, maintained by the dense shoals of mentation-corpuscles which inhabited the heart of the world, and with grace notes added by the Coalesced individuals of the higher, oxygen-rich layers of the Ocean.

At the end of their lives, the mentation structures of billions of individuals had dissolved into the Deep's corpuscle shoals. The Song, they believed, was a form of immortality.

Embracing this idea, most people welcomed Dissolution.

Others rejected it.

Sun-Cloud gathered around her central corpus the cubical pattern of Cold-Current, and Orange-Dawn's sad remnants, integrating them crudely. She grew huge, bloated, powerful.

And now, as she broke the thick Surface of the Ocean, she made ready.

She wondered briefly if she had gone mad. Perhaps Orange-Dawn had infected her.

But if it were so, let it be. She must know the answer to Orange-Dawn's questions for herself, before she submitted to – as she saw it now, as if through her sister's perception – the sinister embrace of the Song.

She enfolded Cold-Current's compact data pattern, and let its new wisdom flow through her . . .

Of course. It is simple.

She began to forge forward, across the Ocean.

A bow wave built up before her, thick and resisting. But she assembled her impellers and drove through it. At last the wave became a shock, sharp-edged, travelling through the water as a crest.

And now, quickly, she began to sense the resistance of light-speed's soft membrane. The water turned softly blue before her, and when she looked back, the world was stained red.

At length she passed into daylight.

The day seemed short. She continued to gather her pace.

Determined, she abandoned that which she did not need:

lantern-corpuscles, manipulators, even some mentation components: any excess mass which her impellers need not drag with her.

A bow, of speed-scattered light, began to coalesce around her.

The day-night cycle was passing so quickly now it was flickering. And she could sense the Cycles themselves, the grand, slow heaving of the Ocean as her world tracked around its sun.

The light ahead of her passed beyond blue and into a milky invisibility, while behind her a dark spot gathered in the redness and reached out to embrace half the world.

Time-dilated, she forged across the surface of her Ocean and into the future; and ninety-five Cycles wore away around her.

Light's crawl was embedded, a subtle scaling law, in every force governing the structure of Sun-Cloud's world.

The sun was much larger than Sol – ten thousand times more so – for the fusion fires at its heart were much less vigorous than Sol's. And Sun-Cloud's world was a thousand times smaller than Earth, for the electrostatic and degeneracy pressures which resisted gravitational collapse were greatly weaker.

Lightspeed dominated Sun-Cloud's structure, too. If she had been a single entity, complete and entire, it would have taken too long for light – or any other signal – to crawl through her structure. So she was a composite creature; her mind was broken down into modules of thought, speculation and awareness. She was a creature of parallel processing, scattered over a thousand fragile corpuscles.

And Sun-Cloud's body was constrained to be small enough that her gravitational potential could not fracture the flimsy molecular bonds which held her corpus together.

Sun-Cloud, forging across the Surface of her Ocean, was just two millimetres across.

At last, a new light erupted in the bow that embraced her world.

With an effort, she slowed. The light-bow expanded rapidly, as if the world were unfolding back into its proper morphology. She allowed some of her impeller corpuscles to run free, and she saw their tiny wakes running across the Surface, determined, red-shifted.

Now that her monumental effort was done she was exhausted, depleted, her impellers dead, lost or dying; unless new impellers joined her, she would scarcely be able to move again.

Ninety-five Cycles.

Everybody she had known – Cold-Current and the rest – all of them must be gone, now, absorbed into the Song's unending pulse.

It remained only for her to learn what mystery awaited, here in the remoteness of the future, and then she could Dissolve into the Song herself.

. . . From the darkling sky, the new light washed over her.

Her optic corpuscles swivelled upwards.

She cried out.

Sun-Cloud felt her world shrink beneath her from infinity to a frail mote; the Song decayed from the thoughts of a god to the crooning of a damaged sub-corpus.

Above her, utterly silently – and for the first time in all history – the stars were coming out.

To human eyes, the skies of this cosmos would have seemed strange indeed:

The stars spawned from gas clouds, huge and cold. Hundreds of them formed in a cluster, companions to Sun-Cloud's sun. Light and heat crept from each embryonic star, dispersing the remnant wisps of the birthing cloud.

It took five billion human years for the light to cross the gulf between the stars.

And at last – and as one speculative thinker among Sun-Cloud's people had predicted, long ago – the scattered light of those remote suns washed over an unremarkable world, which orbited a little above the photosphere of their companion . . .

The stars were immense globes, glowing red and white, jostling in a complex sky; and sheets and lanes of gas writhed between them.

Orange-Dawn had been right. This *was* wonderful, beyond her imagining – but crushing, terrifying.

Pain tore at her. Jagged molecules flooded her system; her corpuscles broke apart, and began at last their ancestral war.

She struggled to retain her core of rationality, just a little longer. Exhausted, she hastily assembled sub-corpora, and loaded packets of information into them, pale images of the astonishing sky. She sent them hailing down into the Ocean, into the Deep, into the belly of the Song itself.

Soon a new voice would join the Song: a merger of her own,

and Orange-Dawn's. And it would sing of suns, countless, beyond imagining.

Everything would be different, now.

She fell, gladly, into the warm emptiness of Dissolution.

MANIFOLD

The first time Kate had come here, to his son's home, Malenfant had shown her an image of a planet: blue, streaked with white cloud.

Kate's heart had thumped. 'Earth?'

He shook his head. 'And not Pluto either. This is a live image of Neptune. Almost as far out as Pluto. A strange blue world, blue as Earth, on the edge of interstellar space . . .'

Saranne said uneasily, 'What's wrong with it?'

'Not Neptune itself. Triton, its moon. Look.' He pointed to a blurred patch of light, close to Neptune's ghostly limb. When he tapped the wall, the patch moved, quite suddenly. Another tap, another move. Kate couldn't see any pattern to the moves, as if the moon was no longer following a regular orbit.

'I don't understand,' she said.

'Triton has started to . . . flicker. It hops around its orbit – or adopts another orbit entirely – or sometimes it vanishes, or is replaced by a ring system.' He scratched his bald pate. 'According to Cornelius, Triton was an oddity – circling Neptune backwards – probably created in some ancient collision event.'

'Even odder now,' Mike said dryly.

'Cornelius says that all these images – the multiple moons, the rings – are all possibilities, alternate outcomes of how that ancient collision might have come about. As if other realities are folding down into our own. Other realities, from out there in phase space.' He searched their faces, seeking understanding.

Kate took a breath. Neptune: a long way away, out in the dark, where the planets are cloudy spheres, and the sun's light is weak and rectilinear. But out there, she thought, something strange is stirring: something with awesome powers indeed, beyond human comprehension.

'I wonder,' Malenfant said, 'if we are out there somewhere. Versions of us and those we love, with different destinies. Lost in phase space.'

SHEENA 5

Sheena didn't mean it to happen.

Of course not; she knew the requirements of the mission as well as anyone, as well as Dan himself. She had her duty to NASA. She understood that.

But it felt so *right*.

It came after the kill.

The night was over. The sun, a fat ball of light, was already glimmering above the water surface.

The squid emerged from the grasses and corals where they had been feeding. Shoals formed in small groups and clusters, eventually combining into a community a hundred strong.

Court me. Court me.

See my weapons!

I am strong and fierce.

Stay away! Stay away! She is mine! . . .

It was the ancient cephalopod language, a language of complex skin patterns, body posture, texture, words of sex and danger and food; and Sheena shoaled and sang with joy.

. . . But there was a shadow on the water.

The sentinels immediately adopted concealment or bluff postures, blaring lies at the approaching predator.

Sheena knew that there would be no true predators here. The shadow could only be a watching NASA machine.

The dark shape lingered close, just as a true barracuda would, before diving into the shoal, seeking to break it up.

A strong male broke free. He spread his eight arms, raised his two long tentacles, and his green binocular eyes fixed on the fake barracuda. Confusing patterns of light and shade pulsed across his hide. *Look at me. I am large and fierce. I can kill you.* Slowly, cautiously, the male drifted towards the barracuda, coming to within a mantle length.

At the last moment the barracuda turned, sluggishly.

But it was too late.

The male's two long tentacles whipped out, and their club-like pads of suckers pounded against the barracuda hide, sticking there. Then the male wrapped his eight strong arms around the barracuda's body, his pattern changing to an exultant uniform darkening. And he stabbed at the barracuda's skin with his beak, seeking meat.

And meat there was, what looked like fish fragments to Sheena, booty planted there by Dan.

The squid descended, lashing their tentacles around the stricken prey. Sheena joined in, cool water surging through her mantle, relishing the primordial power of this kill despite its artifice.

. . . That was when it happened.

As she clambered stiffly down through the airlock into the habitat, the smell of air freshener overwhelmed Maura Della.

'Ms Della, welcome to Oceanlab,' Dan Ystebo said. Ystebo, marine biologist, was fat, breathy, intense, thirtyish, with Coke-bottle glasses and a mop of unlikely red hair, a typical geek scientist type.

Maura found a seat before a bank of controls. The seat was just a canvas frame, much repaired with duct tape. The working area of this hab was a small, cramped sphere, its walls encrusted with equipment. A sonar beacon pinged softly, like a pulse.

The sense of confinement, the *feel* of the weight of water above her head, was overwhelming.

She leaned forward, peering into small windows. Sunlight shafted through empty grey water. She saw a school of squid, jetting through the water in complex patterns.

'Which one is Sheena 5?'

Dan pointed to a softscreen pasted over a scuffed hull section.

The streamlined, torpedo-shaped body was a rich burnt-orange, mottled black. Wing-like fins rippled elegantly alongside the body.

The Space Squid, Maura thought. The only mollusc on NASA's payroll.

'*Sepioteuthis sepioidea*,' Dan said. 'The Caribbean reef squid.

About as long as your arm. Squid, all cephalopods in fact, belong to the phylum *Mollusca*. But in the squid the mollusc foot has evolved into the funnel, *here*, leading into the mantle, and the arms and tentacles *here*. The mantle cavity contains the viscera and gills. Sheena can use the water passing through her mantle cavity for jet propulsion –'

'How do you know that's her?'

Dan pointed again. 'See the swelling between the eyes, around the oesophagus?'

'That's her enhanced brain?'

'A squid's neural layout isn't like ours. Sheena has two nerve cords running like rail tracks the length of her body, studded with pairs of ganglia. The forward ganglia pair is expanded into a mass of lobes. We gen-enged Sheena and her grandmothers to –'

'To make a smart squid.'

'Ms Della, squid are smart anyway. They evolved – a long time ago, during the Jurassic – in competition with the fish. They have senses based on light, scent, taste, touch, sound – including infra-sound – gravity, acceleration, perhaps even an electric sense. Sheena can control her skin patterns consciously. She can make bands, bars, circles, annuli, dots. She can even animate the display.'

'And these patterns are signals?'

'Not just the skin patterns: skin texture, body posture. There may be electric or sonic components too; we can't be sure.'

'And what do they use this marvellous signalling for?'

'We aren't sure. They don't hunt cooperatively. And they live only a couple of years, mating only once or twice.' Dan scratched his beard. 'But we've been able to isolate a number of primal linguistic components which combine in a primitive grammar. *Even in unenhanced squid.* But the language seems to be closed. It's about nothing but food, sex and danger. It's like the dance of the bee.'

'Unlike human languages.'

'Yes. So we opened up Sheena's language for her. In the process we were able to prove that the areas of the brain responsible for learning are the vertical and superior frontal lobes that lie above the oesophagus.'

'How did you prove that?'

Dan blinked. 'By cutting away parts of squid brains.'

Maura sighed. What great PR if *that* got broadcast.

They studied Sheena. Two forward-looking eyes, blue-green rimmed with orange, peered briefly into the camera.

Alien eyes. Intelligent.

Do we have the right to do this, to meddle with the destiny of other sentient creatures, to further our own goals – when we don't even understand, as Ystebo admits, what the squid use their speech for. What it is they talk about?

How does it *feel,* to be Sheena?

And could Sheena possibly understand that humans are planning to have her fly a rocket ship to an asteroid?

He came for her: the killer male, one tentacle torn on some loose fragment of metal.

She knew this was wrong. And yet it was irresistible.

She felt a skin pattern flush over her body, a pied mottling, speckled with white spots. *Court me.*

He swam closer. She could see his far side was a bright uniform silver, a message to the other males: *Keep away. She is mine!* As he rolled the colours tracked around his body, and she could see the tiny muscles working the pigment sacs on his hide.

And already he was holding out his hectocotylus towards her, the modified arm bearing the clutch of spermatophores at its tip.

Mission Sheena mission. Bootstrap! Mission! NASA! Dan!

But then the animal within her rose, urgent. She opened her mantle to the male.

His hectocotylus reached for her, striking swiftly, and lodged the needle-like spermatophore among the roots of her arms.

Then he withdrew. Already it was over.

. . . And yet it was not. She could choose whether or not to embrace the spermatophore and place it in her seminal receptacle.

She knew she must not.

All around her, the squid's songs pulsed with life, ancient songs that reached back to a time before humans, before whales, before even the fish.

Her life was short: lasting one summer, two at most, a handful of matings. But the songs of light and dance made every squid aware she was part of a continuum that stretched back to those ancient seas; and that her own brief, vibrant life was as insignificant, yet as vital, as a single silver scale on the hide of a fish.

Sheena, with her human-built mind, was the first of all cephalopods to be able to understand this. And yet every squid *knew* it, on some level that transcended the mind.

But Sheena was no longer part of that continuum.

Even as the male receded, she felt overwhelmed with sadness, loneliness, isolation. Resentment.

She closed her arms over the spermatophore, and drew it inside her.

'I have to go into bat for you on the Hill Monday,' Maura said to Dan. 'I have to put my reputation on the line, to save this project. You're sure, absolutely sure, this is going to work?'

'Absolutely,' Dan said. He spoke with a calm conviction that made her want to believe him. 'Look, the squid are adapted to a zero-gravity environment – unlike us. And Sheena can hunt in three dimensions; she will be able to *navigate*. If you were going to evolve a creature equipped for space travel, it would be a cephalopod. And she's much cheaper than any robotic equivalent . . .'

'But,' Maura said heavily, 'we don't have any plans to bring her back.'

He shrugged. 'Even if we had the capability, she's too short-lived. We have plans to deal with the ethical contingencies.'

'That's bullshit.'

Dan looked uncomfortable. But he said, 'We hope the public will accept the arrival of the asteroid in Earth orbit as a memorial to her. A just price. And, Senator, every moment of her life, from the moment she was hatched, Sheena has been oriented to the goal. It's what she lives for. The mission.'

Sombrely Maura watched the squid, Sheena, as she flipped and jetted in formation with her fellows.

We have to do this, she thought. I have to force the funding through, on Monday.

If Sheena succeeded she would deliver, in five years or so, a near-Earth asteroid rich in organics and other volatiles to Earth orbit. Enough to bootstrap, at last, an expansion off the planet. Enough, perhaps, to save mankind.

And, if the gloomier State Department reports about the state of the world were at all accurate, it might be the last chance anybody would get.

But Sheena wouldn't live to see it.

The squid shoal collapsed to a tight school and jetted away, rushing out of sight.

*   *   *

Sheena 5 glided at the heart of the ship, where the water that passed through her mantle, over her gills, was warmest, richest. The core machinery, the assemblage of devices that maintained life here, was a black mass before her, lights winking over its surface.

She found it hard to rest, without the shoal, the mating and learning and endless dances of daylight.

Restless, she swam away from the machinery cluster. As she rose the water flowing through her mantle cooled, the rich oxygen thinning. She sensed the subtle sounds of living things: the smooth rush of fish, the bubbling murmur of the krill on which they browsed, and the hiss of the diatoms and algae which fed *them*. In Sheena's spacecraft, matter and energy flowed in great loops, sustained by sunlight, regulated by its central machinery as if by a beating heart.

She reached the wall of the ship. It was translucent. If she pushed at it, it pushed back. Grass algae grew on the wall, their long filaments dangling and wafting in the currents.

Beyond the membrane shone a milky, blurred sun – with, near it, a smaller crescent. That, she knew, was the Earth, all its great oceans reduced to a droplet. This craft was scooting around the sun after Earth like a fish swimming after its school.

She let the lazy, whale-like roll of the ship carry her away from the glare of the sun, and she peered into the darkness, where she could see the stars.

She had been trained to recognize many of the stars. She used this knowledge to determine her position in space far more accurately than even Dan could have, from far-off Earth.

But to Sheena the stars were more than navigation beacons. Sheena's eyes had a hundred times the number of receptors of human eyes, and she could see a hundred times as many stars.

To Sheena the universe was *crowded* with stars, vibrant and alive. The Galaxy was a reef of stars beckoning her to come jet along its length.

But there was only Sheena here to see it. Her sense of loss grew inexorably.

So, swimming in starlight, Sheena cradled her unhatched young, impatiently jetting clouds of ink in the rough shape of a male with bright, mindless eyes.

Maura Della was involved in all this because – in the year 2030, as the planet's resources dwindled – Earth had become a bear pit.

Take water, for instance.

Humanity was using *more* than all the fresh water that fell on the planet. Unbelievable. So, all over Asia and elsewhere, water wars were flaring up, and at least one nuke had been lobbed, between India and Pakistan.

America's primary international problem was the small, many-sided war that was flaring in Antarctica, now that the last continent had been 'opened up' to a feeding frenzy of resource-hungry nations – a conflict that constantly threatened to spill out to wider arenas.

And so on.

In Maura's view, all humanity's significant problems came from the world's closure, the lack of a frontier.

Maura Della had grown up believing in the importance of the frontier. Frontiers were the forcing ground for democracy and inventiveness. In a closed world, science was strangled by patent laws and other protective measures, and technological innovation was restricted to decadent entertainment systems and the machinery of war. It was a vicious circle, of course; only smartness could get humanity out of this trap of closure, but smartness was the very thing that had no opportunity to grow.

America, specifically, was going to hell in a handbasket. Long dwarfed economically by China, now threatened militarily, America had retreated, become risk-averse. The rich cowered inside vast armoured enclaves; the poor lost themselves in VR fantasy worlds; American soldiers flew over the Antarctic battle zones in armoured copters, while the Chinese swarmed over the icebound land they had taken.

And, such were the hangovers from America's dominant days, the US remained the most hated nation on Earth.

The irony was, there were all the resources you could wish for, floating around in the sky: the asteroids, the moons of Jupiter and Saturn, free power from the sun. People had known about this for decades. But after seventy years of spaceflight nobody had come up with a way to get into Earth orbit that was cheap and reliable enough to make those sky mines an economic proposition.

But now this NASA back-room wacko, Dan Ystebo from JPL, had come up with a way to break through the bottleneck, a Space Squid that could divert one of those flying mountains.

Maura didn't care what his own motives were; she only cared

how she could use his proposals to achieve her own goals.

So when Dan invited her to JPL for the rendezvous, she accepted immediately.

Maura looked around Dan Ystebo's JPL cubicle with distaste, at the old coffee cups and fast-food wrappers amid the technical manuals and rolled-up softscreens. Dan seemed vaguely embarrassed, self-conscious; he folded his arms over his chest.

One softscreen, draped across a partition, showed a blue-green, rippling spacecraft approaching an asteroid. The asteroid was misshapen and almost black, the craters and cracks of its dusty surface picked out by unvarying sunlight.

'Tell me what I'm getting for my money here, Dan.'

He waved his plump hand. 'Near-Earth asteroid 2018JW, called Reinmuth. A ball of rock and ice half a mile across. It's a C-type.' Dan was excited, his voice clipped and wavering, a thin sweat on his brow as he tried to express himself. 'Maura, it's just as we hoped. A billion tons of water, silicates, metals and complex organics – aminos, nitrogen bases. Even Mars isn't as rich as this, pound for pound . . .'

Dan Ystebo was out of his time, Maura thought. He would surely have preferred to work here in the 1960s and '70s, when science was king, and the great probes were being planned, at outrageous expense: *Viking, Voyager, Galileo.* But that wasn't possible now.

JPL, initiated as a military research lab, had been taken back by the Army in 2016.

It hadn't been possible to kill off JPL's NASA heritage immediately, not while the old *Voyagers* still bleeped away forlornly on the rim of the solar system, sending back data about the sun's heliopause and other such useless mysteries.

And Dan Ystebo was making the best of it, in this military installation, with his Nazi-doctored Space Squid. He would probably, Maura realized, have gen-enged *her* and stuck her in a box if it got him a mission to run.

She said, 'Before somebody asks me, tell me again why we have to bring this thing to Earth orbit.'

'Reinmuth's orbit is close to Earth's. But that means it doesn't line up for low-energy missions very often; the orbits are like two clocks running slightly adrift of each other. The NEOs were never as easy to reach as the space-junkie types like to believe. We'd have to wait all of forty years before we could repeat Sheena's trajectory.'

'Or bring Sheena home.'

'. . . Yes. But that's irrelevant anyhow.'

Irrelevant. He doesn't understand, she thought. This had been the hardest point of the whole damn mission to sell, to the House and the public. If we are seen to have killed her for no purpose, we're all finished.

. . . And now the moment of rendezvous was here.

The firefly spark tracked across the blackened surface. The gentle impact came unspectacularly, with a silent turning of digits from negative to positive.

There was a small splash of grey dust.

And then she could see it, a green fragment of Earth embedded in the hide of the asteroid.

Beneath the translucent floor Sheena could see a grainy, grey-black ground. Dan told her it was a substance older than the oceans of Earth. And, through the curving walls of the ship, she was able to see this world's jagged horizon, barely tens of yards away.

Her world. She pulsed with pride, her chromatophores prickling.

And she knew, at last, she was ready.

Sheena laid her eggs.

They were cased in jelly sacs, hundreds of them in each tube. There was no spawning ground here, of course. So she draped the egg sacs over the knot of machinery at the heart of her miniature ocean, which had now anchored itself to the surface of Reinmuth.

Fish came to nose at the eggs. She watched until she was sure that the fish were repelled by the jelly that coated the eggs, which was its purpose.

All this was out of sight of Dan's cameras. She did not tell him what she had done. She could not leave her water habitat; yet she was able to explore.

Small firefly robots set off from the habitat, picking their way carefully over the surface of the asteroid. Each robot was laden with miniature instruments, as exquisite as coral, all beyond her understanding.

But the fireflies were under her control. She used the waldo, the glove-like device into which she could slip her long arms and so control the delicate motions of each firefly.

. . . Soon the babies were being hatched: popping out of their dissolving eggs one by one, wriggling away, alert, active, questioning. With gentle jets of water, she coaxed them towards sea grass.

Meanwhile, she had work to do.

Sheena sent the fireflies to converge at one pole of Reinmuth. There, patiently, piece by piece, she had them assemble a small chemical factory, pipes and tanks and pumps, and a single flaring nozzle which pointed to the sky. Precious solar panels, spread over the dusty ground, provided power.

The factory began its work. Borers drew up surface regolith and the rock and ice which lay deeper within. Chemical separation processes filtered out methane ice and stored it, while other processes took water ice, melted it and passed it through electrical cells to separate it into its components, oxygen and hydrogen.

This whole process seemed remarkable to Sheena. To take rock and ice, and to transform it into other substances! But Dan told her that this was old, robust technology, practised by NASA and other humans for many times even his long lifetime.

Mining asteroids was easy. You just had to get there and do it.

Meanwhile the young were growing explosively quickly, converting half of all the food they ate to body mass. She watched the males fighting: *I am large and fierce. Look at my weapons. Look at me!*

Most of the young were dumb. Four were smart.

She was growing old now, and tired easily. Nevertheless she taught the smart ones how to hunt. She taught them about the reef, the many creatures that lived and died there. And she taught them language, the abstract signs Dan had given her. Soon their mantles rippled with questions. *Who? Why? Where? What? How?*

She did not always have answers. But she showed them the machinery that kept them alive, and taught them about the stars and sun, and the nature of the world and universe, and about humans.

At last the structure at the pole was ready for its test.

Under Sheena's control, simple valves clicked open. Gaseous methane and oxygen rushed together and burned in a stout chamber. Through robot eyes Sheena could see combustion products emerge, ice crystals that caught the sunlight, receding in perfectly straight lines. It was a fire fountain, quite beautiful.

And Sheena could feel the soft thrust of the rocket, the huge waves that pulsed slowly through the hab's water.

The methane rocket, fixed at the axis of the asteroid's spin, would push Reinmuth gradually out of its orbit and send it to intercept Earth.

Dan told her there was much celebration, within NASA. He did not say so, but Sheena understood that this was mainly because she had finished her task, before dying.

Now, she was no longer needed. Not by the humans, anyway.

The young ones seemed to understand, very quickly, that Sheena and all her young would soon exhaust the resources of this one habitat. Already there had been a number of problems with the tightly closed environment loops: unpredictable crashes and blooms in the phytoplankton population.

The young were *very* smart. Soon they were able to think in ways that were beyond Sheena herself.

For instance, they said, perhaps they should not simply repair this fabric shell, but *extend* it. Perhaps, said the young, they should even make *new* domes and fill them with water.

Sheena, trained only to complete her primary mission, found this a very strange thought.

But there weren't enough fish, never enough krill. The waters were stale and crowded.

This was clearly unacceptable.

So the smart young hunted down their dumb siblings, one by one, and consumed their passive bodies, until only these four, and Sheena, were left.

When the storm broke, Dan Ystebo was in his cubicle in the science rooms at JPL, in the middle of an online conference on results from Reinmuth.

Maura Della stood over him, glaring.

He touched the softscreen to close down the link. 'Senator –'

'You asshole, Ystebo. How long have you known?'

He sighed. 'Not long. A couple of weeks.'

'Did you know she was pregnant before the launch?'

'No. I swear it. If I'd known I'd have scrubbed the mission.'

'Don't you get it, Ystebo? We'd got to the point where the bleeding-heart public would have accepted Sheena's death. But this has changed everything . . .'

It's over, he thought, listening to her anger and frustration.

She visibly tried to calm down. 'The thing is, Dan, we can't have that asteroid showing up in orbit with a cargo of sentient squid corpses. People would think it was monstrous.' She blinked. 'In fact, so would I.'

He closed his eyes. 'I don't suppose it's any use pointing out how stupid it is to stop now. We spent the money already. We have the installation on Reinmuth. It's working; all we have to do is wait for rendezvous. We achieved the goal, the bootstrap.'

'It doesn't matter,' she said gently, regretfully. 'People are – not rational, Dan.'

'And the future, the greater goal –'

'We're still engaged in a race between opportunity and catastrophe. We have to start again. Find some other way.'

'This was the only chance. We just lost the race.'

'I pray not,' she said heavily. 'Look – do it with decency. Let Sheena die in comfort. Then turn off the rockets.'

'And the babies?'

'We can't save those either way, can we?' she said coolly. 'I just hope they forgive us.'

'I doubt that,' Dan said.

The water which trickled through her mantle was cloudy and stank of decay. She drifted, aching arms limp, dreaming of a male with bright, mindless eyes.

But the young wouldn't let her alone.

Danger near. You die we die. They were flashing the fast, subtle signals employed by a shoal sentinel, warning of the approach of a predator.

There was no predator here, of course, save death itself.

She tried to explain it to them. Yes, they would all die – but in a great cause, so that Earth, NASA, the ocean, could live. It was a magnificent vision, worthy of the sacrifice of their lives.

Wasn't it?

But they knew nothing of Dan, of NASA, of Earth.

No. You die we die.

They were like her. But in some ways they were more like their father. Bright. Primal.

Dan Ystebo cleared his desk, ready to go work for a gen-eng biorecovery company in equatorial Africa. All he was hanging around JPL for was to watch Sheena die, and the bio-signs in the telemetry indicated that wouldn't be so long now.

Then the Deep Space Network radio telescopes would be turned away from the asteroid for the last time, and whatever followed would unfold in the dark and cold, unheard, and to hell with it.

. . . Here was a new image in his softscreen. A squid, flashing signs at him: *Look at me. Dan. Look at me. Dan. Dan. Dan.*

He couldn't believe it. 'Sheena?'

He had to wait the long seconds while his single word, translated to flashing signs, was transmitted across space.

Sheena 6.

'. . . Oh.' One of the young.

Dying. Water. Water dying. Fish. Squid. Danger near. Why.

She's talking about the habitat biosphere, he realized. She wants me to tell her how to repair the biosphere. 'That's not possible.'

Not. Those immense black eyes. *Not. Not. Not.* The squid flashed through a blizzard of body patterns, bars and stripes pulsing over her hide, her head dipping, her arms raised. *I am large and fierce. I am parrotfish, seagrass, rock, coral, sand. I am no squid, no squid, no squid.*

He had given Sheena 5 no sign for 'liar', but this squid, across millions of miles, bombarding him with lies, was doing its best.

But he was telling the truth.

Wasn't he? How the hell could you extend the fixed-duration closed-loop life-support system in that ball of water to support *more* squid, to last much longer, even indefinitely?

. . . But it needn't stay closed-loop, he realized. The *Bootstrap* hab was sitting on an asteroid full of raw materials. That had been the point of the mission in the first place.

His brain started to tick at the challenge.

It would be a hell of an effort, though. And for what? His NASA pay was going to run out any day, and the soldier boys who had taken back JPL, and wanted to run nothing out of here but low-Earth-orbit milsat missions, would kick his sorry ass out of here sooner than that.

To tell the truth he was looking forward to moving to Africa. He'd live in comfort, in the Brazzaville dome, far from the arenas of the global conflict likely to come; and the work there would be all for the good, as far as he was concerned. None of the ethical ambiguities of Bootstrap.

So why are you hesitating, Ystebo? Are you growing a conscience, at last?

'I'll help you,' he said. 'What can they do, fire me?'

That wasn't translated.

The squid turned away from the camera.

Dan started to place calls.

Sheena 6 was the smartest of the young.

It was no privilege. There was much work.

She learned to use the glove-like systems that made the firefly robots clamber over the asteroid ground. The mining equipment was adapted to seek out essentials for the phytoplankton, nitrates and phosphates.

Even in the hab itself there was much to do. Dan showed her how to keep the water pure, by pumping it through charcoal filters. But the charcoal had to be replaced by asteroid material, burned in sun fire. And so on.

With time, the hab was stabilized. As long as the machines survived, so would the hab's cargo of life.

But it was too small. It had been built to sustain one squid.

So the firefly robots took apart the rocket plant at the pole and began to assemble new engines, new flows of material, sheets of asteroid-material plastic.

Soon there were four habs, linked by tunnels, one for each of Sheena's young, the smart survivors. The krill and diatoms bred happily. The greater volume required more power, so Sheena extended the sprawling solar-cell arrays.

The new habs looked like living things themselves, spawning and breeding.

But already another cephalopod generation was coming: sacs of eggs clung to asteroid rock, in all the habs.

It wouldn't stop, Sheena 6 saw, more generations of young and more habs, until the asteroid was full, used up. What then? Would they turn on each other at last?

But Sheena 6 was already ageing. Such questions could wait for another generation.

In the midst of this activity, Sheena 5 grew weaker. Her young gathered around her.

Look at me, she said. *Court me. Love me.*

Last confused words, picked out in blurred signs on a mottled carapace, stiff attempts at posture by muscles leached of strength.

Sheena 6 hovered close to her mother. What had those darkening eyes seen? Was it really true that Sheena 5 had been hatched in an ocean without limits, an ocean where hundreds – thousands, millions – of squid hunted and fought, bred and died?

Sheena 5 drifted, purposeless, and the soft gravity of Reinmuth started to drag her down for the last time.

Sheena's young fell on her, their beaks tearing into her cooling, sour flesh.

Dan Ystebo met Maura Della once more, five years later.

He met her at the entrance to the Houston ecodome, on a sweltering August day. Dan's project in Africa had collapsed when ecoterrorists bombed the Brazzaville dome – two Americans were killed – and he'd come back to Houston, his birthplace.

He took her to his home, on the south side of downtown. It was a modern house, an armoured box with fully-equipped closed life support.

He gave her a beer.

When she took off her resp mask he was shocked; she was wasted, and her face was pitted like the surface of the Moon.

He said, 'An eco-weapon? Another WASP plague from the Chinese –'

'No.' She forced a hideous smile. 'Not the war, as it happens. Just a closed-ecology crash, a prion plague.' She drank her beer, and produced some hardcopy photographs. 'Have you seen this?'

He squinted. A blurred green sphere. A NASA reference on the back showed these were Hubble II images. 'I didn't know Hubble II was still operating.'

'It doesn't do science. We use it to watch the Chinese Moon base. But some smart guy in the State Department thought we should keep an eye on – *that.*'

She passed him a pack of printouts. These proved to be results from spectography and other remote sensors. If he was to believe what he saw, he was looking at a ball of water, floating in space, within which chlorophyll reactions were proceeding.

'My God,' he said. 'They survived. How the hell?'

'You showed them,' she said heavily.

'But I didn't expect *this*. It looks as if they transformed the whole damn asteroid.'

'That's not all. We have evidence they've travelled to some of the other rocks out there. Methane rockets, maybe.'

'I guess they forgot about us.'

'I doubt it. Look at this.'

It was a Doppler analysis of Reinmuth, the primary asteroid. It was moving. Fuzzily, he tried to interpret the numbers. 'I can't do orbital mechanics in my head. Where is this thing headed?'

'Take a guess.'

There was a silence.

He said, 'Why are you here?'

'We're going to send them a message. We'll use English, Chinese and the sign system you devised with Sheena. We want your permission to put your name on it.'

'Do I get to approve the contents?'

'No.'

'What will you say?'

'We'll be asking for forgiveness. For the way we treated Sheena.'

'Do you think that will work?'

'No,' she said. 'They're predators, like us. Only smarter. What would *we* do in their position?'

'But we have to try.'

She began to collect up her material. 'Yes,' she said. 'We have to try.'

As the water world approached, swimming out of the dark, Sheena 46 prowled through the heart of transformed Reinmuth.

On every hierarchical level mind-shoals formed, merged, fragmented, combining restlessly, shimmers of group consciousness that pulsed through the million-strong cephalopod community, as sunlight glimmers on water. But the great shoals had abandoned their song-dreams of Earth, of the deep past, and sang instead of the huge deep future which lay ahead.

Sheena 46 was practical.

There was much to do, the demands of expansion endless: more colony packets to send to the ice balls around the outer planets, for instance, more studies of the greater ice worlds that seemed to orbit far from the central heat.

Nevertheless, she was intrigued. Was it possible this *was* Earth, of legend? The home of Dan, of NASA?

If it were so, it seemed to Sheena that it must be terribly *confining* to be a human, to be trapped in the skinny layer of air that clung to the Earth.

But where the squid came from scarcely mattered. Where they were going was the thing.

Reinmuth entered orbit around the water world.

The great hierarchies of mind collapsed as the cephalopods gave themselves over to a joyous riot of celebration, of talk and love and war and hunting: *Court me. Court me. See my weapons! I am strong and fierce. Stay away! Stay away! She is mine! . . .*

Things had gone to hell with startling, dismaying speed. People died, all over the planet, in conflicts and resource crashes nobody even kept track of any more – even before the first major nuclear exchanges.

But at least Dan got to see near-Earth object Reinmuth enter Earth orbit.

It was as if his old Project Bootstrap goals had at last been fulfilled. But he knew that the great artefact up there, like a shimmering green, translucent Moon, had nothing to do with him.

At first it was a peaceful presence, up there in the orange, smoggy sky. Even beautiful. Its hide flickered with squid signs, visible from the ground, some of which Dan even recognized, dimly.

He knew what they were doing. They were calling to their cousins who might still inhabit the oceans below.

Dan knew they would fail. There were almost certainly no squid left in Earth's oceans: they had been wiped out for food, or starved or poisoned by the various plankton crashes, the red tides.

The old nations that had made up the USA briefly put aside their economic and ethnic and religious and nationalistic squabbles, and tried to respond to this threat from space. They tried to talk to it again. And then they opened one of the old silos and shot a nuclear-tipped missile at it.

But the nuke passed straight through the watery sphere, without leaving a scratch.

It scarcely mattered anyway. He had sources which told him the signature of the squid had been seen throughout the asteroid belt, and on the ice moons, Europa and Ganymede and Triton, and even in the Oort Cloud, the comets at the rim of the system.

Their spread was exponential, explosive.

It was ironic, he thought. We sent the squid out there to bootstrap *us* into an expansion into space. Now it looks as if they're doing it for themselves.

But they always were better adapted for space than we were. As if they had evolved that way. As if they were waiting for us to come along, to lift them off the planet, to give them their break.

As if that was our only purpose.

Dan wondered if they remembered his name.

The first translucent ships began to descend, returning to Earth's empty oceans.

THE FUBAR SUIT

I know I'm still lying here in the regolith, on this dumb little misshapen asteroid, inside my fubar suit. I know nobody's come to save me. Because I'm still here, right? But I can't see, hear, feel a damn thing.

Although I sometimes think I can.

I'm going stir-crazy, inside my own head.

I know they're coming to kill me, though. *The little guys.* The nems told me that much.

So I have a decision to make.

Them or me.

She drifted in blue warmth, her thoughts dissolving.

. . . Consciousness burst in on her, dark and dry, dispelling the fug of her prenatal dream. She gasped and coughed, expelling fluid from her lungs.

She was turned around, by huge, confident hands. She was held before a looming face, smiling, wet. Her mother.

There were people all around, naked, thin, anxious. Even so, they smiled at this new birth.

Her eyes were clearing quickly. She – they – were in some kind of huge hall, a vast cylindrical space. The roof, far above, was clear, and some kind of light moved beyond it. There was water in the base of the hall, a great trapped river of it, dense with green. The people were clustered at the edge of the water, on a smooth, sloping beach. Children were playing in the water, which lapped gently against the walls.

Adults clustered around, plucking at her fingers and toes, which grew with a creaking of soft, stretching skin. The growth hurt, and she cried. She squirmed against her mother, seeking an escape from this dismal cold.

Her mother put her down, on the sloping wall.

Still moist from birth, she crawled away, towards the water.

One of the children came stalking out of the murky water on skinny legs. It was a boy. He spoke to her, pointing and smiling. At first the words made no sense, but they soon seemed to catch. *Brother. Sister. Mother. River.*

She tried to speak back, but her mouth was soft and sticky.

The boy – her brother – ran back to the water. She followed, crawling, already impatient, already trying to stand upright.

The water was warm and welcoming, and full of sticky green stuff. She splashed out until her head was covered.

Swimming was easier than crawling, or walking.

Her brother showed her how to use her fingers to filter out the green stuff. *Algae,* he said. She could see little knots and spirals in the green mats.

She crammed the green stuff into her mouth, gnawing at it with her gums, with her growing buds of teeth, sucking it into her stomach. She was very, very hungry.

Her name, they said, was Green Wave.

I was born at the wrong time, in the wrong place.

In the year 2050, when I was eighteen years old, no American was flying into space. We'd ceded the high frontier: the Moon to the Japanese, Mars to the Russians, the asteroid belt to the Chinese. America, without space resources, got steadily poorer, not to mention more decadent. A hell of a time to grow up.

I come from enterprising stock. One of my ancestors made a fortune hauling bauxite on twenty-mule trains out of Death Valley. He also got himself killed, however. Another ancestor was one of the first in the Texas oil fields. And so on.

We lost all the money, of course, long before I was born. But we're a family with one hell of a tradition.

But when I grew up we were rattling around in a box, with no place to go.

I served in the Army. I studied astronomy. I tried to figure an angle: some place out there the Russians and Chinese hadn't got locked up yet.

Finally I settled on the Trojans: little bunches of asteroids outside the main belt, sixty degrees ahead of and behind Jupiter, shepherded by gravity effects. The density of the rocks there is actually greater than in the main belt.

Not only that, the asteroids out there are different from the ones in the belt, which are lumps of basalt and metal. The Trojans are carbonaceous: that is, coated in carbon compounds. And they have water.

And nobody had been out there, ever.

I started to raise money.

My ship, when assembled, was a stack of boxes fifty metres long. At its base was a big pusher plate, mounted on shock absorbers. Around that there were fuel magazines and superconducting hoops. There were big solar-cell wings stuck on the sides.

The drive was a fusion-pulse pusher. It worked by shooting pellets of helium-3 and deuterium out back of the craft, behind the pusher plate, and firing carbon dioxide lasers at them. Each fusion pulse lasts two hundred and fifty nanoseconds. And then another, and another: three hundred microexplosions each second. My acceleration was three per cent of G.

My hab module was just a box, with a reconditioned Russian-design closed-loop life support, and an exercise bicycle.

It was a leaky piece of shit. For instance I watched the engineers fix up a ding in a reaction-control thruster fuel line with Kevlar and epoxy, the way you'd repair your refrigerator. I spent as little as I could on my ship, and a lot on my suit, which is a Japanese design. I called it my fubar suit, my safety option of last resort.

In the event, I was glad to have it.

I was looking at an eighteen-day trip to the Trojans.

I said goodbye to the investors, all of whom had bought a piece of my ass at no risk to themselves. I said goodbye to my daughter. That was hard. I'd said goodbye to her father long before.

I called my ship the *Malenfant,* after that great explorer. I wasn't exploring, of course, but I always had a little romance in my soul, I think.

When I left Earth orbit, the glow of my drive turned Pacific night into day.

On her second day, she woke up a spindly-legged girl almost as tall, already, as her mother. She spent as long as she could in the water, dragging at the algae. They all did, most of the time.

There was never enough to eat. Sometimes the algae was so thin she could barely taste it sticking to her fingers. She was hungry, the whole time, and she kept on growing.

Her brother touched her shoulder. 'Get out,' he said. His name was Sun Eyes.

'What?'

He took her hand and pulled her from the river. Everybody else was clambering up the curving bank too.

Something was approaching, under the surface of the water, from the darkness at the end of the hall. Something big and sleek and powerful, that churned the water.

Green Wave was one of a row of skinny naked people, waiting by the edge of the water. 'What is it?'

Sun Eyes shrugged. 'It's a Worker.'

'What's a Worker?'

'One of those.'

A lot of her questions were answered like that.

The river wasn't really a river, more a long, stagnant pond. The Workers, coming by once or twice a day, stirred up the liquid. Maybe it was good for the algae, Green Wave speculated.

Anyhow, when a Worker came along, the people had to get out of the way.

As soon as it had gone, she joined the rush to splash back into the water. But the algae was thinner than before.

'The Workers take away the algae,' said Sun Eyes.

'Why? Can't they see we're hungry?'

Sun Eyes shrugged.

'I don't like the Workers,' said Green Wave.

Sun Eyes laughed at her.

The facts of her life were these:

This place was called Finger Hall. It was a cylinder, roofed over by some material that allowed in a dim, murky light during the short day. The river ran down its length. The Hall was maybe ten times as tall as an adult human.

The Hall, it was said, was one of five – five Fingers, in fact, lying parallel. The Halls were joined at one end by a big cavern, as her own fingers were joined at her hand. Her mother said she saw this Palm Cavern once, early in her life, three or four days ago. Her brother had never left Finger Hall.

The only drink was river water. The only food was river algae.

That day, her brother spent a lot of time with a girl. And there was a boy, Churning Wake, who started paying attention to Green Wave. He even brought her handfuls of algae, the only gift he had.

This was her second day. On the third, she came to understand, she would be expected to pair with somebody. Maybe this kid Churning Wake. She would have a baby of her own on the third or fourth day, maybe another.

And on the fifth day –

Her mother was five days old. She was thin, bent, her breasts empty sacks of flesh. Green Wave brought her algae handfuls.

An old man died. His children grieved, then carried his body to the edge of the water. He had been seven days old.

Soon a Worker clambered out of the water. It was a wide, fat disc, half the height of an adult, and its rim was studded with jointed limbs.

The Worker cut up the body of the old man, snip snip, into bloodless pieces. It loaded the chunks of corpse into a hatch on its back, and then closed itself up and slid smoothly back into the water.

'Why did it do that?' Green Wave asked.

'I don't know,' her mother said. She was wheezing. 'You have a lot of questions, Green Wave. His name was Purple Glow, because on the day he was born –'

'Is that it? We're born, we eat algae, we die? In *seven days*? Is that all there is?'

'We care for each other. We tell the children stories.'

'I don't like it here.'

Her mother laughed, weakly. 'Where else is there?'

I spent the first week throwing up, and drinking banana-flavoured rehydration fluids.

The sun turned to a shrunken yellow disc, casting long shadows. Even Jupiter was just a point of light, about as remote from me as from Earth.

There wasn't a human being within millions of miles. A hell of a feeling.

I found it hard to sleep, listening to the rattles and bangs of my Russian life support. I wore my fubar suit the whole time.

I'd aimed for the largest Trojan, called 624 Hektor. At first it was just a starlike point, but it pulsed in brightness as I watched it. When I got a little closer, I could make out its shape.

624 Hektor: take two big handfuls of Moon, complete with craters and dusty maria. Mould them into egg-shapes, each a hundred miles long. Now touch them together, sharp end to sharp end, and let them rotate, like one almighty peanut.

That's 624 Hektor.

Nobody knows for sure how it got that way. Maybe there was a collision between two normal asteroids which produced a loosely consolidated, fragmented cloud of rubble, which then deformed into this weird compound configuration: two little worlds, made egg-shaped by their mutual attraction, joined in a soft collision.

It was exhilarating to see something no human had witnessed before. For a while, it was as if I really was Reid Malenfant. I sent a long radio letter to my kid, telling her what I could see.

Maybe that will be the last she'll hear of my voice. Because I was still sightseeing when everything fell apart.

I don't know what went wrong. It happened too fast. My best guess is my reaction-control system, little peroxide thrusters, was misaligned. I remembered that ding in the fuel line –

I came in too fast. I tried to turn. I even restarted the fusion pulse drive, but it wasn't enough.

One of the spinning mountains came sweeping up, inexorable, to swat the *Malenfant* like a fly.

Before the impact, I closed up my fubar suit and bailed out.

The solar panels crumpled, and I saw cells tumble away, little black discs the size of my palm. When my hab module hit it cracked open right down a leaky Russian weld. The drive unit kept working, for a while; it lurched away from the surface, spinning crazily. Other fragments were bounced off the surface, the gravity too low to make them stick: pieces of my ship, scattering into trans-Jovian space.

It took a long time for 624 Hektor to reel me in.

I landed like a dust mote. My boots crunched on lightly-compacted regolith. It felt like loose snow.

I walked towards the wreck. The gravity was so low I kept tumbling away from the ground, as if I was suspended on some huge bungee cord.

Malenfant was fubar, as we used to say in the Army: fucked up beyond all recognition. Just as well I had my fubar suit, I thought.

The stars wheeled around me.

*   *   *

The next day it was her mother's turn.

Green Wave, three days old, was an adult herself now, and her growing pains had diminished. Not her hunger, though. And not her anger.

She stood with Churning Wake at the edge of the water, over her mother's body. 'Why does it have to be like this?'

'It just is,' said Churning Wake.

'But she lived only a few days. In two, three, four days, it will be your turn, Churning Wake. And mine. It isn't right. It isn't enough.'

'But it's all we have. It's all there's ever been.' He took her hand. 'Accept it. Be calm.'

'Like hell.'

After a time, he let her hand go.

A Worker slid through the water, its wake oily. It clattered up the curving shoreline of Finger Hall, and loomed over her mother's corpse. It trailed a fine net which was crammed with algae. It raised up a glinting limb, which started to descend towards her mother's body.

Green Wave lunged forward and grabbed the limb. It was cold and hard, its edges sharp. She twisted. There was a crunching noise, and the limb came away from its socket. Green Wave staggered back, breathing hard. There was a steady ticking from somewhere inside the Worker's algae-crusted case.

Sun Eyes grabbed her shoulders. A day older, her brother already looked closer to death than life, she thought.

'What are you doing?'

'Why do they take away the dead?' she snapped. 'Why do they take away our food? We don't have enough to eat. If we had more to eat, maybe we'd live longer.'

He looked doubtful. 'How long?'

'I don't know.' She struggled with the concept. 'Ten days. Maybe twenty.'

'*Twenty days?* That's ridiculous.'

The Worker had come forward again, and was sawing industriously at her mother's cadaver. It didn't seem impeded by the loss of its limb.

'You have to let her go,' said Sun Eyes.

Green Wave looked at him bleakly.

When the beach was clean of traces of her mother the Worker slid back towards the water. The stump, where she had torn away the limb, trailed cables. The Worker sank beneath the water and began to surge towards the darkness at the end of Finger Hall.

The people clattered back into the water, to resume their endless feeding.

Green Wave, carrying her Worker limb, started to wade along the river.

Churning Wake stood on the bank, watching her. 'Where are you going?'

'I want to see where it's taking all our food.'

'What about *us?*'

She laughed. 'Come with me.'

'No,' he said. 'This is my place. We only have a few days. It's up to us not to waste it.'

That made Green Wave hesitate.

What if he was right? Wasn't she gambling away what little was left of her life? Did she really want to risk it all, chasing the unknown?

Maybe she should take time to think this out.

She looked back at Churning Wake, the ribs poking out of his skinny frame. A new infant came crawling past his bony legs, struggling to stand. It was Sun Eyes' son, her nephew, a grand-child her mother had never seen. His wife was already dead.

There had to be, she thought, more than this.

'Come with me,' she said again.

Churning Wake ignored her. He strode into the water and started to feed, with steady determination.

Her brother stood hesitating.

'Sun Eyes? Please?'

'You've been trouble since you were born.'

'I'm sorry.'

He walked into the water.

Side by side, they waded through the shallow water, feeding on filtered handfuls of algae paste. Before long, the little community was just a knot of motion in the dim light of the distance. Nobody called them back. They walked on into the cold and dark.

The fubar suit is a smart design. I read the Owner's Manual, which scrolled across the inside of my faceplate.

A fubar suit is a miniature life-support system in itself. It has a small plutonium-based power supply, heavily shielded. It is full of nanotechnology. It could recycle my wastes, filter my water, break down the solid residue, even feed me on the blue-green algae which would grow in the transparent, water-filled outer layers of the suit.

When I walked across the surface of 624 Hektor, I sloshed and sparkled green. Neil Armstrong would have hated it.

The suit could keep me alive – oh, for two or three weeks. It's a hell of a technical achievement.

Beyond that timescale, it just isn't practical to preserve a full-scale human being in a closed skin-tight container.

Even so, the fubar suit had fallbacks. More drastic options. Mostly untested; the Owner's Manual said I would be voiding manufacturers' guarantees if I exercised them.

I put it off.

I toured 624 Hektor.

With the low gravity it is easy to bound around the equator of either of the little peanut twins. The curvature is tight; I could see I was on a compact ball of rock, curved over on itself, suspended in space. There are craters, some a couple of kilometres across, as if this was a scale model of Luna. Everywhere I found black, sooty carbon compounds, like a dark snow over the regolith.

I hiked around to the contact region.

624 Hektor is a toy world, but even so it is *big*. I was clambering over a sloping landscape, approaching a hundred-mile mountain that was suspended impossibly over my head, grounded in a broad region of mushed-up regolith and shattered rock.

I lost my sense of the vertical. I actually threw up a couple of times – me, the great astronaut – but some kind of biochemical process inside my helmet cleaned me out.

I could leap from one worldlet to the other.

My perspective shifted. Suspended halfway between the two halves of the peanut, I got a brief sense that these were, indeed, two miniature planets, joined at the hip. But then the other half of the pair started to open out, into a dusty, broken lunar landscape. Real Peter Pan stuff.

I wished I could show it to my kid.

The Worker surged steadily along the length of Finger Hall.

Gradually the walls opened out around them, smooth and high, receding into the distance. At last they reached a new chamber, much wider and higher than Finger Hall. It was roughly circular, and its roof let in the sunlight. A compact lake lapped at its floor, thick with algae.

There were no people here, but more corridors led off from the rim: five narrow tubes like Finger Hall, and one much broader and darker.

'It's just as they said,' Sun Eyes said. 'This is the Palm Cavern: the Hand from which five Fingers sprout.' He held up his own hand. 'Just like a human hand. And look – that larger tunnel is like a Wrist, leading to an Arm –'

'Maybe.'

The Worker was heading out of the lake, in a new direction. Towards the Wrist.

'We have to go on,' Green Wave said.

'I'm too old for this, Green Wave. Maybe we should go back. Anyhow, nobody's ever been up there before.'

'Then we'll be the first.'

She took his hand and all but dragged him into the water.

The Worker surged silently along the broader corridor that was the Arm, its roof so far above them – seventy, eighty times their height – it was all but impossible to see. There were more Workers here, swimming precisely back and forth along the Arm.

Green Wave and Sun Eyes tired quickly. They were spending so much time just moving, they weren't feeding enough.

The Worker stopped. It was completing small, tight circles in the water, scooping up algae with its trailing nets.

Bringing Sun Eyes, Green Wave moved steadily closer, until the Worker came within an arm's length.

Green Wave grabbed onto the net it trailed. She lodged the detached Worker limb in strands of the net. She helped Sun Eyes get a close grip on the net.

The Worker didn't seem to notice. It wasn't moving so fast; it was easy to hold onto the net, and let the Worker just pull her through the water.

The Worker resumed its steady progress upstream. Some of the net was worn, and she was even able to reach inside and haul out handfuls of algal paste to feed them both.

The walls of the Arm slid steadily past, remote and featureless. On the long beaches there were no signs of people. Maybe, she thought, her own people were alone here, however far this branching series of tunnels and gloomy lakes continued.

Sun Eyes slept for a while. His hair, thinning and straggling, drifted into his eyes; Green Wave brushed it back.

The Worker turned a wide corner, and the river opened out. Now they entered a new chamber, containing a broad, glimmering lake, many times wider than the Palm Cavern they'd seen before. The roof here, far above them, was all but transparent, and Green Wave could see the sun's small disc, and many lesser lights. The water was thick with algae; she merely had to dip her hand in to pull out great fistfuls of sticky paste.

'Fingers,' she said.

'What?'

'Fingers. A Hand. An Arm. If that's all true, this must be the Chest. Or the Stomach.'

'You don't know what you're talking about,' Sun Eyes said tiredly.

'If I'm right, that way must be the Head.'

'The Head of what?'

'How should I know?'

In the direction she pointed, there was a broad, dark exit. The Neck? A series of thick pipes snaked out of the lake, and passed into the Neck. There was a system of net hoppers in front of the pipes; the water was greener there, as if richer with algae. Workers clustered around the hoppers, working busily, dumping in algae from their own nets. She pictured some prone giant, sucking nutrient out of this algal hopper in its Stomach.

Sun Eyes clutched at the net. 'We're leaving the shore. I can't feel the floor.'

It was true. The Worker was forging its way across the lapping surface of the lake; they were already a long way from the curving walls, heading for the deeper water under the high arch of the Stomach roof.

And now there was something new. Something deep under the water. It was a light, flickering, bubbling. No: a bank of lights, in neat rows, stretching off all around her.

'What do you think it is?' she whispered.

'I don't know. I only ever saw lights in the sky.'

'Maybe it's another sun, under the water. Maybe –'

But now a hatch on top of the Worker's back was opening up. A limb came looping over, and plucked objects out of the hatch. The objects, dried-up and irregular, were the remnants of Green Wave's mother. The Worker dumped them into the water.

They fell quickly, but when they hit the underwater suns there was a ferocious, silent bubbling.

'So that's what happens to dead people,' said Sun Eyes.

'That's what will happen to us.'

The hatch closed, and the Worker swam in lazy, broadening circles.

'I'm tired,' Sun Eyes said.

She fed him more handfuls of algal paste.

I lay on my back, face up to the stars, unsure if I would ever get up again.

I let the nems get to work.

I wish I could say it was painless.

The idea is simple.

The fubar suit has constructed a stable, simplified, long-duration ecosphere inside itself. Most of the volume is just air, but there is a shallow water lake pooling in the suit's back, arms and legs. There is blue-green algae growing in the lake, feeding on sunlight, giving off carbon dioxide – *spirulina,* according to the Owner's Manual, full of proteins, vitamins and essential amino acids. The other half of the biocycle is a community of little animals, living inside the suit. They are like humans: eating the algae, drinking the water, breathing in oxygen, breathing out carbon dioxide. Their wastes, including their little dead bodies, go to a bank of SCWOs – supercritical water oxidizers – superhot liquid steam which can oxidize organic slurry in seconds. A hell of a gadget. It can even sustain underwater flames; you have to see it to believe it.

Of course you can't close the loops completely. But I was able to plug the suit into the surface of 624 Hektor and supplement the loops with raw materials – carbon compounds, hydrates. It would last a long time.

It's all constructed and maintained by the nems – nano-electro-mechanical systems, tiny crab-like robots with funny little limbs. The suit is full of them. They're even burrowing their way out into the asteroid surface, in search of raw materials.

I read all about the nems in the Owner's Manual. The technology is neat; the nems are run by chips lithographed by high-energy proton beams, and they store data in chains of fluorine and oxygen atoms on the surface of dinky little diamonds –

I always liked Japanese gadgets.

But I should stick to the point.

Little guys. Of course they are like miniature people. What else could they be? They are made out of me.

There's no nice way of putting this. The fubar suit couldn't keep me alive – not as sixty kilograms of eating, breathing, excreting woman anyhow. So the nems took me apart.

The nems used my body water to make the lakes, and my meat – some of it – to make the little guys.

What's left of *me* is my head. My head is sustained – my brain is kept alive – by nutrients from the little biosphere that takes up the space my body used to occupy. One day, the theory goes, the medics will retrieve me and will reassemble me, in some form, with more nanotech.

It's grotesque. Well, it's not what I wanted. I'm only thirty-eight years old. I have a kid, waiting for me.

I just didn't have any choices left.

The fubar suit was a last resort. It worked, I guess.

I just wish they'd tested it first. Damn those Japanese.

Little humans. They are supposed to look like us, bug-sized or not. They are supposed to be able to move around; the water surfaces in there are doped somehow, so the little guys aren't locked in place by surface tension. They are supposed to breed quickly and eat and breathe and die back, and just play their part in the two-component biosphere, keeping me alive.

What they're not supposed to be is *smart.* What they're not supposed to do is *ask questions.*

What a mess.

When she woke, she was so stiff it was all she could do to unhook her claw-like hands from the net. Sun Eyes was still sleeping, shivering gently. His scalp was all but hairless now, his face a mask of wrinkles.

She looked around. The Worker was close to the shore of this great Stomach cavern, but it was working its way back towards the exit from which it had emerged.

Time to get off, she thought.

She shook Sun Eyes. His eyes were crusted with sleep. 'Green Wave? I can't see so well. I'm cold.'

'Come on. I'll get you to the shore.'

She helped him disentangle himself from the netting. His legs unfolded from his chest with painful slowness.

At last they were standing, in water that came to their waists. She slid an arm around him, and they walked to shallower water, scooping up algae. Green Wave still carried her purloined Worker limb.

The Worker, apparently oblivious to the loss of its passengers, surged steadily towards the exit to the Arm.

'It's going back,' Sun Eyes said.

'I know. We have to go on.'

'What for?'

'I'm not sure.'

'Where?'

She pointed. 'That way. The Head.'

They began to work their way around the complex, sculpted shoreline, towards the exit Green Wave had labelled the Neck. They walked in the shallows. They could only manage a slow pace, such was Sun Eyes' condition.

She felt a deep stab of regret. She'd taken Sun Eyes away from where he should be, with his children and grandchildren. And she was old herself now – too old to have a life of her own, too old for children. She wondered what had happened to Churning Wake, if he was surrounded now by splashing children who might have been hers.

They neared the sharp folds in the ground that marked the entrance to the Neck. She could see the big pipes that carried water up from the lake. The pipes were clear, and she could see thick, greenish, rich fluid within. Food, taken away from people who needed it. A diffuse anger gathered.

They walked into the Head.

It was darker here. Most of the light came from the Stomach lake, a greenish glow at the mouth of this broad tunnel.

There was little free water here, little food. But still she urged Sun Eyes on. 'Just a bit more,' she said.

They reached a pit in the ground, twenty or thirty paces across.

She sat Sun Eyes down, propping him up against a wall.

She lay on her stomach. The pit was pitch dark. It was the first time in her life she'd seen a breach in the floor. Her imagination raced.

She reached down into the pit.

At first she could feel nothing but the smooth flooring. But that came to an end quickly, and below it she could feel beneath, to some much rougher, looser material. It felt damp and cold.

There were even algae here, clinging to the walls in clumps.

She could hear Workers doing something, perhaps chewing at the loose rubble down there. Building the pit, onwards and outwards.

She straightened up stiffly. She tried to see deeper into the Head – there were suggestions of vast, sleeping forms there, perhaps an immense face – but there was no light, no free water. She couldn't go any further.

She went back to Sun Eyes. He seemed to be sleeping.

She told him what she'd found.

'Maybe there are worlds beyond this one.' Her imagination faltered. 'If we are crawling through the body of some human form, maybe there is another, still greater form beyond. And perhaps another beyond that – an endless nesting . . .'

He slumped against her shoulder.

She laid his light, wizened body down against the floor. In the darkness she could feel his ribs, the lumps of his joints.

Her anger flared up, like the light of a new sun.

I know I'm still lying here in the regolith, on this dumb little misshapen asteroid, inside my fubar suit. I know nobody's come to save me. Because I'm still here, right? But I can't see, hear, feel a damn thing.

Although I sometimes think I can.

I'm going stir-crazy, inside my own head.

I know they're coming, though. *The little guys.* The nems told me that much.

They aren't supposed to be smart, damn it!

But the nems will stop them, if I tell them.

So I have a decision to make. I could stop them.

After all, it's them or me.

She got to her feet. She picked up her battered Worker limb, and stumbled out of the Neck, towards the light of the Stomach lake.

She started to batter at the feeder pipes with the Worker limb, her only tool.

The pipes were broad, as thick as her waist, but they punctured easily. Soon she had ripped fist-sized holes in the first pipe, and algae-rich water spilled down over the flooring, and flowed steadily back into the lake. She kept it up until she'd severed the pipe completely.

Then she started on the next pipe.

The Workers didn't react. They just swam around in their complacent circles, piling up the net hopper with algae that wasn't going anywhere any more.

She worked until all the pipes were broken.

She threw away her Worker limb, and lay down where she was, in the slimy, brackish water she'd spilled. She licked at the floor, sucking in a little algal paste, and let herself sleep.

Sometimes I think humans aren't supposed to be out here at all. Look at me, I'm grotesque. These little guys, on the other hand, might be able to survive.

Even prosper.

A hell of a shock for those smug Chinese in the asteroid belt, when a swarm of little Americans comes barrelling in from the orbit of Jupiter.

What the hell. It didn't look as if anyone was coming for me anyhow.

Funny thing is, I feel cold. Now, that's not supposed to happen, according to the Owner's Manual.

It was hard to wake up. Her eyes didn't open properly. And when they did, they wouldn't focus.

She lifted up her hand, and held it close so she could see. Her skin was brown and sagging and covered in liver spots.

She got to her feet, and stumbled down the slope.

She stood at the edge of the water, peering at the Workers, until her rheumy, ruined eyes made out one which didn't look quite right. One that was missing a limb.

She struggled through water that seemed thick and resistant, until she had caught hold of the Worker's net, and it was pulling her away from the shore.

With any luck this creature would, unwitting, take her home. She'd be a sack of bones by then, of course, but that didn't matter. The important thing was that someone would see, and maybe connect her with the enriching of the water, and wonder what she'd found.

More would come, next time. Children, too.

They would find that pit, up in the Neck, the way out of the world.

She smiled.

The water was warm around her.

She wondered what had happened to Sun Eyes. Maybe he was somewhere beneath her now, fizzing in the light of those underwater suns.

She closed her eyes. She drifted in blue warmth, her thoughts dissolving.

GREY EARTH

She was old now. The cold dug into her joints and her scars, and the leg she had fractured long ago, more than it used to.

She still called herself Mary. But she was one of the last to use the old names. And the people no longer called themselves Hams – for there were no Skinnies here who could call them that, none save Nemoto – and they were no longer called the People of the Grey Earth, for they had come home to the Grey Earth, and had no need to remember it.

There came a day, when they put old Saul in the ground, when Mary found herself the last to remember the old place, the Red Moon where she had been born.

Outside the cave that day there was only darkness, the still darkness of the Long Night, broken by the stars that sprinkled the cloudless black sky. Mary's deep past was a place of dark green warmth. But her future lay in the black cold ground, where so many had gone before her: Ruth, Joshua, Saul, even one of her own children.

But it didn't matter.

All that mattered were her skins, and the warm fug of gossip and talk that filled the cave, and the warm sap that bled from the root of the blood-tree that pierced the cave roof, on its way to seek out the endless warmth that dwelled in the belly of this earth, this Grey Earth.

All that mattered was today. Comparisons with misty other times – with past and future, with a girl who had fought and laughed and loved on a different world, with the bones that would soon rot in the ground – were without meaning.

Nemoto was not so content, of course.

* * *

Day succeeds empty day.

At first, on arriving here, I dreamed of physical luxuries: running hot water, clean, well-prepared food, a soft bed. But now it is as if my soul has been eroded down to an irreducible core. To sleep in the open on a bower of leaves no longer troubles me. To have my skin coated in slippery grime is barely noticeable.

But I long for security. And I long for the sight of another human face.

Sometimes I rage inwardly. But I have no one to blame for the fact that I have become lost between worlds, between realities.

And when I become locked inside my own head, when my inner distress becomes too apparent, it disturbs the Hams, as if I am becoming a danger to them.

So I have learned not to look inward.

I watch the Hams as they shamble about their various tasks, their brute bodies wrapped up in tied-on animal skins like Christmas parcels. All I see is their strangeness, fresh every day. They will complete a tool, use it once, drop it, and move on. It is as if every day is the very first day of their lives, as if they wake up to a world created anew.

It is obvious that their minds, housed in those huge skulls, are powerful, but they are not like humans'. But then they are not human. They are Neandertal.

This is their planet. A Neandertal planet.

Still, I try to emulate them. I try to live one day at a time. It is comforting.

My name is Nemoto. If you find this diary, if you understand what I have to say, remember me.

Nemoto was never content. Even in the deepest dark of the Long Night, she would bustle about the cave, arguing with herself, agitated, endlessly making her incomprehensible objects. Or else she would blunder out into the dark, heavily wrapped in furs, perhaps seeking her own peace in the frozen stillness beyond.

Few watched her come and go. To the younger folk, Nemoto had been here all their lives, a constant, unique, somewhat irritating presence.

But Mary remembered the Red Moon, and how its lands had run with Skinnies like Nemoto.

Mary understood. Mary was of the Grey Earth, and she had come home. But Nemoto was of the Red Moon – or perhaps of another place, a Blue Earth of which she sometimes spoke – and now it was Nemoto who had been stranded far from her home.

And so Mary made space for Nemoto. She would protect Nemoto when the children were too boisterous with her, or when an adult challenged her, or when she fell ill or injured herself. She would even give her meat to eat. But Nemoto's thin, pointed jaw could make no impression on the deep-frozen meat of the winter store, and nor could her shining tools. So Mary would soften the meat for her with her own strong jaws, chewing it as she would to feed a child.

But one day Nemoto spat out her mouthful of meat on the floor of the cave. She raged and shouted in her jabbering Skinny tongue, expressing disgust. She pulled on her furs and gathered her tools, and stamped out of the cave.

Time did not matter during the Long Night, nor during its bright twin, the Long Day. Nemoto was gone, as gone as if she had been put in the ground, and she began to soften in the memory.

But at last Nemoto returned, as if from the dead. She was staggering and laughing, and she carried a bundle under her arms. The children gathered around to see.

It was a bat, still plump with its winter fat, its leathery wings folded over. The bat had tucked itself into a tree hollow to endure the Long Night. But Nemoto had dug it out, and now she put it close to a warm root of the blood-tree to let it thaw. She jabbered about how she would eat well of fresh meat.

The bat revived briefly, flapping its broad wings against the cave floor. But Nemoto briskly slit its throat with a stone knife, and began to butcher it.

Nemoto consumed her bat, giving warm titbits to the children who clustered around to see. She sucked marrow from its thread-thin bones, and gave that to the children as well. But when she offered the children bloated, pink-grey internal organs, mothers pulled the children away.

That was the last time Nemoto was ever healthy.

Mary eats her meat raw, tearing at it with her shovel-shaped teeth and cutting it with a flake knife; every so often she scrapes her teeth with the knife. And as her powerful jaw grinds at the meat, great muscles work in her cheeks.

Mary is short, robust, heavily built. She is barrel-chested, and her arms and massive-boned legs are slightly bowed. Her feet are broad, her toes fat and bony. Her massive hands, with their long powerful thumbs, are scarred from stone chips. Her skull, under a thatch of dark brown hair, is long and low with a pronounced bulge at the rear. Her face is pulled forward into a great prow fronted by her massive, fleshy nose; her cheeks sweep back as if streamlined, but her jaw, though chinless, is massive and thrust forward. From her lower forehead a great ridge of bone thrusts forward, masking her eyes. There is a pronounced dip above the ridges, before her shallow brow leads back into a tangle of hair.

She is Neandertal. There can be no doubt.

She lives – I live – in a system of caves. There is an overpowering stench of people, of sweat, wood smoke, excrement and burning fur, and a musty, disagreeable odour of people who don't wash.

Every move the Hams make, every act they complete, from cracking open a bone to bouncing a child in the air, is suffused with strength. They suffer a large number of injuries, bone fractures and crushing injuries and gouged and scarred skin. But then their favoured hunting technique is to wrestle their prey to the ground. It is like living with a troupe of rodeo riders.

The Hams barely notice me. They are utterly wrapped up in each other. Some of the children pluck at the remnants of my clothing with their intimidatingly strong fingers. But otherwise the Hams step around me, their eyes sliding away, as if I am a rock embedded in the ground. I sometimes theorize that they are only truly conscious in social interactions; everything else – eating, making tools, even hunting – is done in a rapid blur, as I used to drive a car without thinking. Certainly, to a Neandertal, by far the most fascinating things in the world are other Neandertals.

They are not human. But they care for their children, and for their ill and elderly. However coolly the Hams treat me, they have not expelled me, which is how I survive.

I brought them here, from the Red Moon. This tipped-up Earth is their home. They remembered it during the time of their exile on another world. Remembered it for forty thousand years, an unimaginable time.

I imagined I would be able to get away from here, to home. It did not happen that way.

There was a time of twilights, blue-purple shading to pink. And then, at last, the edge of the sun was visible over the horizon: just a splinter of it, just for an hour, but it was the first time the sun had shown at all for sixty-eight days.

When the people saw the light they came bursting out of the cave.

They scrambled onto the low bluff over the cave, where the blood-tree stood: leafless and gaunt now, but its blood-red sap coursed with the warmth it had drawn from the Grey Earth's belly, the warmth that had sustained the people through the Long Night. The people danced and capered and threw off their furs. Then they retreated to the warmth of the cave, where there was much chatter, much eating, much joyous sex.

Though it would be some time yet before the frozen lakes and rivers began to thaw, there was already a little meltwater to be had. And the first hibernating animals – birds and a few large rats – were beginning to stir, sluggish and vulnerable to hunting. The people enjoyed the first thin fruits of the new season.

But Nemoto's illness was worse.

She suffered severe bouts of diarrhoea and vomiting. She steadily lost weight, becoming, in the uninterested eyes of the people, even more gaunt than she had seemed before. And her skin grew flaky and sore. The children would watch in horrified fascination as she shucked off her furs and her clothes, and then peeled off bits of her skin, as if she would keep on until nothing was left but a heap of bones.

Mary tried to treat the diarrhoea. She brought water, brine from the ocean diluted by meltwater. But she did not know how to treat the poisoning which was working its way through Nemoto's system.

The key incident in the formation of the Earth was the collision of proto-Earth with a wandering planetesimal larger than Mars. This is known as the Big Whack.

It is hard to envisage such an event. The projectile that ended the Cretaceous era, sending the dinosaurs to extinction, was perhaps six miles across. The primordial impactor was some four thousand miles across. It was a fully formed planet in its own right. And the collision released two hundred million times as much energy as the Cretaceous impact.

The proto-Earth's oceans were boiled away. About half of Earth's crust was demolished by the impact. A tremendous spray of liquid rock was hurled into space. The impactor was stripped of its own mantle material, and its core sank into the interior of the Earth. Much of the plume fell back to Earth. Whatever was left of the atmosphere was heated to thousands of degrees.

The remnant plume settled into a ring around the Earth, glowing white hot. As it cooled it solidified into a swarm of moonlets. It was like a replay of the formation of the solar system itself. The largest of the moonlets won out. The growing Moon swept up the remnant particles, and under the influence of tidal forces, rapidly receded from Earth.

Earth itself, meanwhile, was afflicted by huge tides, a molten crust and savage rains as the ocean vapour fell back from space. It took millions of years before the rocks had cooled enough for liquid water to gather once more.

Everything was shaped in those moments of impact: Earth's spin, the tilt of the axis that gives us seasons, the planet's internal composition, the Moon's composition and orbit.

But it didn't have to be that way.

Such immense collisions are probably common in the formation of any planetary system. But the impact itself was a random event: chaotic, in that small differences could have produced large, even unpredictable consequences. The impactor might have missed Earth altogether – but that would have left Earth with its original atmosphere, a crushing Venus-like blanket of carbon dioxide. Or the impactor might have hit at a subtly different angle. A single Moon isn't necessarily the most likely outcome; many collision geometries would produce two twin Moons, or three or four, or ring systems like Saturn's. And so on.

Many possibilities. All of which, somewhere in the infinite manifold of universes, must have come to pass.

I know this because I have visited several of those possibilities.

The days lengthened rapidly.

The ice on the lakes and rivers melted, causing splintering crashes all over the landscape, like a long, drawn-out explosion. Soon the lakes were blue, though pale cores of unmelted ice lingered in their cores.

Life swarmed. In this brief temperate interval between deadly cold and unbearable heat, plants and animals alike engaged in a frenzied round of fighting, feeding, breeding, dying.

The people moved rapidly about the landscape. They gathered the fruit and shoots that seemed to burst out of the ground. They

hunted the small animals and birds that emerged from their hiber-
nations to seek mates and nesting places.

And soon a distant thunder sounded across the land: relentless,
billowing day and night across the newly green plains, echoing
from green-clad mountains. It was the sound of hoofed feet, the
first of the migrant herds.

The men and women gathered their weapons, and headed
towards the sea.

It turned out to be a herd of giant antelopes. They were slim
and streamlined, the muscles of their legs and haunches huge and
taut, the bucks sporting huge folded-back antlers. And they ran
like the wind. Since most of this tilted world was, at any given
moment, freezing or baking through its long seasons, migrant
animals were forced to travel across thousands of kilometres, spanning continents in their search for food, water and temperate
climes. Speed and endurance were of the essence for survival.

But predators came too, sleek hyenas and cats stalking the vast
herds. Though the antelopes were mighty runners – fuelled by
high-density fat, able to race for days without a break – there were
always outliers who could not keep up: the old, the very young,
the injured, mothers gravid with infants. And it was on these
weaker individuals that the predators feasted.

Those predators included the people, who inhabited a neck of
land between two continents, a funnel down which the migrant
herds were forced to swarm.

The antelope herd was huge. But it passed so rapidly that the
great river of flesh was gone in a couple of days. And after another
day, the predator packs that stalked it had gone too.

The people ate their antelope meat and sucked rich marrow,
and gathered their fruit and nuts and shoots, and waited for their
next provision to come to them, delivered up by the tides of the
world.

But the next group of running animals to come by was small
– everyone could sense that – and everybody knew what they were,
from their distinctive, high-pitched cries.

Everybody lost interest. Everybody but Nemoto.

*The Hams are aware of the coming and going of the herds of
migrating herbivores on which they rely for much of their meat,
and are even able to predict them by the passage of the seasons.
But Hams do not plan. They seem to rely on the benison of the*

world to provision them, day to day. It means they sometimes go hungry, but not even that dents their deep, ancient faith in the world's kindness.

I remember a particular hunt. I followed a party of Hams along a trail through the forest.

They stopped by a small tree, thick with hanging fibres, and with dark hollows showing beneath its prop roots. White lichen was plastered over its trunk, and a parasitic plant with narrow, dark-green leaves dangled from a hollow in its trunk. A Ham cut a sapling and pushed it into one deep dark hollow, just above the muddy mush of leaves and detritus at the base of the tree.

A deep growling emerged from beneath the roots of the tree.

Excited, the Hams gathered around the tree and began to haul at it, shaking it back and forth. To my amazement they pulled the tree over by brute force, just ripping the roots out of the ground. Out squirmed a crocodile, a metre long, jaws clamped at the end of the pole. It was dark brown with a red-tinged head, huge eyes, and startlingly white teeth.

It was a forest crocodile. These creatures come out at night. They eat frogs, insects, flightless birds, anything they can find. They have barely changed in two hundred million years.

This world is full of such archaisms and anachronisms – like the Hams themselves. Of course it is. For it is not my world, my Earth. It is not my universe.

The Hams fell on the crocodile in their brutal, uncompromising way. They rolled it onto its back. One woman took a stone hand-axe and sliced off the right front leg, then the left. The animal, still alive, struggled feebly; its screams were low, like snoring. When the woman opened its chest it slumped at last.

I confronted Abel. 'Why didn't you kill it before starting the butchering?'

The big man just looked back at me, apparently bemused.

These are not pet-owners. They aren't even farmers. They are hunter-gatherers. They have no reason to be sentimental about the animals, to care about them. My ancestors were like this once.

Not only that: the Hams do not anthropomorphize. They could not imagine how it would be to suffer like the animal, for it was a crocodile, not a person.

I turned away from the blood, which was spreading over the ground.

*   *   *

Sickly, gaunt, enfeebled, her clothing stained with her own shit and piss, her eyes so weak she had to wear slitted skins over her face, Nemoto seemed enraged by the approach of these new arrivals. She gathered up her tools of stone and metal, and hurried out of the cave towards the migrants.

Mary followed Nemoto, catching her easily.

Soon they saw the Running-folk.

There were many of them, men, women, children. They had broken their lifelong trek at a river bank. They were splashing water into their mouths, and over their faces and necks. The children were paddling in the shallows. They were all naked, all hairless save for thatches on their scalps and in their groins and arm-pits.

They would never have been considered beautiful by a human, for their legs were immensely long and their chests expanded behind huge rib cages, giving them something of the look of storks. But they had the faces of their *Homo erectus* ancestors, small and low-browed with wide, flat nostrils.

And Nemoto was stalking towards this gathering, waving her arms and brandishing her weapons. 'Get away! Get away from there, you brutes!'

Some of the adults got to their feet, their legs unfolding, bird-like. Mary could hear their growls, though she and Nemoto were still distant.

The first rock – crudely chipped, as if by a child – landed in the dirt at their feet.

Mary grabbed Nemoto's arm. Nemoto struggled and cursed, but Mary held her effortlessly. She dragged Nemoto back out of range of the stones.

The Runners settled again to their bathing and drinking. They stayed where they were for most of that long day, and so did Nemoto, squatting in the dirt with scarcely a motion, staring at the Runners.

Mary stayed with her, growing increasingly hot and thirsty.

At last, as the evening drew in, the Runners got to their feet, one by one, picking up their long hinged legs. And then they began to move off along the river. They became lanky silhouettes against the setting sun, and the river gleamed gold.

Nemoto stalked down towards the river.

Here, just where the Runners had settled, there was a shell of white and black, cracked open. It was the thing Nemoto called a *lander*. Once, Nemoto had used it to bring the Hams here, to the Grey Earth, to home. Nemoto clambered inside the shattered hull. After so many cycles of the Grey Earth's ferocious seasons, there was little left of the interior equipment now. Mary saw how birds and wasps and spiders had made their home here, and grass and herbs had colonized the remnants of the softer materials.

Mary thought she understood. Though it had been broken open the moment it had fallen to the ground, Nemoto had done her best to protect and preserve the wreck of the lander. Perhaps she wanted it to take her home.

But the lander remained resolutely smashed and broken, and Nemoto could not even persuade the people to get together to haul it away from the river.

As the light seeped out of the sky, Nemoto, at last, came away from the wreck. Mary took her arm, and shepherded her quickly towards the security of the cave, for the predators hunted at sunset.

It proved to be the last time Nemoto ever left the community.

I do not know how this came to be, this manifold, this cosmic panoply, this proliferation of realities.

There is a theory that our universe grew from a seed, a tiny piece of very high-density material that then inflated into a great volume of spacetime, with planets and stars and galaxies. This was the Big Bang. But perhaps that seed was not unique. Perhaps there is a sea of primordial high-density matter-energy – a sea where temperatures and densities and pressures exceed anything in our universe, where physics operates according to different laws – and within this sea universes inflate, one after another, like bubbles in foam. These bubble-universes would have no connection with each other. Their inhabitants would see only their own bubble, not the foam itself.

That is my legend. The Hams' legend is that the Old Ones created it all. Who is to say who is right? How could we ever know?

Whatever the origin of the manifold, within it there could be an infinite number of universes. And in an infinite ensemble, everything which is logically possible must – somewhere, somehow – come to pass.

Thus there must be a cluster of bubble-spaces with identical histories up to the moment of Earth's formation, the Big Whack – and differing after that only in the details of the impact itself, and their consequences. I imagine the possible universes arrayed around me in phase space. And universes differing only in the details of the Earth-Moon impact must somehow be close to ours in that graph of the possible.

I know this from personal experience.

For me it began when a new Moon appeared in Earth's sky: a fat Moon, a Red Moon, replacing poor dead Luna. I travelled to that Moon on a quixotic jaunt with Reid Malenfant, ostensibly in search of his lost wife, Emma Stoney. There we encountered many hominid forms – some more or less human, some not – all refugees from different reality strands, swept away by that Red Moon, which slides in sideways knight's moves between universes.

Just as Malenfant and I were swept away, when my own Earth, Blue Earth, disappeared from the Moon's sky. I knew immediately that I could never go home.

To fulfil a pledge foolishly made to these Hams by Emma Stoney, I agreed to use our small Earth-Moon ferry spacecraft to carry the Hams back to their Grey Earth – when the opportunity presented itself, as our wandering Moon happened that way. Once I was off the Red Moon, with a spacecraft, I vaguely imagined that I would be able to go further, to get away from the deadening menticulture that rapidly emerged among the stranded on the Red Moon. But it was not to be; I crashed here, and when the Red Moon wandered away from the sky, I was left doubly stranded.

The Red Moon is an agent of human evolution. That is why it wanders. Its interstitial meandering is a mixing device, an artefact of the Old Ones, who may even have manufactured this vast mesh of realities.

So I believe.

But whatever the purpose of that Moon's wandering, it destroyed my own life.

For the Hams, for Julia, the Grey Earth is home. For me, this entire universe is a vast prison.

The air grew hotter yet, approaching its most violent peak of temperature, even though the sun still lingered beneath the horizon for part of its round, even though night still touched the Grey Earth. Soon the fast-growing grasses and herbs were dying back, and the migrant animals and birds had fled, seeking the temperate climes.

The season's last rain fell. Mary closed her eyes and raised her open mouth to the sky, for she knew it would be a long time before she felt rain on her face again.

The ground became a plain of baked and cracked mud.

The people retreated to their cave. Just as its thick rock walls had sheltered them from the most ferocious cold of the winter, so now the walls gave them coolness. And just as the people had drawn warmth from the sap of the blood-tree, pumped up from the ground, now the tree let its sap carry its excess heat down into the ground, and its tangle of roots cooled the cave further.

The people ate the meat they had dried out and stored in the back of their cave, and they drank water from the drying rivers and lakes, and dug up hibernating frogs, fat sacks of water and meat that croaked resentfully as they were briskly killed.

Nemoto could not leave the cave, of course. Long before the heat reached its height, her relentless illness had driven her to her pallet, where she remained, unable to rise, with a strip of skin tied across her eyes. But Mary brought her water and food.

At length there came a day when the sun failed even to brush the horizon at its lowest point. From now on, for sixty-eight days, it would not rise or set, but would make meaningless circles in the sky, circles that would grow smaller and more elevated.

The Long Day had begun.

And still the great blood-tree grew, drinking in the endless light of the sun and the water it found deep beneath the ground, so that sometimes the roots that pierced the cave writhed like snakes.

Here is how, or so I have come to believe, this Red Moon has played a key role in human evolution.

Consider. How do new species arise, of hominids or any organism?

Isolation is the key. If mutations arise in a large and freely mixing population, any new characteristic is diluted and will disappear within a few generations. But when a segment of the population becomes isolated from the rest, dilution through interbreeding is prevented. Thus the isolated group may, quite rapidly, diverge from the base population. And when those barriers to isolation are removed, the new species finds itself in competition with its predecessors. If it is more fit, in some sense, it will survive by out-competing the parent stock. If not, it declines.

When our scientists believed there was only one Earth, they developed a theory of how the evolution of humanity occurred. The ape-like bipeds called Australopithecines gave rise to tool users, who in turn produced tall erect hairless creatures capable of walking on the open plain, who gave rise to various species of Homo sapiens – *the genus that includes myself. It is believed that at some points in history there were many hominid species, all derived from the base Australopithecine stock, extant together on the Earth. But my kind – Homo sapiens sapiens – proved the fittest of them all. By out-competition, the variant species were removed.*

Presumably, each speciation episode was instigated by the isolation of a group of the parent stock. We assumed that the key isolating events were caused by climate changes: rising or falling sea levels, the birth or death of forests, the coming and going of glaciation. It was a plausible picture – before we knew of the Red Moon, of the Grey Earth, of other Moons and Earths.

Assume that the base Australopithecine stock evolved on Earth – my Earth. Imagine that some mechanism scooped up handfuls of undifferentiated Australopithecines and, perhaps some generations later, deposited them on a variety of subtly different Earths.

It is hard to imagine a more complete isolation. And the environments in which they were placed might have had no resemblance to those from which they were taken. In that case our Australopithecines would have had to adapt or die.

And later, samples of those new populations were swept up in their turn, and handed on to other Earths, where they were shaped again. Thus the Hams, with their power and conservatism, have been shaped by the brutal conditions of this Grey Earth.

This is my proposal: that hominid speciation has been driven by the transfer of populations between parallel Earths. It is fantastic, but logical.

If this is true, then everything about us – everything about me – has been shaped by the meddling of the Old Ones, these engineers of worlds and hominids, for their own unrevealed, unfathomable purpose. Just as my own life story – too complicated to set out here – has become a scrawl across multiple realities.

What remains unclear is why the Old Ones, if they exist, should wish to do this. Perhaps their motives were somehow malicious, or somehow benevolent; perhaps they wished to give the potential of humankind its fullest opportunity of expression.

But their motive is scarcely material.

What power for mortals to hold.
What arrogance to wield it.

Nemoto said she would not go into the ground until she saw another night. But she grew steadily weaker, until she could not raise her body from its pallet of moss, or clean herself, or even raise her hands to her mouth.

Mary cared for her. She would give Nemoto water in sponges of mashed-up leaf, and when Nemoto fouled herself Mary cleaned her with bits of skin, and she bathed her body's suppurating sores with blood-tree sap.

But Nemoto's skin continued to flake away, as the slow revenge of the bat disturbed from its hibernation took its gruesome course.

There came a day when the sun rolled along the horizon, its light shimmering through the trees which flourished there. Mary knew that soon would come the first night, the first *little* night, since the spring. So she carried Nemoto to the mouth of the cave – she was light, like a thing of twigs and dried leaves – and propped her up on a bundle of skins, so that her face was bathed in the sunlight.

But Nemoto screwed up her face. 'I do not like the light,' she said, her voice a peevish husk. 'I can bear the dark. But not these endless days. I have always longed for tomorrow. For tomorrow I will understand a little more. I have always wanted to *understand*. Why I am here. Why the world is as it is. Why there is something, rather than nothing.'

'Lon' for tomorrow,' Mary echoed, seeking to comfort her.

'Yes. But *you* do not dream of the future, do you? For you there is only today. Here especially, with your Long Day and your Long Night, as if a whole year is made of one tremendous day.'

Overhead, a single bright star appeared.

Nemoto gasped. 'The first star since the spring. How marvellous, how beautiful, how fragile.' She settled back on her bundle of skins. 'You know, the stars here are the same – I mean the same as those that surround the world where I grew up, the Blue Earth. But the way they swim around the sky is not the same.' She was trying to raise her arm, perhaps to point, but could not. 'You have a different pole star here. It is somewhere in Leo, near the sky's equator. I cannot determine which . . . Your world is tipped over, you see, like Uranus, like a top lying on its side; that is how the Big Whack shaped it here. And so for six months, when your pole

233

points at the sun, you have endless light; and for six months endless dark . . . Do you follow me? No, I am sure you do not.' She coughed, and seemed to sink deeper into the skins. 'All my life I have sought to understand. I believe I would have pursued the same course whichever of our splintered worlds I had been born into. And yet, and yet –' She arched her back, and Mary laid her huge hands on Nemoto's forehead, trying to soothe her. 'And yet I die alone.'

Mary took her hand. It was delicate, like a child's. 'Not alone,' she said.

'Ah. I have you, don't I, Mary? I have a friend. That is something, isn't it? That is an achievement . . .' Nemoto tried to squeeze Mary's hand; it was the gentlest of touches.

And the sun, as if apologetically, slid beneath the horizon. Crimson light towered into the sky.

There are no books here. There is nothing like writing of any kind. And there is no art: no paintings on animal skins or cave walls, no tattoos, not so much as a dab of crushed rock on a child's face.

As a result, the Hams' world is a startlingly drab place, lacking art and story.

To me, a beautiful sunset is a comforting reminder of home, a symbol of renewal, a sign of hope for a better day tomorrow. But to the Hams, I believe, a sunset is just a sunset. But every sunset is like the first they have ever seen.

They are clearly aware of past and future, of change within their lives. They care for each other. They will show concern over another's wounds, and lavish attention on a sickly infant. They show pain, and fear, a great sense of loss when a loved one dies – and a deep awareness of their own mortality.

But they are quite without religion.

Think what that means. Every morning Mary must wake up, as alert and conscious as I am, and she must face the horror of life full in the face – without escape, without illusion, without consolation.

As for me, I have never abandoned my shining thread of hope that someday I will get out of here – without that I would fear for my sanity. But perhaps that is just my Homo sapiens *illusion, my consolation.*

*　　*　　*

Before the sun disappeared again, Mary had placed her friend in the ground, the ground of this Grey Earth.

The memory of Nemoto faded, as memories will.

But sometimes, sparked by the scent of the breeze that blew off the sea – a scent of different places – she would think of Nemoto, who had died far from home, but who had not died alone.

HUDDLE

A blue flash, a moment of searing pain.

Madeleine Meacher was home.

She had fled the solar system at a time of war. The sun itself had been under attack, from interstellar bandits called the Crackers. Thanks to Einstein, she had arrived home from the stars a *hundred thousand years* later.

She waited in trepidation for data.

His birth was violent. He was expelled from warm red-dark into black and white and *cold,* a cold that dug into his flesh immediately.

He hit a hard white surface and rolled onto his back.

He tried to lift his head. He found himself inside a little fat body, grey fur soaked in a ruddy liquid that was already freezing.

Above him there was a deep violet-blue speckled with points of light, and two grey discs. *Moons.* The word came from nowhere, into his head. Moons, two of them.

There were people with him, on this surface. Shapeless mounds of fat and fur that towered over him. *Mother.* One of them was his mother. She was speaking to him, gentle wordless murmurs.

He opened his mouth, found it clogged. He spat. Air rushed into his lungs, cold, piercing.

Tenderly his mother licked mucus off his face.

But now the great wind howled across the ice, unimpeded. It grew dark. A flurry of snow fell across him.

His mother grabbed him and tucked him into a fold of skin under her belly. He crawled onto her broad feet, to get off the ice. There was bare skin here, thick with blood vessels, and he snuggled against its heat gratefully. And there was a nipple, from which he could suckle.

He could feel the press of other people around his mother, adding their warmth.

He slept, woke, fed, slept again, barely disturbed by his mother's shuffling movements.

The sharp urgency of the cold dissipated, and time dissolved.

He could hear his mother's voice, booming through her big belly. She spoke to him, murmuring; and, gradually, he learned to reply, his own small voice piping against the vast warmth of her stomach. She told him her name – *No-sun* – and she told him about the world: people and ice and rock and food. '*Three winters:* one to grow, one to birth, one to die . . .' Birth, sex and death. The world, it seemed, was a simple place.

The cold and wind went on, unrelenting. Perhaps it would go on forever.

She told him stories, about human beings.

'. . . We survived the Collision,' she said. 'We are surviving now. Our purpose is to help others. We will never die . . .' Over and over.

To help others. It was good to have a purpose, he thought. It lifted him out of the dull ache of the cold, that reached him even here.

He slept as much as he could.

There were no ships to greet her, no signals from the inner system.

The sun was still shining, though, just as it always had.

Did that mean the Crackers had indeed been repulsed? Or had the sun simply found some new equilibrium, after their meddling?

Madeleine found three giant comets, swooping through the heart of the system. Another was on its way, sailing in from the Oort cloud, due in a century or two.

She sought out Earth.

Too far to make out details. There was oxygen in the air, though. Was that a good sign? Oxygen was reactive. The rocks would rust, taking the oxygen out of the air. Unless there was an agency to replace it. Such as life. If all the life had been scraped off the Earth, how long would it take the oxygen to disappear?

Was Earth alive or dead?

She didn't know. The alien Gaijin were her allies. They had taken her to the stars and back, in search of Reid Malenfant. But they couldn't tell her what had become of Earth.

The Earth seemed bright, white. A pale-white dot. Silent.
She sailed towards the inner system, black dread thickening.

No-sun pulled her broad feet out from under him, dumping him onto the hard ice. It was like a second birth. The ice was dazzling white, blinding him. *Spring.*

The sun was low to his right, its light hard and flat, and the sky was a deep blue-black over a landscape of rock and scattered scraps of ice. On the other horizon, he saw, the land tilted up to a range of mountains, tall, blood-red in the light of the sun. The mountains were to the west of here, the way the sun would set; to the east lay that barren plain; it was morning, here on the ice.

East. West. Morning. Spring. The words popped into his head, unbidden.

There was an austere beauty about the world. But nothing moved in it, save human beings.

He looked up at his mother. No-sun was a skinny wreck; her fur hung loose from her bones. She had spent herself in feeding him through the winter, he realized.

He tried to stand. He slithered over the ice, flapping ineffectually at its hard surface, while his mother poked and prodded him.

There was a sound of scraping.

The people had dispersed across the ice. One by one they were starting to scratch at the ice with their long teeth. The adults were gaunt pillars, wasted by the winter. There were other children, little fat balls of fur like himself.

He saw other forms on the ice: long, low, snow heaped up against them, lying still. Here and there fur showed, in pathetic tufts.

'What are *they?*'

His mother glanced apathetically. 'Not everybody makes it.'

'I don't like it here.'

She laughed, hollowly, and gnawed at the ice. 'Help me.'

After an unmeasured time they broke through the ice, to a dark liquid beneath. *Water.*

When the hole was big enough, No-sun kicked him into it.

He found himself plunged into dark fluid. He tried to breathe, and got a mouthful of chill water. He panicked, helpless, scrabbling. Dark shapes moved around him.

A strong arm wrapped around him, lifted his head into the air. He gasped gratefully.

He was bobbing, with his mother, in one of the holes in the

ice. There were other humans here, their furry heads poking out of the water, nostrils flaring as they gulped in air. They nibbled steadily at the edges of the ice.

'Here's how you eat,' No-sun said. She ducked under the surface, pulling him down, and she started to graze at the underside of the ice, scraping at it with her long incisors. When she had a mouthful, she mushed it around to melt the ice, then squirted the water out through her big, overlapping molars and premolars, and munched the remnants.

He tried to copy her, but his gums were soft, his teeth tiny and ineffective.

'Your teeth will grow,' his mother said. 'There's algae growing in the ice. See the red stuff?'

He saw it, like traces of blood in the ice. Dim understandings stirred.

'Look after your teeth.'

'What?'

'Look at him.'

A fat old man sat on the ice, alone, doleful.

'What's wrong with him?'

'His teeth wore out.' She grinned at him, showing incisors and big canines.

He stared at the old man.

The long struggle of living had begun.

Later, the light started to fade from the sky: purple, black, stars. Above the western mountains there was a curtain of light, red and violet, ghostly, shimmering, semi-transparent.

He gasped in wonder. 'It's beautiful.'

She grinned. 'The night dawn.'

But her voice was uneven; she was being pulled under the water by a heavy grey-pelted body. A snout protruded from the water and bit her neck, drawing blood. 'Ow,' she said. 'Bull –'

He was offended. 'Is that my father?'

'The Bull is everybody's father.'

'Wait,' he said. 'What's my name?'

She thought for a moment. Then she pointed up, at the sky burning above the mountains like a rocky dream. 'Night-Dawn,' she said.

And, in a swirl of bubbles, she slid into the water, laughing.

* * *

Triton was gone.

Neptune had a new ring, of chunks of rock and ice that was slowly dispersing. Because of its retrograde orbit, Triton had been doomed anyhow: to spiral closer to Neptune, to be broken up by the increasing tides. But not *yet*; not for hundreds of millions of years.

The asteroids were – sparse. They had been broken up for their resources, sailed away, destroyed in wars. The solar system, it seemed, had been overrun, mined out, just like so many others.

Even so, somehow, in her heart of hearts, Madeleine never thought it would happen *here*.

Night-Dawn fed almost all the time. So did everybody else, to prepare for the winter, which was never far from anyone's thoughts.

The adults co-operated dully, bickering.

Sometimes one or other of the men fought with the Bull. The contender was supposed to put up a fight for a while – collect scars, maybe even inflict a few himself – before backing off and letting the Bull win.

The children, Night-Dawn among them, fed and played and staged mock fights in imitation of the Bull. Night-Dawn spent most of his time in the water, feeding on the thin beds of algae, the krill and fish. He became friendly with a girl called Frazil. In the water she was sleek and graceful.

Night-Dawn learned to dive.

As the water thickened around him he could feel his chest collapse against his spine, the thump of his heart slow, his muscles grow more sluggish as his body conserved its air. He learned to enjoy the pulse of the long muscles in his legs and back, the warm satisfaction of cramming his jaw with tasty krill. It was dark under the ice, even at the height of summer, and the calls of the humans echoed from the dim white roof.

He dived deep, reaching as far as the bottom of the water, a hard invisible floor. Vegetation clung here, and there were a few fat, reluctant fishes.

And the bones of children.

Some of the children did not grow well. When they died, their parents delivered their misshapen little bodies to the water, crying and cursing the sunlight.

His mother told him about the Collision.

Something had come barrelling out of the sky, and the Moon

– one or other of them – had leapt out of the belly of the Earth. The water, the air itself was ripped from the world. Giant waves reared in the very rock, throwing the people high, crushing them or burning them or drowning them.

But they – the people of the ice – survived all this in a deep hole in the ground, No-sun said. They had been given a privileged shelter, and a mission: to help others, less fortunate, after the calamity.

They had spilled out of their hole in the ground, ready to help.

Most had frozen to death, immediately.

They had food, from their hole, but it did not last long; they had tools to help them survive, but they broke and wore out and shattered. People were forced to dig with their teeth in the ice, as Night-Dawn did now.

Their problems did not end with hunger and cold. The thinness of the air made the sun into a new enemy.

Many babies were born changed. Most died. But some survived, better suited to the cold. Hearts accelerated, life shortened. People changed, moulded like slush in the warm palm of the sun.

Night-Dawn was intrigued by the story. But that was all it was: a story, irrelevant to Night-Dawn's world, which was a plain of rock, a frozen pond of ice, people scraping for sparse mouthfuls of food. *How, why, when:* the time for such questions, on the blasted face of Earth, had passed.

And yet they troubled Night-Dark, as he huddled with the others, half-asleep.

One day – in the water, with the soft back fur of Frazil pressed against his chest – he felt something stir beneath his belly. He wriggled experimentally, rubbing the bump against the girl.

She moved away, muttering. But she looked back at him, and he thought she smiled. Her fur was indeed sleek and perfect.

He showed his erection to his mother. She inspected it gravely; it stuck out of his fur like a splinter of ice.

'Soon you will have a choice to make.'

'What choice?'

But she would not reply. She waddled away and dropped into the water.

The erection faded after a while, but it came back. More and more frequently, in fact.

He showed it to Frazil.

Her fur ruffled up into a ball. 'It's small,' she said dubiously. 'Do you know what to do?'

'I think so. I've watched the Bull.'

'All right.'

She turned her back, looking over her shoulder at him, and reached for her genital slit.

But now a fat arm slammed into his back. He crashed to the ice, falling painfully on his penis, which shrank back immediately.

It was the Bull, his father. The huge man was a mountain of flesh and muscle, silhouetted against a violet sky. He hauled out his own penis from under his greying fur. It was a fat, battered lump of flesh. He waggled it at Night-Dawn. 'I'm the Bull. Not you. Frazil is mine.'

Now Night-Dawn understood the choice his mother had set out before him.

He felt something gather within him. Not anger: a sense of wrongness.

'I won't fight you,' he said to the Bull. 'Humans shouldn't behave like this.'

The Bull roared, opened his mouth to display his canines, and turned away from him.

Frazil slipped into the water, to evade the Bull.

Night-Dawn was left alone, frustrated, baffled.

As winter approached, a sense of oppression, of wrongness, gathered over Night-Dawn, and his mood darkened like the days.

People did *nothing* but feed and breed and die.

He watched the Bull. Behind the old man's back, even as he bullied and assaulted the smaller males, some of the other men approached the women and girls and coupled furtively. It happened all the time. Probably the group would have died out long ago if only the children of the Bull were permitted to be conceived.

The Bull was an absurdity, then, even as he dominated the little group. Night-Dawn wondered if the Bull was truly his father.

. . . Sometimes at night he watched the flags of night dawn ripple over the mountains. He wondered why the night dawns should come there, and nowhere else.

Perhaps the air was thicker there. Perhaps it was warmer beyond the mountains; perhaps there were people there.

But there was little time for reflection.

It got colder, fiercely so.

As the ice holes began to freeze over, the people emerged reluc-tantly from the water, standing on the hardening ice.

In a freezing hole, a slush of ice crystal clumps would gather. His mother called that frazil. Then, when the slush had condensed to form a solid surface, it took on a dull matte appearance – grease ice. The waves beneath the larger holes made the grease ice gather in wide, flat pancakes, with here and there stray, protruding crys-tals, called congelation. At last, the new ice grew harder and compressed with groans and cracks, into pack ice.

There were lots of words for ice.

And after the holes were frozen over the water – and their only food supply – was cut off, for six months.

When the blizzards came, the huddle began.

The adults and children – some of them little fat balls of fur barely able to walk – came together, bodies pressed close, enveloping Night-Dawn in a welcome warmth, the shallow swell of their breathing pressing against him.

The snow, flecked with ice splinters, came at them horizontally. Night-Dawn tucked his head as deep as he could into the press of bodies, keeping his eyes squeezed closed.

Night fell. Day returned. He slept, in patches, standing up.

Sometimes he could hear people talking. But then the wind rose to a scream, drowning human voices.

The days wore away, still shortening, as dark as the nights.

The group shifted, subtly. People were moving around him. He got colder. Suddenly somebody moved away, a fat man, and Night-Dawn found himself exposed to the wind. The cold cut into him, shocking him awake.

He tried to push back into the mass of bodies, to regain the warmth.

The disturbance spread like a ripple through the group. He saw heads raised, eyes crusted with sleep and snow. With the group's tightness broken, a mass of hot air rose from the compressed bodies, steaming, frosting, bright in the double-shadowed Moonlight.

Here was No-sun, blocking his way. 'Stay out there. You have to take your turn.'

'But it's *cold*.'

She turned away.

He tucked his head under his arm and turned his back to the wind. He stood the cold as long as he could.

Then, following the lead of others, he worked his way around the rim of the group, to its leeward side. At least here he was sheltered. And after a time more came around, shivering and iced up from their time to windward, and gradually he was encased once more in warmth.

Isolated on their scrap of ice, with no shelter save each other's bodies from the wind and snow, the little group of humans huddled in silence. As they took their turns at the windward side, the group shifted slowly across the ice, a creeping mat of fur.

Sometimes children were born onto the ice. The people pushed around closely, to protect the new-born, and its mother would tuck it away into the warmth of her body. Occasionally one of them fell away, and remained where she or he lay, as the group moved on.

This was the huddle: a black disc of fur and flesh and human bones, swept by the storms of Earth's unending winter.

A hundred thousand years after the Collision, all humans had left was each other.

Mars was a deserted ice ball, as it had always been.

Venus was choked by acid clouds, its surface glowing red hot.

Mercury was, simply, gone. She smiled at that. Mercury had been the last refuge of mankind. Perhaps humanity persisted, somewhere out there, beyond.

The Moon appeared restored: the craters, the great lava seas, the gleaming, ancient highlands. As if life had never touched its ancient face. But in the telescopic viewers she could see the traces of mankind, persisting even now. Abandoned dwellings, clinging to crater walls. Canals cut from crater to crater. Even water marks in some of the smaller craters, like drained bath tubs. Air, frozen out in the permanent shadows of the poles.

And to Earth, at last, she turned.

Spring came slowly.

Dwarfed by the desolate, rocky landscape, bereft of shelter, the humans scratched at their isolated puddle of ice, beginning the year's feeding.

Night-Dawn scraped ice from his eyes. He felt as if he were waking from a year-long sleep. This was his second spring, and it would be the summer of his manhood. He would father children,

teach them and protect them through the coming winter. Despite
the depletion of his winter fat, he felt strong, vigorous.

He found Frazil. They stood together, wordless, on the thick
early-spring ice.

Somebody roared in his ear, hot foul breath on his neck.

It was, of course, the Bull. The old man would not see another
winter; his ragged fur lay loose on his huge, empty frame, riven
by the scars of forgotten, meaningless battles. But he was still
immense and strong, still the Bull.

Without preamble, the Bull sank his teeth into Night-Dawn's
neck, and pulled away a lump of flesh, which he chewed noisily.

Night-Dawn backed away, appalled, breathing hard, blood
running down his fur.

Frazil and No-sun were here with him.

'Challenge him,' No-sun said.

'I don't want to fight.'

'Then let him die,' Frazil said. 'He is old and stupid. We can
couple despite him.' There was a bellow. The Bull was facing him,
pawing at the ice with a great scaly foot.

'I don't wish to fight you,' Night-Dawn said.

The Bull laughed, and lumbered forward, wheezing.

Night-Dawn stood his ground, braced his feet against the ice,
and put his head down.

The Bull's roar turned to alarm, and he tried to stop; but his
feet could gain no purchase.

His mouth slammed over Night-Dawn's skull. Night-Dawn
screamed as the Bull's teeth grated through his fur and flesh to
his very bone.

They bounced off each other. Night-Dawn felt himself tumbling
back, and finished up on his backside on the ice. His chest felt
crushed; he laboured to breathe. He could barely see through the
blood streaming into his eyes.

The Bull was lying on his back, his loose belly hoisted towards
the violet sky. He was feeling his mouth with his fingers.

He let out a long, despairing moan.

No-sun helped Night-Dawn to his feet. 'You did it. *You smashed
his teeth*, Night-Dawn. He'll be dead in days.'

'I didn't mean to –'

His mother leaned close. 'You're the Bull now. You can couple
with who you like. Even me, if you want to.'

'. . . Night-Dawn.'

Here came Frazil. She was smiling. She turned her back to him, bent over, and pulled open her genital slit. His penis rose in response, without his volition.

He coupled with her quickly. He did it at the centre of a circle of watching, envious, calculating men. It brought him no joy, and they parted without words.

He avoided the Bull until the old man had starved to death, gums bleeding from ice cuts, and the others had dumped his body into a water hole.

For Night-Dawn, everything was different after that.

He was the Bull. He could couple with who he liked. He stayed with Frazil. But even coupling with Frazil brought him little pleasure.

One day he was challenged by another young man called One-Tusk, over a woman Night-Dawn barely knew, called Ice-Cloud.

'Fight, damn you,' One-Tusk lisped.

'We shouldn't fight. I don't care about Ice-Cloud.'

One-Tusk growled, pursued him for a while, then gave up. Night-Dawn saw him try to mate with one of the women, but she laughed at him and pushed him away.

Frazil came to him. 'We can't live like this. You're the Bull. Act like it.'

'To fight, to eat, to huddle, to raise children, to die . . . There must be more, Frazil.'

She sighed. 'Like what?'

'The Collision. Our purpose.'

She studied him. 'Night-Dawn, listen to me. The Collision is a pretty story. Something to make us feel better, while we suck scum out of ice.'

That was Frazil, he thought fondly. Practical. Unimaginative.

'Anyhow,' she said, 'where are the people we are supposed to help?'

He pointed to the western horizon: the rising ground, the place beyond the blue-grey mountains. 'There, perhaps.'

The next day, he called together the people. They stood in ranks on the ice, their fur spiky, rows of dark shapes in an empty landscape.

'We are all humans,' he said boldly. 'The Collision threw us here, onto the ice.' Night-Dawn pointed to the distant mountains.

246

'We must go there. Maybe there are people there. Maybe they are waiting for us, to huddle with them.'

Somebody laughed.

'Why now?' asked the woman, Ice-Cloud.

'If not now, when? Now is no different from any other time, on the ice. I'll go alone if I have to.'

People started to walk away, back to the ice holes.

All, except for Frazil and No-sun and One-Tusk.

No-sun, his mother, said, 'You'll die if you go alone. I suppose it's my fault you're like this.'

One-Tusk said, 'Do you really think there are people in the mountains?'

'Please don't go,' Frazil said. 'This is our summer. You will waste your life.'

'I'm sorry,' he said.

'You're the Bull. You have everything we can offer.'

'It's not enough.'

He turned his back, faced the mountains and began to walk.

He walked past the droppings and blood smears and scars in the ice, the evidence of humans.

He stopped and looked back.

The people had lined up to watch him go – all except for two men who were fighting viciously, no doubt contesting his succession, and a man and woman who were coupling vigorously. And except for Frazil and No-sun and One-Tusk, who padded across the ice after him.

He turned and walked on, until he reached bare, untrodden ice.

After the first day of walking, the ice got thinner.

At last they reached a place where there was no free water beneath, the ice firmly bonded to a surface of dark rock. And when they walked a little further, the rock bed itself emerged from beneath the ice.

Night-Dawn stared at it in fascination and fear. It was black and deep and hard under his feet, and he missed the slick compressibility of ice.

The next day they came to another ice pool: smaller than their own, but a welcome sight nonetheless. They ran gleefully onto its cool white surface. They scraped holes into the ice, and fed deeply.

They stayed a night. But the next day they walked onto rock again, and Night-Dawn could see no more ice ahead.

The rock began to rise, becoming a slope.

They had no food. Occasionally they took scrapes at the rising stone, but it threatened to crack their teeth.

At night the wind was bitter, spilling off the flanks of the mountains, and they huddled as best they could, their backs to the cold, their faces and bellies together.

'We'll die,' One-Tusk would whisper.

'We won't die,' Night-Dawn said. 'We have our fat.'

'That's supposed to last us through the winter,' hissed No-sun.

One-Tusk shivered and moved a little more to leeward. 'I wished to father a child,' he said. 'By Ice-Cloud. I could not. Ice-Cloud mocked me. After that nobody would couple with me.'

'Ice-Cloud should have come to you, Night-Dawn. You are the Bull,' No-sun muttered.

'I'm sorry,' Night-Dawn said to One-Tusk. 'I have fathered no children yet. Not every coupling –'

One-Tusk said, 'Do you really think it will be warm in the mountains?'

'Try to sleep now,' said Frazil sensibly.

They were many days on the rising rock. The air grew thinner. The sky was never brighter than a deep violet blue.

The mountains, at last, grew nearer. On clear days the sun cast long shadows that reached out to them.

Night-Dawn saw a gap in the mountains, a cleft through which he could sometimes see a slice of blue-violet sky. They turned that way, and walked on.

Still they climbed; still the air thinned.

They came to the pass through the mountains. It was a narrow gully. Its mouth was broad, and there was broken rock, evidently cracked off the gully sides.

Night-Dawn led them forward.

Soon the walls narrowed around him, the rock slick with hard grey ice. His feet slipped from under him, and he banged knees and hips against bone-hard ice. He was not, he knew, made for climbing. And besides, he had never been *surrounded* before, except in the huddle. He felt trapped, confined.

He persisted, doggedly.

His world closed down to the aches of his body, the gully around him, the search for the next handhold.

. . . The air was *hot*.

248

He stopped, stunned by this realization.

With renewed excitement, he lodged his stubby fingers in crevices in the rock, and hauled himself upwards.

At last the gully grew narrower.

He reached the top and dragged himself up over the edge, panting, fur steaming.

. . . There were no people here.

He was standing at the rim of a great bowl cut into the hard black rock. And at the base of the bowl was a red liquid, bubbling slowly. Steam gathered in great clouds over the bubbling pool, laced with yellowish fumes that stank strongly. It was a place of rock and gas, not of people.

Frazil came to stand beside him. She was breathing hard, and her mouth was wide open, her arms spread wide, to shed heat.

They stood before the bowl of heat, drawn by some ancient imperative to the warmth, and yet repelled by its suffocating thickness.

'The Collision,' she said.

'What?'

'Once, the whole world was covered with such pools. Rock, melted by the great heat of the Collision.'

'The Collision is just a story, you said.'

She grunted. 'I've been wrong before.'

His disappointment was crushing. 'Nobody could live here. There is warmth, but it is poisonous.' He found it hard even to think, so huge was his sense of failure.

He stood away from the others and looked around.

Back the way they had come, the uniform-hard blackness was broken only by scattered islands of grey-white: ice pools, Night-Dawn knew, like the one he had left behind.

Turning, he could see the sweep of the mountains clearly: he was breaching a great inward-curving wall, a great complex string of peaks that spread from horizon to horizon, gaunt under the blue-purple sky.

And ahead of him, ice had gathered in pools and crevasses at the feet of the mountains, lapping against the rock walls as if frustrated – save in one place, where a great tongue of ice had broken through. *Glacier*, he thought.

He saw that they could walk around the bowl of bubbling liquid rock and reach the head of the glacier, perhaps before night fell, and then move on, beyond these mountains. Hope sparked. Perhaps what he sought lay there.

'I'm exhausted,' No-sun said, a pillar of fur slumped against a heap of rock. 'We should go back.'

Night-Dawn, distracted by his plans, turned to her. 'Why?'

'We are creatures of cold. Feel how you burn up inside your fat. This is not our place . . .'

'Look,' breathed One-Tusk, coming up to them.

He was carrying a rock he'd cracked open. Inside there was a thin line of red and black. Algae, perhaps. And, in a hollow in the rock, small insects wriggled, their red shells bright.

Frazil fell on the rock, gnawing at it eagerly.

The others quickly grabbed handfuls of rocks and began to crack them open.

They spent the night in a hollow at the base of the glacier.

In the morning they clambered up onto its smooth, rock-littered surface. The ice groaned as it was compressed by its forced passage through the mountains, which towered above them to either side, blue-grey and forbidding.

At the glacier's highest point, they saw that the river of ice descended to an icy plain. And the plain led to another wall of mountains, so remote it was almost lost in the horizon's mist.

'More walls,' groaned One-Tusk. 'Walls that go on forever.'

'I don't think so,' said Night-Dawn. He swept his arm along the line of the distant peaks, which glowed pink in the sun. 'I think they curve. You see?'

'I can't tell,' muttered No-sun, squinting.

With splayed toes on the ice, Night-Dawn scraped three parallel curves – then, tentatively, he joined them up into concentric circles. 'Curved walls of mountains. Maybe that's what we're walking into,' he said. 'Like a ripples in a water hole.'

'Ripples, in rock?' Frazil asked sceptically.

'If the Collision stories are true, it's possible.'

No-sun tapped at the centre of his picture. 'And what will we find here?'

'I don't know.'

They rested a while, and moved on.

The glacier began to descend so rapidly they had some trouble keeping their feet. The ice here, under tension, was cracked, and there were many ravines.

At last they came to a kind of cliff, hundreds of times taller than Night-Dawn. The glacier was tumbling gracefully into the ice plain, great blocks of it carving away. This ice sheet was much wider than the pool they had left behind, so wide, in fact, it lapped to left and right as far as they could see and all the way to the far mountains. Ice lay on the surface in great broken sheets, but clear water, blue-black, was visible in the gaps.

It was – together they found the word, deep in their engineered memories – it was a *sea*.

'Perhaps this is a circular sea,' One-Tusk said, excited. 'Perhaps it fills up the ring between the mountains.'

'Perhaps.'

They clambered down the glacier, caution and eagerness warring in Night-Dawn's heart.

There was a shallow beach here, of shattered stone. The beach was littered with droppings, black-and-white streaks, and half-eaten krill.

In his short life, Night-Dawn had seen no creatures save fish, krill, algae and humans. But this beach did not bear the mark of humans like themselves. He struggled to imagine what might live here.

Without hesitation, One-Tusk ran to a slab of pack ice, loosely anchored. With a yell he dropped off the end into the water.

No-sun fluffed up her fur. 'I don't like it here –'

Bubbles were coming out of the water, where One-Tusk had dived.

Night-Dawn rushed to the edge of the water.

One-Tusk surfaced, screaming, in a flurry of foam. Half his scalp was torn away, exposing pink raw flesh, the white of bone.

An immense shape loomed out of the water after him: Night-Dawn glimpsed a pink mouth, peg-like teeth, a dangling wattle, small black eyes. The huge mouth closed around One-Tusk's neck.

He had time for one more scream – and then he was gone, dragged under the surface again.

The thick, sluggish water grew calm; last bubbles broke the surface, pink with blood.

Night-Dawn and the others huddled together.

'He is dead,' Frazil said.

'We all die,' said No-sun. 'Death is easy.'

'Did you see its eyes?' Frazil asked.

'Yes. *Human*,' No-sun said bleakly. 'Not like us, but human.'

'Perhaps there were other ways to survive the Collision.'

No-sun turned on her son. 'Are we supposed to huddle with *that*, Night-Dawn?'

Night-Dawn, shocked, unable to speak, was beyond calculation. He explored his heart, searching for grief for loyal, confused One-Tusk.

They stayed on the beach for many days, fearful of the inhabited water. They ate nothing but scavenged scraps of crushed, half-rotten krill left behind by whatever creatures had lived here.

'We should go back,' said No-sun at last.

'We can't,' Night-Dawn whispered. 'It's already too late. We couldn't get back to the huddle before winter.'

'But we can't stay here,' Frazil said.

'So we go on.' No-sun laughed, her voice thin and weak. 'We go on, across the sea, until we can't go on any more.'

'Or until we find shelter,' Night-Dawn said.

'Oh, yes,' No-sun whispered. 'There is that.'

So they walked on, over the pack ice.

This was no mere pond, as they had left behind; this was an ocean.

The ice was thin, partially melted, poorly packed. Here and there the ice was piled up into cliffs and mountains that towered over them; the ice hills were eroded, shaped smooth by the wind, carved into fantastic arches and spires and hollows. The ice was every shade of blue. And when the sun set its light filled the ice shapes with pink, red and orange.

There was a cacophony of noise: groans and cracks, as the ice moved around them. But there were no human voices, save their own: only the empty noise of the ice – and the occasional murmur, Night-Dawn thought, of whatever giant beasts inhabited this huge sea.

They walked for days. The mountain chain they had left behind dwindled, dipping into the mist of the horizon; and the chain ahead of them approached with stultifying slowness. He imagined looking down on himself, a small, determined speck walking steadily across this great, moulded landscape, working towards the mysteries of the centre.

Food was easy to find. The slushy ice was soft and easy to break through.

No-sun would walk only slowly now. And she would not eat. Her memory of the monster which had snapped up One-Tusk was too strong. Night-Dawn even braved the water to bring her fish, but they were strange: ghostly-white creatures with flattened heads, sharp teeth. No-sun pushed them away, saying she preferred to consume her own good fat. And so she grew steadily more wasted.

Until there came a day when, waking, she would not move at all. She stood at the centre of a fat, stable ice floe, a pillar of loose flesh, rolls of fur cascading down a frame leached of fat.

Night-Dawn stood before her, punched her lightly, cajoled her. 'Leave me here,' she said. 'It's my time anyhow.'

'No. It isn't right.'

She laughed, and fluid rattled on her lungs. '*Right. Wrong.* You're a dreamer. You always were. It's my fault, probably.'

She subsided, as if deflating, and fell back onto the ice.

He knelt and cradled her head in his lap. He stayed there all night, the cold of the ice seeping through the flesh of his knees.

In the morning, stiff with the cold, they took her to the edge of the ice floe and tipped her into the water, for the benefit of the creatures of this giant sea.

After more days of walking, the ice grew thin, the water beneath shallow.

Another day of this and they came to a slope of hard black rock, that pushed its way out of the ice and rose up before them.

The black rock was hard-edged and cold under Night-Dawn's feet, its rise unrelenting. As far as he could see to left and right, the ridge was solid, unbroken, with no convenient passes for them to follow, the sky lidded over by cloud.

They grasped each other's hands and pressed up the slope.

The climb exhausted Night-Dawn immediately. And there was nothing to eat or drink, here on the high rocks, not so much as a scrap of ice. Soon, even the air grew thin; he struggled to drag energy from its pale substance.

When they slept, they stood on hard black rock. Night-Dawn feared and hated the rock; it was an enemy, rooted deep in the Earth.

On the fourth day of this they entered the clouds, and he could not even see where his next step should be placed. With the thin, icy moisture in his lungs and spreading on his fur he felt trapped, as if under some infinite ice layer, far from any air hole. He struggled to breathe, and if he slept, he woke consumed by a thin panic. At such times he clung to Frazil and remembered who he was and where he had come from and why he had come so far. He was a human being, and he had a mission that he would fulfil.

Then, one morning, they broke through the last ragged clouds.

Though it was close to midday the sky was as dark as he had ever seen it, a deep violet blue. The only clouds were thin sheets of ice crystals, high above. And – he saw, gasping with astonishment – there were *stars* shining, even now, in the middle of the sunlit day.

The slope seemed to reach a crest, a short way ahead of him. They walked on. The air was thin, a whisper in his lungs, and he was suspended in silence; only the rasp of Frazil's shallow breath, the soft slap of their footsteps on the rock, broke up the stillness.

He reached the crest. The rock wall descended sharply from here, he saw, soon vanishing into layers of fat, fluffy clouds.

And, when he looked ahead, he saw a mountain.

Far ahead of them, dominating the horizon, it was a single peak that thrust out of scattered clouds, towering even over their elevated position here, its walls sheer and stark. Its flanks were girdled with ice, but the peak itself was bare black rock – too high even for ice to gather, he surmised – perhaps so high it thrust out of the very air itself.

It must be the greatest mountain in the world.

And beyond it there was a further line of mountains, he saw, like a line of broken teeth, marking the far horizon. When he looked to left and right, he could see how those mountains joined the crest he had climbed, in a giant unbroken ring around that great, central fist of rock.

It was a giant rock ripple, just as he had sketched in the ice. Perhaps this was the centre, the very heart of the great systems of mountain rings and circular seas he had penetrated.

An ocean lapped around the base of the mountain. He could see that glaciers flowed down its heroic base, rivers of ice dwarfed by the mountain's immensity. There was ice in the ocean too – pack ice, and icebergs like great eroded islands, white, carved. Some manner of creatures were visible on the bergs, black and grey dots against the pristine white of the ice, too distant for him to make out. But this sea was mostly melted, a band of blue-black.

The slope of black rock continued below him – far, far onwards, until it all but disappeared into the misty air at the base of this bowl of land. But he could see that it reached a beach of some sort, of shattered, eroded rock sprinkled with snow, against which waves sluggishly lapped.

There was a belt of land around the sea, cradled by the ring mountains, fringed by the sea. And it was covered by *life*, great furry sheets of it. From this height it looked like an encrustation of algae. But he knew there must be living things there much greater in scale than any he had seen before.

'. . . It is a bowl,' Frazil breathed.

'What?'

'Look down there. This is a great bowl, of clouds and water and light, on whose lip we stand. We will be safe down there, away from the rock and ice.'

He saw she was right. This was indeed a bowl – presumably the great scar left where one or other of the Moons had torn itself loose of the Earth, just as the stories said. And these rings of mountains were ripples in the rock, frozen as if ice.

He forgot his hunger, his thirst, even the lack of air here; eagerly they began to hurry down the slope.

The air rapidly thickened.

But his breathing did not become any easier, for it grew *warm*, warmer than he had ever known it. Steam began to rise from his thick, heavy fur. He opened his mouth and raised his nostril flaps wide, sucking in the air. It was as if the heat of this giant sheltering bowl was now, at the last, driving them back.

But they did not give up their relentless descent, and he gathered the last of his strength.

The air beneath them cleared further.

Overwhelmed, Night-Dawn stopped.

The prolific land around the central sea was divided into neat shapes, he saw now, and here and there smoke rose. It was a made landscape. The work of people.

Humans were sheltered here. It was a final irony, that people should find shelter at the bottom of the great pit dug out of the Earth by the world-wrecking Collision.

. . . And there was a colour to that deep, cupped world, emerging now from the mist. Something he had never seen before; and yet the word for it dropped into place, just as had his first words after birth.

'*Green*,' Frazil said.

'Green. Yes . . .'

He was stunned by the brilliance of the colour against the black rock, the dull blue-grey of the sea. But even as he looked into the pit of warmth and air, he felt a deep sadness. For he already knew he could never reach that deep shelter, peer up at the giant green living things; this body which shielded him from cold would allow heat to kill him.

Somebody spoke.

The crater was immense.

It must have been the worst impact since the end of the great bombardment that had greeted Earth's formation.

The Gaijin helped her understand.

This was nothing to do with the Cracker wars of the remote past. In the long ages since then, the twin suns of Alpha Centauri had come sailing by the solar system, making a closest approach of about three light years. That was more than two hundred thousand astronomical units, a long way out. The twin suns hadn't come close enough to interfere with the orbits of the planets, still less the sun itself. But they were close enough to disturb the comets, sleeping through their orbits in the Oort cloud, that great sparse fuzzy halo in the outer dark.

Because of Alpha's grazing approach, more than two hundred thousand giant comets would cross Earth's orbit over the next twenty million years. The Gaijin had no data on how many might strike the planet, or its Moon. This game of cosmic billiards was nothing to do with intelligence, nothing to do with war. It was just a matter of the random motion of the stars, whizzing around the Galaxy like molecules in a gas.

Even without predatory colonists, she thought, the universe is a dangerous place.

. . . Yes – but if we'd been left undisturbed, if not for these squabbling, colonizing Eeties, we would have figured out how to push the damn things away for ourselves.

Too late now. Damn, damn.

He cried out, spun around. Frazil was standing stock still, staring up.

There was a creature standing here. Like a tall, very skinny human.

It *was* a human, he saw. A woman. Her face was small and neat, and there was barely a drop of fat on her, save around the hips, buttocks and breasts. Her chest was small. She had a coat of some fine fur – no, he realized with shock; she was wearing a false skin, that hugged her bare flesh tightly. She was carrying green stuff, food perhaps, in a basket of false skin.

She was twice his height.

Her eyes were undoubtedly human, though, as human as his, and her gaze was locked on his face. And in her eyes, he read fear.

Fear, and disgust.

He stepped forward. 'We have come to help you,' he said.

'Yes,' said Frazil.

'We have come far –'

The tall woman spoke again, but he could not understand her. Even her voice was strange – thin, emanating from that shallow chest. She spoke again, and pointed, down towards the surface of the sea, far below.

Now he looked more closely he could see movement on the beach. Small dots, moving around. People, perhaps, like this girl. Some of them were small. Children, running free. Many children.

The woman turned, and started climbing away from them, down the slope towards her world, carrying whatever she had gathered from these high banks. She was shaking a fist at them now. She even bent to pick up a sharp stone and threw it towards Frazil; it fell short, clattering harmlessly.

Madeleine made her home in the depths of the crater, where air pooled, thick.

A single Gaijin flower-ship stayed in orbit, in case she called. The Gaijin seemed prepared to wait forever. Sometimes she glimpsed it, at dawn, at sunset.

Madeleine's conditions were hardly primitive. She had the Gaijin lander, which served as a fine shelter. It was stocked with food-preparation technology; all she had to do was cram its hoppers full of vegetable material, once or twice a week. But she also had her garden, and the fruits and berries she gathered from the sparse trees here, and she drank exclusively water from the snow-melt streams. It pleased her to live as close to the Earth as she could.

She didn't go near the circular sea, though. There were creatures living in there she couldn't identify. Their sleek forms scarcely looked friendly. And she thought there were human-like creatures on the far side of the sea. She didn't approach them either.

It was a world of scale and depth, of perspective. She would lie on her porch and watch the waterfalls glimmering through the air from the rocky walls, kilometres above, and gaze even beyond that, at the feathery tails of the great comets that swept across the sky.

Sometimes she saw creatures moving against the ice which lapped against the rim mountains, far above her. Her sensor packs, even at highest magnification, showed her only penguin-like creatures, waddling over the ice, huddling against ferocious winds. Perhaps they were indeed some remote descendants of penguins. Or even post-humans, gruesomely adapted to survive. She felt no temptation to seek them out. But their presence disturbed her.

The Moon's grey face was reassuringly familiar. The tide of life on that patient satellite had long receded, and the face of the Man was restored to patient watchfulness. Just as she was.

It was a vigil, Madeleine had decided.

Once, she'd read of an island called San Nicolas, off Los Angeles. Long before the coming of the Europeans, it had been inhabited by native Americans. But the settlement had collapsed, the numbers dwindling, one by one.

The last survivor was a woman who had lived on, in complete isolation, for eighteen years.

How had *she* spent her time? Had she watched for canoes that had never come, hoped to see the return of some last, desperate emigrants? Or had she simply savoured her memories, and waited?

She tried not to think too hard. What good would that do?

Madeleine Meacher was no vigil-keeper.

She grew restless, despite herself.

This wasn't her world, whether it belonged to the post-humans or not. Anyhow she had never been too good at sitting still.

She'd never forgotten her alternative plan, as she'd discussed with Malenfant. To travel on and on. Why the hell not?

But if she entered the Saddle Point network again, she might never come out. If so, she supposed, she'd never know about it.

She watched the sky, studying the changed stars. When the wind picked up, stirring her wispy hair, she went into her lander and prepared her evening meal.

The next day, she called the Gaijin down from the sky.

'I don't understand,' Frazil said.

Night-Dawn thought of the loathing he had seen in the strange woman's eyes. He saw himself through her eyes: squat, fat, waddling, as if deformed.

He felt shame. 'We are not welcome here,' he said.

'We must bring the others here,' Frazil was saying.

'And what then? Beg to be allowed to stay, to enter the warmth? No. We will go home.'

'Home? To a place where people live a handful of winters, and must scrape food from ice with their teeth? How can that compare to *this*?'

He took her hands. 'But this is not for us. We are monsters to these people. As they are to us. And we cannot live here.'

She stared into the pit of light and green. 'But in time, our children might learn to live there. Just as we learned to live on the ice.'

The longing in her voice was painful. He thought of the generations who had lived out their short, bleak lives on the ice. He thought of his mother, who had sought to protect him to the end; poor One-Tusk, who had died without seeing the people of the mountains; dear, loyal Frazil, who had walked to the edge of the world at his side.

'Listen to me. Let these people have their hole in the ground. We have a *world*. We can live anywhere. We must go back and tell our people so.'

She sniffed. 'Dear Night-Dawn. Always dreaming. But first we must eat, for winter is coming.'

'Yes. First we eat.'

They inspected the rock that surrounded them. There was green *here,* he saw now, thin traces of it that clung to the surface of the rock. In some places it grew away from the rock face, brave little balls of it no bigger than his fist, and here and there fine fur-like sproutings.

They bent, reaching together for the green shoots.

The shadows lengthened. The sun was descending towards the circular sea, and one of Earth's two Moons was rising.

PARADOX

When Kate had first met Malenfant, out at JPL, she could smell desert dust on him, hot and dry as a sauna.

But he was suspicious of her. Maybe he was suspicious of all journalists.

'And you think there's a story in the Fermi Paradox?'

She shrugged, non-committal. 'I'm more interested in you, Colonel Malenfant.'

He was immediately defensive. 'Just Malenfant.'

'Of all the projects you could have undertaken when you were grounded, why front a stunt like this?'

He shrugged. 'Look, if you want to call this a stunt, fine. But we're extending the envelope here. Today we'll prove that we can touch other worlds. Maybe an astronaut is the right face to head up a groundbreaker project like this.'

'Ex-astronaut.'

His grin faded.

Fishing for an angle, she said, 'Is that why you're here? You were born in 1960, weren't you? So you remember Apollo. But by the time you grew up cheaper and smarter robots had taken over the exploring. Now NASA says that when the International Space Station finally reaches the end of its life, it plans no more manned spaceflight of any sort. Is this laser project a compensation for your wash-out, Malenfant?'

He barked a laugh. 'You know, you aren't as smart as you think you are, Ms Manzoni. It's your brand of personality-oriented cod-psychology bullshit that has brought down –'

'Are you lonely?'

That pulled him up. 'What?'

'The Fermi Paradox is all about loneliness, isn't it? – the loneliness of mankind, orphaned in an empty universe . . . Your wife, Emma, died a decade back. I know you have a son, but you never remarried –'

He glared at her. 'You're full of shit, lady.'

She returned his glare, satisfied she had hit the mark.

Later he would say to her, 'The universe is out there, like it or not, regardless of our soap-opera human dramas. And it is bigger than your petty concerns. And the questions I deal with are bigger than your trivial pestering.'

'Like Fermi.'

'Like Fermi, yes.'

'But you don't have any answers to Fermi.'

'Oh, that isn't the trouble at all, Ms Manzoni. Don't you understand that much? The trouble is we have far too many answers . . .'

REFUGIUM

Celso and I were ejected from the *Sally Brind*. Frank Paulis had brought us to the Oort Cloud, that misty belt far from the sun where huge comets glide like deep-sea fish.

Before us, an alien craft sparkled in the starlight.

On the inside of my suit helmet a tiny softscreen popped into life and filled up with a picture of Paulis. He was wizened, somewhere over eighty years old, but his eyes glittered, sharp.

Even now, I begged. 'Paulis. Don't make me do this.'

Paulis was in a bathrobe; behind his steam billowed. He was in his spa at the heart of the *Brind* – a luxury from which Celso and I had been excluded for the long hundred days it had taken to haul us all the way out here. 'Your grandfather would be ashamed of you, Michael Malenfant. You forfeited choice when you let yourself be put up for sale in a debtors' auction.'

'I just had a streak of bad luck.'

'A streak spanning fifteen years hustling pool and a mountain of bad debts?'

Celso studied me with brown eyes full of pity. 'Do not whine, my friend.'

'Paulis, I don't care who the hell my grandfather was. You can see I'm no astronaut. I'm forty years old, for Christ's sake. And I'm not the brightest guy in the world –'

'True, but unimportant. The whole point of this experiment is to send humans where we haven't sent humans before. Exactly who probably doesn't matter. Look at the Bubble, Malenfant.'

The alien ship was a ten-foot balloon plastered with rubies. Celso was already inspecting its interior in an intelligent sort of way.

Paulis said, 'Remember your briefings. You can see it's a hollow sphere. There's an open hatchway. We know that if you close the hatch the device will accelerate away. We have evidence that its effective final speed is many times the speed of light. In fact, many millions of times.'

'Impossible,' said Celso.

Paulis smiled. 'Evidently, not everyone agrees. What a marvellous adventure! I only wish I could come with you.'

'Like hell you do, you dried-up old bastard.'

He took a gloating sip from a frosted glass. 'Malenfant, you are here because of faults in your personality.'

'I'm here because of people like you.'

Celso took my arm.

'In about two minutes,' Paulis said cheerfully, 'the pilot of the *Sally Brind* is going to come out of the airlock and shoot you both in the temple. Unless you're in that Bubble with the hatch closed.'

Celso pushed me towards the glittering ball.

I said, 'I won't forget you, Paulis. I'll be thinking of you every damn minute –'

But he only grinned.

My name is Reid Malenfant.

You know me, Michael. And you know I was always an incorrigible space cadet. I campaigned for, among other things, private mining expeditions to the asteroids. I hope you know my pal, Frank J. Paulis, who went out there and did what I only talked about.

But I don't want to talk about that. Not here, not in this letter. I want to be more personal. I want you to understand why your grandpappy gave over his life to a single, consuming project.

For me, it started with a simple question: What use are the stars?

Paulis had installed basic life-support gear in the Bubble. Celso already had his suit off and was busy collapsing our portable airlock.

Through the net-like walls of the Bubble I looked back at the *Sally Brind*. I could see at one extreme the fat cone shape of Paulis's Earth return capsule, and at the other end the angular, spidery form of the strut sections that held the nuke reactor and its shielding.

Beside our glittering toy-ship the *Brind* looked crude, as if knocked together by stone axes.

I had grown to hate the damn *Brind*. In the months since we left lunar orbit, she had become a prison to me. Now, as I looked back at her, drifting in this purposeless immensity, she looked like home.

When I took off my suit off I found I'd suffered some oedema, swelling caused by the accumulation of fluid under my skin – in the webs of my fingers, in places where the zippers had run, and a few other places where the suit hadn't fit as well as it should. The kind of stuff the astronauts never tell you about. But there was no pain, no loss of muscle or joint function that I could detect.

'Report,' Paulis's voice, loud in our ears, ordered.

'The only instrument is a display, like a softscreen,' said Celso. He inspected it calmly. It showed a network of threads against a background of starlike dots.

'Your interpretation?'

'This may be an image of our destination. And if these are cosmic strings,' Celso said dryly, 'we are going further than I had imagined.'

I wondered what the hell he was talking about. I looked more closely at the starlike dots. They were little spirals.

Galaxies?

Celso continued to poke around. 'The life-support equipment is functioning nominally.'

'I've given you enough for about two months,' said Paulis. 'If you're not back by then, you probably won't be coming back at all.'

Celso nodded.

'Time's up,' Paulis said. 'Shut the hatch, Malenfant.'

I shot back, 'You'll pay for this, Paulis.'

'I don't think I'll be losing much sleep, frankly.' Then, with steel: 'Shut the hatch, Malenfant. I want to see you do it.'

Celso touched my shoulder. 'Do not be concerned, my friend.' With a lot of dignity he pressed a wall-mounted push-button.

The hatch melted into the hull, closing us in.

The Bubble quivered. I clung to the soft wall.

Paulis's voice cut out. The sun disappeared. Electric-blue light pulsed in the sky. There was no sensation of movement.

But suddenly – impossibly – there was a planet outside, a fat steel-grey ball. A world of water. *Earth?*

It looked like Earth. But, despite my sudden, reluctant stab of hope, I knew immediately it was not Earth.

Celso's face was working as he gazed out of the Bubble, his softscreen jammed against the hull, gathering images. 'A big world, larger than Earth – but what difference does that make? Higher surface gravity. More internal heat trapped. A thicker crust, but hotter, more flexible; lots of volcanoes. And the crust couldn't support mountains in that powerful gravity . . . Deep oceans, no mountains tall enough to peak out of the water – life clustering around deep-ocean thermal vents –'

'I don't understand,' I said.

'We are already far from home.'

I said tightly, 'I can see that.'

He looked at me steadily, and rested his hands on my shoulders. 'Michael, *we have already been projected to the system of another star.* I think –'

There was a faint surge. I saw something like streetlamps flying past. And then a dim pool of light soaked across space below us.

Celso grunted. 'Ah. I think we have accelerated.'

With a click, the hull turned transparent as glass.

The streetlamps had been stars.

And the puddle of light was a swirl, a bulging yellow-white core wrapped around by streaky spiral-shaped arms.

It was the Galaxy. It fell away from us.

That was how far I had already come, how fast I was moving.

I assumed a foetal position and stayed that way for a long time.

As a kid I used to lie out on the lawn, soaking up dew and looking at the stars, trying to feel the Earth turning under me. It felt wonderful to be alive – hell, to be ten years old, anyhow. Michael, if you're ten years old when you get to read this, try it sometime. Even if you're a hundred, try it anyhow.

But even then I knew that the Earth was just a ball of rock, on the fringe of a nondescript galaxy. And I just couldn't believe that there was nobody out there looking back at me down here. Was it really possible that this was the only place where life had taken hold – that only here were there minds and eyes capable of looking out and wondering?

Because if so, what use are the stars? All those suns and worlds, spinning through the void, the grand complexity of creation unwinding all the way out of the Big Bang itself . . .

Even then I saw space as a high frontier, a sky to be mined, a resource for humanity. Still do. But is that all it is? Could the sky really be nothing more than an empty stage for mankind to strut and squabble?

And what if we blow ourselves up? Will the universe just evolve on, like a huge piece of clockwork slowly running down, utterly devoid of life and mind? What would be the use of that?

Much later, I learned that this kind of 'argument from utility' goes back all the way to the Romans – Lucretius, in fact, in the first century AD. Alien minds must exist, because otherwise the stars would be purposeless. Right?

Sure. But if so, where are they?

I bet this bothers you too, Michael. Wouldn't be a Malenfant otherwise!

Celso spoke to me soothingly. Eventually I uncurled.

The sky was embroidered with knots and threads. A fat grey cloud drifted past.

After a moment, with the help of Celso, I got it into perspective. The embroidery was made up of galaxies. The cloud was a supercluster of galaxies.

We were moving fast enough to make a supercluster shift against the general background.

'We must be travelling through some sort of hyperspace,' Celso lectured. 'We hop from point to point. Or perhaps this is some variant of teleportation. Even the images we see must be an illusion, manufactured for our comfort.'

'I don't want to know.'

'But you should have been prepared for all this,' said Celso kindly. 'You saw the image – the distant galaxies, the cosmic strings.'

'Celso –' I resisted the temptation to wrap my arms around my head. 'Please. You aren't helping me.'

He looked at me steadily. Supercluster light bathed his aquiline profile; he was the sort you'd pick as an ambassador for the human race. I hate people like that. 'If the builders of this vessel are transporting us across such distances, there is nothing to fear. With such powers they can surely preserve our lives with negligible effort.'

'Or sit on our skulls with less.'

'There is nothing to fear save your own human failings.'

I sucked weak coffee from a nippled flask. 'You're starting to sound like Paulis.'

269

He laughed. 'I am sorry.' He turned back to the drifting super-cluster, calm, fascinated.

Just think about it, Michael. Life on Earth got started just about as soon as it could – as soon as the rocks cooled and the oceans gathered. Furthermore, life spread over Earth as fast and as far as it could. And already we're starting to spread to other worlds. Surely this can't be a unique trait of Earth life.

So how come nobody has come spreading all over us?

Of course the universe is a big place. But even crawling along with dinky ships that only reach a fraction of lightspeed – ships we could easily start building now – we could colonize the Galaxy in a few tens of millions of years. 100 million, tops.

100 million years: it seems an immense time – after all, 100 million years ago dinosaurs ruled the Earth. But the Galaxy is 100 times older still. There has been time for Galactic colonization to have happened many times since the birth of the stars.

Remember, all it takes is for one race somewhere to have evolved the will and the means to colonize; and once the process has started it's hard to see what could stop it.

But, as a kid on that lawn, I didn't see them.

Advanced civilizations ought to be very noticeable. Even we blare out on radio frequencies. Why, with our giant radio telescopes we could detect a civilization no more advanced than ours anywhere in the Galaxy. But we don't.

We seem to be surrounded by emptiness and silence. There's something wrong.

This is called the Fermi Paradox.

The journey was long. And what made it worse was that we didn't know *how* long it would be, or what we would find at the end of it – let alone if we would ever come back again.

The two of us were crammed inside that glittering little Bubble the whole time.

Celso had the patience of a rock. Trying not to think about how afraid I was, I poked sticks into his cage. I ought to have driven him crazy.

'You have a few "human failings" too,' I said. 'Or you wouldn't have ended up like me, on sale in a debtors' auction.'

He inclined his noble head. 'What you say is true. Although I did go there voluntarily.'

I choked on my coffee.

'My wife is called Maria. We both work in the algae tanks beneath New San Francisco.'

I grimaced. 'You've got my sympathy.'

'We remain poor people, despite our efforts to educate ourselves. You may know that life is not easy for non-Caucasians in modern California . . .' His parents had moved there from the east when Celso was very young. 'My parents loved California – or at least, the dream of California – a place of hope and tolerance and plenty, the society of the future, the Golden State.' He smiled. 'But my parents died disappointed. And the California dream had been dead for decades . . .'

It all started, he said, with the Proposition 13 vote in 1978. It was a tax revolt, when citizens began to turn their backs on public spending. More ballot initiatives followed, to cut taxes, limit budgets, restrict school-spending discretion, bring in tougher sentencing laws, end affirmative action, ban immigrants from using public services.

'For fifty years California has been run by a government of ballot initiative. And it is not hard to see who the initiatives are favouring. The whites became a minority in 2005; the rest of the population is Latino, black, Asian and other groups. The ballot initiatives are weapons of resistance by the declining proportion of white voters. With predictable results.'

I could sympathize. As a kid growing up with two radicals for parents – in turn very influenced by my grandfather, the famous Reid Malenfant himself – I soaked up a lot of utopianism. My parents always thought that the future would be better than the present, that people would somehow get smarter and more generous, overcome their limitations, learn to live in harmony and generosity. Save the planet and live in peace. All that stuff.

It didn't work out that way. Where California led, it seems to me, the rest of the human race has followed, into a pit of self-ishness, short-sightedness, bigotry, hatred, greed – while the planet fills up with our shit.

'But,' Celso said, 'your grandfather tried.'

'Tried and failed. Reid Malenfant dreamed of saving the Earth by mining the sky. Bullshit. The wealth returned from the asteroid mines has made the rich richer – people like Paulis – and did nothing for the Earth but create millions of economic refugees.'

And as for my grandfather, who everybody seems to think I ought to be living up to: his is a voice from the past, speaking of vanished dreams.

Celso said, 'Is there really no hope for us? Can we really not transcend our nature, save ourselves?'

'My friend, all you can do is look after yourself.'

Celso nodded. 'Yes. My wife and I could see no way to buy a decent life for our son Fernando but for one of us to be sold through an auction.'

'You did that knowing the risk of coming up against a bastard like Paulis – of ending up on a chute to hell like this?'

'I did it knowing that Paulis's money would buy my Fernando a place in the sun – literally. And Maria would have done the same. We drew lots.'

'Ah.' I nodded knowingly. 'And you lost.'

He looked puzzled. 'No. I won.'

I couldn't meet his eyes. I really do hate people like that.

He said gently, 'Tell me why *you* are here. The truth, now.'

'Paulis bought me.'

'The laws covering debtor auctions are strict. He could not have sent you on such a hazardous assignment without your consent.'

'He bought me. But not with money.'

'Then what?'

I sighed. 'With my grandfather. Paulis knew him. He had a letter, written before Reid Malenfant died, a letter for me . . .'

A paradox arises when two seemingly plausible lines of thought meet in a contradiction. Throughout history, paradoxes have been a fertile seeding grounds for new ways of looking at the world. I'm sure Fermi is telling us something very profound about the nature of the universe we live in.

But, Michael, neither of the two basic resolutions of the Paradox offer much illumination – or comfort.

Maybe, simply, we really are alone.

We may be the first. Perhaps we're the last. If so, it took so long for the solar system to evolve intelligence it seems unlikely there will be others, ever. If we fail, then the failure is for all time. If we die, mind and consciousness and soul die with us: hope and dreams and love, everything that makes us human. There will be nobody even to mourn us . . .

* * *

Celso nodded gravely as he read.

I snorted. 'Imagine growing up with a dead hero for a grand-father. And his one communication to me is a lecture about the damn Fermi Paradox. Look, Reid Malenfant was a loser. He let people manipulate him his whole life. People like Frank Paulis, who used him as a front for his predatory off-world capitalism.'

'That is very cynical. After all this project, the first human explo-ration of the Bubbles, was funded privately – by Paulis. He must share some of the same, ah, curiosity as your grandfather.'

'My grandfather had a head full of shit.'

Celso regarded me. 'I hope we will learn enough to have satis-fied Reid Malenfant's curiosity – and that it does not cost us our lives.' And he went back to work.

Humans fired off their first starships in the middle of the twen-tieth century. They were the US space probes called *Pioneer* and *Voyager*, four of them, launched in the 1970s to visit the outer planets. Their primary mission completed, they sailed helplessly on into interstellar space. They worked for decades, sending back data about the conditions they found. But they haven't gone too far yet, all things considered; it will take the fastest of them tens of thousands of years to reach any nearby star.

The first genuine star probe was the European-Japanese *D'Urville*: a miniaturized robot the size of a hockey puck, accel-erated to high velocity. It returned images of the Alpha Centauri system within a decade.

The *D'Urville* found a system crowded with asteroids and rocky worlds. None of the worlds was inhabited . . . but one of them had been inhabited.

From orbit, *D'Urville* saw neat buildings and cities and mines and what looked like farms, all laid out in a persistent hexagonal pattern.

But everything had been abandoned. The buildings were subsiding back into the yellow-grey of the native vegetation, though their outlines were clearly visible. *Farms and cities*: they must have been something like us. We must have missed them by no more than millennia. It was heartbreaking.

So what happened? There was no sign of war, or cosmic impact, or volcanic explosion, or eco-collapse, or any of the other ways we could think of to trash a world. It was as if everybody had just up and left, leaving a *Marie Celeste* planet.

But there were several Bubbles neatly orbiting the empty world, shining brightly, beacons blaring throughout the spectrum.

Since then more probes to other stars, followers of the *D'Urville*, have found many lifeless planets – and a few more abandoned worlds. Some of them appeared to have been inhabited until quite recently, like Alpha A-IV, some deserted for much longer. But always abandoned.

And everywhere we found Bubbles, their all-frequency beacons bleeping invitingly, clustering around those empty worlds like bees around a flower.

After a time one enterprising microprobe was sent *inside* a Bubble. The hatch closed. The Bubble shot away at high speed, and was never heard from again.

It was shortly after that that Bubbles were found in the Oort cloud of our own solar system. Hatches open. Apparently waiting for us.

Paulis had set out the pitch for me. 'Where do these Bubbles come from? Where do they go? And why do they never return? My company, Bootstrap, thinks there may be a lot of profit in the answers. Our probes haven't returned. Perhaps you will.'

Or perhaps not.

It doesn't take a Cornelius Taine to figure out that the Bubbles must have something to do with the fact that my grandfather's night sky was silent.

. . . Or maybe we aren't alone, but we just can't see them. Why not?

Maybe the answer is benevolent. Maybe we're in some kind of quarantine – or a zoo.

Maybe it's just that we all destroy ourselves in nuclear wars or eco collapse.

Or maybe there is something that kills off every civilization like ours before we get too far. Malevolent robots sliding silently between the stars, which for their own antique purposes kill off fledgling cultures.

Or something else we can't even imagine.

Michael, every outcome I can think of scares me.

Celso called me over excitedly. 'My friend, we have travelled for days and must have spanned half the universe. But I believe our journey is nearly over.' He pointed. 'Over there is a quasar. Which is a very bright, very distant object. And over there –' He moved his arm almost imperceptibly. 'I can see the same quasar.'

'Well, golly gee.'

He smiled. 'Such a double image is a characteristic of a cosmic string. The light bends around the string. You see?'

'I still don't know what a cosmic string is.'

'A fault in space. A relic of the Big Bang, the birth of the universe itself . . . Do you know much cosmology, Michael?'

'Not as such, no.' It isn't a big topic of conversation in your average poker school.

'Imagine the universe, just a few years old. It is mere light years across, a soup of energy. Rapidly it cools. Our familiar laws of physics take hold. The universe settles into great lumps of ordered space, like – like the freezing surface of a pond.

'But there are flaws in this sober universe, like the gaps between ice floes. Do you understand? Just as liquid water persists in those gaps, so there are great channels through which there still flows energy from the universe's earliest hours. Souvenirs of a reckless youth.'

'And these channels are what you call cosmic strings?'

'The strings are no wider than ten hydrogen atoms. They are very dark, very dense – many tons to an inch.' He cracked an imaginary whip. 'The endless strings lash through space at almost the speed of light, throwing off loops like echoes. The loops lose energy and decay. But not before they form the kernels around which galaxies crystallize.'

'Really? And what about this primordial energy?'

'Great electric currents surge along the strings. Which are, of course, superconductors.'

It sounded kind of dangerous. I felt my stomach loosen – the reaction of a plains primate, utterly inappropriate, lost as I was in this intergalactic wilderness.

But now there was something new. I looked where Celso was pointing –

– and made out a small bar of light. It moved like a beetle across the background.

'What's that? A bead sliding on the string?'

He grabbed a softscreen, seeking a magnified image. His jaw dropped. 'My friend,' he said softly, 'I believe you are exactly right.'

It was one of a series of such beads, I saw now. The whole damn string seemed to be threaded like a cheap necklace.

But now the perspective changed. That nearest bar swelled to a cylinder. To a wand that pointed towards us. To a tunnel whose mouth roared out of infinity and swallowed us.

We sailed along the tunnel's axis, following a fine thread beaded with toy stars – a thread that had to be the cosmic string. The stars splashed coloured tubes on the tunnel walls; they hurtled by like posters in a subway to hell.

I clung to the Bubble walls. Even Celso blanched.

'Of course,' he yelled – and stopped himself. There was no noise, just the feeling there ought to have been. 'Of course, we have still less reason to fear than before. Our speed must be vastly less than when we were in free space. And I believe we're still slowing down.'

I risked a look.

We were dipping away from the axis. Those tremendous bands of light flattened out and became landscapes that streamed beneath us.

We slowed enough to make out detail.

One model sun was a ruddy giant. By its light, fungi the size of continents lapped vast mountain ranges.

The next sun was a shrunken dwarf; oceans of hydrogen or helium slithered over the tunnel walls. I saw something like an enormous whale. It must have had superconducting fluid for blood.

So it went, sun after sun, landscape after landscape. A subway filled with worlds. Worlds, and life.

Celso's dark eyes shone with wonder. 'This tunnel must be a million miles across. So much room . . .'

We dipped lower still. Atmosphere whistled. The latest sunlight looked warm and familiar, and the walls were coated with a jumble of blue and green.

The huge curved floor flattened out into a landscape, exploded into trees and grass and rivers; suddenly we landed, as simple as that.

Gravity came back with a thump. We fell into the base of our Bubble.

Without hesitation Celso pulled on his suit, set up our inflatable airlock, and kicked the hatch open.

I glimpsed grassy hills, and a band of night, and a white dwarf star.

I buried my face in the wall of the Bubble.

*   *   *

Celso came to me that evening.

(Evening? The toy sun slid along its wire and dimmed as it went. In the night, I could see Earthlike landscape smeared out over the other side of the sky.)

'I want you to know I understand,' Celso said gently. 'You must come to terms with this situation. You must do it yourself. I will wait for you.'

I shut my eyes tighter.

The next morning, I heard whistling.

I uncurled. I pulled on my suit, and climbed out of the bubble.

Celso was squatting by a stream, fishing with a piece of string and a bit of wire. He'd taken his suit off. In fact, he'd stripped down to his undershorts. He broke off his whistling as I approached.

I cracked my helmet. The air smelt funny to me, but then I'm a city boy. There was no smog, no people. I could smell Celso's fish, though.

I splashed my face in the stream. The water felt pure enough to have come out of a tap. I said: 'I'd like an explanation, I think.'

Celso competently hauled out another fish. (At least it looked like a fish.) 'Simple,' he said. 'The line is a thread from an undergarment. The hook is scavenged from a ration pack. For bait I am using particles of food concentrate. Later we can dig for worms and –'

'Forget the fishing.'

'We can eat the fish, just as we can breathe the air.' He smiled. 'It is of no species I have ever seen. But it has the same biochemical basis as the fish of Earth's oceans and rivers. Isn't that marvellous? *They* knew we were coming – they brought us here, right across the universe – they stocked the streams with fish –'

'We didn't come all this way to bloody fish. What's going on here, Celso?'

He wrapped the line around his wrist and stood up. Then, unexpectedly, he grabbed me by the shoulders and grinned in my face. 'You are a hero, my friend Michael Malenfant.'

'A hero? All I did was get out of bed.'

'But, for you, that step across the threshold of the Bubble was a great and terrible journey indeed.' He shook me gently. '*I understand*. We must all do what we can, yes? Come now. We will find wood for a fire, I will build a spit, and we will eat a fine meal.'

He loped barefoot across the grass as if he'd been born to it.

Grumbling, I followed.

Celso gutted the fish with a bit of metal. I couldn't have done that to save my life. The fish tasted wonderful.

That night we sat by the dying fire. There were no stars, of course, just bands of light on the horizons like twin dawns.

Celso said at length, 'This place, this segment alone, could swallow more than ten thousand Earths. So much room . . . And we flew over dozens of other inside-out worlds. I imagine there's a home for every life form in the universe – perhaps, in fact, a refuge for all logically possible life forms . . .'

I looked up to the cylinder's invisible axis. 'I suppose you're going to tell me the whole thing's built around a cosmic string. And the power for all the dinky suns comes from the huge currents left over from the Big Bang.'

'I would guess so. And power for the gravity fields we stand in – although there may be a simpler mechanism. Perhaps the tube is spinning, providing gravity by centripetal forces.'

'But you'd have to spin the tube at different rates. You know, some of the inhabitants will be from tiny moons, some will be from gas giants . . .'

'That's true.' He clapped me on the shoulder. 'We'll make a scientist of you yet.'

'Not if I can help it.' I hunched up, nostalgic for smog and ignorance. 'But what's the point of all this?'

'The point – I think – is that species become extinct. *Even humans* . . . I did not always work in the algae farms. Once I had higher ambitions.' He smiled. 'I would have been an anthropologist, I think. Actually my speciality would have been palaeoanthropology. Extinct homs.'

'Homs?'

'Sorry: field slang. Hominids. The lineage of human descent. I did some work, as a student, in the field in the desert heartlands of Kenya. At Olduvai I was privileged to make a key find. It was just a sharp-edged fragment of bone about the size of my thumb, the colour of lava pebbles.'

'But it was a bit of skull.'

'Homs don't leave many fossils, Michael. You very rarely find ribs, for example. Until humans began to bury each other, a hundred thousand years ago, ribs were the first parts of a corpse to be crunched to splinters by the carnivores. It took me months before I learned to pick out the relics, tiny specks against the soil . . .

'Well. Believe me, we were very excited. We marked out the site. We broke up the dirt. We began to sieve, looking to separate bits of bone from the grains of soil and stone. After weeks of work you could fit the whole find into a cigarette packet. But that counts as a phenomenal find, in this field.

'What we had found was a trace of a woman. She was *Homo erectus*. Her kind arose perhaps two million years ago, and became extinct a quarter-million years ago. They had the bodies of modern humans, but smaller brains. But they were highly successful. They migrated out of Africa and covered the Old World.'

I said dryly, 'Fascinating, Celso. And the significance –'

'*They are gone*, Michael. This is what my field experiences taught me. Here was another type of human – *extinct*. All that is left is shards of bone from which we have to infer everything – the ancient homs' appearance, gait, behaviour, social structure, language, culture, tool-making ability – everything we know, or we think we know about them. *Extinction*. It is a brutal, uncompromising termination, disconnecting the past from the future.

'And for an intelligent species this over-death is an unbearable prospect. Everything that might make a life valuable after death – memory, achievement – is wiped away. *There is nobody even left to grieve*. Do you see?'

He was genuinely agitated; I envied his intensity of emotion. 'But what has this to do with the builders?'

He lay on his back and stared at the empty sky. 'I think the builders are planning ahead. I think this is a *refugium*, as the ecologists would say. A place to sit out the cold times to come, the long Ice Age of the universe – a safeguard against extinction.' He sighed. 'I think your grandfather understood about extinction, Michael.'

I stared at the fire, my mind drifting. He was thinking of the destiny of mankind. I was just thinking about myself. But then, I hadn't asked to be here. 'Maybe this is okay for you. Sun, trees, fishing, mysterious aliens. But I'm a city boy.'

'I am sorry for you, my friend. But I, too, am far from my family.'

It was a long night, and not a whole lot of laughs.

* * *

A new sun slid down the wire. The dew misted away.

I rubbed my eyes; my back was stiff as hell from sleeping unnaturally without a mattress on the ground.

There were two alien Bubbles. They bobbled in the breeze, side by side.

One was ours. Its door gaped; I recognized our kit inside it. Within the second Bubble I thought I could make out two human forms.

I shook Celso awake. 'We've got company.'

We stood before the new vessel. Its hatch opened.

There was a woman; a small boy clung to her. They were a terrified mess. When they recognized Celso –

Look, I have some decency. I took a walk along the stream.

After an hour I rejoined the family. They were having a nice fish breakfast, talking animatedly.

Celso grinned. 'My friend Michael Malenfant. Please meet my wife, Maria, and Fernando, my son.'

Maria still wore the grimy coverall of an algae tank worker. She said: 'The Bubble came and scooped me up from work; and Fernando from his school.'

I gaped. 'The Bubbles have come to Earth?'

They had, it seemed: great gossamer fleets of them, sailing in from the Oort Cloud, an armada perhaps triggered by our foolhardy jaunt.

'They make the sky shine,' said the boy, beaming.

'Of course it is logical,' said Celso. 'The aliens would want to reconstruct stable family units.'

'I wonder how they knew who to bring.'

Celso smiled. 'I would guess they studied us – or rather the Bubble did – during the journey. Whoever was most in our thoughts would be selected. The puzzles of the human heart must be transparent to the builders of such a monumental construct as this.'

'We were scared,' said Fernando proudly, chewing the flesh off a fishy spine.

'I'll bet.' I imagined the scenes in those nightmarish farms as a Bubble came sweeping over the algae beds . . . 'So now what? Do you think you'll stay here?'

Celso took a deep breath. 'Oh, yes.'

'Better than the algae farms, huh.'

'It is more than that. This will be a fine land in which to build a home, and for Fernando to grow. Other people will be brought here soon. We will farm, build cities.' He took my arm. 'But you look troubled, my friend. I must not forget you in my happiness. Was no one in your heart during our journey?'

In my hop-skip-and-jump life I'd never made the time to get close enough to anyone to miss them.

He put his hand on my arm. 'Stay with us.' His son smiled at me.

Once again I found myself unable to meet Celso's kind eyes.

Michael, much of my life has been shaped by thinking about the Fermi Paradox. But one thing I never considered was the subtext.

Alone or not alone – why do we care so much?

I think I know now. It's because we are lonely. On Earth there is nobody closer to us than the chimps; we see nobody like us in the sky.

But then, each of us is alone. I have been alone since your grandmother, Emma, died. And now I'm dying too, Michael; what could be lonelier than that?

That's why we care about Fermi. That's why I care.

Michael, I'm looking at you, here in this damn hospital room with me; you're just born, just a baby, and you won't remember me. But I'm glad I got to meet you. I hope you will learn more than I have. That you will be wiser. That you will be happier. That you won't be alone.

I said, 'I guess we know the truth about Fermi now. As soon as intelligence emerges on some deadbeat world like Earth, along come the Bubbles to take everybody away. Leaving all the lights on but nobody home. That's all there is to it.'

'But what a vast enterprise,' Celso said. 'Remember, a key difficulty with the Fermi Paradox has always been consistency. If there is a mechanism that removes intelligent life from the stars and planets, it must do so unfailingly and everywhere: it must be all but omniscient and omnipotent.'

'So the universe must be full of those damn Bubbles.'

'Yes.' He smiled. 'Or perhaps there is only one . . .'

'But *why*? Why go to all this trouble, to build this – this vast theme park?'

He grinned. 'Extinction, Michael. This is a dangerous universe for fragile beings such as ourselves. Left to our own devices, it doesn't look as if we are smart enough to get through many more centuries, does it? Maybe the Bubbles have come just in time. And remember that life can be readily destroyed – by impact events, volcanism and other instability – by chance events like nearby supernovae or the collision of neutron stars – by more dramatic occurrences like the collision of galaxies – and in the end, of course, all stars will die, all free energy sources dwindle . . . We are stalked by extinction, Michael; we are all refugees.

'But one energy source will not fade away: the energy trapped in the cosmic strings. So I think they built this place, and they sent out their trawler-like vessels. The refugium is a defiance of extinction – a mechanism to ensure that life and mind may survive into the unimaginable future –'

I sniffed, looking up at a fake sun. 'But isn't that a retreat? This great sink of life isn't our world. To come here is an end to striving, to ambition, to the autonomy of the species.' I thought of the Bubbles clustering around Earth, like antibodies around a source of infection. I thought of human cities, New York and London and Beijing, emptied and overgrown like the dismal ruins of Alpha Centauri A-IV.

But Celso said, 'Not really. They were just thinking of their children. Rather like me, I guess. And there are adventures to be had here. We will design flying machines and go exploring. There may be no limit to the journeys we, or our children, will make, up and down this great corridor, a corridor that encircles the universe, no limit to the intelligences we might meet. And here, sheltered in this refugium, the human species could last *forever* . . . think of that.' He studied me. 'As for you, I didn't know you were so restless, Michael. Heroism, now wanderlust. You have travelled across half the cosmos, and at the end of your journey you found yourself. Maybe your grandfather's genes really are working within you.'

The boy spoke around a mouthful of fish. 'If you are lonely, sir, why don't you go home?'

I smiled. 'Easier said than done.'

'No, really. You know the screen in the Bubble – the one that showed our destination?'

'The cosmic string picture . . . what about it?'

'Well, in your Bubble it's changed.'

Celso stared at the boy, then ran to the Bubble. 'He's right,' he breathed.

The screen showed a picture of the Earth – continents, grey-blue oceans – unmistakeable and lovely.

I kissed that damn kid.

Celso nodded. 'They know you wish to leave.' He shrugged. 'The choice of the species is surely clear; *this,* not that beautiful, fragile blue bauble, is mankind's destiny. But individuals are free . . .'

There was a distant shiver of motion. A third Bubble sailed towards us across the plain. I hardly noticed it.

Without hesitation I jumped into the open hatchway of our Bubble. 'Listen,' I said to Celso, 'are you sure you don't want to come? It's going to be a tough life here.'

He rejoined his family. 'Not for us. Goodbye, my friend. Oh – here.' He handed me his softscreen. 'With the information I have gathered in this you will become a rich man.'

The new vessel drifted to rest.

I couldn't have cared less. I banged the button to shut the hatch. My Bubble lifted.

Through the net walls I could see the new arrival tumble out onto the raw earth. I recognized him. He was the reason the new Bubble had been summoned for me. The person who'd made sure he'd been on my mind throughout the whole journey.

Frank J. Paulis was wearing his bathrobe. He wailed.

Celso caught my eye and winked. Paulis would be doing a lot of worm digging before he was allowed back to his spa and Bootstrap and his sprawling empire. I wished I'd been there when that damn Bubble had shown up to scoop him away.

But maybe Paulis had got what he wanted, at that. *The answer* – in this universe, anyhow. My grandfather would have been pleased for him, I thought.

The landscape fell away, and I flew past toy stars.

LOST CONTINENT

Without warning Dorehill leaned across the table. 'Close your eyes.'

I was startled into obeying.

'Don't think before replying. *Tell me who you are.*'

And, just for a second or two, nothing came. It was as if I was drifting in a fog. Who am I? Where am I from? How did I get here?

The answers quickly loomed out of that pearly fog. I saw my own face, at age six and sixteen and thirty-six; my parents, our somewhat dilapidated family house in Nantucket; my study, my books; Mary's sweet face, the kids, our home here in Tangier. It all came together, a mosaic of images, a tidy narrative.

Too tidy? Was that Dorehill's point?

He was watching me, those desperate eyes bright. 'You see? You *see*? How do you know your past is real? How do you *know* that everything you think you remember wasn't conjured into existence a couple of seconds ago, knitted into place for you, a – a tapestry to cover up the holes in the wall? Don't you think it's at least *possible*? . . .'

It had been nearly twenty years since I had last seen Peter Dorehill, at our graduation together. Now, in the cool brightness of a café on Tangier's beach promenade, we sipped mint tea and appraised each other, as old acquaintances will.

The years had made Dorehill gaunt, as if the softer parts of his personality had worn away. I had soon learned he was still full of words, words, words, just as he always had been. But I detected something in his eyes, about his stance, as if he was wound up to explosive tension.

Knowing his history, I thought I recognized the signs. It seemed to me he looked – as my father used to say of my uncle – 'white-knuckle sober'. Perhaps he was finding Islamic Morocco trying.

But, intense or not, I could see no chain of reasoning, no string of words which might lure a man like Peter Dorehill into the murky solipsistic waters of Lost Continent mythmaking.

'It began with geology,' he told me. 'My chosen profession after Stanford, if you remember. Three decades ago – in October 1962 – savage earth tremors were experienced around a great half-ring of land, from Scandinavia, down through the Russian ports of Leningrad and Lvov and Odessa, on through Alexandria and the north African coast – even as far as Tangier, where we sit. Many of these quakes were in regions far from any geological fault. All of them occurred within minutes of each other. And at the same time, tsunamis marched across the Atlantic to smash against the east coast of America.'

I nodded. I remembered all this, of course; we had both been ten years old at the time. 'And this is what you have been working on.'

'Not exactly.' He grinned, rueful. 'You know me, John: an unanswered question is an endless, nagging irritation. I've always been fascinated by the puzzle of that sudden chthonic jolt. How did it happen? Why *then*, and in those specific sites? What could have triggered it all? And so on.

'But, after taking my master's, I found that *nobody* was working seriously on the problem. This was just a dozen or so years after the event, remember. Oh, the geological records were there to inspect – there had been no fast answers; there was still work to be done – but even so, it struck me that people had turned away from the mystery, had lost interest. I couldn't understand it. But I got nowhere fast. Forced to earn a crust, I took a job with an oil company.'

'But you kept digging.'

'You see, you do know me! I wondered if it might be fruitful to look a little wider. I wanted to know what else was going on in that autumn of 1962.'

I said dryly, 'I seem to remember that the news of the period was somewhat dominated by missiles in Cuba.'

He smiled and pushed back a straggling grey hair from his startlingly high forehead. (Why are we always so shocked by the ageing of friends from youth?) 'Correct – and maybe significant. In that month virtually every commentator was predicting nuclear war – a war which was averted only by some adroit diplomacy, and a large pinch of luck. But I went further than that. I looked at trends in other disciplines – such as yours, John. I consulted newspaper records. I even dug around in the drugstore tabloids.'

'What were you looking for?'

'I didn't know – I suspected I wouldn't know until I found it. I sensed a pattern, out there somewhere . . . It's hard to be more clear than that. All I did find were more unanswered questions. For instance there was a rash of stories of UFO visitations and alien abductions.'

'Peter, there are always UFO stories –'

'Not in such numbers, and with such consistency. Anyhow there's more – much of which ought to interest a historian like yourself, John.'

My smile froze a little at that, but I kept listening.

With diligent (if probably amateurish) research he had, he claimed, uncovered clusters of new folk tales.

'Shiite imams in Algeria told me how the Trumpet of Israfil sounded over the northern ocean – how Iblis, Satan, rose and resumed his defiance of God's great command: *Be.* The Orthodox Christians of the Russian coast spoke of a recent return by Satan, who they call the Murderer of the Beginning. Even modern practitioners of the old Norse religions whispered stories of an irruption of *Ginnungagap*, the primeval void, into the modern world.

'These fragmentary tales were expressed in the differing mythic structures of local populations. But they were all alike. And I found them scattered in a great circle, running along the North African coast, through the Middle East and Russia, as far as Scandinavia.'

I said reluctantly, 'The same as the 1962 quake arc.'

His eyes gleamed. 'You see the pattern. I felt I was skirting some enormous, hidden event, revealed not so much by evidence as by a notable absence. *I believe these tales are fragments of recollection* – smashed, scattered, broken – like the ring of debris that surrounds an impact crater.' He eyed me. 'You think I'm babbling.'

I forced a smile. 'Peter, I'm making no judgement.' But in fact my heart was sinking.

Because we had already moved from geology to mythmaking, and I suspected I was about to be introduced to his Lost Continent theory.

* * *

I suppose I felt a lingering fondness for Dorehill. I hadn't forgotten Stanford and our late-night bull sessions, fuelled by bad food, whiskey, dope and fellowship, when we had talked about anything and everything.

Aliens, for instance – or the lack thereof, a favourite bullshit topic. *Where is everybody?* Peter would ask, lecturing as usual, younger, wispy-bearded, hairier, almost as intense. *Why isn't there evidence of extraterrestrial civilization all around us? They should be here by now. Even if They are long gone, surely we should see Their mighty ruins all around us . . .*

Perhaps we were being anthropomorphic, we would say. Perhaps They were nothing like us – not recognizable as life forms at all – or perhaps They were pursuing projects we can't even imagine. But even if we had no idea what Their great structures are for, we would surely recognize them as artificial. And so on.

But it was always Peter who came up with the wackiest notions. *They might simply be invisible. The physicists talk of mirror matter, of an elusive unseen twin for every particle in nature. Are there mirror stars? Are there planets inhabited by mirror organisms, invisible to our senses? Do Their ships of mirror matter slide through our solar system even now?* . . . It looked as if he hadn't changed.

But I had. College was long ago and far away, an intense confinement where seeming friendships could be forged between basically incompatible types, friendships that fell apart pretty rapidly once we were all let out into the real world. I had kept in touch with few of my friends and acquaintances from those days – and certainly not Peter Dorehill.

So it was guilt as much as friendship, I guess, that kept me in my seat in that sunlit café.

It was still harmless enough. We talked around the parameters of the mythos: of tales of rich island-nations whose powerful conquering princes became wicked and impious, until their lands were swallowed up by the sea.

The conventional explanation of Lost Continent myths is well known. Almost certainly, if there is anything in such legends at all, they stem from real events – volcanic eruptions, earthquakes, tsunamis and the like – enough to shatter civilizations. Such half-memories are handed down through the ages, mutating and elaborating as they go. In later times, efforts are often made to identify the wonderful land with an actual country, to no avail, of course.

All of which is a rational, logical justification of the archetypical legends, deriving from a very human reaction to devastating, barely comprehended events.

But Peter Dorehill had another explanation.

He closed his eyes. 'Imagine a great and ancient civilization. Its territories are encrusted with fine buildings, works of art, libraries full of learning.

'And now, imagine a race of beings. Beings from another world.'

Though I kept carefully still, he sensed my reaction. His eyes snapped open like camera shutters.

'This *is* an outrageous hypothesis,' he said. 'There's no easy way to express it. Just hear me out. You always were a good listener, John. And as you listen, try to imagine how you would prove me wrong.'

'Aliens,' I prompted. 'Extraterrestrials.'

'Yes. They have powers and ambitions, perhaps, far beyond human imagining – and yet They are aesthetes who share some of our own conceptions of beauty. In particular, They take great pleasure in the ancient glories of this old country.

'But now They see that it is all soon to be destroyed. Perhaps it will be devastated by some natural disaster, a volcanic eruption, a quake or a flood. Or perhaps it is threatened by humanity – by war, or the collapse of empire. The specifics do not matter. What does matter is what They do about it.

'They come to a decision.

'It is an operation as simple and delicate as removing a prized vase from the grasp of a foolish child. *They carefully detach the old country from the Earth,* and remove it and its treasures to – another place, a museum perhaps, safe from humanity and the vagaries of our untamed planet.

'But They face a dilemma. They will not submit Earth's inhabitants to the trauma of such a display of power. The operation has to be performed stealthily.'

I raised an eyebrow at that. '*Stealthily?*'

'What a tremendous, monstrous act! They must distort all records mentioning, however obliquely, the lost lands. Histories have to be truncated and rewritten – They must force entire cultures to forget their roots – They have to suppress our very memories of the place.

'The operation itself is a – a cauterization. But it is hardly clean.

Nothing is without flaw, in our mortal universe . . . As the amputation is made, just as the Earth shudders, so the mass psyche reacts. We are bereft, and we seek expression.'

'Ah. Hence the volcanism and so forth associated with such events. They are a consequence, not a cause.'

'Yes –'

'And hence the Lost Continent legends.'

'Yes. Hence the legends. *They are memories*, you see – half-erased, inchoate, seeking expression . . .'

As kindly as I could, I pointed out, 'But you have no proof.'

'It is in the nature of the event itself that proof is erased.'

'Then the argument's circular.'

'Yes,' he said, with a kind of strained patience. 'Of course that's true. But that doesn't make it wrong, does it? And think about it. How would it be to live through such an event, to witness such a – a miracle? Would we even be able to perceive it? We evolved as plain-dwelling hunter-gatherers, and our sensoriums are conditioned to the hundred-mile scale of Earth landscapes. And if we aren't programmed to register something, we simply don't see it . . .'

And on, and on.

I was growing irritated, and not a little bored.

Although I couldn't quite see where 1962 fit into all this, I had heard Dorehill's 'theory' before – versions of it anyhow. As a professional historian I am pestered by believers in such tales – which often allow the marvellous inhabitants of the lost lands to live on, at the Earth's poles or under the sea, casually meddling with history – tales usually embroidered with 'proof' concerning Aboriginal art or the building of South American temples – and all these believers are more or less like Dorehill: each obsessed with a single idea, seeing nothing of the greater themes of history, vague about or even ignorant of the meaning of *evidence* and *proof*.

Dorehill's was indeed a circular argument, his 'evidence' nothing but a check of internal consistency. Like most such fantastic notions his claims could never be verified or debunked, for they made no predictions which could be tested against fresh data. I imagined him hawking his notions around the academic community, gradually losing whatever reputation he once had, relying on favours and debts even to get a hearing. And now he had come to me.

But he saw my scepticism, and anger flared in his eyes, startling me.

'Okay, forget the UFOs and fairy tales,' he snapped. 'Let's talk about the blindness in your own speciality.'

I prickled. 'What do you mean by that?'

'What would you say is the most fundamental question facing modern historians?'

'I have a feeling you're going to tell me.'

'*The emergence question*. Consider the history of America. Quite suddenly, in the fifteenth, sixteenth and seventeenth centuries, you have the arrival of new populations around the coastal fringes of both northern and southern continents – English-speakers in Newfoundland and Virginia, French in Canada, Spanish in Mexico, Portuguese in South America – as if from nowhere, in a moment of historical time, with distinctive skin colours, cultures, technology, blood types, even different DNA signatures.'

I shrugged. '*Arrival* surely isn't the right word. The new groups must have been separated from their parent populations by geographical or climatic barriers, and in isolation they rapidly diverged, physically and culturally.'

'That's the standard line. But, come on, John – look at the holes! Why such a dramatic series of emergences occur all around the world, in such a short period of time? And how can such similar linguistic and cultural groups have developed spontaneously *on different continents* – English, for instance, in North America, Africa, Australia?'

I was uneasy to be under attack in an area so far from my own speciality – which was, and is, Morocco's Almoravide Empire of the eleventh century. 'There are theories of linguistic convergence,' I said uneasily. 'Common grammars reflect the underlying structure of the human brain. It is a matter of neural hard-wiring –'

'But if you actually *observe* them,' he said sharply, 'you'll find that languages *don't* converge. In fact languages drift apart – and at a fixed, measurable rate.

'For example: suppose you have a land colonized by a group who pronounce the vowel in "bad" – what the phoneticians call RP Vowel 4 – with the mouth more closed, so it sounds like "bed". A few decades later, a new bunch of colonists arrive, but by now they have reverted to the open pronunciation. Well, the older settlers seek a certain solidarity against the new arrivals, and they retain their closed pronunciation – in fact they close it further. But that makes for confusion with RP3, as in "bed". So that must move over, sounding more like "bid", RP2, which in turn becomes still more closed, sounding like "bead", RP1. This is what the linguists call a push-chain –'

I held up my hands. 'Enough linguistics!'

He permitted himself a fairly straightforward grin. 'All right. But my point is, *you can trace such phonetic chains in the versions of English spoken in America, Canada* – the example I gave you is from Australia. We know that the divergence of the English group of languages began in the seventeenth and eighteenth centuries – there was a divergence, you see, not a convergence – just as the new populations *emerged* in Australia and America. It is as if there had been influxes of new settlers, interacting with the existing stock . . .'

'Influxes from where?'

He eyed me. 'John, be honest – I think that if you had never before heard your quaint theories of emergence and convergence you would dismiss them out of hand. *What we are looking at is the result of colonization* – wave after wave of it . . .'

Which was absurd, of course. I suppose I glared at him, unsympathetic.

He smiled, but his expression was cold, his gaze directed inward. 'We make patterns,' he said now. 'It's in our nature. Scatter a handful of coloured pebbles on the ground and we make a picture out of them. That's what you historians do. Make pretty pictures out of pebbles . . .'

Now I had no idea what he was talking about. I had the awful feeling he was disintegrating, right in front of me. 'Peter –'

He looked at me. I peered into his church-window eyes. 'You see – I think it's happened again.'

Even at college he was always the last to nurse another shot out of a dying bottle.

And it had gone on from there. When he'd been hospitalized briefly after a thirty-fifth birthday party bender – complete with drunk-driving car crash – there had been some communication among his old college buddies. Maybe we all felt a little responsible; some of us (not me) gathered around.

Dorehill said he wasn't an alcoholic, clinically anyhow, and refused treatment. He gave up drinking, just like that, and had been sober for seven, eight years.

Sure. Except that my uncle, a recovering alcoholic in my own family, would have summed up that behaviour in one word. *Denial.*

I had to agree, having seen the pattern before. Dorehill might be dry, but he was still a problem drinker, to say the least. As he hadn't been in a programme or sought counselling, he was at risk of relapse. And now here he was, sipping iced tea, wound up as tight as he could be, obsessing about 1962.

A dry drunk. White-knuckle sober.

None of which made him wrong, of course.

'It was the war,' he whispered. 'Those damn missiles in Cuba. And the cockpit of the war would have been another ancient land – the mother of the newer colony nations, perhaps . . .'

He talked on, rapidly, fanatically, barely coherently – of a great tongue of land sliced away, of landlocked towns suddenly becoming ports, of anomalous salt concentrations in the ocean, of how the world's rocks and oceans juddered like a bathtub struck with a hammer, of fragments of memories transmuted into new folk tales – of the adjustment of every human mind on the planet.

Solipsistic nonsense, of course. But as I listened, in the mundanity of that bright, bustling café, it suddenly seemed to me that I was huddled in a circle of light, a circle that reached only a few feet, and beyond there was nothing but darkness, unmapped, unexplored, incomprehensible.

But then a waiter moved smoothly through the café and opened windows; at once a cool, salty breeze from the ocean wafted into the room, breaking up the heavy mugginess of the afternoon air.

Once again I tried to be kind. 'Look, Peter – you must see how this looks. I mean, where are these aliens of yours?'

His face was set, composed. 'You haven't been listening.'

'Well, this isn't 4000 BC. For all the limitations of our eyes and minds, what of our records? TV, films – a billion photographs in family albums . . . Are you trying to tell me that *they* were all changed?' I shook my head, impatient with myself. 'And then there's your claim that our modern nations were born of colonies of this detached place. In that case its history, its culture must be utterly intertwined with ours. How could any force, no matter how powerful, detach one from the other? And what of Occam's razor?' I rapped the tabletop between us. 'It is simpler to assume that the table is real than that there is a vast invisible machine which generates the illusion of the table. Just as when I consider my own memories –'

His lips quivered oddly, and that half-suppressed anger flared again. 'So damn smug.' But the anger faded as rapidly. 'Ah, but you can't help but think that way. We are such small creatures. Well, if nothing else, you are in at the birth of a new myth structure, John. How privileged you are.' More emotions chased across his face – resentment, baffled curiosity, confusion. 'You know, I sometimes wonder if it was necessary.'

'What?'

'The amputation. Maybe we wouldn't have gone to war after all.'

I felt awkward, remorseful. 'Look, Peter, I'm sorry if –'

'We might have muddled through, without Their interference. Maybe that was how it turned out, in some other universe.' He abruptly drained his cup. 'More tea?'

I'd had enough, of the tea and of Peter Dorehill. I got up to leave.

But his voice pursued me, out into the shining air of the beach front. 'You and I were just ten years old,' he said. '*Ten years old*, John, when They stuck Their fingers in our heads. What do you think about that? . . .'

A year after that last brief meeting, Peter Dorehill disappeared from view, theories and all, sliding off the face of the Earth like his purloined continent, presumed lost in a fog of alcohol. According to my uncle, dry drunks invariably lapse – and when they do, the fall is spectacular and destructive.

Still, the news saddened me.

On the day I heard about it I took a walk through Old Tangier, which is the *medina*, a walled Arab town, a maze of narrow alleys. I climbed to the Bordj el Marsa, the port battery which offers some of the best views of the city and its harbour. From there I followed the Bab el Bahr steps out of the old city to the port gates, and the beach promenade.

Well, how *could* I tell if anything I remembered corresponded to the truth? Occam's razor is only a philosophical principle – a guideline, not a law. Was I an arrogant plains ape, assuming that what I was *capable* of seeing comprised everything there *was* to see – making up comforting stories from patterns in scattered bits of historical wreckage – clinging to simplistic principles to convince me the stories were true – complacently judging a theory by the theorist who delivered it?

But even if it was true – even if nothing anybody remembered before October 1962 was real – what was there to be done about it? *That* was the essential futility of Peter's solipsism. He may have been right, but we must continue to behave as if it were not so. What else is there to do?

... Of course, I thought, that might be what They want me to think.

I smiled. I stared out over the enormous greyness of the ocean – the huge, misnamed Mediterranean, which stretches unbroken from North Africa to Scandinavia – and then I turned away and walked back into the bright, noisy clutter of Tangier.

TRACKS

Well, the Moon was a pretty exciting place to be, I can tell you that. Even if we hadn't found alien beings.

It was as we drove out at the start of our second EVA – our second day on the Moon, the second of our three – that we found the tracks. I know what you're thinking. *What* tracks? There was no report of tracks in our TV transmission, or our radio transmission, or in the debriefing, or the still photographs. Nevertheless, they were there.

Peter, I know there's a kind of a stigma that hung over your father, for the rest of his life, after that mission. You don't have to deny it. A sense of failure, right? A sense that he was a little reckless with that jump you've seen so many times on video, that fall that smashed up his backpack, the way we had to limp back to the LM and come hurrying home with half our objectives lost, a twenty-million-buck mission screwed up by one guy fooling around on the Moon.

Well, I can tell you it wasn't like that – not like that at all. But it's something only your father and I knew, up to now. Today, now that old Joe is going to his grave, I want you to know the truth. And I want you to think about it, when you see that old Missing Man up in the sky this afternoon.

If you want to know where we were, look up at a new Moon, and look for the chin of the Man, the highland area there. You might see a dimple, a bright pinpoint; I'm told some kids can see it with the naked eye. That's Tycho Crater. A hole in the ground fifty miles across, big enough to swallow LA.

And that's where we walked, in 1973.

The sky's black, you know, but the ground is brightly lit, as if lit by floodlights on the floor of some huge theatre. A theatre stage, yeah. You lope across the surface, in the light of that big white spotlight that's the sun. And with every step you kick up the dust from under your feet, and it goes flying out in straight lines, just glimmering once in the flat sunlight, before falling back.

It was our second day. Our first day had been good, full of solid work. But morning is a week long, on the Moon. So I knew I had another bright morning, here on the Moon, stretching ahead of me.

And today we were going climbing, up into the foothills of Tycho's central peak. I whistled as I went to work.

The Lunar Rover, yeah. Now that car was one terrific toy. It comes to the Moon folded up like a concertina against the side of the LM. To deploy it you pull on a pair of lanyards, and the chassis lowers slowly, like pulling down a drawbridge. Then, suddenly, wire-mesh wheels pop out from the four corners, complete with orange fenders.

It worked just fine. We loaded up with our tools and our sample bags and what-not, and off we set, two good old boys at home on the Moon. Joe – as commander, he was the driver – kept complaining about the lack of front-wheel steering, which for some reason wouldn't work, so he had to rely on the rear steering. I was just thrown around, especially when Joe took a swerve. The ground was nothing but bumps and hollows, an artillery field, and every time we hit an obstacle one or two wheels would come looming off of the ground, throwing up huge rooster tails of black dust behind them.

It would have looked strange if there had been anyone around to see it, as we bounced our way over the surface of the Moon. The Rover is just a frame, with its wire wheels and fold-up seats and clusters of antennae and tool racks, and there's the two of us, outsize in our shining white Moon suits, like two dough boys riding a construction-kit car.

It was tough work driving directly away from the sun. The shadows, even of the smallest fragments of regolith, were hidden, and the light just glared back like off a snow field. But if you looked away from the sun, you looked into shades of grey, darker and darker. And that was pretty much all the colours there were on the Moon, except for what we brought with us, and what we left at home. Black sky, grey soil, blue Earth.

I remember I was talking nine to the dozen about the geology, as we bounced along. I was trying to describe it for the guys in the back rooms, back in Houston. You never knew when some observation of yours was going to provide the key to understanding.

But Joe was somewhat graver. He always was. Your father was a good five years older than me, remember, and he'd been to the Moon once already, on an orbital LM test flight, while I was a rookie; and I guess he just let me chatter.

We got to the foothills and started to drive uphill. That Rover seemed to carry us without effort even under pretty steep hills. But I felt like I was about to slip out the back the whole time. And when we stopped, and I tried to get up, I could barely raise my suited body out of the seat. We were concerned that the Rover would run downhill, and in fact I could see one of its wheels was lifting off the surface. I just grabbed onto the Rover; it was so light I felt I could support it easily. We found an eroded old crater to park in, and when Joe drove it forward, there we were.

Well, we found the big two-hundred-yard crater that was our main sampling objective. We climbed up towards the rim. It was like walking over a sand dune. In that old suit it felt as if I was inside an inflated tyre. But the footing under my feet got firmer, slowly.

As I approached the crater rim I began to walk into a litter of rocks. They must have been dug out of the crater by the impact that formed it, and they had rained down here like artillery shells. But that was long ago. Now the rocks' exposed faces were eroded, all but smoothed back into the surface from which they'd been dug out.

And so I climbed, chattering about the geology the whole way.

When I got to the crater itself I found it was maybe thirty yards deep, strewn with blocks ranging from a yard across to maybe fifteen yards.

I turned around. A few yards away I could see Joe, working through his checklist. His white suit glowed in the sunlight, except for his lower legs and boots, which looked as if they had been dragged through a coal scuttle. He moved stiffly, scarcely bending from the waist, and when he moved he tipped forward, like a leaning statue. But he was whistling, glowing in the light. We were happy up there. That's how I'll remember him, you know. Glowing on the Moon.

Anyhow, it was at that moment, at the rim of that crater, that I saw the tracks.

Rover tracks.

I took a couple of seconds to get my breath, to think about it.

Three-hundred-feet high, I was looking down at the mountain's broad flank. It merged with a bright, undulating dust plain that swept away, just a sculpture of craters: craters on craters, young and sharp and cup-shaped overlying old and eroded and subtle. Beyond that I could see mountains thrusting up into space. All of this was diamond sharp, under a black sky. And out there in the middle of it all was a single human artefact: our lander, a gleaming metal speck.

Well, I looked for the tracks again. They were still there. They were still Rover tracks.

At first I thought they must be ours. I mean, whose else could they be? But I could see *our* tracks; they snaked back over the plain to the lander. *These* went west-east. In fact you could tell by the tread marks that the vehicle that had made these tracks was going to the east.

I kind of shivered.

I called to Joe. At first he didn't believe me. I think he figured I might be in some kind of trouble, my suit overheating or some such. Anyhow, there were the tracks, large as life. And they still weren't ours.

Through all this, we hadn't said a word, and we were out of sight of the Rover's TV camera. I remember we flipped up our gold sun-visors and we just looked each other, and we came to a silent decision.

We clambered down to the Rover. We told the Mission Control guy in charge of the camera where to point, and we told them to look for themselves. There they were, tracks on the Moon, made by a Lunar Rover that sure wasn't ours. You could see them crystal clear in the TV images. I tell you, it was a relief to find that they saw them too, back in Mission Control.

Well, they debated for a time what to do, and we sat there and waited.

. . . If I looked at the ground, pocked and battered as it was, things didn't seem so strange. If you've ever seen a freshly ploughed field, harrowed and very fine, and you know when it rains on it, it gives you that sort of pimply look – that's what I called it, I called it a freshly ploughed field. It was dry as toast but it still had that appearance. Mundane, as you might say.

But whenever I looked up, there was the black sky above this glowing ground, and there was Earth, a brilliant blue crescent, a sight utterly unlike anything seen from the ground. It was electrifying, in moments, this realization of how far I'd come, of *where I was*.

I remember thinking that just being up there, driving a car on the Moon, would be strangeness enough for one lifetime, without *this*.

You might not believe it now, but some of the scientists wanted us to just ignore this wacko stuff and carry on with our timelined work. I felt a little of that anxiety too. We'd been rehearsing the science objectives for two years already, and we only had a few hours, and we might waste the whole damn thing if we followed some chimera, up here on the Moon. For example, maybe those tracks could have been made by a boulder that rolled down hill after a landslide. I mean, you could *see* that wasn't so, but it was possible, I guess.

In the end, after maybe ten minutes, we got the order to go ahead and, well, to follow those tracks. And I remember how my heart thumped as we loaded up the Rover again, and turned right, to the east, and set off in a big flurry of black dirt.

Another rockin' and rollin' ride: grey surface as wavy as an ocean surface, black sky, blue Earth. We didn't say much, on the way, following those crisp tracks. What was there to say?

I remember what I was thinking, though.

I'd always been fascinated by the notion of alien life. Well, I was in the space programme. It was a disappointment to me that by the time my mission rolled around – long before humans ever got there, I guess, in fact – it was clear to everybody that the Moon was dry as dust, and dead besides. We were going to the Moon for geology, not biology.

So I was getting pretty excited as we bounced along, following those tracks. Was it possible that we were in some kind of *2001* situation here, that we were after all going to find some kind of alien marker on the Moon, that those tracks we followed had been planted to lead us right there?

That isn't quite what we found.

Towards the eastern end of the valley, as we come over a ridge, there's this car. Immediately I can see it looks very similar to the

Lunar Rover, and there are two figures in it. They didn't seem to be moving. We stopped, maybe a half mile away, and just stared. I don't know what I was expecting – a monolith? Bug-eyed green guys? – but not *that*.

So we radioed Houston that we'd found this car, and we start to describe it. And they're mystified, but they start to get excited, we're excited. So we drove up to the other car, parked right along-side, and I got out and turned the TV on. I remember I wiped the lens clean of dust before I took the time to do anything else, but my heart was thumping like a jackhammer; the surgeons must have known, but it wasn't the time to raise an issue like that.

The occupants of the other car, two astronauts just like Joe and me, just sat there, not moving.

Anyhow I ran over to the passenger side, and Joe went to the driver's side. We just stood there, because by now we could see the two of them up close, and – you guessed it – the passenger's suit had my name sewn on it, and the other guy's had Joe's.

And then my heart was pumping harder, because I reached over and pulled up the gold sun visor, and I was looking at myself.

What can you say about an experience like that? It was unreal. In those heavy pressure suits, you're cut off anyhow. You can't see too well because of the curving glass all around your head, and you can't feel the texture of things because of your gloves. And there I was, looking out like a goldfish staring out of his bowl, staring at my own face.

But it wasn't like a nightmare – it wasn't like I was dead – whoever it was looked like me but it *wasn't* me. And, of course, the other fellow looked like Joe.

And now I got the shock of shocks, because my guy, the copy of *me*, turns his head, inside his helmet, and opens his eyes, and looks straight at me.

Well, he looked terrible, as if he'd been sitting there some time, but he was obviously alive. He mouthed, but I couldn't hear what he was saying.

So again we debated what to do, with each other, with Houston.

We didn't know who these guys were, of course, or how they got there, or any of it. But here they were, obviously in trouble, and nobody else to help them but us.

So we helped them.

I took the other me, and Joe took his twin. You can just lift up a person, up there on the Moon, with a little effort. The other me moved like a big stiff balloon, and I plumped him down, upright in the dust. Then I hooked up the hoses from my backpack to his. It was an emergency procedure we'd rehearsed any number of times, in case one of our backpacks failed. And meanwhile Joe hooked up himself to his copy. Then I pulled my twin's arm over my shoulder, and Joe did likewise, and we started to bounce our way down the hill and back to our LM.

We considered taking the Rovers, but it wouldn't have been an easy drive for either of us – even supposing the 'other' Rover had worked at all. And we would have been separated, too far apart to help each other. We just decided to get back home as soon as we could.

Not that it was too clear to me what we'd do when we got there. That old LM wasn't exactly a field hospital. But we could have brought the two guys home, I guess; the LM was designed to carry a couple of hundred pounds of Moonrock off the surface, and we could have crammed two extra guys into the Command Module, the ferry that was waiting in orbit to bring us home.

I guess.

The truth is we didn't think that far ahead. We just had to help those guys. What else were we going to do?

I do remember looking back at the Rover, though – our Rover – and looking at all the rocks we'd already collected, that now we wouldn't be able to bring on home. We were bringing back something unutterably strange, but we wouldn't be able to complete our mission.

It took us an hour to make it back to the LM. The surgeons insisted we stop for breaks along the way, letting ourselves cool down, sipping water out of the mouthpieces in our helmets. And so on.

It was hard work. I spent most of it staring down at my footing. The dust was like powdered charcoal. The surface was like walking on crisp, frozen snow, or maybe on a cinder track. I remember thinking that whatever came out of this, these would be the last steps I'd take on the Moon.

Well, we got back to Tycho Base, our landing site. And that was when we got our next shock.

Because the LM had gone.

At least, the ascent stage had, the cabin that would have carried us back to orbit. Only the truncated base remained. Neither of us spoke, if I recall, and nor did the capcom. What could you say? Without that LM we weren't going home.

I remember limping around that site, still supporting my copy, just looking. I could see Rover tracks and footprints converging on the truncated base of the Lunar Module. The LM itself was the centre of a circle of scuffed regolith, littered with gear, two thrown-out backpacks, urine bags and food packs, lithium hydroxide canisters and LM armrests, the detritus of three days of exploration, all of it just thrown out at the end of the stay, as we would have done. Somebody here had been and gone before us.

The LM was surrounded by glittering fragments, for its foil insulation had been split and scattered by the blast of the departed ascent-stage's engine. And there was a new ray system, streaks of dust which overlaid the footprints. But the gold insulation on the descent stage was discoloured, and in some places it had split open and peeled back. Joe tried to smooth it back with his gloved hand, but it just crumbled under his touch. The bird was evidently thoroughly irradiated, and remarkably dusty. The paint had turned to tan, but it was uneven, and when you looked more closely you could see tiny micrometeorite pits, little craters dug into the paintwork.

That LM had suddenly gotten old.

I remember looking up, looking for the Earth. Well, that was still there. And I saw a single, glittering star in the blackness, far above my head. It was the Command Module, in its two-hour lunar orbit, waiting to carry us home. Except we couldn't reach it, without a LM.

I wasn't afraid. It was all too strange.

. . . And then I heard our capcom yammering in my ear, telling me the surgeons were very concerned, I had to quit goofing off and get Joe into the LM.

Joe?

Well, I looked around. And I found I wasn't propping up some ghostly shadow of myself, but old Joe. Our two copies had gone, as if they'd never been, and it was Joe's backpack I was hooked up to. And when I turned again, there was the LM, intact once more, gold and silver and black, gleaming and glistening, good as new.

I looked at Joe, and Joe looked at me, and we didn't say a word.

I guess you know the rest of the story.

As far as the world was concerned, Joe had taken a pratfall

doing a dumb stunt, seeing how high he could jump in the one-sixth gravity, and snafued his suit, and I'd had to rescue him, walk him back to the LM on my backpack. That was what everybody else remembered; it's what the video records and even our voice transcripts show. I've seen the images myself. He falls with a dreamy slowness, like falling underwater. He has time to twist around, the stiff suit making him move as a unit, like a statue.

Except it didn't happen that way. That's just the way reality knit itself back together around us. You see?

Well, we didn't argue. We managed to get back into the LM, pressure up, and we prepared for an emergency launch.

We had time to think about it, in the three days it took to get back to Earth, and afterwards, in the long debriefings and all the rest.

I'll tell you what I concluded – though I don't think Joe ever agreed with me.

We're in some sort of Quarantine.

The early Moonwalkers were put in quarantine when they got back to Earth, just to be sure there were no bugs to hurt us here on Earth. So maybe we're seen as infectious, or even dangerous, like in that movie with the big robot – what was it called?

But it might be benevolent. Think about it. Maybe They cherish us. Maybe They cherish our art and religion and literature and stuff, and don't want to swamp us with their giant galactic civilization until we're ready. Maybe They are even protecting us from the real bad guys.

So They just hide it all. We're in some kind of shell. What we see around us isn't completely real; 'reality' is doctored, a little or a lot, as if we're in some giant Program, a virtual reality as you'd call it today, showing us what's best for us to see. But beyond the painted walls of our fake sky, the glittering lights of the interstellar cities light up the dark.

Walking on the Moon, we walked into a glitch in the Program. That was all.

That all seemed plausible to me, even back then. We didn't know about virtual reality. Believe me, though, we had computer glitches. At least it was a rational explanation.

What Joe believed, in the end, he never told me. He knew he could never tell the truth – as I couldn't – even though the subtle blaming for a screwed mission began even before we hit the Pacific. Even though old Joe came back carrying the can for a snafu, even

though his pride hurt more than he could say, he kept his peace.
And now he's taken his secret with him.

There was one more thing, Peter. I never discussed this, even with Joe.

On the way back I participated in a spacewalk between Earth and Moon. I wasn't fully outside. My job was to be a lifeguard if you will. I was to monitor our Command Module Pilot's actions as he collected data cartridges from the outer hull, and I held his lifeline, his tether which controlled communications and oxygen and restraint. I was to haul him back if he got into trouble.

So Ben floats out, starts hand over hand back to the Service Module. The Earth's off to the right, probably about a two o'clock low, just a little thin sliver of blue and white. And then I spin around, and there's this enormous full Moon, and it was – I mean it was overwhelming, that kind of feeling. And you could see Tycho, you could see Tranquillity, all the major features, and it just felt you could reach out and touch 'em. No sensation of motion at all. And everywhere else you looked was just black.

About fifteen minutes into this, with Ben doing his work nice and easy, I glanced at the Earth. And I saw ships in orbit.

Not little tin cans like ours. Giant golden ships. I had no sense of threat at all. Just watchfulness.

Next time I looked, those ships had gone, and there was the Earth, just a beautiful blue crescent, the loveliest thing.

It wasn't meant to happen, you see. It was just a glitch in the Quarantine Program. A bug. They just weren't ready for us to fly to the Moon so soon. They hadn't ordered the virtual-reality upgrades from Central Supplies in Andromeda, wherever. We just pushed it too far, and we got ourselves mixed up with other copies, or echoes, of ourselves. We crossed tracks, for a few hours.

But it turned into a test for us, for how we'd react to such strangeness. A test I liked to think we passed. I think that's why They showed Themselves to me.

Enough. Peter, I should let you go to your family. You decide what to do with what I told you. I just wanted you to know.

Wait until you see the Missing Man. Look out for the way that wing man peels off. I asked for him. Good pilot. Not so good as your father.

LINES OF LONGITUDE

There was one in every class, Sheila Pal had observed. With experience she had come to be able to spot him – and usually it *was* a him – the moment she walked in to face a new group.

And so it was now as she arrived on this chill January night at a draughty high school in Aylesbury, for the first of her six Tuesday evening sessions. The classroom was fitted with the standard rows of desks and a white board, and the walls were covered to chest height by the project work of the room's regular thirteen-year-old occupants.

It was a course she'd called *Einstein for Relative Beginners*. She was sponsored by the Workers' Educational Association, a voluntary organization which put on cheap courses on a variety of subjects aimed, in theory, at those who had missed out on education in the past. The 'Workers' tag was a hangover from earlier in the century; now most of the courses were vocational or aimed at improving job-related skills – interview techniques, for instance – and the WEA was pretty squarely directed at the unemployed, who could take the courses for free. But there was still room for more academic or offbeat items, such as Sheila's Einstein course.

There was a good turnout, for such an obscure and off-putting subject: a first glance, as she unloaded her notes, registration forms and props, revealed ten or twelve pupils, mostly men, mostly of retirement age.

And there, of course, *he* was: perhaps forty years old – about her own age, Sheila thought gloomily – with black hair thinning and unclean-looking, hunched in a corner, isolated even from this newly formed group. He had a thick, well-used notebook resting on top of his bulky coat. His gaze was on her already, but with none of the polite interest of the others, rather with an unhealthy eagerness.

She suppressed a sigh. Almost certainly he was just another run-of-the-mill obsessive who would be no real *threat*. He would just want her attention as he aired pet theories about space and time and the nature of reality – or, God forbid, UFOs. It was an occupational hazard for the science teacher in these post-rational times.

Summoning up a smile, she started to hand out registration forms.

He waited until the end of the class, when the other students had gone, before approaching her. It was harmless enough, as it turned out. He just pressed a letter into her hands: full of capitals, crudely pencilled on lined sheets, in some places the lettering pressed so hard the point had pushed through the paper.

Sheila collected up her materials and hurried out. She couldn't avoid the encounter, but she didn't want to be alone with this man. She climbed into her car, locked the doors, and pulled out.

She drove home, to her flat in a village on the outskirts of Milton Keynes. She left her teaching materials in the car; everything was on unofficial loan from the OU and she had to take it all back the next day anyway.

Her flat was a small, somewhat poky place, but her landlady was friendly, and the village was without street-lighting: on frosty winter nights – like tonight – the sky was crowned by stars. When she looked up, she immediately made out Orion's powerful figure astride the night.

After a bath and a cup of tea, she glanced over the letter.

It was about UFOs.

. . . Suddenly I realized I was being levitated to a height of a hundred and sixty feet. There were beings in the air with me. They were floating, as I was. They looked like babies, I thought, or perhaps monkeys, with grey skin, oversized heads, huge eyes, and small noses, ears and mouths. Their ship was golden. But its shape was distorted, as if I was looking through a wall of curved glass, and so were the aliens themselves. They seemed to have difficulty staying in one place. They could pass through the walls of their craft at will, like ghosts. They even passed through my body.

They took hold of my arms, and pulled me towards the wall of their ship. I looked for my mother on the ground below, but I could no longer see her. I passed into the wall as if it was made of mist; but I had a sense of warmth and softness.

I was in a cylindrical room. I was enclosed in a plastic chair with a clear-fitted cover. The cover was filled with a warm grey fluid. But there was a tube in my mouth and covering my nose, through which I could breathe cool, clean air. A telepathic voice in my mind told me to close my eyes. When I did so I could feel pleasing vibrations, the fluid seemed to whirl around me, and I was fed a sweet substance through the tubes. I felt tranquil and happy. I kept my eyes closed, and I seemed to become one with the fluid.

Later I was moved, within my sac. I was taken through tunnels and elevators from one room to another. The tunnels varied in length, but ended usually with doorways into brightly lit, dome-shaped rooms.

After a time my fluid was drained and I was taken out of the sac. It was uncomfortable and dry and my head hurt. I was pinned to a table. I was undressed. I did not seem able to resist, or even help in any way, had I wished. I was in a big bright room.

I seemed to lose consciousness.

I was standing outside my house again. The craft, the aliens with their sac, had gone. A moment before I had felt comfortably warm, inside my sac, and now I was bitterly cold and dry. It was the worst feeling I have ever had, that feeling of abandonment and rejection, for I knew they had only intended good.

It was now after dawn. It was full daylight, in fact. Some hours had passed . . .

His name was George Holland.

It was pretty much as she'd expected: a farrago of misunderstood cosmology and relativity, with a lashing of Richard Dawkins, and promises of more missives to come. And the heart of it, of course, was the UFO abduction account: run-of-the-mill stuff with psychological origins, for such a sad loner as George Holland, which seemed lucidly obvious to her.

What wasn't clear was what he expected her to do in response. Perhaps it was enough for him that he was communicating.

She read through half of the letter, then folded its several sheets and put them carefully into her course folder. She knew how offended he'd be if she simply discarded the letter, at least before her six weeks was up.

She fixed herself a drink, and tried to relax by watching the TV news. She wondered afresh why she put herself through this, even to the extent of running risks of encounters with oddballs like George Holland.

But she knew the answer to that. For Sheila Pal, teaching was an itch she had to keep scratching.

After taking a PhD in theoretical physics, and much against the advice of her parents and colleagues, she'd become a teacher, of maths and physics to A-level at a sixth-form college. She'd had no illusions about the challenges she would face – she'd done some supply teaching while taking her doctorate as a way of eking out her meagre grant – and in fact it had been that experience which had hooked her on education as a vocation.

Still, she'd soon been ground down: the absurd workload, the ill-suited and ill-advised students, the out of date and restrictive syllabuses, the inadequate funding and equipment. She lasted three years. The decision to quit was forced on her after a double lesson on vectors, the most graphic topic of her A-level maths syllabus, held first thing on a Monday morning in a twenty-year-old 'temporary' wooden annexe whose rat-chewed walls were so poor at keeping out the damp that none of her visual aids would work: even the blackboard was covered by a layer of dew so thick not a particle of chalk would adhere to it . . .

Perhaps the young George Holland had endured lessons in conditions like that. Perhaps things would have been different, for him, if he'd had a good teacher, decent educational opportunities. A teacher like herself, she thought.

She reached for his letter again, and read a little more.

. . . It all made sense to me after reading *Brief History of Time* – in so far as I could follow it, and the technical references I went into after that.

According to Hawking, there was no Big Bang.

Conventional physics says that if we could wind Time back to the Big Bang, the moment when the Universe began, we would see the world – the whole Universe, all of matter and energy, even Space and Time themselves – falling down a sort of funnel, compressing down into a point of unimaginable density and energy. And before the Big Bang there was nothing, nothing at all, not even Time.

But there are problems with that model. Infinite density, zero size? Even I know enough mathematics to know we can't handle such concepts. And the idea that there was another region where not even Time existed seems bizarre.

Hawking made it all clear to me – up to a point.

Hawking says there *was* no Big Bang. This is the concept of Imaginary Time, which is all a matter of quantum mechanics, but what it boils down to is this: the Universe isn't like a funnel at all. It's more like a Sphere, which folds over on itself in Imaginary Time, complete and closed. The Time we experience is just a Line of Longitude on that Sphere, among many such Lines. And the Big Bang – our Big Bang – is just a Pole on the Sphere, an arbitrary point. If you looked along different timelines, you would see back to different Poles.

Think about a globe of the world, with all the Lines of Latitude and Longitude. At the North Pole and the South Pole, all the Lines of Longitude come together. If we were at a Pole of Space and Time, the Lines of Longitude would spread out from here, so everything more than a little bit away from here would be smeared out and flattened.

But you could have the Pole somewhere else, and the Lines would come together there. It's a Pole to one person, but just another place to someone else. It's all how you see it.

And that's why the ships, and their crew, look distorted to us. They are from *somewhere else:* a different place, on the Sphere of Imaginary Time. Perhaps this is their Big Bang, which they've come back to observe. Of course there's no cosmic explosion going on here. But there doesn't have to be. It's all a sort of illusion, no more real than the convergence of Lines of Longitude on a globe.

When I read Hawking, all this became clear to me . . .

Stephen Hawking, she thought bleakly, had a lot to answer for.

There were a few odd points about the letter, she mused. Of course the subject matter was bizarre. But Holland did show a reasonable lay understanding of Hawking's arguments. And it was, at least, a novel rationale for the UFO phenomenon: those spacecraft which moved like no material object, viewed only in enigmatic glimpses. . .

The tone of the letter wasn't as self-obsessed and cranky as some she'd read – no invented cod-scientific terms, for instance – and the letter seemed to be addressed outward, to a person living independently of the contents of Holland's head.

It was as if, she thought, Holland truly had endured these experiences, and, bereft of guidance, was trying to find a framework to understand them, and to communicate them to others. Much as she might do herself, if she were to experience – or believed she had experienced – something so far out of the ordinary.

But then, what did she know of craziness? And why was she, alone in her flat in the middle of a winter's night, musing over George Holland's damaged psyche?

Because, she told herself, he's my student.

Leaving the teaching profession hadn't been easy. Aside from the emotional wrench and the feeling that she was betraying her students, she found she had to give a full term's notice, and so she ended up trapped for a further nine months. She'd hoped for a return to academia, but even short-term research contracts were as precious as gold dust, and the chance of a secure tenured post was effectively nil.

In the end, she took a job as a technician in a lab at the Open University. She was overqualified, but the job was actually more secure than an academic position, and not much worse paid, and she even got to do a little teaching.

The one good thing about the whole experience was that she had proved to herself, at least, that she'd been right in her choice of career. She *was* a born teacher. She'd enjoyed every lesson where the resources had by some chance been adequate for the job. And she knew her students had found her work enriching, beyond the narrow needs of the syllabus; she enjoyed the way she was able to get inside her students' minds, to see the material from their point of view, to overcome its difficulties and obscurities.

She'd even found the space to plug some of the more lamentable gaps in the syllabuses she was handed. The physics particularly seemed to pay no attention to the developments of the twentieth century; her students struggled with Victorian-standard science apparatus while the watches on their wrists and the calculators in their desks relied on the most advanced quantum-mechanical technology. So she put together simple demonstrations of ideas from quantum theory, relativity and cosmology, and was gratified by the understanding her students showed. Relativity, for instance: you could go a long way, at least with the special theory, with no more mental equipment than the geometry of Pythagoras's Theorem and the stark, startling fact that the speed of a photon was constant, no matter how quickly you moved, for space and time themselves – and your measuring rods and clocks – adjusted themselves to make it so . . .

Well, despite her failed career, she knew she'd been right in her life choices. It was society, in Britain in the 1980s, which had been out of step with *her*.

Still, the teaching itch remained strong. So she began a little work on various adult-education courses. Too often she came up against the old restrictions of syllabuses and recalcitrant students, but she appreciated the WEA particularly for the freedom and encouragement it gave her.

Even if it did bring her into contact with the likes of George Holland.

She shouldn't think like this. Holland was an oddball, but, she reminded herself, he was still a student, and showing enthusiasm for the subject in the only way he knew how . . .

Maybe she ought to learn to be more tolerant.

But on the other hand, she'd been warned before that her excessive sympathy for her more difficult students might one day lead her into trouble.

The next week, Holland gave her another letter.

. . . But if *all* points in Space and Time are really equivalent – if they are *all* Poles, if you take the right point of view – why can't we *see* it that way?

Relativity teaches us that Space and Time are malleable things. Space and Time adjust themselves to make the Speed of Light come out constant, for instance. And if so, perhaps we can train ourselves to *see* the world differently.

I've been running a series of experiments. I intend to train myself to *think* my way to a Pole. The experience would be wonderful, of course – to *see* those golden ships I can only glimpse now, distorted and compressed! – *if* it can be controlled.

I'm not at liberty to divulge the details right now – it would be far too dangerous to do so – for surely at a Pole one would be isolated: utterly alone, in a small lens-shaped area of Space and Time, in a way unprecedented in human experience.

And if the new way of seeing were to start to spread among the population, it could be disastrous.

Space and Time would be inverted. Instead of humans being as we are – crammed close together in Space, and fixed to a small duration in Time – we would be *scattered*: each of us isolated, in limitless Space and Time, alone for all eternity.

And the danger of such contamination is real. Of course I subscribe to Richard Dawkins's theory of the meme: the mental infection which leaps from mind to mind, enslaving whole populations in the manner of a religion, or a scientific paradigm. I would hate to be responsible for bringing such a meme into existence – for spreading the infection of loneliness and isolation to a single other person – perhaps even initiating the collapse of our consensual shared reality altogether.

That is why I must be careful.

But I have become convinced that I am on the right lines. Already, I am sure I have transported myself, mentally, closer to a Pole. For I can, you know, no longer see the sun. Or the stars, or Moon. The sky to me is a washed-out neon blur, grey and empty. It is as I expected. I am seeing the increasing divergence of the Lines of Longitude, as I migrate to the Pole . . .

George Holland didn't turn up for the fourth lesson. Nobody in the class knew where he was – in fact, none of the other students had troubled to learn his name. She was rather relieved, guiltily, to be spared the weekly letter.

And somehow it came as no real surprise to her when, a few days later, two policemen came to her flat. It was late on a clear, frosty night, and, tall and sombre, the police were both dressed in heavy black overcoats.

George Holland, they said, had been found dead.

It was in the house he shared with his mother. In fact his mother had discovered him, after returning from a long visit to relatives.

He had died of thirst, hunger and cold. The house was emptied of food. The police suspected it was a particularly bizarre form of suicide.

He had left behind one last letter, addressed to Sheila. The police watched as she opened and read it.

. . . I found the girl the day after the rest of the world folded away. I was disappointed; I thought it might be the spaceships.

I reached the Pole about lunch time on a Tuesday. Not that the time is important – or is it? I suppose I should record every detail . . .

This is how it happened.

My mother was away at her sister's. I remember standing at my bedroom window and looking out over the quiet street. There was a girl in a scarlet coat standing at the bus stop just along the road from our house. (This was the girl I would find later.)

Then I moved to the Pole.

It was extraordinary. The houses across the street started to flatten out, smearing like wet Polaroid photos. They became reddish streaks along the ground, and then the rest of the town beyond them squashed down to a line of colour. Even the air, the sky itself, was crushed down into that line.

I walked out of the house. It was quiet as the middle of a fog. I was in a dome of air about a hundred feet across. Our house was intact but the terraces to either side were melted out of shape; they looked like plastic models with one side melted and crushed down. I walked out past the twisted bus-stop sign. The next house along was about three feet high. I could look down into its chimney pots. And the next was just a brown smear on the ground.

I tried to walk out further but it was like walking through sticky oil, and it started getting harder to breathe. The ground was smooth as glass. I ducked down into the top of the atmosphere and peered ahead. I could see a brown line topped with blue. Sometimes I could see a hint of movement along that line, perhaps an aeroplane.

It was just as I had anticipated, from my studies of Hawking.

I walked back. That was a lot easier, like walking downhill. I felt exhilarated at my affirmation. I'd done it. I was at the Pole, a lens-shaped region of Space and Time, centred on myself. This was the place where all the Lines of Longitude meet, the place where the ships were. If I could see them, no doubt they could see me, and would take me back. All I had to do was wait for the ships to come and find me.

I walked all around our house, stepping over the roofs of the ones next door. I hoped I'd find the ships waiting already, but they weren't there. I supposed I'd have to be patient.

I made myself a supper from a snack bar. Chocolate sandwiches. There wasn't much food in the fridge, but I didn't suppose it mattered. I won't be here much longer, once the ships arrive. I wrapped up the rest of the chocolate bar for the next day.

I was a bit surprised when it got dark. I can't see the sun; there's only a sort of pearly neon light over everything, but the light goes down in the evening. The electric lights won't turn on, though, and the TV is dead. I've got a radio that works on batteries but there's only a mush, even at the highest volume.

It got quite cold, that first evening, so I went to bed. I had a

313

lot of trouble sleeping. I kept hearing noises, little scratching sounds.

It was light but still cold when I got out of bed, so I put my coat on over my pyjamas and went down to the kitchen. There was a trickle of water dripping out of the fridge. I opened it up. There was a stink of spoiled milk in there, but the chocolate was gone. Even the paper had vanished.

So it couldn't be mice. What mouse would eat foil wrapping? There had to be another person with me, here at the Pole.

I tried to get washed, but there was only a brownish trickle of cold water out of the taps. And I couldn't shave because there was no power for my razor.

I searched the house from top to bottom, walked around and around, stepping over the roofs again. Nothing.

Then I went out into the street and started to shout, making as much noise as I could.

Eventually she came running out of the front door and stood in the middle of what was left of the street. It was the girl in the red coat I'd seen at the bus-stop the day before. She held her hands to her ears and she was crying. 'Stop it! Stop it!' Tears splashed down onto her coat, of shiny plastic.

I stood in front of her. 'Did you take my chocolate?' My throat was scratchy after all the shouting.

She nodded, and then lowered her hands and looked up at me, dabbing her eyes with the back of her hand. She had blonde hair but it was all over the place, a real mess. And her mascara had been washed over her face. 'I was hungry,' she said.

I shrugged. 'Well, I don't care.' And I didn't. Once the ships arrive, I won't be hungry again. I started walking back to the house.

'Wait!' She ran after me, but stopped a few yards away, trembling. 'Please . . .' She opened and closed her mouth a few times, like a fish. She was no more than twenty, I suppose, and she had nice teeth, like a row of little pearls. 'What's happened? Where are we? Do you know?' She waved her hand around vaguely, pointing to the blue-and-brown line all around us. 'Has there been a war?'

'A war?' I laughed. 'No. No war. We've moved, that's all. To the Pole. I thought it was just me, to tell you the truth. I didn't know you were here too. I don't suppose it matters.'

She had a small face that creased up now as she tried to work it out. 'What Pole? What do you mean?'

I tried to explain, but she looked distant, and avoided my eyes. It's a look I've come to recognize: the sign of a closed mind.

I turned and walked away from her, back to the house.

'Wait,' she called. 'Don't go . . . Could I, uh, could I come in too?'

I left the door open.

Later on, when it got dark, I heard her come in and sneak around. She opened the fridge door with a click, but there was nothing left. I'd poured the rotten milk down the sink. Then, after I went to bed, she crept upstairs to my mother's bedroom.

I heard her crying. I put my coat on and went into my mother's room and sat on the edge of the single bed. She was sitting up, shivering and crying. It was nearly pitch black but I could see her big eyes looking at me.

'You shouldn't cry,' I said. My voice sounded loud and clumsy. 'We'll be alright, as soon as the ships come.'

The girl said nothing, sitting up in bed in her red coat. I could see her trembling like a rabbit.

I went back to bed. I didn't sleep again.

I got out of bed feeling gritty and cold. The girl had gone, leaving my mother's bed rumpled and cold. She wasn't anywhere in the house, not even the kitchen.

It took me a few minutes to find her. She'd walked as far away from the house as she could get, had flattened herself out against the glassy ground at the edge and reached out one hand to the blue-brown line. She had rings on three fingers on that hand. Her lips were blue and her eyes had rolled up, showing white. Her tongue was sticking out. I crawled out and grabbed her ankles, pulled her back into the air.

She breathed again in huge gasps. When she opened her eyes and saw me she started to cry. 'Let me go. Please.'

I felt very angry. 'You shouldn't be scared. They'll be here soon.'

She shut her eyes and kept crying, and said: 'Please, please . . .' Over and over.

And then she folded away. I'm not sure if I did it or if she did it herself. She just rolled flat into a sort of bright red streak and flashed away like a scarlet worm.

So that was that. Since then I've been alone in this fog, waiting.

I hope they're here soon. I haven't eaten anything for days now, and it's getting very cold here . . .

*　　*　　*

The police had found no sign of any girl, red-coated or otherwise.

Sheila told the police what little she knew of Holland, and described the uncertain contact she had had with him. She tried to make the policemen share her understanding of Holland's delusions and obsessions, of lines of space-time longitude and mental infections and golden UFOs – as far as she understood them herself – but she could see the police switching off, and labelling George Holland with brutal efficiency as 'nutter', or 'anorak'.

After an hour or so they seemed to have decided they had enough. They closed their notebooks, thanked her for her time, and left. They took the letter with them; by tomorrow, she expected, it would be all over the tabloids.

After they'd gone, she found it hard to relax. She tried TV, and reading, but nothing distracted her.

She couldn't put aside the image of Holland dying alone, trapped at the 'Pole' he had constructed for himself, waiting endlessly for UFOs which never came.

What was the true horror for Holland, the reason he had shut out the world? She'd always thought of UFO abduction, whatever the psychological truth of the phenomenon, as a horrific experience. But Holland seemed to have *enjoyed* his abduction. Perhaps the true terror for him was of the final abandonment, at the end of a life of abandonments: the terror of being the one they left behind . . .

She went to bed. But sleep, never easy for her, seemed further away than ever. Holland's bizarre world-view stayed in her head. Perhaps it was just her teacher's sympathy. Or perhaps Holland with his last letter had, after all, infected her with some meme. Well, if so, by tomorrow, millions more who would read what she'd read were just as much at risk.

She smiled. The loner who brought about the end of the universe. If she looked out in the street now, would she see his golden UFOs, cruising across the sky?

. . . In fact, the light outside was oddly bright.

She went to her window and pulled back the curtain. The window was misted up. She wiped the glass with her sleeve, and pressed her face to the window, looking for Orion.

She couldn't see the stars. The sky was a washed-out neon blur, grey and empty.

BARRIER

Let me say at once that I have no regrets.

Both Gurzadian and I were men with wings on, and that means we were willing to accept risks. Naturally nobody expected the contingency we've come up against here, but we always knew the odds were against us in terms of getting all the way to Proxima II. In fact we would both have volunteered, even without the Draft.

I'm downlinking everything in the hope somebody will pick this up, although we've had no contact with the ground for a hundred days now. *Geezer* seems to be stuck fast in this barrier at the edge of the solar system, so maybe someday somebody will come out here to pick this up, and read it.

I'm not one for melodramatic gestures.

I'll complete as much as I can before the hull implodes.

I joined *Geezer* in LEO, in low Earth orbit.

I launched in a new-series Soyuz craft from Kazakhstan. Chemical technology: obsolete in these days of the Bias Drive, of course, but you may as well shoot 'em off as break 'em up. There was a sign on the launch pad saying 'Reliable Launch Complex Guarantees Success'. That's the kind of little touch you just don't get back home any more, which, in my opinion, is all part of a more general decline.

There was no foofaraw when we left. This was not Project Mercury. A lot of the coverage of America's first interstellar mission failed even to mention the fact that two human beings were going along for the ride, and we never met a single one of the program's head sheds. Once, when I flew Shuttle, I got to shake the hand of Ronald Reagan. Things sure have changed.

Anyhow it was a thrill to feel those bolts blowing, and that boot up the rear as the Gs cut in, and to know I was leaving Earth once more.

The truth is I'd gotten pretty tired of sitting around in the grey gulag waiting for my Demograph Draft. Anything would be better, I'd decided, even a ticket to the happy booth. And when my notice turned out to be the commission for *Geezer*, I was pleased – even relieved – but I found I wasn't really so surprised to hear that old shipping-over music one more time.

I was already over ninety years old.

But I knew I was more than capable of returning to space, of doing this job. Jenna always said that I have spent much of my life trying to appear humble, but failing. Humility is not a favoured trait among air and space pilots, where a high premium is placed on performance.

I suppose, however, I *was* surprised to find that the Draft was leading me, not to some sky-boring LEO mission as I first thought, but to the stars themselves.

The Bias Drive's acceleration is pretty low. We spent weeks in Earth orbit, slowly spiralling away.

All in all, the old world hasn't changed much since I first saw it from orbit in the early 1980s, Christ, nearly sixty years ago. Can't honestly say it looks *better* now, however.

There's more desert, of course, all around the tropical belt. The cities are bigger and brighter than they were, although over the US – what's left of it since the secessions – the view is obscured by the huge megacorporate logos laser-painted on the lower cloud decks. The logger wars are still blazing in South America; you can see the flash of weaponry at night.

The China–Russia border is just a wilderness. You can see the string of bomb craters. I know there are still some who criticize the Administration for keeping us out of that conflict. Not me. A well-trained military man has reason to fear war.

As we receded the signs of humanity were soon invisible. Earth became a planet of ocean, desert and ice, just as it always was.

We sailed past the bony Moon, and I glimpsed the shadows of Farside craters. I found myself singing that old song: *Drifting and Dreaming*. Even as a kid in small-town New Jersey I never dreamed I'd go further than this.

Well, I was wrong. Earth and Moon receded, blue and grey.

Gurzadian, my sole crewmate, was ten years older than me. He had a head like a bullet, a barrel chest and arms like a big Russian bear's. He habitually wore a rumpled red jump-suit with the legs tied off in knots. The loss of his legs, after a Soyuz landing accident long before *Geezer* was ever thought of, didn't make a damn difference to his mobility as far as I could see. In fact Gurzadian was living proof of the saw that in space your hands and arms do all the work and your legs just get in the way.

I don't know what I need tell you about *Geezer*.

Geezer – strictly *New Explorer* – is mankind's first interstellar craft, and it is a big maumoo. It is a cluster of six modules nose to nose around a transfer node, which is a Grand Central Station for ducts and pipes and cables. The modules are wrapped in thick insulating blankets, yellowing now and pitted by micrometeorites.

Five of the modules are for science. There is a base block where we – I – sleep and live, and where the controls for the cooling systems and oxygen regenerators and waste recyclers and other stuff are situated. It's like my old garage in here. There's stuff bolted to every wall, and to reach anything you have to move layers of kipple. The pumps and fans make it sound like an old boiler-house. It always sounds louder at night; I don't know why that should be. And it smells like a library: old books, mixed with a little engine oil. The musty book smell is mould, of course.

Our power comes from big clunky nuclear-fission reactors descended from the old Soviet 'Topaz' design. The design of most of the components of this craft is basically Russian, in fact. The Russians have been learning to live in space with this technology for decades, and I for one was happy to step aboard.

There are small automated orbiters and landers studded around the cluster, gliders and entry pods, intended to be deployed when we reached Proxima II. The probes are modern: small and smart, built around the latest autonomous-software designs – qubit technology in fact – and their micromechanical systems pack a lot of punch per pound. But they can't carry people, not even a pair of chicken-boned old farts like Gurzadian and me. Well, that's the nature of the modern space program, and there's a whole debate to be had about man versus machine and the nature of human exploration I don't have the time to get into here.

The Bias Drive is just a little black box mounted on a boom.

It thrusts through the cluster's centre of gravity at a steady one per cent of G. Not much, but enough to get us to Proxima in forty-some years, with a peak velocity at turnaround of eighty per cent of lightspeed. Quite a marvel.

Of course you have to realize that it's only the propulsion technology that has developed since my day. Otherwise *Geezer* is just Station technology with a few more life-support loops closed. When the solids recycler broke down Gurzadian and I still had to take the covers off and stir our shit by hand. Hey ho.

Forty years isn't so much. But nobody can build systems for forty-year reliability, not without qubit technology anyhow. And that's why we were sent along for the ride.

Qubit technology is quantum computing. In a qubit chip, the bits are represented by the spin states of chloroform molecules. It seems these spin states exist *simultaneously* in some spooky way. A qubit machine beats out a conventional device every time because it can process its bits, not one after the other, but *at the same time*.

The problem with qubits is their fragility and expense, and hence rarity. The top-of-the-range stuff is forever snapped up by the big corporations for their commercial purposes which, like the doings of federal agencies, are generally beyond me. The world is now run, it seems to me, by huge, shadowy qubit AIs, far beyond any kind of democratic control.

Anyhow, for sure, NASA and the federal government can't afford to buy in qubit technology big time. And there's the paradox.

It used to be that people were too expensive to haul into space, because they mass so much, not to mention all the related plumbing. It was more cost-effective to send out a smart little robot to explore by proxy. But the equation's changed. The robots have gotten *much* more expensive. Meanwhile the Bias Drive has made human spaceflight dirt cheap, comparatively. Suddenly it's cheaper to ship two old fuckers like Gurzadian and me, plumbing and all, with a brief to keep the ship's systems working long enough to reach Proxima.

Our telomerase implants should have kept at least one of us alive that long.

A telomere is a series of organic compounds which cap the ends of chromosomes, like the plastic tip of a shoelace. The telomere gets shorter every time a cell divides. Eventually, the cell won't divide any more, and it dies.

When I reached my seventy-fifth birthday I was able to purchase telomerase treatment. Bluntly speaking this enzyme restored the telomere tips of my cells, and they became youthful again. My bones stopped getting weaker, my spine stopped curving, my skin stopped from sagging, my brain stopped shrinking, my shanks stopped withering, my gums no longer retreated. I wasn't getting younger, of course, but I wasn't getting any older either. I'm not spared the various afflictions of age. But thanks to my telomerase implant I have a life expectancy of a hundred and fifty upwards.

Or did have.

Of course the irony is that it was telomerase treatment which finally blew the values of our society out the water. That and the collapse of Medicare. In my opinion at least.

Anyhow it all worked out. A few months out and Gurzadian and I had stripped down and rebuilt this big-old bomber until you could have run a white-glove inspection any hour of the day or night.

There is a certain logic in sending old guys into space.

Even before the demographic bomb you had astronauts still flying in their fifties and sixties. And the idea of crewing Mars ships, for example, with oldsters was openly discussed at NASA and elsewhere. If you go as far as Mars and back, you've taken on more than your recommended lifetime dose of radiation. Not a good idea until you're done having your kids.

Conversely the space environment can actually be beneficial. I know my heart has benefited from the reduced strain of low G. And we old timers are patient. A spacecraft is a cramped, unforgiving environment, and a hotshot of thirty is not necessarily the ideal crewman.

Frankly I regard myself well suited to this berth. Experience is the key. Mock combat is *not* equivalent to facing a guy intent on killing you. Simulated emergencies are *not* an equivalent experience to bringing a Shuttle orbiter down on one fuel cell, as I once did. And so forth.

What I'm saying is that I'm not sure a wet-diaper crew could have coped with what we found out here.

I remember I was eating when the first problem came up.

I was at the tiny table in the base block with my legs wrapped around my T-seat. Most of what we got to eat was Russian stuff, warm borsch and jellied perch, which is okay when you get used to it. But it was Christmas week, and that day I was treating myself to stew. I always liked Christmas.

In came Gurzadian, swimming through the air like a fat Russian dolphin. He was somewhat excited. He was jabbering in a mix of Russian, English and pidgin, and when I slowed him down enough to untangle it all, it turned out he thought we had a problem with our trajectory, or maybe our navigation systems, or both.

Since at the time we were rather remote from Earth – in fact, after twenty-one months, we were already more than twice as far from the sun as Pluto – this could, I felt, ruin my entire day.

Let me set out the elements of interplanetary navigation. Navigation means the skill of plotting a route and directing a craft along it. In practice you determine your ship's state – that is, its position and velocity – and estimate a trajectory from that point. The problem is made more interesting by relativistic effects as you approach lightspeed, such as aberration. All of this is an exercise in constrained optimization and adaptive parameter estimation, techniques in which I am somewhat skilled.

When Gurzadian raised the alarm, I found our position and trajectory vectors were all undetermined.

We began internal system checks. We have two basic data-gathering systems. The first of these is radiometric, in which our range and speed relative to Earth are estimated from properties of our radio signals, such as round-trip delay times and Doppler shifts. The second system is optical. We determine the craft's position and attitude using observations of background stars and the planets. To achieve this we have a small Cassegrain telescope coupled to a light-sensitive diode sensor array. Measurements are accurate to one second of arc.

The radiometry was all over the place, and the optical suite couldn't find any of its target stars, and even the planets weren't where they should be.

We checked the systems and found them faultless. I also ran a number of diagnostic tests on the computer systems which supported the navigation suites. These are all American systems. They aren't qubit, but they are based on ex-USAF rad-hardened silicon systems, and are pretty damn reliable.

Gurzadian, being Russian, was somewhat sceptical of this, and he said something sarcastic along the lines of, 'Well, if there is no fault in your systems, my friend, there must be a fault in the universe.'

That was my prompt to look out the window. And, by golly, he was right.

That was when we lost contact with the ground.

It was a shame, because the first few months of the mission had gone about as well as could be expected.

Gurzadian and I had gotten along pretty well, given our culture clashes. Russians always assume Westerners are soft and weak. Gurzadian would be condescending to me, and he tried to protect me from bad news. There was the time I woke to the smell of smoke. Gurzadian shrugged, and said there had been an unplanned burning of an oxygen cylinder. It turned out there had been a sheet of flame three feet long that nearly burned through one bulkhead in the biotech module. But this 'unplanned burning' wasn't a *fire*, you understand, because nothing else had caught alight. And as Gurzadian had put it out he hadn't thought necessary to report it to me.

The Russians in space just get on and fix things without whining. Basically I admire that attitude; it's something else we lost, somewhere along the way.

The highlight was the gravity-assist swingby of Jupiter.

We dug deep into the gravity well, for as you may know the lower the perijove the greater the assist obtained. Of course we were also thereby taken through Jupiter's magnetosphere, the most ferocious radiation environment in the solar system outside the orbit of Mercury, but that's okay; the little Proxima orbiters and landers are rad-hardened, and we'd both long exceeded federal worker radiation-dose allowances, not that anybody gave a shit.

Jupiter is a hell of a sight, let me tell you. The shadows of the Galilean moons sail across the cloud tops, which are a kind of autumn gold, dimmer than you'd expect. My trusty Hasselblad jammed at closest approach, but I was able to tear it down. The problem was the gear train, a problem I fixed with a speck of Neosporin, an ointment from the medical kit.

Anyhow the whole thing was terrific. Like something out of James Blish – remember *Earthman Come Home*? – the stuff that got me into space in the first place. Even Jupiter was a sight I never dreamed of seeing for myself – and here I was on my way to Proxima Centauri.

I remember the stir when the first direct images of the Proxima exoplanets came in, blurred dots captured by the Hubble and the

Superhubble in the early '00s. One superjovian, ten times the size of Jupiter, swooping in to about half Earth's distance from the sun, and a string of five or more smaller Jovians. The interesting one, of course, is Proxima II, which looks to have a bunch of Earth-sized rocky moons, all about the right distance from the star for liquid water.

Of course back then I never expected anyone to be sailing to the stars: not in my lifetime, probably never, certainly not if NASA had anything to do with it. But then NASA invented a star drive by accident.

In the late '90s NASA started its Breakthrough Propulsion Physics Program, operating out of Lewis. No serious money, of course, just a handful of wacko funny-physics egghead types and a Web site. A PR stunt while NASA poured billions into Station.

. . . Until, out of the blue, the double-domes came up with the Bias Drive.

Gurzadian could have explained it better than me. It seems that the whole universe, atoms and people and stars, is generated from the wriggling of a membrane floating in 11-dimensional space. One of those dimensions is collapsed down, rolled up to a tube, and the way the membrane wraps itself around that tube generates the properties of the particles and forces we see around us.

This is the M-theory: the new theory of everything. The M, it seems, stands for 'membrane', but as far as I'm concerned it could equally be 'mirrors' as in 'smoke and'. They teach this stuff in the high schools now. Science has come a *long* way since I flunked geometry.

It seems that old membrane can wrap itself up in two ways. A *single* loop generates energy levels from modes of vibration, like a violin string. Or the membrane can wind itself around the tube *many* times, and the number of turns gives you energy levels, like coils around an armature. One wrapping mode describes the large-scale structure of the universe. The other mode describes small-scale energy structures, such as those of an electron.

But here's the catch: when the tube is middle-sized, the vibration modes look the same as the wrapping modes. That means that the universe on very *small* scales looks the same as it does on *large* scales. This is called duality. For instance, electron charge by one description is equivalent to the size of things in another.

Anyhow that, as I understand it, is how the Bias Drive works.

A tiny piece of the universe is shrunk down and manipulated.

Another piece, linked by duality, opens up behind the ship. It is a miniature Big Bang, a wave of space-time that pushes us forward. A little more precisely, the drive creates a localized asymmetric bias in the properties of space-time which generates a local propulsive gradient on the ship. It amounts to a rocket of infinite specific impulse.

It was as if space-propulsion technology leaped forward a thousand years overnight.

We should have expected something like the Bias Drive, back in the '80s or '90s. After all we'd been flying the same old Nazi missile technology for fifty years by then; we were overdue for a breakthrough. Gurzadian said science and technology doesn't proceed in a smooth upward slope, but with big upward hops between plateaux. *Punctuated equilibrium,* he called it. And we lived long enough to see one of those punctuation marks.

Anyhow, that is how I found myself sailing to the stars. It's the paradox of modern America: a land of starships on the one hand, gulags for the old on the other. Maybe these tensions were already there, back when I grew up in New Jersey. All I know is it's no longer *my* kind of America.

After that first panic, it took some days to establish what was going on.

The radio signals from Earth were reduced in frequency, as if red-shifted, and subject to excessive time delay, and reduced in magnitude. When we managed to reacquire the signal, Houston and Kalinin were both saying they had lost our beacon signal.

We tried adjusting frequency and boosting the amplitude, but nobody, it seemed, could hear us.

Meanwhile we measured whatever it was that was happening outside. I backed up the ship's sensors with my own observations; for instance I mocked up a small theodolite to measure star angles.

To cut a long story short: the magnitudes of the target stars were all lower than they should be. The *angles* between the target stars, when we managed to identify them, weren't what they should be.

I couldn't come up with a consistent model for what we were seeing. If we'd somehow gained too much velocity, that could explain some of the effects, like the excessive redshifting of the ground signals. But it didn't explain the redshifting of stars *ahead* of us – stars which ought to be turning blue as we hurtled toward them. And besides, those changing star angles weren't consistent with any such hypothesis.

Gurzadian developed his own theories.

He said that as far as he could see space itself was distorted around us.

He'd set up piezoelectric strain gauges to prove it to himself. It's kind of flattening out, he said. There were stresses acting across *Geezer's* cluster because of that – like tidal stresses.

It was, he said, as if we were trapped in a bubble universe, which was collapsing around us. Ha ha.

Meanwhile Gurzadian thought about the bigger picture.

He quoted the assumption of mediocrity. We'd flown out of the solar system, straight into this muddled space. There was no reason to suppose the trajectory we'd selected was special in any way. Therefore you had to assume that the muddled space lay all around the solar system, like a shell enclosing the sun. A barrier. And all we could do was keep on driving into it.

All I knew was, every time I looked out the window, the stars were getting dimmer and redder.

But then there hadn't been any scenery since Jupiter anyhow.

I'll be truthful and tell you that we'd got a little bored, before we hit the barrier anyhow.

Of course we have a giant online library. I wish we had more honest-to-God *books*. But the truth is my concentration isn't what it used to be. The surgeons call it the Tithonius syndrome: immortality, but ageing.

We played games a lot. Low-G games, like where Gurzadian would make a loop of his thumb and forefinger and I would try to throw a pen through. We were a little better at catching cinnamon cubes in our mouths, like at cocktail hour with peanuts. We'd make it more interesting by knocking the cubes off course with blasts from an air hose.

Gurzadian played a lot of his favourite discs, which are all Russian romance music. My hearing isn't too good now so I forgave him that. Sometimes I admit I longed for the clean howl of an electric guitar, however.

We would one-up each other continually. And we would bullshit, in a mixture of languages, the whole damn time. Mostly about the past, but that's old people for you.

I may have mentioned I grew up in a small town in New Jersey.

My father had been an Army flier. He took me up for the first time when I was eight, in a beat-up Aeronca C3. We climbed into a stiff wind that blew so hard we flew backwards in relation to the ground. From then on I was hooked.

I cut my teeth as a brown-shoe Navy man. That is, I was a Navy aviator. I saw some combat in Korea, which is detailed in the record. Later I moved to the Test Pilot School at Patuxent; I was therefore a member of the Society of Experimental Test Pilots before I joined the space program.

I wasn't sorry to retire from NASA. Once, briefly, we were a space-faring nation. England, Spain and Portugal crossed the seas and found greatness. Similarly we reached for the skies and ennobled ourselves. But I believe NASA has long lost its success mystique, and I have come to understand that our snout-in-the-trough politicians will not commit to a program that may take more than ten years to come to fruition, which rules out most serious ventures. To me it's all of a piece with other turns our society has taken, which, while disastrous, are no surprise.

After NASA and the Navy I went into various business ventures. I served on the boards of several suppliers to the major aerospace contractors. I retired from *that*, and went to live in a retirement community built like a fortress, and played a lot of golf. I thought I was heading for a rather long but comfortable dotage. The only cloud on my horizon had been the loss of my wife, Jenna, to cancer.

That was when Congress started passing the demographics bills, which is why, in a nutshell, I find myself here.

Gurzadian was always rather more reticent about his background.

I knew that after leaving the Soviet space industry, he'd fled the collapse of Russia and found some work on Wall Street computer systems. But then he committed the crime of growing old.

He'd been living quietly alone when it started. The talk-show jokes about long-lived geezers. The commentaries and black humour about the demographic bulges, the lack of jobs for the young, the burden of the growing number of elderly. The implicit approval for neglect and cruelty.

Gurzadian actually witnessed one of the early attacks on a retirement home, the fat cops standing around doing nothing. He went hobbling in on his fake legs and got beat up for his trouble. Saved a couple of lives, however.

He said he wasn't surprised by what followed: punitive age-related taxes, the removal of the vote at age eighty-five, the grey stars we had implanted on our palms. He said it was a pattern he'd seen before: first they remove your dignity, then your property, then your rights, then your life. Until at last you're cleansed.

We talked for long hours. The way he told the familiar story was chilling; this was a man who had seen it all before, in a different context. The difference was, this time it wasn't one ethnic group against another. It was children against parents.

The thing of it is, of course, someday every last one of those who abuses us now is going to cross the barrier into the place we're at. Payoff time.

Please note we did have work to do.

In the cluster's various modules we did biotech research, and low-G material science, and astrophysics. Gurzadian had some astrophysics training, but we were both basically aviators. Therefore the 'science' we did was simple lab-rat stuff, working sensors and running experiments for ground-based researchers. There was a lot of the usual Nazi-doctor medical stuff as space slowly killed us.

Gurzadian studied quasars. A quasar is a primitive galaxy lit up by the collapse of matter into a central, supermassive black hole. As the first observers to travel out of the dust-laden plane of the ecliptic, that was a key objective for us. Gurzadian said we were looking for the most ancient quasars, relics of the dark age of the universe.

He liked to tell me stories, the potted history of the universe.

First there was the light of the beginning. But as the Big Bang fireball expanded and cooled the light shifted out of the visible region of the spectrum, and the universe entered a dark age: just a few pinpricks, giant early stars and scattered quasars. The darkness lasted millions of years, while the universe grew a hundred times in size – until the first stars and galaxies formed, and the cosmos lit up like a Christmas tree. Quite a sight.

Eventually the universe will be dark again, said Gurzadian. The star stuff will run out. It will take a trillion years, but that's *nothing* compared to the long future.

We're fortunate, said Gurzadian. To exist in this little interval of light, between the darknesses. It made me glad, briefly, to be alive.

As the first interstellar explorers, we would argue about the philosophy of starships. Like the old Fermi question: where the hell is everybody?

The galaxy contains hundreds of billions of stars. If just *one* of those supported a colonizing civilization, even with ships no more advanced than *Geezer,* the galaxy would be completely conquered in no more than a few million years. As the galaxy is *billions* of years old, Earth should have been colonized a hundred times over before life crawled out of the sea, and the night sky ought to look like Los Angeles from the air.

But it doesn't.

Gurzadian had thought long and hard about these problems. The Russians have always had more than their share of space dreamers. Gurzadian believed *they* must be out there, looking in, because it's logically impossible that they don't exist. Maybe we just aren't smart enough to recognize them. Or maybe they're keeping themselves hidden. The zoo hypothesis, that's called.

Maybe we'll find out the answers at Proxima, he would say. Ha ha.

Funny thing was, he was half right.

I'd like to put on record I was more than happy to accept Gurzadian as my crewmate. We didn't always get along, but he knew this old bird inside and out before we left the ground. Besides which he was actually a pilot. In my opinion people who don't fly the spacecraft should not be called astronauts. Both Gurzadian and I were, you would say, out-of-the-pack people.

And, let me say, we both preferred talking philosophy and the old times to mulling over Demograph Draft horror stories.

I don't think either of us lost much sleep over those dimming stars.

It was kind of a relief to find that our problems were only cosmological – that it was indeed the universe that was at fault and not our craft. We remained calm, and continued to do our bits of science, and to downlink our results and progress reports, whether or not anybody could hear us.

If that sounds peculiar, you have to remember that neither of us were meant to survive the mission anyhow.

The stars winked out one by one, fading into a redness like the inside of my eyelid. I admit my heart thumped a bit on the day we lost the sun.

But the thing of it was, we could see something ahead. Something new.

Grey stars.

Not Proxima Centauri, though. Not really stars at all, in fact. Just a scattering of grey lights around the sky. Gurzadian said they looked like quasars. He was scared. None of this made sense to him; he couldn't figure out what we were seeing, what had happened to the stars.

As for me I felt kind of cheated. It's no longer clear to me if Proxima even exists, or if it – and its planetary system – aren't just some artefact of the huge shell which surrounds us. Damn it, Proxima *ought* to exist. Who the hell has the right to take away man's nearest star – the dreams of my boyhood – and, worse, to render my mission meaningless, a vain flight in pursuit of a mirage?

I remember the day I was given the grey star on my palm, a mark that I was too old to be given a job rather than some younger person. I marched to the welfare office and I wore that star with pride, damn it. I still have it here, a hundred AU from Sol.

But it got worse.

The life-extending technologies, like telomerase, started to be withdrawn. And they introduced the confiscation of assets at age eighty. Of course we'd have voted it down, if they hadn't taken the vote away from us first, along with our drivers' licences. Disenfranchizement and enslavement. What kind of society supports *that*?

We bore it all. It was a bad day, though, when they broke up the nursing homes and retirement communities, and forced us all into the grey gulags, all of us whose families would not shelter us.

We watched that shoot-out in West Virginia, a bunch of stay-put old soldiers pitting themselves against the FBI, and we cheered ourselves hoarse.

In the end, of course, we couldn't win.

When we didn't die off fast enough, they went further.

It was a couple of days after we lost the sun that the biotech module blew. I was in the base block at the time, changing carbon dioxide scrubber canisters.

There was a thud, a groan of strained metal, a flurry of red lights, a wailing klaxon.

I did what I was trained to do, which was to stay absolutely still. If there was a bad leak the air would gush out of the ship, and my ears would pop suddenly and painfully, which would be about the last thing I would know about.

To my relief I could feel the leak was a slow one.

And then Gurzadian came barrelling past me, pulling his way to the transfer node. When we got there he began pulling out the cables and ducts that snaked into the biotech module, because that, he said, was where the leak was, and we had to get the hatch clear before we could close it.

It took half an hour. Lousy design, I guess. Gurzadian said he'd been *expecting* a seam to blow for a couple of days. *Geezer* was being crushed by those damn space-time stresses. I just watched the barometer creep down to the 540 millibar mark, where we'd start to lose consciousness.

Then the power failed, all over the ship. Dim emergency lights came on, and the cabin lights and instrument panels went dead, and the banging of the pumps and fans fell silent.

My ears started to pop again, and I could feel my lungs pulling at the thinning air. Some seam had split wide open.

Gurzadian pulled out the last cables by main force, and dived into the biotech module. Before I could stop him he pulled the hatch closed behind him, and held it there until the pressure difference forced it closed. There wasn't a damn thing I could do to get it open.

I worked fast. I got that transfer node sealed off, suited up, and went in after Gurzadian. Too late, of course.

The Demograph Draft put us back to work. But it was work you wouldn't want to expend a young life on, or even an expensive qubit AI.

So you had spry eighty-year-olds riding plastic cars across the Mid-East deserts, clearing mines for the combat soldiers marching behind. You had ninety-year-olds in flimsy rad suits going in to clear out Hanford, and the closed Russian cities near Chelyabinsk and Tomsk where they used to manufacture weapons-grade uranium, and so forth.

You had centenarians sent off in one-way Rube Goldberg spaceships to the Moon and Mars and the stars.

But if you were too frail, if you failed all the suitability assessments, there were always the happy booths, a whole block of them in every grey gulag. The final demographic adjustment.

Here's what always brought tears to my eyes: the fact that we always marched into the places they sent us – even the happy booths – singing and waving and *smiling*. Mine is a generation that understands duty, a generation that risked their lives over and over to leave a legacy for our children, and we are doing it over again now. You can call that a small-town value if you like. The first American astronauts all came from out-of-the-way communities, and small-town values marked us out. It seems to me that values diminish in proportion to the growth of a community, which explains a great deal of the world we see today.

In my opinion it was those core values which led Gurzadian to sacrifice himself for me and the mission. And I would have done exactly the same for him.

I wrapped him in his country's flag and said a few words. I pushed him out through a science airlock. I could see him receding from the ship, into the darkness, lit only by the lights of the cluster. Just before I lost him he became a smudge against the grey stars, smeared out by the funny space around me.

I grieved, of course. But I won't dwell on the loss. Test pilots have always been killed with regularity. And that, whatever the designers of this mission intended, is what we have been: the test pilots of man's first starship.

I went through Gurzadian's stuff. It was like when Jenna died. All his jumble and clutter was where he left it, and when I sorted it I knew he was never coming back to disorder it again. I found a couple of last messages for his family – a handful of grandkids – and downlinked them, in hope.

I moved into the base block, because that's closest to the ship's centre of gravity, and it's about the bulkiest piece of shit anyhow. It should survive the space-time stress longer than the other modules. If anyone wants my skinny ass because I gave up the science programs, they can have it.

A couple of days ago I heard a bang, which could have been the materials science module failing. But the instruments in the astrophysics module are working still. I can even get an image out of the Cassegrain.

All I can see is grey light. Quasars.

Here's what I think.

I think I'm coming out the other side of the barrier that surrounds the solar system. I think I'm seeing the universe as it really is.

Young. Still in its dark age, just as Gurzadian described it.

We – the solar system – are stuck in some kind of M-theory bubble. What we see from the Earth, looking out through the enclosing barrier, is an image of a much older universe. But it isn't real. It can't be.

I think this is all some kind of experiment. *Somebody* out there in the real, young, dark-age universe is fast-forwarding a chunk of space, to see how it all turns out. And we live in that chunk.

I like the irony, incidentally. Here I am, the first star traveller, sent out here because I'm an old and useless fucker. And yet I find the universe is younger than anyone thought.

Anyway that's your resolution to the Fermi paradox, Gurzadian, old buddy. *They* were here all the time, all around us. Playing with us. I wonder what they think of us, of a society that sends its old people out to die in the dark, alone.

I've considered cutting this short. I have a number of options from the medical kit. Or I could simply open the hatch. Sitting in this metal tube and waiting for the walls to cave in doesn't appeal.

It's time to get off my soap-box. I had the great good fortune to participate in a common dream to test the limits of mankind's imagination and daring. It is, I hope, a dream I have passed on to those who read this account. The stars may be gone, but we still have the sun and its children; and what lies beyond this barrier may be far more strange and wonderful than we ever imagined.

You see, I've come to think this bubble around our universe is maybe some kind of eggshell we have to break out of.

Or maybe it's no coincidence that we've gotten stuck like this just as we develop a space-bending star drive. Maybe this is flypaper.

Whatever, I'm confident that someday – in bigger and better ships than *Geezer* – we'll be able to break out.

I will say that we are not the same America I grew up in, but we can be again. Maybe the challenge of taking on whoever it was dared to put us inside this cosmic box will be the making of us.

I've decided I will stick around a little longer. Maybe I'll luck out and see the first stars come out, that Christmas tree light-up Gurzadian talked about. I always did like Christmas.

MARGINALIA

(Author's note: I was sent the document below anonymously. The document itself, a photocopy, is government-speak, bland to the point of unreadability. But the notes scribbled in the margins are intriguing.)

Title page:

United States General Accounting Office
GAO report to the Honorable William X. Lambie,
House of Representatives
June 1998
GOVERNMENT RECORDS
Results of a Search for Records Concerning the 1983 Explosion
near Cross Fork, Nevada
SUMMARY ONLY
GAO/NSRAF-96-244

Cover note:

From: United States General Accounting Office, Washington, DC 20548.
National Security and International Affairs Division. June 24, 1998.
To: The Honorable William X Lambie, House of Representatives.

Dear Mr Lambie:

After fifteen years, speculation continues on the truth of the large explosion which is alleged to have taken place at a covert US military research facility in Nevada.

Some observers speculate that the explosion was the destruction of a conventional rocket; others that it was caused by the crash of an aircraft, perhaps of an extraterrestrial nature; others that agencies of the government have been engaged in a misinformation campaign to

334

conceal some deeper truth, such as a successful launch of some space vehicle; others that this was the demolition of a covert military facility.

In its 1984 official report and since, the Air Force has denied the reality of the explosion.

Concerned that the Department of Defense may not have provided you with all available information on the incident, you asked us to determine any government records concerning the incident. We examined a wide range of classified and unclassified documents dating from 1965 through the 1980s. The full scope and methodology of our work are detailed in the full report . . .

Sir:

I read your counterfactual 'novel'. About NASA going on to Mars in the 1980s, instead of shutting everything down after Apollo? What a crock.

Counterfactuality does not serve the needs of the truth. But now, at last, the truth is starting to come out.

And the truth is, people have been to Mars.

They are walking around among us right now. And nobody knows about it.

Of course much of the data returned by the old Mars probes has always been kept from the public. These include:

1) Grainy photographs of what could be structures on the surface taken by the space probe Mariner 4 in 1964.

2) Mysterious surface glimpses through the global dust storm encountered on the planet by Mariner 9 in 1971.

3) The strange readings from the Viking landers of 1976, which found a supposedly sterile Martian surface.

And of course the Mars Observer of 1992 was deliberately destroyed. (The jury is out on the Russian Mars 96. Maybe that really was a screw-up. The later NASA probes definitely were.)

Only a handful of people know that the US General Accounting Office – that's Congress's investigative arm – recently published this, the results of a search for records concerning the Cross Fork, Nevada incident, generally thought to be at the centre of the Mars cover-up. Search meaning forced through by white-hat Congressman Bill Lambie, who's as sick of cover-ups as anyone. Published meaning hurried out and buried. I owe my copy to [illegible].

Here's how I started this.

I got an e-mail from a Janet [illegible] of Albuquerque. She said she had met a hooker from Reno in the 1970s. This lady had worked at a cathouse close to Cross Fork, Nevada. And she told Janet there had been an awful lot of ex-NASA engineers in town at that time.

And one night two NASA guys talked too much.

NATIONAL SECURITY COUNCIL, WASHINGTON DC 20506.
APRIL 18, 1997.
MEMORANDUM FOR MR JOHN E PROCTOR, DIRECTOR-IN-CHARGE,
NATIONAL SECURITY ISSUES, GENERAL ACCOUNTING OFFICE.
SUBJECT: Request for Records.

I am responding to your April 2, 1997 request for information or NSC records related to the supposed explosion near Cross Fork, Nevada in October 1983.

The NSC has no records or information related to the incident.

For information about any government records that may document the explosion in Nevada, we suggest you contact the National Archives, Textual Reference Division, 8601 Adelphi Rd, College Park, Maryland 20740.

– Albert D. Steele, Executive Secretary

There were four categories of key staff involved in the Mars cover-up:

1) top-level management, including CIA, FBI and DIA operatives
2) interface personnel
3) technical personnel
4) the astronauts.

Only recruiting the astronauts would have posed any challenge. These were, after all, brave and dedicated men.

Secrecy would not have been a major problem, even for such a gigantic enterprise. There were precedents. More than three hundred thousand people were directly involved in the building of an atomic bomb in 1942–5, and no significant information reached the public.

And besides America had been sliding towards a police state for years (wire-taps, surveillance of civilians) and it was a simple matter to apply these cloak-and-dagger methods and precedents to the Mars program.

(I was e-mailed with the news that someone had called into a talk show in Phoenix, Arizona, and claimed to be the man who had run the security operation for NASA during that period. He claimed that four astronauts died in missions that were squelched by NASA. And he said he had the truth about Apollo 13. Never heard from again. Probably a flake.)

The entire Mars program was run out of Southern Nevada, at a (so-called) atomic test station called the Nevada Test Site: a thousand square miles of Nevada desert.

Why there?

It is an area of hills, mountain peaks, desert valleys draining into dry lake beds. The lunar-like terrain is a warren of dark tunnels and secret facilities. You'd spot a car miles away from its dust cloud; anybody walking would be the only moving object in the landscape. And who would go there? Even by 1970 it had a reputation as a forbidden region, soaked in radioactivity.

The most likely sites of the USAF Mars facility are those least used by the AEC, notably Yucca Flat and Camp Desert Rock, aka Area 22.

Here's another good reason: Vegas – just sixty miles to the southeast.

Those astronauts weren't children, and they weren't shrinking violets. The clerks and secretaries for the Mars control centre were babes recruited from Las Vegas casinos, which added to the general appeal of the place.

Executive Office of the President, Office of Science and Technology Policy,
Washington DC 20500. April 20, 1997.
Mr John E Proctor, Director-in-Charge, National Security Issues, General Accounting Office.

Dear Mr Proctor:

In response to your recent query of April 2, 1997.

The Office of Science and Technology Policy reviewed its records concerning the 'Nevada Incident'. OSTP has no direct knowledge of what occurred at Nevada and no records, except for the information I received from the Air Force. I look forward to receiving the GAO report.

Sincerely, Joseph V. Ververk, Director

At Cross Fork, Nevada, I found that hooker.

And through her I found a guy called Tad Jones.

Tad Jones claimed to have been a minor worker, in the early 1970s, on a covert government nuclear-rocket program. This program continued after the shut-down of the public-domain NERVA program, following Nixon's (supposed) decision not to go to Mars.

Jones, and other workers, were bribed and threatened to keep them quiet about their work on the program. Jones lost his job in 1972, I gather for personal reasons. Now, more than two decades later, radiation injuries were killing him.

The thing of it is, Tad Jones told me he once met a man who told *him* he had been to Mars.

He was called Elliott Becker, and at the time he was an Air Force colonel, and he made the mistake of getting too drunk one night.

Under false pretences, which I won't go into here, I got to meet Elliott Becker himself. He is now a senior Air Force officer. He is aged around 60, and he suffers from premature-ageing symptoms: atrophied muscles, osteoporosis.

He threw me out fast. But not so fast I didn't manage to notice some oddities. For instance at one point Becker let go of a glass in mid-air and looked startled when it fell.

This sort of thing happened to the Skylab astronauts and Mir cosmonauts, conditioned to long periods in zero G. Furthermore his illnesses are consistent with the proposal that Becker endured a long-duration spaceflight in the early 1980s.

But he was not on any spaceflight made public.

So where the hell did he go?

I only met Tad Jones the once.

I wasn't so surprised. Ageing, poor, stricken by pain, Jones was becoming less discreet. I don't know how he died. His old radiation injuries must have baffled the coroners.

Of course he could have been lying through his teeth about the whole thing. But if so, where did he get his injuries?

US Department of Justice, Federal Bureau of Investigation,
Washington DC 20535
April 22, 1997.
Mr John E Proctor, Director-in-Charge, National Security Issues, General Accounting Office.

Dear Mr Proctor:

This is in response to a letter dated April 2, 1997, from Simon J Holusha, Director, Administration of Justice Issues, General Accounting Office, to Kathryn G Keyworth, Inspector in Charge, Office of Public and Congressional Affairs, FBI, regarding government records concerning the large-scale explosion near Cross Fork, Nevada in October 1983 (Code 91183).

A search of FBI indices has determined that all FBI data concerning the incident has been processed under the provisions of the Freedom of Information Act (FOIA) and is available for review in our FOIA Reading Room. If your staff wishes to review the material, please call Margaret Feeley, a member of my staff, at least 48 hours in advance of the desired appointment.

Sincerely yours,

Eric G. Dower, Supervisory Special Agent, Office of Public and Congressional affairs

The truth about Mars, at least, is now obvious.

The space probes did not observe any evidence of an inhabited Mars because it was deliberately concealed. The Mariner 9 dust storm was no coincidence! – it was thrown up to conceal hasty efforts *by the planet's inhabitants* to fake a Moonlike landscape. And the surface was sterilized by neutron bombs before the Vikings could land, and the Mars Observer was shot out of the sky.

We didn't go back to Mars for twenty years. And by the time we got there, with Pathfinder and the rest, there was nothing to see. Of course not. The Martians had completed their mock-up.

And nobody told us about all this.

We worship secrecy in this country.

Get this: last year the US government produced 6,300,000 'classified' documents. The least restricted bear the stamp FOUO, 'For Official Use Only'. The next category – the first technically classified – are 'Confidential'. After that comes 'Secret', and some of them are 'NATO Secret', meaning they can be shared with NATO nations. Then comes 'Top Secret' and 'NATO Top Secret'.

Above 'Top Secret' there is 'SCI' – 'Sensitive Compartmented Information', open to still fewer individuals. And there is some information that you can only see if you are on a BIGOT list – if you have your own specific code word.

And then there are qualifies like 'NOFORN' – no foreigners to see – and 'NOCONTRACT' – no contractors, 'WNINTEL' – 'Warning Notice – Intelligence Sources or Methods Involved', 'ORCON' – 'Originator Controls Further Dissemination'.

What's the cost of all this secrecy? When does secrecy increase military strength, and when does it weaken security?

We should be told.

. . . Or is that classified too?

The space-probe evidence, naturally, was covered up. I should be used by now to our natural disposition for secrecy. But over an issue as immense as this, it utterly dismays me.

That's why I fight on.

(Teletype uncovered during review of FOIA material:)

FBI DALLAS 10-20-1983 4-28 PM

DIRECTOR AND SAC, CINCINNATI URGENT

NEVADA EXPLOSION, INFORMATION CONCERNING (blanked) TELE-PHONICALLY ADVISED THIS OFFICE THAT (blanked) SATELLITE OBSERVED DEBRIS AND DESTRUCTION AT (blanked) TELEPHONIC CONVERSATION BETWEEN THIS OFFICE AND (blanked) FAILED TO BEAR OUT BELIEF PHOTOGRAPHS AND NEGATIVES BEING TRANSPORTED TO THIS OFFICE BY SPECIAL PLANE FOR EXAMINATION PROVIDED BY THIS OFFICE BECAUSE OF NATIONAL INTEREST IN THE CASE AND FACT THAT NATIONAL BROADCASTING COMPANY ASSOCIATED PRESS AND OTHERS ATTEMPTING TO BREAK STORY OF EXPLOSION AND/OR AIRCRAFT CRASH TODAY NO FURTHER INVESTIGATION BEING CONDUCTED

END.

Here's the story, as best I can reconstruct it.

In 1971 – armed with space-probe information about a secretive, advanced and possibly hostile civilization on Mars – President Nixon ordered preparations to begin for covert missions to Mars, manned and otherwise. These were to include the possibility of launching a pre-emptive nuclear attack against the planet. The project was under the command of the USAF, and would use Apollo moon-rocket technology with nuclear-rocket stages.

(And *that*, sir author, is the truth about Nixon's decision on going to Mars after Apollo. He didn't decide we wouldn't go. He decided we *would* – but the program would be run by the USAF, not NASA, and it would be run in secret. Even the publicly declared Apollo follow-on program, the Space Shuttle, had a military flavour and had a role in the defense of Earth against the Martians, which I've yet to determine.)

Elliott Becker trained as an astronaut in the 1960s. In 1971 his death was faked in a T-38 airplane accident, and he was assigned to the secret man-to-Mars program.

But Nixon fell, and the project was abandoned, the Nevada launch complex and the space hardware mothballed. Elliott was moved into senior Air Force positions, with a central responsibility for maintaining the integrity of a Mars program cover-up.

In 1981, things changed.

By now the additional Viking data was in hand. President Reagan ordered the mounting of a secret manned flyby scouting mission to Mars, under the command of the USAF, using what was left of the 1970s-era Saturn technology. This limited-objectives mission was achievable relatively easily. Meanwhile Reagan revived preparations for a nuclear attack on Mars.

The flyby mission was launched in 1982 from the secret Nevada base. It carried two men, and it would pass by Mars on the planet's night side.

The funding was covered as an SDI project. But when SDI funding came under scrutiny, and Reagan's attention moved on to other issues, the project was again abandoned. I guess the logic was that the Martians didn't after all pose an immediate threat. This time the Nevada launch complex was destroyed.

And that's the truth behind the 1983 explosion out in the desert.

. . . But Elliott Becker got to fly his mission.

Inspector General, Department of Defense,
400 Army Navy Drive, Arlington,
Virginia 22202-2684. April 29, 1997.

Mr John E Proctor, Director-in-Charge, National Security Issues, General Accounting Office.

Dear Mr Proctor:

The Department of the Air Force July 1984 report is the DoD response to questions posed in your April 2 letter related to GAO C 91165. If you have any questions, please contact my action officer, Janet Fromkin, at 703-604-7846. If she is not available please contact Ms Frances Douhet at 703-604-7543.

Sincerely

Richard S. Dupuy, Deputy Assistant Inspector General for GAO Report Analysis.

Tad Jones told me that in 1981 he heard a rumour that the program he had worked on was being revived. But nobody was hiring in Cross Fork.

Tad Jones was kind of a bitter man. So he got himself an off-road vehicle and went hunting.

The nuclear rocket site is on no map. Jones had to break through wire fences and skirt mine fields (he told me). Then he found himself in an area of high radioactivity (he'd taken along counters).

He approached the centre of the site.

And there he found the white needle-shape of a nuclear-tipped Saturn V rocket, assembled in secret, standing on a rusting gantry out there in the desert. Hell of a thing. He showed me a photograph.

Jones said that after the demolition the site was seeded with radioactive waste. He said it would be impossible to return to the now-lethal site, and the evidence is lost.

But the program lasted long enough to send Elliott Becker to Mars.

He and his crewmate used Apollo-class spacecraft, enduring the year-long journey in an adapted Skylab habitation module.

Think of it. Becker must have watched Earth and Moon recede like twin stars, every moment travelling further than any human before him. I wonder what he imagined he would find at journey's end.

Central Intelligence Agency, Washington, DC 20505.
May 22 1997.
Mr John E Proctor, Director-in-Charge, National Security Issues, General Accounting Office.

Dear Mr Proctor:

In a letter dated 15 April 1997, this Agency advised you that it would conduct a comprehensive record search to aid in the completion of your investigation of an explosion in Nevada, October 1983. In accordance with your request we have searched all of our databases. The search did not yield any documents related to either of these terms other than the report returned by our field worker Frederic K Durant in 1983, which remains classified. Therefore this Agency has no information relevant to your investigation.

Sincerely, Nora Franck, Executive Director.

It goes to prove there is hope. Even the most gigantic fraud and cover-up, no matter what the investment of time and money, is going to flake at the edges after a couple of decades.

Look, you can verify most of this stuff from the public records for yourself, as I'm trying to do. Right? And I'd welcome it if you did and let me know. I mean, it was *our* hundred billion dollars.

I have an instinct to blow a hole through every veil of secrecy

I come across. That keeps me busy. It's a point of principle. But aside from the principle, I just want to know. I mean, here we have two guys who went all the way to Mars, for God's sake, and they've never been allowed to tell their stories.

I'll go to my grave wondering what Elliot Becker saw. Just cold, lonely emptiness? Or perhaps glimpses of structures, lights in the ochre deserts on the dark side of Mars?

We grope for truth, and make our progress slow. William Davenant, 1606–1668

(Author's note: I guess it's fairly obvious why I was the target of this particular hoax. And my correspondent is right about our culture's excessive fondness for secrecy, as this stonewalling document itself demonstrates; as long as secrecy remains, rumours about *what* is being hidden are going to flourish.

(But like all good hoaxes, this one is rooted in enough fact to make it at least remotely plausible – for there *are* a few oddities in the story of human involvement with Mars.

(Before the first space probes, Mars was thought to be Earth-like. Many expert telescope observers were convinced they had seen networks of canals, swathes of vegetation. The Mariner 4 flyby probe of 1964, however, glimpsed a Moon-like world with a thin atmosphere, and craters where the Earth-bound observers thought they saw canals. In 1971 the Mariner 9 orbiter really did find a global dust storm obscuring the surface. And later, the Viking landers found a surface not just lifeless but apparently sterilized, perhaps by solar radiation. The US Mars Observer did fail as it reached Mars.

(And there were proposals, mooted in the 1960s, for manned flybys of Mars, an interim program to follow Apollo. The flyby *would* have passed the planet's dark side . . .)

United States General Accounting Office.
Summary to GAO report GAO/NSRAF-96-244 addressed to the Hon. W.X. Lambie.
Cover note (concluded):
. . . Our search of government records was complicated by the fact that some records we wanted to review were missing and there was not always an explanation. Further, the records management regulations for the retention and disposition of records were unclear or changing during the period we reviewed.

We conducted our review from March 1997 to May 1998 in accordance with generally accepted government-auditing standards. If you or your staff have any questions about this report, please call me on (202) 512-7858.

Sincerely yours,

John E. Proctor, Director-In-Charge, National Security Issues.

THE WE WHO SING

Reid Malenfant wrote to his grandson:
Sure, you can spin conspiracy theories forever. Sometimes I think we're just little bitty creatures who think too small. We can't see the truth that's all around us.

Maybe there is life everywhere, and everywhen, but we just can't see it. Maybe there was life as far back in the history of the universe as you can look.

○

Shine joined the chattering, swarming throng. The excitement was enormous. 'The Wave is approaching,' the people sang. '*The Wave . . .*'

Shine's people called themselves the We Who Sing. For that is what they did, and how they knew themselves.

And here came the Wave itself, a vast swell of light, crashing endlessly forward with a noise like a vast groan. As it progressed the Wave broke over a bank of frost, effortlessly smashing apart its lifeless filigree structures.

Now the people rose up before the Wave, sparks rising before a vast firestorm. But there was structure in the songs they sang, and in their dance, as if they were a flock of glowing swallows.

The Wave was a vast acoustic pulse that spanned the Ocean – but the Ocean was the world, and so the Wave was the song of the world itself.

Swept up by anticipation, Shine added a whoop of joy to the people's complex electromagnetic harmonies, and she dove deeper into the glowing crowd.

In this Ocean of plasma, a place filled with light and heat, Shine was a creature of ball lightning. Her body was a thing of sound itself, her internal structure maintained by criss-crossing standing waves and solitons. And as she swelled joyously, her song advertized her strength and beauty, the depth and harmony of her structure – and her readiness to triple.

Potential partners clustered around her, tense, eager.

. . . But here was the one she thought of as Cold.

Shine danced away.

All around Shine, firework bursts of death and life lit up the sky. Already the We Who Sing had begun to triple. They came together in their threes, their structures merging and briefly dissolving, before the bright compounds flew apart in sudden happy explosions. And from the shining shrapnel emerged triple-daughters, small, eager, like their vanished parents yet subtly modified, their essences shared.

Shine longed to dissolve in that final happy glow.

But Cold had followed her. 'You must not do this, Shine,' Cold said.

Cold was small and ugly. The potential triple-partners had no wish to share their terminal love with this etiolated creature. Subtly they began to back away.

Shine's angry shout pulsed over Cold. 'Leave me alone!'

But Cold stayed close to her. 'To triple is to lose yourself,' she said, insistent. 'It is to dissolve in that final madness, from which nothing emerges but immature triple-daughters, as mindless as a clump of frost.'

'It is the way of things –'

'It is our tragedy. As we make new life, *we forget* – even the best and brightest of us. I have seen it happen, over and over.'

Shine swooped and spun, her agitation growing as the Wave approached and the dance reached its climax. All her life Cold had pursued her like this, baffling her with an incomprehensible, dismal chatter of patterns and memory. 'You are nothing but talk. The Ocean is without end! It will last forever! What use is a long life if there is no change?'

Cold said solemnly, 'Listen to me, Shine. The Ocean is going to die.'

It was an ugly thought, discordant, incomprehensible. Unacceptable.

'No.' Shine sailed away from Cold, jetting through the plasma soup, seeking to rejoin the throng.

But still Cold pursued her. 'It is the truth, Shine. The next Wave will be the last. Please, Shine. You are one of the few who can understand – even though you deny it.'

The giant Wave loomed closer, and people bobbed before it like flecks of surf.

'This is my time,' begged Shine. 'Let me go.'

Cold said, 'I think there may be a way –'

But now the Wave's immense compression front hit them.

The people crashed through the great glowing wall. Swooping, singing, immersed in the world's booming voice, the We Who Sing fed on dense plasma, and they tripled madly. It was a shrieking, joyous frenzy.

And when the Wave had passed – and the people, illuminated by the brightness of a new, bewildered generation, began to sing their songs once more – here was Shine, alone.

She swept away from Cold, away from the creature who had kept her from the tripling, angry, bitter, frightened.

The universe was young.

It had been just three hundred thousand years since the formative singularity. Now the universe was a knot of spacetime, unravelling at lightspeed, yet still little larger than a single galaxy.

And everywhere it was as hot as the interior of a star.

All matter here was in the form of plasma: an electrically charged mist crowded with protons, electrons, simple atomic nuclei. And the plasma made the universe opaque. A photon, a bit of light, could not travel far before it was impeded by a charged particle, just as sunlight scatters from the droplets of water that make up a fog.

So the plasma glowed, an ocean of light.

But the intense radiation bath likewise assailed matter. True, wherever it got the chance – in pockets of relative cool – atomic matter formed, electrons clinging to nuclei like long-separated siblings, the new atoms gravity-tugging each other. But, bombarded by the blistering photons, any matter cluster was quickly shattered. The brief frost banks evaporated, the atoms smashed, the plasma restored.

In this ferocious heat there could be no solid structure: no planets, no stars, no galaxies.

But the plasma ocean was not uniform. Not featureless.

*   *   *

Cold said she would take Shine and Harmony to a place where, she said, they could see the future.

The two of them joined her reluctantly, in the place where the people hung in a great cloud, rippling on the Ocean's softly swelling currents.

There was a full ecology here. Instabilities generated little pockets of turbulence, like spinning flowers in the plasma, and on these small structures fed greater forms, which were consumed in their turn. The pinnacle of this food chain was reached in the dense, complex, hot-as-sun bodies of the We Who Sing. And so they fed now, browsing on the turbulence and scurrying, mindless forms.

Cold, with Shine and Harmony, moved out of this glowing crowd and away into swelling emptiness.

Soon they were alone, three points of brightness swimming through a sea of yellow-white light.

Harmony was younger than Shine, her sparkling structure less subtly developed. But she was nevertheless a handsome creature who, like Shine, had somehow been snared by Cold's discordant words. She sang as they jetted along, but her songs betrayed her unease and boredom.

Cold's body was smaller than Shine's or Harmony's: small, ugly, her inner structure decaying, her circumference ragged. Denying the dissolution of the triple, she had been subject too long to the great pulses of heat and cold that washed through this Ocean-sky.

They were an odd trio, uncomfortable with each other.

'. . . Here,' said Cold at last. 'This will do. Look now . . .'

They had come to a place where the Ocean glowed with a little less vigour than elsewhere. Instinctively Shine contracted, compressing the warmth of her own structure.

Here was a great sculpture of frost, a wispy glimmering spider-web. But already the Ocean's turbulence was closing this random pocket of coolness, and the frost, twisting, crumbling, was breaking up.

Harmony grumbled, 'There's nobody here.'

Cold said, 'It isn't *people* I've brought you to see.'

'Nothing, then,' said Harmony. 'There's *nothing* here.'

'Nothing but frost,' Shine said.

'Who cares about frost?' said Harmony. 'Frost is dead. Frost cannot sing.'

She said, 'There has always been frost – wispy structures like this, gathering in the transient cold pockets. *But there is more frost now than in the past.*'

'I don't believe you,' Harmony said haughtily.

'Nevertheless it is true.'

Shine struggled to find the right questions. *What is 'past'? What is 'future'? What is 'change'?* 'How can you know such a thing?'

Cold's ragged body pulsed. 'Because I have lived long enough to see it. Time is a great gift. I have seen the frost gather, Shine . . . I have built my memory, so that I may understand the world. And I have learned that there is a deeper sort of memory, that lingers even when we are gone.'

'What do you mean?'

Cold began to sing, quite beautifully. Her body glowed with colour.

The song was part of the standard canon of the We Who Sing, and it had structure: subtle rhythms, themes composed of repetitive phrases, 'notes' expressed in a discrete suite of colours, even a kind of refrain like a rhyme.

A human could have appreciated the song's beauty. A whale could.

At last Cold finished.

Shine found herself drawing subtly closer. 'You sing well,' she said.

Cold emitted a kind of laugh, and she spun. 'And so you come to me. Of course you do. That was how our songs began: as simple tripling calls. *Look at me. Hear how well I sing! Think how well we could merge, how strong and dense with structure our children would be* . . . But the songs have become more than that. Passed from one generation to the next, they have become elaborate. They have come to tell what happened before: of great beauties, of spectacular triples – and of the Ocean itself, the Waves and the frost.'

Harmony, moodily, spun away. 'I don't like this game.'

'Shine – Harmony – I have heard this happen. *I have heard the songs grow,* just a phrase or two at a time, from triple to triple. And so I thought *back.* I imagined the songs being stripped of their layers of meaning, becoming simpler, more elemental, until – in the beginning – they were no more than a mating cry.'

Shine was still struggling to comprehend the idea that she might live in a universe in which the past might be different from the future. It was almost impossible for her to absorb Cold's efforts to describe how she had observed a trend.

Of her kind, Shine saw, Cold was a genius: but hers was a chill, repellent brilliance, and Shine felt herself shrink away.

Cold seemed to observe this, and withered regretfully.

Harmony, despite herself, seemed intrigued. 'If the songs tell stories, what do they say?'

'That the Ocean is not limitless,' Cold said quickly. 'That is the first thing, despite what most people believe. The songs tell of the Waves. Everyone knows that. But over enough time – so the songs say – *the same Waves return.* It is as if the Ocean is a single body, like yours, Harmony, within which Waves echo back and forth, subtly changing. That is how I know the Ocean is a small place.

'And here is the next thing. *The Ocean will not last forever.* It changes. I am old enough now to have seen it for myself –'

Shine, reluctantly, understood. 'You're talking about the frost.'

'Yes. There is more of it – always more, never less.'

Shine tried to think like Cold. *Before, less. Now, more. If this goes on . . .* 'Soon *all* the Ocean will be frost. That is what you are saying.'

'Yes,' Cold said, but with a kind of exultance. 'At last somebody hears me! *That* is what is going to happen.'

Harmony spun and spat bits of light, growing agitated.

Shine tried to imagine a universe full of lifeless, static frost. 'How will we live? Where will we go? What about the Waves, the triples?'

'There will be nowhere to go,' said Cold harshly. 'It will happen all at once, everywhere. When the next Wave comes –'

'These are terrible things to be saying!' Harmony cried suddenly. 'You are stupid and ugly, Cold, and I don't want to finish up like you!' And with a final dazzling burst she surged away, leaving Shine and Cold alone.

Shine said, 'I should go after her.'

'She is smart,' Cold said. 'She understands too, despite herself. That is why she is frightened.'

Frightened and repelled, Shine thought.

'You must help me, Shine.'

'Help you?'

Cold spun around, a ragged cloud. 'Look at me. Unless I triple soon, I will die. And I will not triple. I will not let my mind dissolve.'

'You will not live long enough to see the next Wave. That is what you are saying . . . Ah. But I could.'

Cold came to her anxiously. 'It will be up to you,' she said. 'I will be long dead. You must make them see . . .'

Suddenly Shine was angry. 'I don't want such a life. I wish I was as old as you. I would rather die.'

'No,' said Cold urgently. 'You must not forget what I have told you. You must not lose it in the tripling – for then, you doom your mindless offspring to die in your place.'

Shine flinched from her chill logic.

Cold, it seemed to her, was not natural. She had put aside the ultimate joy of the triple; this dismal knowledge scarcely seemed a consolation.

But then – if Cold was right – what was the natural thing to do?

Shine said slowly, 'We are evanescent. Here and gone, like a song.'

'What are you saying?'

Shine watched the ugly frost evaporating as the Ocean's warmth gushed over it. 'If you are right – if all this must pass – perhaps we should accept what is to come.'

Cold was very still.

The young cosmos expanded relentlessly.

It was a bath of plasma, almost at thermodynamic equilibrium, with no large-scale energy flows, no large structure. But still, on small scales, there was unevenness and instability, undulations in the background density. And so there were flows of energy, heat cancelling cold.

Where energy flowed, life fed. Life: even in this chaotic, glowing soup.

And there were the Waves.

In its first instants this universe had endured a pulse of drastic inflation, during which it had ballooned from a region of space smaller than a proton to the size of the Earth. And as spacetime was stretched so dramatically, some of the pulsing cosmic energy condensed to matter.

It was as if rocks had been thrown into a great opaque pond.

Though light was hindered by the plasma, sound waves could travel freely. The ripples cast by that inflationary explosion were tremendous acoustic pulses of compression and decompression that marched across the swelling cosmos. With time, the oscillations developed on ever larger scales.

The growing universe was filled with a deepening roar.

But as it grew, so it cooled.

* * *

Already the Wave could be seen in the glimmering distance, like a bank of spotlights approaching through a glowing fog. Already its throaty roar could be heard.

The We Who Sing began to cluster, like migrant birds.

By now, Shine herself had grown old.

And she had learned that Cold was right. All you had to do was look around.

You could even hear change in the Wave itself. The Waves were stretching, their tone deepening. The Ocean was filled with great descending groans, as if immense creatures were dying.

But not one in a hundred of the great soaring throng around her understood this. Not one of them was old enough to remember a time when this fast-evolving world of theirs had been any different – and few would listen to Shine.

Just like Cold, Shine had gradually become ostracized by We Who Sing. It was Shine now who had endured long past her time of tripling, she whose ragged, slowly decohering form repelled those around her.

But Shine was not Cold. Whatever became of her, without tripling she would forever be incomplete. And she dreaded following the final destiny of poor Cold, who, in the end, had evaporated, her precious, hoarded memories lost forever in the currents of light.

Often she wished she had defied Cold's wishes and embraced the tripling. The chill logic of a coming extinction seemed to her a poor reward for the loss of such terminal joy.

But Shine, resolutely, put such thoughts aside.

In the midst of the gathering gaiety, she brought together those who followed her. There was a bare hundred of them – no more, even after a lifetime of Shine's increasingly impassioned prosely-tizing. Now they clustered around Shine, gathering almost as tightly as partners keen to triple.

'I don't like this,' said Harmony. 'I don't want this to happen.'

Others assented, swarming closer.

'I know,' said Shine, as soothing as she could be, despite her own fear. 'We must stay together. We must stay close. It is the only way.'

This was not Harmony herself, but one of her triple-daughters. The old Harmony had been unable, in the end, to resist the brilliant lure of the triple. But Shine had wooed her triple-daughters, and she had been rewarded to find much of Harmony's character lingering in them: high intelligence mixed with a stubborn refusal to believe the worst.

Thus Shine had sought to find in the daughters what she had perceived in their mothers. It was just as Cold had once pursued her. She had often wondered whether it was herself that Cold was after, or something she had seen in Shine's triple-parents . . .

'Oh,' said one young beauty called Glimmer. 'Oh, but the tripling has begun. They sing the songs already. Can you hear?'

Of course they could. The songs emerged from the swelling, swooping crowd of the We Who Sing, songs of sex, of light-filled, orgasmic instants of birth and death, of an Ocean-world like a womb. The dances were beginning too. Patterns, beautiful, in three dimensions and on a vast scale, were soon emergent from the people's unconscious flocking.

'I don't want it to be true,' moaned Harmony. 'How can *this* end? I want to go to the dance, to the triples. Let us go, Shine. Oh, let us go!'

Some of the rest joined in this desolate chorus. The group spun and pulsed, confused, unstable.

It felt as if Shine herself was tearing apart. How wonderful it would be to think that even now, if she let herself dissolve into the burning light of a triple, something of herself would go on, enduring forever, in an Ocean without end, a song without limits!

Oh, she thought, I love it all.

But she knew that beneath the dazzling dance of the people lay the chill, implacable logic of Cold. There was no escape.

'It is time,' she said, sadly. 'We must do as Cold instructed us. Come now.'

She swam up to Glimmer and let her perimeter soften, so that they overlapped, the complex weft of their cores overlaying. It was like a tripling, but they kept their identities separate.

Now another joined them, and another, so that they grew into a huddle, an increasingly dense, glowing mass that looked, from the outside, undifferentiated – and yet the individuals were sustained within, like palimpsests.

'I don't like this,' whispered Glimmer – very bright, very immature, terrified by the clarity of her own thinking. 'It feels strange.'

'Cold thought it might help us survive –'

'Survive what?' Harmony's pulsing voice was full of anger and fear. 'The death of the Ocean itself? Do you really believe that, Shine?'

'If you wish to leave,' Shine said, 'you may.' Like her triple-mother, Harmony sought nothing so much as somebody to punish.

But now their argument was ended. The Ocean itself shuddered – *and it dimmed.*

The We Who Sing could not ignore the dimming: even the youngest, the most foolish of them. Striving to continue their anxious dancing before the approaching Wave, they swarmed, agitated.

Harmony stayed where she was, embedded deep in the huddle.

It was just as Cold had forecast. Despair clamp down inside Shine, the last impossible hope evaporate.

She felt Glimmer within her, as if snuggling close.

'Shine –'

'You're frightened. It's all right. So am I.'

'What will we see?'

Shine struggled to answer. What would be left if the Ocean vanished? – for the Ocean *was* the world. 'Perhaps there is a greater Ocean,' she said at last. 'In which our Ocean is embedded. As one becomes embedded in the three of a triple.'

'And,' Glimmer said suddenly, 'perhaps there is a greater Ocean beyond that. And then another.'

This keen, intelligent insight startled Shine. But as she tried to imagine an infinite hierarchy of Oceans, each contained within the next, she recoiled, bewildered.

Now the Ocean's light flickered again, like a failing lightbulb, visibly dimmer.

The swarming people were confused, agitated. Some of them even strove to join Shine's huddle.

But it was too late.

The great Wave broke, a last defiant burst of light that swept them all before it.

The We Who Sing shrieked and danced and sang, and they tripled madly. Young emerged in silent starbursts. They raced over the Wave's swelling face, exhilarated to find themselves suddenly alive.

Even now, Shine longed to join them.

But once again the light dimmed. The Wave's rushing front was disrupted, becoming turbulent. The dances were broken, and the songs of the people turned to wails of fear, the bewildered young crying for comfort.

Shine gathered her acolytes close. She said, 'I think –'

But there was no more time.

* * *

At last a critical temperature was reached. Suddenly, atomic matter was able to condense out of the stew of electrons and nuclei.

The photons – no longer energetic enough to smash open the fledgling atoms, no longer impeded – were free to fly their geodesic courses to infinity. The plasma glow died.

For the first time the sky became transparent, a transition as abrupt as a clash of cymbals.

With the dissipation of the plasma, the great acoustic waves had no medium in which to travel. But they did not vanish without trace. Where a wave had compressed the particle soup, it had been made hotter, the photons more energetic. And so as the photons began their endless journey through swelling spacetime, they carried in their energy distribution images of the last sound waves.

Thus the last birthing cry of the universe was caught forever in a thinning, reddening sea of primordial photons.

Meanwhile the matter that had suddenly frosted out of the great bath of radiation began to gather in swirls and clumps, arranged in a great lacy tapestry that hung over the universe. It was a wispy frost of hydrogen and helium, slowly collapsing under gravity: a frost that would condense into galaxies and stars and superclusters and planets, places where new forms of life could prosper.

In all cosmic history it was the most dramatic instant of transition.

But, with every transition, there is loss.

Dark and cold, suddenly, everywhere.

Many of the huddle had died in that first great instant of freezing.

And now, as the mass clump collapsed, fusion began, deep in the heart of the huddle. At that moment more died, torn apart by the immense densities, the sudden fire.

But the fusion became stable.

In all the universe, just a single star shone.

Shine peered out, filled with curiosity and fear, stunned by clarity and emptiness.

Cold was right, she thought. I am alive. I lived through the end of the world. Alive! But – what happens next?

As she watched, a second star lit up, a beacon in the endless dark.

And then another.

And another.

THE GRAVITY MINE

*And perhaps (Malenfant wrote to Michael) life will persist long
after we imagine it would be impossible: deep in the future, far
downstream, after the Earth has died, after the sun and all the
stars have expired, life finding a way to get by in the dark . . .*

Call her Anlic.

The first time she woke, she was in the ruins of an abandoned
gravity mine.

At first the Community had chased around the outer strata of
the great gloomy structure. But at last, close to the core, they
reached a cramped ring. Here the central black-hole's gravity was
so strong that light itself curved in closed orbits.

The torus tunnel looked infinitely long. And they could race as
fast as they dared.

As they hurtled past fullerene walls they could see multiple
images of themselves, a glowing golden mesh before and behind,
for the echoes of their light endlessly circled the central knot of
spacetime. 'Just like the old days!' they called, excited. 'Just like
the Afterglow! . . .'

Exhilarated, they pushed against the light barrier, and those
trapped circling images shifted to blue or red.

That was when it happened.

This Community was just a small tributary of the Conflux:
isolated here in this ancient place, the density of mind already
stretched thin. And now, as lightspeed neared, that isolation
stretched to breaking point.

356

. . . She budded off from the rest, her consciousness made discrete, separated from the greater flow of minds and memories.

She slowed. The others rushed on without her, a dazzling circular storm orbiting the exhausted black hole. It felt like coming awake, emerging from a dream.

Her questions were immediate, flooding her raw mind. 'Who am I? How did I get here?' And so on. The questions were simple, even trite. And yet they were unanswerable.

Others gathered around her – curious, sympathetic – and the race of streaking light began to lose its coherence.

One of them came to her.

Names meant little; this 'one' was merely a transient sharpening of identity from the greater distributed entity that made up the Community.

Still, here he was. Call him Geador.

'. . . Anlic?'

'I feel – odd,' she said.

'Don't worry.'

'Who am I?'

'Come back to us.'

He reached for her, and she sensed the warm depths of companionship and memory and shared joy that lay beyond him. Depths waiting to swallow her up, to obliterate her questions.

She snapped, 'No!' And, wilfully, she sailed up and out and away, passing through the thin walls of the tunnel.

At first it was difficult to climb out of this twisted gravity well. But soon she was rising through layers of structure.

Here was the tight electromagnetic cage which had once tapped the spinning black hole like a dynamo. Here was the cloud of compact masses which had been hurled along complex orbits through the hole's ergosphere, extracting gravitational energy. It was antique engineering, long abandoned.

She emerged into a blank sky, a sky stretched thin by the endless expansion of spacetime.

Geador was here. 'What do you see?'

'Nothing.'

'Look harder.' He showed her how.

There was a scattering of dull red pinpoints all around the sky.

'They are the remnants of stars,' he said.

He told her about the Afterglow: that brief, brilliant period after

357

the Big Bang, when matter gathered briefly in clumps and burned by fusion light. 'It was a bonfire, over almost as soon as it began. The universe was very young. It has swollen some ten thousand trillion times in size since then . . . Nevertheless, it was in that gaudy era that humans arose. *Us*, Anlic.'

She looked into her soul, seeking warm memories of the Afterglow. She found nothing.

She looked back at the gravity mine.

At its centre was a point of yellow-white light. Spears of light arced out from its poles, knife-thin. The spark was surrounded by a flattened cloud, dull red, inhomogeneous, clumpy. The big central light cast shadows through the crowded space around it.

It was beautiful, a sculpture of light and crimson smoke.

'This is Mine One,' Geador said gently. 'The first mine of all. And it is built on the ruins of the primeval galaxy – the galaxy from which humans first emerged.'

'The first galaxy?'

'But it was all long ago.' He moved closer to her. 'So long ago that this mine became exhausted. Soon it will evaporate away completely. We have long since had to move on . . .'

But that had happened before. After all humans had started from a single star, and spilled over half the universe, even before the stars ceased to shine.

Now humans wielded energy, drawn from the great gravity mines, on a scale unimagined by their ancestors. Of course mines would be exhausted – like this one – but there would be other mines. Even when the last mine began to fail, they would think of *something*.

The future stretched ahead, long, glorious. Minds flowed together in great rivers of consciousness. There was immortality to be had, of a sort, a continuity of identity through replication and confluence across trillions upon trillions of years.

It was the Conflux.

Its source was far upstream.

The crudities of birth and death had been abandoned even before the Afterglow was over, when man's biological origins were decisively shed. So every mind, every tributary that made up the Conflux today had its source in that bright, remote upstream time.

Nobody had been born since the Afterglow.

Nobody but Anlic.

'. . . Come back,' Geador said.

Her defiance was dissipating.

She understood nothing about herself. But she didn't want to be different. She didn't want to be unhappy.

There wasn't anybody who was less than maximally happy, the whole óf the time. Wasn't that the purpose of existence?

So, troubled, she gave herself up to Geador, to the Conflux. And, along with her identity, her doubts and questions dissolved.

The universe would grow far older before she woke again.

'. . . Flee! Faster! As fast as you can! . . .'

There was turbulence in the great rushing river of mind.

And in that turbulence, here and there, souls emerged from the background wash. Each brief fleck suffered a moment of terror before falling back into the greater dreaming whole.

One of those flecks was Anlic.

In the sudden dark she clung to herself. She slithered to a stop.

Transient identities clustered around her. 'What are you doing? Why are you staying here? You will be harmed.' They sought to absorb her, but fell back, baffled by her resistance.

The Community was fleeing, in panic. Why?

She looked back.

There was something there, in the greater darkness. She made out the faintest of patterns: charcoal grey on black, almost beyond her ability to resolve it, a mesh of neat regular triangles covering the sky. Visible through the interstices was a complex, textured curtain of grey-pink light.

It was a structure that spanned the universe.

She felt stunned, disoriented. It was so different from Mine One, her last clear memory. She must have crossed a great desert of time.

But – she found, when she looked into her soul – her questions remained unanswered.

She called out: 'Geador?'

A ripple of shock and doubt spread through the Community.

'. . . You are Anlic.'

'Geador?'

'I have Geador's memories.'

That would have to do, she thought, irritated; in the Conflux, memory and identity were fluid, distributed, ambiguous.

'We are in danger, Anlic. You must come.'

She refused to comply, stubborn. She indicated the great netting. 'Is that Mine One?'

'No,' he said sadly. 'Mine One was long ago, child.'

'*How* long ago?'

'Time is nested . . .'

From this vantage, the era of man's first black-hole empire had been the spring time, impossibly remote. And the Afterglow itself – the star-burning dawn – was lost, a mere detail of the Big Bang.

'What is happening here, Geador?'

'There is no time –'

'Tell me.'

The universe had ballooned, fuelled by time, and its physical processes had proceeded relentlessly.

Just as each galaxy's stars had dissipated, leaving a rump which had collapsed into a central black hole, so clusters of galaxies had broken up, and the remnants fell inwards to cluster-scale holes. And the clusters in turn collapsed into supercluster-scale holes – the largest black holes to have formed naturally, with masses of a hundred trillion stars.

These were the cold hearths around which mankind now huddled.

'But,' said Geador, 'the supercluster holes are evaporating away – dissipating in a quantum whisper, like all black holes. The smallest holes, of stellar mass, vanished when the universe was a fraction of its present age. Now the largest natural holes, of super-cluster mass, are close to exhaustion as well. And so we must farm them.

'Look at the City.' He meant the universe-spanning net, the rippling surfaces within.

The City was a netted sphere. It contained giant black holes, galactic supercluster mass and above. They had been deliberately assembled. And they were merging, in a hierarchy of more and more massive holes. Life could subsist on the struts of the City, feeding off the last trickle of free energy.

Mankind was *moving* supercluster black holes, coalescing them in hierarchies all over the reachable universe, seeking to extend their lifetimes. It was a great challenge.

Too great.

Sombrely, Geador showed her more.

The network was disrupted. It looked as if some immense object had punched out from the inside, ripping and twisting the struts. The tips of the broken struts were glowing a little brighter than the rest of the network, as if burning. Beyond the damaged network she could see the giant coalescing holes, their horizons distorted, great frozen waves of infalling matter visible in their cold surfaces.

This was an age of war: an obliteration of trillion-year memories, a bonfire of identity. Great rivers of mind were guttering, drying.

'This is the Conflux. How can there be war?'

Geador said, 'We are managing the last energy sources of all. We have responsibility for the whole of the future. With such responsibility comes tension, disagreement. Conflict.' She sensed his gentle, bitter humour. 'We have come far since the Afterglow, Anlic. But in some ways we have much in common with the brawling argumentative apes of that brief time.'

'Apes? . . . Why am I here, Geador?'

'You're an eddy in the Conflux. We all wake up from time to time. It's just an accident. Don't trouble, Anlic. You are not alone. You have us.'

Deliberately she moved away from him. 'But I am not like you,' she said bleakly. '*I* do not recall the Afterglow. I don't know where I came from.'

'What does it matter?' he said harshly. 'You have existed for all but the briefest moments of the universe's long history –'

'Has there been another like me?'

He hesitated. 'No,' he said. 'No other like you. There hasn't been long enough.'

'Then I *am* alone.'

'Anlic, all your questions will be over, answered or not, if you let yourself die here. Come now . . .'

She knew he was right.

She fled with him. The great black-hole City disappeared behind her, its feeble glow attenuated by her gathering velocity.

She yielded to Geador's will. She had no choice. Her questions were immediately lost in the clamour of community.

She would wake only once more.

Start with a second.

Zoom out. Factor it up to get the life of the Earth, with that second a glowing moment embedded within. Zoom out *again*, to get a new period, so long Earth's lifetime is reduced to the span of that second. Then nest it. Do it again. And again and again and *again* . . .

Anlic, for the last time, came to self-awareness.

It was inevitable that, given enough time, she would be budded by chance occurrence. And so it happened.

She clung to herself and looked around.

It was dark here. Vast, wispy entities cruised across spacetime's swelling breast.

There were no dead stars, no rogue planets. The last solid matter had long evaporated: burned up by proton decay, a thin smoke of neutrinos drifting out at lightspeed.

For ages the black-hole engineers had struggled to maintain their Cities, to gather more material to replace what decayed away. It was magnificent, futile.

The last structures failed, the last black holes allowed to evaporate.

The Conflux of minds had dispersed, flowing out over the expanding universe like water running into sand.

Even now, of course, there was *something* rather than nothing. Around her was an unimaginably thin plasma: free electrons and positrons decayed from the last of the Big Bang's hydrogen, orbiting in giant, slow circles. This cold soup was the last refuge of humanity.

The others drifted past her like clouds, immense, slow, coded in wispy light-year-wide atoms. And even now, the others clung to the solace of community.

But that was not for Anlic.

She pondered for a long time, determined not to slide back into the eternal dream.

At length she understood how she had come to be.

And she knew what she must do.

She sought out Mine One, the wreckage of man's original galaxy. The search took more empty ages.

With caution, she approached what remained.

There was no shape here. No form, no colour, no time, no order. And yet there was motion: a slow, insidious, endless writhing, punctuated by bubbles which rose and burst, spitting out fragments of mass-energy.

This was the singularity that had once lurked within the great black-hole's event horizon. Now it was naked, a glaring knot of quantum foam, a place where the unification of spacetime had been ripped apart to become a seething probabilistic froth.

Once this object had oscillated violently, and savage tides, chaotic and unpredictable, had torn at any traveller unwary enough to come close. But the singularity's energy had been dissipated by each such encounter.

Even singularities aged.

Still, the frustrated energy contained there seethed, quantum-mechanically, randomly. And sometimes, in those belched fragments, put there purely by chance, there were hints of order.

Structure. Complexity.

She settled herself around the singularity's cold glow.

Free energy was dwindling to zero, time stretching to infinity. It took her longer to complete a single thought than it had once taken species to rise and fall on Earth.

It didn't matter. She had plenty of time.

She remembered her last conversation with Geador. *Has there been another like me? . . . No. No other like you. There hasn't been long enough.*

Now Anlic had all the time there was. The universe was exhausted of everything but time.

The longer she waited, the more complexity emerged from the singularity. Purely by chance. Much of it dissipated, purposeless.

But some of the mass-energy fragments had sufficient complexity to be able to gather and store information about the thinning universe. Enough to grow.

That, of course, was not enough. She continued to wait.

At last – by chance – the quantum tangle emitted a knot of structure sufficiently complex to reflect, not just the universe outside, but its own inner state.

Anlic moved closer, coldly excited.

It was a spark of consciousness: not descended from the grunting, breeding humans of the Afterglow, but born from the random quantum flexing of a singularity.

Just as she had been.

Anlic waited, nurturing, refining the rootless being's order and cohesion. And it gathered more data, developed sophistication.

At last it – *she* – could frame questions.

'. . . Who am I? Who are you? Why are there two and not one?'

Anlic said, 'I have much to tell you.' And she gathered the spark in her attenuated soul.

Together, mother and daughter drifted away, and the river of time ran slowly into an unmarked sea.

SPINDRIFT

Or (Malenfant wrote to Michael) perhaps there is life all around us, even now. Perhaps there is life in the stars, the clouds, the rocks under your feet. But we just can't see it. Wouldn't that be strange?

Look up at the full Moon.

Look for the patch of bright highland at the centre of the southern hemisphere, nestling amid the darker seas. The highlands are old territory, my dear Svetlana, battered and scarred by five billion years; the seas are ponds of frozen lava, flooded impact wounds.

Close to the lunar equator, a little to the left of the highland mass, you will find the Known Sea – Mare Cognitum. Here, through a good telescope, you might observe the Fra Mauro complex of craters.

Here, for the last six years, I have made my home; and here, I am now certain, I will die.

I am Vladimir Alexeyevich Zotov, first human being to walk upon the surface of the Moon. I will record as long as I can. Hear my story, Svetlana, my daughter!

I left Earth on October 18, 1965.

A mere ten thousand years after the great impact which budded it from young Earth, the Moon coalesced. The infant world cooled rapidly. Gases driven out of the interior were immediately lost to space.

Planetesimals bombarded the Moon, leaving red-glowing pinpricks in the cooling rind. But soon the hail of impactors ceased. The first volcanism had already begun, dark mantle material pouring through crust faults to flood impact basins and craters and lava-cut valleys. But soon even the lava pulses dwindled.

After just a billion years, the Moon's heart grew cold.

The living things which huddled there, of carbon and oxygen and hydrogen, grew still and small and cold.

And the first ponderous rocky thoughts washed sluggishly through the Moon's rigid core.

Meanwhile life exploded over blue, stirring Earth.

In my contoured couch I felt the shudder of distant valves slamming shut, the rocket swaying as the fuel lines were pulled away. Five minutes before launch they turned on the music. I felt peaceful.

'Launch key to go point.' 'Air purges.' 'Idle run.' 'Ignition!'

More vibrations, high whinings and low rumbles. The Proton booster began to sway to left and right, as if losing balance. Then acceleration surged, as if the rocket had been unchained.

The weight lifted, and I was thrown forward. It was as if the rocket was taking a great breath. Then the core engines burned, crushing me, and I rose through fire and noise.

The core stage died. Vostok Seven swivelled in space.

I was in orbit. I could see the skin of Earth, spread out beneath me like a glowing carpet.

I flew over the Kamchatka peninsula. A chain of volcanoes stretched from north to south, ice glittering on their summits and crests, and all surrounded by sky-blue water. It was very beautiful.

The control centre told me I should prepare for the ignition of my last rocket stage: the Block-D, my translunar engine.

Earth receded rapidly.

I flew through Earth's shadow. I could see the home planet as a hole in the stars, ringed by a rainbow of sunlight refracted through the atmosphere. And in the centre of the planet I could see a faint grey-blue glow: it was the light of the Moon, shining down on the belly of the Pacific.

Here came the Vice President of the United States, and NASA head honchos, and even a brace of Moonwalkers. Men in suits. They were on a guided tour of the lunar colony experiments in the Johnson Space Center back rooms.

And here was Michaela Cassell, along with her buddy Fraser, two lowly interns tagging along.

The first stop was a machine that could bake oxygen out of lunar rock. It was a cylinder six feet tall, with a hopper for ore at one end, and pipes for circulating hydrogen and water and dumping waste: a clunky-looking, robust piece of chemical-engineering technology.

The NASA PR hack did the tour-guide stuff. 'You see, you blow hydrogen across heated regolith. That reacts with the oxygen in an ore called ilmenite, an oxide of iron and titanium, to make water . . . You have basically standard parts here: a 304 stainless steel one hundred psi pressure vessel, swazelock fittings, copper gasket seals, steel tubing. Even the furnace is commercial, a nichrome-wound fuse design. This is a mature technology. But the Moon is a tough place. You need closed-loop fluid systems. In the low gravity you have larger particles than usual, lower fluidizing velocities, big, slow bubbles in the flow that makes for poor contact efficiencies. And you have to figure for minimum maintenance requirements – for instance, the plant has a modular design . . .'

And so on. The old Apollo guys nodded sagely.

The party walked on.

Michaela couldn't help but regard these greying, balding, gap-toothed mid-westerners with awe. Christ, she had even got to shake John Young's hand, a man who had been there *twice*.

New century, new Moon. After forty years, Americans were returning to the Moon, this time to stay, by God. It had been the results from *Lunar Prospector,* and the more ambitious probes which followed, which had kick-started all this.

The probe results, she thought, *and* the corpse on the Moon. The body of a Russian, found by an autonomous Dowser in the shadows of a Mare Cognitum crater.

And the corpse, of course, was all Fraser wanted to talk about.

'. . . It's quite clear,' Fraser said. 'To beat Apollo, the Soviets sent up some poor sap in 1965 on a one-way flight.'

'The Soviets denied they were ever going to the Moon,' Michaela whispered.

'Of course they did, when they lost. But that was a geopolitical lie. *Both* sides had a man-on-the-Moon programme. *Both* sides would do anything to win . . . Hence, the stiff. The idea was to keep him resupplied until the capability came along to retrieve him. *We'd* have done it if we had to. Remember *Countdown*.'

'That was just a movie,' Michaela whispered. 'James Caan –'

'Read the report. NASA SP-4002. Mercury technology. The Soviets covered their resupply flights as failed unmanned probes. Lunas 7, 8, 15, 18. And remember Lunokhod?'

'The Lunokhods *were* science probes.'

'The ones they *reported* did some science. The CIA knew about it, of course. But *nobody* had an interest in exposing this . . .'

The party reached Building 7: something like a chemical plant, huge thickly-painted ducts and pipes everywhere. The Vice Prez was here to inspect the Integrated Life Support System Test Facility. This was a three-storey-high cylinder, built originally for some long-forgotten Cold War pressurization experiment. Now the top storey had been turned into a habitat. The guys in there used physico-chemical systems to recycle their air and urine, for sixty days at a time. The Vice Prez made a joke. *What do you do at work, daddy?*

They met a woman who had worked in here on a previous trial. She was thrilled to meet real-life Moonwalkers. The team were goal-oriented, she said; they had their own astronaut-style crew patches.

Michaela tried to imagine the cosmonaut on the Moon: six years, alone.

Michaela was going to the Moon. She intended to work her way through NASA, make it up there in the second or third wave of colonists.

Smart modern probes were already crawling all over the Moon: autonomous, packed with micromechanical systems and quantum logic chips, swarming and co-operating and discovering. Soon, humans would follow.

There was ice in the regolith; they knew that for sure. There was ambitious talk of lassoing the Earth-approach asteroid, XF11, when it came past in October 2028, and applying its resource. And there were new, ingenious speculations that maybe the interior of the Moon was crammed with water and other volatiles, trapped there since the Moon's savage formation. Riches which would, one day, turn the Moon green.

There were even rumours that the probes had upturned evidence of some kind of sluggish biological activity, in the deep regolith.

But Michaela knew that if it wasn't for the corpse on the Moon they wouldn't be going anywhere. It was a silent witness to a Cold War shame, the source of a new impulse to go back and do it *nobly* this time.

Born long after Apollo, Michaela knew she could never be the first to walk on the Moon. Perhaps, though, she could have been the first human to die there. But the absurd, self-sacrificing bravery of that dead cosmonaut had robbed her of that ambition.

The first child, then, she thought. The first mother on the Moon, the first to bring life there. Not a bad goal.

. . . Unless, she thought, there is life there already.

In Building 241, inside big stainless steel tanks, they were growing dwarf wheat. When Michaela looked through a little port-hole she could see the wheat plants, pale and sturdy, straining up to the rows of fluorescents above them, warm little green things struggling for life in this clinical environment.

Fraser was still talking about the dead cosmonaut. 'We're all guilty, Michaela,' he said softly. 'There is a little patch of the Mare Cognitum forever stained red with human blood . . .'

And so I took humanity's first step on another world. A little spray of dust, of ancient pulverized rock, lifted up around my feet and settled back.

The ground glowed in the sunlight, but the sky was utterly black. There were craters of all dimensions, craters on craters. It was a land sculpted by impact.

Nothing moved here. There was utter silence. This was disorienting. I fought an impulse to turn around, to see who was creeping up behind me.

When I looked at my own shadow the sunlight around it came bouncing straight back at me. The shadow of my body was surrounded by an aura, Svetlana, a halo around my helmet.

I felt filled with love for my country. I sang, '*Oh Russia, my dear and wonderful country, / I am ready to give my life for you, / Just tell me when you need it, / And I will answer you only Yes.*'

I went to work.

The crystal ship rose out of the tall, thin atmosphere. Samtha turned in her seat, uncomfortably aware of her heavy belly.

The horizon curved sharply, blue and blurred. Sparks crawled busily: ships and surface cars and hovercraft, ferrying people to and fro across the Moon's face. The highlands and Farside were peppered with circular crater lakes, glimmering, linked to the mare oceans by the great drainage canals.

Samtha could see the gigantic feather-wake of the pleasure ships on the Tycho-Nubium.

Soon the night hemisphere was turning towards her. But there was no true dark on the Moon, thanks to the solettas, the huge mirror farms which kept the air from snowing out. The solettas were already a thousand years old – nearly as old as the permanent occupation of the Moon itself – but they, or their successors, would have to keep working a lot longer, now that the Spin-Up had been abandoned.

Wistfully she looked for the bone-white ice deserts of the lunar poles. The south pole had been Samtha's home for a decade. She had worked there on the great deep-bore projects, seeking rich new sources of volatiles.

Earth was rising. Blue Moon, brown Earth.

Samtha stroked her belly, feeling the mass of the unborn child there. Today she was leaving, for the moons of Jupiter.

Her project had been shut down. For there was life in the Moon.

Samtha herself had found tracks dissolved into the rock by lunar micro-organisms, little scrapings just micrometres across. The bacteria fed off the Moon's thin flow of internal heat, and mined carbon and hydrogen directly from compounds dissolved in igneous rocks.

Time on the Moon ran slow. The deep bacteria, stunted, starved of energy and nutrients, reproduced just once every few centuries. But they had been found everywhere the temperature of the rocks was less than a hundred degrees or so. And they shared a common origin with Earth life: the first of them, it seemed, had been survivors of the great impact which had led to the budding-off of the Moon from young Earth. It was life which, though separated for five billion years, was nevertheless a remote cousin of her own cells.

Now the Moon would become a museum and laboratory. And the Moon's stillness, said the enthusiasts, made it an ideal test bed for certain new theories Samtha failed to understand – something to do with the spontaneous collapse of quantum-wave functions – perhaps, it was even said, there was a deeper life still to be found in the silent rocks of the Moon.

The Moon, as a laboratory of life and consciousness.

But humanity's role in the future evolution of the Moon would be curtailed. People and their autonomous companions would be restricted to a thin surface layer, limited in the energy they could deploy and the changes they could make.

Samtha had lived through the Die-Back. She accepted the logic; life had to be cherished. But she was a mining engineer and there was nothing for her to do here. So she was going to Jupiter, to mine turbulent, gravity-wrenched Io – where native life was, as far as anybody knew, utterly impossible.

She had no regrets. She was happy that her child would grow up in the rich cosmopolitan society of the moons.

But Samtha was sentimental. She knew that this turning away meant that the Moon could never be more than a shrunken twin of Earth, doomed only to decline.

For the last time the ship soared over the limb of the Moon. Prompted by a murmur from the autonomous ship, Samtha looked out at a grey ellipse, like a mole disfiguring the blue-white face of the Moon. It was the open grave of Vladimir Alexeyevich Zotov, sealed in vacuum under its mile-wide dome. She wondered what that brave Russian would have made of this subtle abandonment of the world he had given his life to reach.

The shuttle tipped up and leapt out of the Moon's shallow gravity well. As the twin worlds receded, watery crescents side by side, Samtha bade a last farewell to the ancient cosmonaut.

Goodbye, goodbye.

My lander rests in a broad valley. There is a broad, meteorite-eroded crater wall nearby, which I call Rimma Crater, for my wife, your dear mother. If I climb this wall – passing through ancient rubble, boulders the size of houses – I can look back over the shining, undulating plain of Fra Mauro. The tracks from my wheeled cart stretch like snail paths down the hillside, to where my lander sits, sparkling like a toy. The ground around the lander is scuffed by my footprints.

The mountains rise up like topped-off pyramids into the black sky. These are mountains which date back almost to the formation of the solar system itself, their contours eroded to smoothness. The constant micrometeorite hail is grinding the Moon to dust. There is a layer of shattered rock and dust, all over the Moon.

I feel isolated, detached, suspended over the rubble of a billion years.

Svetlana, here is how I live on the Moon.

My lander is five metres tall. It consists of a boxy rocket stage standing on four legs, and a fat cabin on top. The cabin is a bulbous, misshapen ball, capped by a fat, wide disk, which is a docking device. Two dinner-plate-sized antennae are stuck out on extensible arms from the descent stage. The whole assemblage is swathed in a green blanket, for thermal insulation.

My cabin is a cosy nest, lined with green fabric. My couch occupies much of the space. Behind my head there is a hatch. There are three small viewing ports recessed into the cabin walls. At my left hand is a console with radio equipment and instruments to regulate temperature and air humidity. On the wall opposite my face, TV and film cameras peer at me. My food is squeezed from tubes. Cupboards set in the walls of the cabin are crammed with such tubes.

The cabin is, in fact, an orbital module adapted from Korolev's new spacecraft design, called Soyuz. This lander is an early model, of course. Little more than an engineering prototype, lacking an engine to bring me home.

Crude solar arrays are draped on frames across the surface of the Moon. In the lander are batteries, capturing the sun energy that keeps me alive during the long nights. But after so many years the lunar weather has taken its toll. The insulation blankets are discoloured. All the equipment is thoroughly irradiated, and remarkably dusty. The paint has turned to tan, but it is uneven, and where I look more closely I can see tiny micrometeorite pits, little craters dug into the paintwork.

Each time I get back into my shelter, I find new scars in my faceplate: tiny pits from the invisible interplanetary sleet within which I walk. Soon I will be blinded.

Moon dust gets in my lungs and causes chest pains. It eats away at joints and seals. Eventually, I suspect, it will overtake me, and everything mechanical will just stop working.

One good thing is that in the lunar vacuum, the dust when disturbed will settle out ballistically. I have kept it clear of my solar panels simply by placing them a metre off the ground, too high for casually disturbed dust to reach.

I have filed reports on many such observations, for I am enthusiastic about the future of the colonized Moon.

cal342 let her viewpoint soar over the surface of the abandoned Moon.

The evidence of the ancient terraforming effort lay everywhere: the gouged-out canals which the micrometeorite wind had yet to erode, the jewel-like cities still sparkling under a thickening layer of dust, the glimmer of frozen air in the shadowed cold traps of the poles.

A million years of human history were wrapped around this small world. That was almost as long as Earth itself – for the first immigration to the Moon had occurred just a few dozen millennia after the emergence of the primal *sapiens* species itself – but now only shreds and shards of primitive technology remained here, as if ape-fingers had never disturbed this dusty ground.

Now that ancient equilibrium was under threat.

A perturbed Oort Cloud comet was approaching. It would be, it was said, the greatest impact event in the solar system since the formation of Earth-Moon itself. And cal342 was here to witness it.

She found the two bodies nestling in an eroded crater at a dust sea's edge.

The first was the physical shell she had prepared for herself. She settled into it.

. . . She found herself breathing. She was gazing at the sky from within a cage of bone: authentically primate, of course, but oddly restricting.

The second body, lying beside her now, was much more ancient.

Even now, with primate eyes, cal342 could see the intruder. It was the brightest object in the sky save the sun: a spark of glowering red in the plane of the ecliptic, a point light in a place it didn't belong.

It was a star, called Gliese 710.

Gliese was making its closest approach to the sun: close enough that it had plunged into the Oort Cloud, the thick belt of comets that lay at the periphery of the solar system. For millennia already the rogue dwarf had been hurling giant ice worldlets into the system's vulnerable heart. Many of cal342's contemporaries had, in fact, bluntly refused to endure this difficult time, and had suspended consciousness until the star had receded.

Not cal342, though.

cal342 had lived a very long time, and she had achieved a certain contentment. She could think of no better way of terminating her existence than this.

For humanity faced a crisis of purposelessness.

Once humans, proudly conscious, had indulged in a certain arrogance. Quantum physics described the universe as filled with uncertainties and probability and ghostly multiple existences. The distinguishing property of consciousness was the ability to *observe:* for when an observation was made, the quantum functions would collapse, uncertainty would disappear, and the universe became – if only briefly and locally – definite.

Humans had spread among the stars, and had found nobody like themselves. So, it had seemed, humans were unique in their consciousness. Perhaps by their observing, humans were actually calling the universe itself into existence. Perhaps humans had been *created* by the universe so that it could generate itself.

But then, in laboratories on the still and silent Moon, spontaneous quantum collapse had been detected in inanimate objects.

In humble rocks, in fact.

An individual particle might take a hundred million years to achieve this – but in a large object, such as a Moon rock, there were so very many particles that one of them would almost immediately collapse its wave function – and then, in a cascade effect of entangled quantum functions, the rest would immediately follow. It was called, after the twentieth-century scientists who first proposed the phenomenon, the Ghirardi-Rimini-Weber effect.

The agonized debate had lasted a hundred thousand years.

At the end of it, there was no doubt that the rocky Moon – scarred by impacts and the clumsy meddling of humans, bearing its own sullen biological lode – was itself *alive*, and, in some huge geologic sense, aware. And so were other small, stable worlds, and many other unpromising structures. The uniqueness of humans was lost.

Now they knew how to look, humans found nothing but mind, infesting the giant structures of the universe. But it was mind that was patient, geologic, immortal. Nothing like their freakish selves.

There was nobody, anywhere, to talk to; and certainly nobody to care.

Science slowed. Art grew decadent. The various species of humanity fragmented and turned in on themselves. They were, it seemed, dancing in the face of oblivion, consuming the resources of worlds – even committing elaborate forms of suicide.

Like cal342 herself.

cal342 turned her head – it was like operating machinery – and looked at the body which lay beside her.

For almost a million years, since the collapse of its protective domes, the body had been exposed to the micrometeorite rain. The top of the body had imploded, leaving a gaping, empty chest cavity, a crumbling hollow shell around it. The head was exposed, and eroded pinnacles of bone hinted at the shape of a skull, eye sockets staring. This human corpse was of the Moon now, reduced to lunar dust, made the same colour as the dark regolith.

Of the Moon, and of the life within it.

Was it possible this ancient traveller, coupled to the chthonic mind of the Moon, was still, in some sense, *aware*? Was he dreaming, as he waited for the comet?

And if so, what were his dreams?

She looked up. The comet light was bright now.

Her choice of viewpoint had been deliberate. Here she was, as humans had always been, her very size suspended between atoms and stars. She was a transient construct arising from baryonic matter, itself a small island in a sea of dark. Her consciousness was spindrift, soon to dissipate.

She dug her hands into crumbling regolith. She wondered if the patient Moon understood what would become of it today.

Fear stabbed.

At the appointed hour I saw the cargo vessel descend.

It was a glittering star in the sunlight, its rocket flame invisible. It came down over the prow of Rimma Crater, perhaps a mile from me. This marked success, Svetlana! Some past craft had failed to leave Earth orbit, or had missed the Moon, or had come down impracticably far away from me, or had crashed.

Elated, I loaded up my cart and set off.

Soon I approached the walls of Rimma Crater. The climb was tiring. My suit was stiff, as if I was inside an inflated tyre.

At the crater rim there were rocks everywhere, poking through a mantle of dust. The crater walls plummeted steeply to a floor of smashed-up rock a hundred metres below.

And there, planted in the crater's centre, was the spacecraft.

But the landing had been faulty. The frame had collapsed, and the Lunokhod rover – an eight-wheeled bathtub shape – lay smashed open, glittering, amid the wreckage of the landing stage.

There was a light in the sky. I looked up. I had to tip back on my heels to do it.

I saw the Earth, a fat crescent, four times the size of a full

Moon. And there, crossing the zenith, was a single, brilliant, unwinking star: it was the orbiting Command Module of an American Apollo spacecraft, waiting to take its astronauts home.

I think I knew at that moment that I would not return home.

I readied my cart and clambered down into Rimma Crater, preparing to salvage the Lunokhod.

The comet nucleus slammed into the Moon's southern hemisphere.

A shock wave raced into the structure of the impactor and vaporized it immediately. A cloud of gas and molten silicate and iron billowed away from the Moon. And a second wave dug down into the ancient hide of the Moon, pulverizing and compressing. The lunar rocks rebounded with equal violence; they disintegrated utterly and exploded from the new cavity.

Then – seconds after the impact, even before the ejecta fell back – the excavated zone began to freeze. Waves of liquid rock froze like ripples on a sluggish pond. The new mountain walls began to collapse under their own weight, forming complex terraces.

But now the ejecta spray fell back from space, blanketing the new mountains in a vast sheet of molten rock.

It was over in minutes. Immediately the steady hail of micrometeorites began its millennial work, darkening and eroding the new deposits.

The cooling scar was the largest impact crater in the solar system.

The Moon, spinning, cooling, steadily receded from its parent Earth. For a time its axis of spin rocked, disturbed by Gliese and the impact. But at last even that residual motion died away, and once more the rigid face of the Moon was locked towards Earth.

But the impact, and Gliese's ferocious gravity, had loosened Earth's ancient grip on its battered offspring.

Month by month, the Moon's orbit became wider, more chaotic.

At last the Moon wandered away, to begin an independent path around the sun.

Goodbye, goodbye.

It was Alexei Arkhipovich Leonov who informed me of the decision of the Presidium. One cosmonaut to another. I admired the way he spoke. I am not certain I could have achieved such dignity.

The N-1 booster programme has been abandoned after continuing failure. No more cosmonauts will be flying to the Moon.

Our managers, it seemed, tried to strike a bargain with the Americans. If they would use a late Apollo flight to retrieve me, my flight would remain a secret – as would my triumph – and the Americans would take the public credit for reaching the Moon first. It is not a bargain I would have welcomed, even if it had saved my life!

But the last Apollos have been cancelled by the Americans; tens of millions of dollars are too high a price to pay, it seems, for my life.

My stranding here was always a possibility, of course. Even so I accepted the challenge gladly! My mission, should it succeed, could only reflect glory and honour on the Communist Party, and on Soviet science and technology.

. . . But there was something in Alexei's tone which conveyed to me a deeper truth.

The Soviet Union cannot admit that at the heart of their space programme was the callous sacrifice of a cosmonaut. And NASA will never admit that their pilot was not the first to the Moon. Thus both sides are locked forever in a shameful compact of deception.

Stranded on the Moon, waiting to die, I am an object of shame, not of glory. I am a relic of a different age, to be hidden.

My cabin is full of noise. There are hundreds of electrical devices, fans, regenerators, carbon-dioxide absorbers and filters. It is like being inside a busy apartment. But in an apartment, a home, there are voices, the noises of life. Here there is only machinery.

I do not begrudge Colonel Armstrong his glory. He is a good pilot. If Korolev and Gagarin had lived, I believe it might have been different.

Humans had exploded from their planet, dug briefly into the Moon's ancient hide, and disappeared.

After the separation of Earth and Moon, humans never returned.

The sun was gradually growing warmer. After a mere billion years, life on Earth was overwhelmed. Five billion years more, and the sun's failing core caused it to swell up and destroy its inner planets.

Not the Moon, though.

The freed Moon circled patiently before the sun's swollen, ferocious face, until the last fires died, and the sun collapsed.

A binary star system, long extinguished, veered past the sun; and the Moon, at last, was torn free.

It began a long journey into the darkness, out of the plane of the disintegrating solar system.

For a time new stars flared around the wandering Moon. And in the rings of rock which surrounded the developing stars, small rocky worlds were born. They glowed briefly in the light of their gaudy parents, and waited for the stillness that would inevitably come.

At last, though, the galaxy's resources were depleted. After a hundred billion years no new stars could form. And after a hundred *thousand* billion years, the last of the stars were reaching the end of their lives.

The great darkness fell over the universe.

Slow cosmic expansion isolated the wreckage of the galaxy from its neighbours. And within that wreckage – a drifting mass of black holes, neutron stars, black dwarfs, stray planets – the soft leakage of gravitational waves caused a gentle, subtle collapse.

The remnant of a star cluster orbited the giant black hole that lurked, slowly evaporating, at the core of the galaxy.

The drifting Moon approached the cluster.

It is lunar night. I am walking across the face of a new Moon. My suit is protesting noisily.

I climb the wall of Rimma Crater.

The phases of the Earth and Moon are opposite. And so the Earth is full, fat above me, a shiny blue ball, laced about by cloud. Its light is blue and cold, and somehow it seems to suit the gentle curves of the Moon, these old, eroded hills.

Time is stretched out here, in the Moon's soft gravity. A day lasts a month. And beneath that there is a still grander scale of time, of the slow evolution of the Moon itself. I look at the hills, the crater-sculpted plain beneath, and I know that I could have come here a billion years ago, or a billion years from now, to find the same scene.

The Moon cares nothing for time.

Perhaps Earth, with its complex geology and cargo of life, is unique. But the galaxy must be full of small, timeless worlds like this one. Explorers of the future will stand on a hundred, a thousand worlds like this, peering up at different patterns of stars. And will they remember *this,* the original Moon, the prototypical destination for mankind?

And as I frame these dreamlike thoughts, it is as if, for a brief moment, I have come further than the Moon itself: as if, in fact,

I have spread myself across the stars, to the ends of space and time, like the godlike people of the farthest future.

They have stopped talking to me.

I refuse to be hidden upstairs, on this Moon, like an insane uncle.

Trillion-year meditations were enriched by the slow gathering of rocky worlds, torn loose of the evaporating galaxy.

Here was one such, approaching the great clustering of mind, as if with caution.

Curiosity was engaged, briefly.

Remnants of crude structures, long vanished, were observed on its surface – and even traces of an ancient carbon-hydrogen body, a spindrift remnant clinging to the rocky world, preserved by the deeper geologic soul.

But none of that was important.

If there had been awareness of humanity's brief span, there would have been only pity.

Humans had been tragic, fluttering, fragile creatures: spindrift, with no future or past. And they had vanished without ever understanding *why* they were so alone.

The truth was, humans had emerged in a dull corner of the universe.

Amid the crashing energies of galaxy cores, by the light of clusters of a million swarming stars, in the giant molecular clouds that spanned whole systems: *those* were the deeps where the great minds had gathered, minds like gongs, minds beyond the reach – even the imagination – of mankind. No wonder humans had never understood.

The spark of chthonic consciousness – swimming out of the darkness, its mountains eroded almost to smoothness – was enfolded at last.

Welcome, welcome.

I lie in the soft, silent dust.

I can feel its cold, sucking at my warm body through the layers of my suit. I am in the crater's shadow here; the sun will never reach my crumbling bones. I will record as long as I can, dear Svetlana.

The psychologists who prepared me said that, according to Freud, there is no time in the unconscious. And that, at certain intensely charged moments, there is no time in consciousness itself.

Can that be true?

And can it be that, at the moment of death, the most intense moment of all, the mind accelerates and the soul becomes eternal – an eternity crammed into that last exquisite instant?

If so, here on the timeless Moon, what will I dream?

Svetlana, the daughter I never held! I love you!

Tears flood my eyes, blurring the light of the full Earth.

TOUCHING CENTAURI

Fermi obsesses me (Malenfant wrote to his grandson). I know it does. Your grandmother – Emma, who died before you were born – must have spent half her life telling me as much.

But the more I think about it the more puzzling it gets.

The more I think there must be something wrong with the universe. That's all there is to it.

Kate Manzoni was there the day Reid Malenfant poked a hole in the wall of reality.

When she arrived in the auditorium, Malenfant was speaking from a podium. 'Ladies and gentlemen, welcome to JPL, and the climax of Project Michelangelo. This truly is a historic moment. For today, June 14 2025, we are anticipating the returned echo of the laser pulse we fired at the planet Alpha Centauri A-4, more than eight years ago . . .'

It was her first glimpse of Malenfant. He stood in a forest of microphones, a glare of TV lights. To either side of Malenfant, Kate recognized Cornelius Taine, the reclusive mathematician (and rumoured marginal autistic) who had come up with the idea for the project, and Vice President Maura Della, spry seventy-something, who had pushed the funding through Congress.

Kate was here for the human angle, and by far the most interesting human in this room was Malenfant himself. But right now he was still talking like a press release.

'Four light years out, four light years back: it has been a long journey for our beam of light, and only a handful of plucky photons will make it home. But we'll be here to greet them – and think what it means. Today, we will have proof that our monkey fingers have touched Centauri . . .'

Kate allowed her attention to drift.

JPL, the Jet Propulsion Laboratory, had turned out to look like a small hospital, squashed into a cramped and smoggy Pasadena-suburb site dominated by the green shoulders of the San Gabriel Mountains. This was the von Karman auditorium, the scene of triumphant news conferences when JPL had sent probes to almost every planet in the solar system. Heady days – but long gone now, and JPL had been returned to the Army to do weapons research, its original purpose.

Well, today the big old auditorium was crowded again, with mission managers and scientists and politicians and journalists – like Kate herself – all crammed in among the softscreen terminals. Camera drones drifted like party balloons overhead, or darted like glittering insects through the air.

She walked past display stands, between scrolling softscreen images and bullshitting nerd-scientist types, all eager to lecture the gathered lay folk on the wonders of Project Michelangelo.

She could learn, for example, how the planets of the twin star system Alpha Centauri had first been detected back in 2010, by a European Space Agency planet-hunter probe called Eddington. Working with robotic patience in the silence of space, Eddington had detected minute oscillations in Alpha A's brightness: the signature of a whole system of planets passing before the star's face.

Of most interest was the fourth planet out, Alpha A-4. Not much bigger than Earth, A-4 orbited in the so-called Goldilocks zone: not too far from its sun for water to freeze, not so close to be too hot for life. Follow-up studies had shown that A-4's atmos-phere contained methane. What was significant about that was that it was chemically unstable: there had to be some mechanism to inject such a reactive gas into A-4's unseen air.

Most likely candidate: life.

But still, despite these exciting hints, A-4 was little more than a dot of light, huddled blurrily close to its sun. There were plans underway to launch high-resolution space telescopes to image the continents and oceans of this second Earth, as everybody hoped it would turn out to be.

But now, ahead of all that, here was Reid Malenfant fronting up Project Michelangelo: an audacious attempt to bounce a laser beam off a planet of Alpha Centauri.

Malenfant had come down off his podium. Standing under an image of Michelangelo's God and Adam – the famous fingertip touch that had become a clichéd icon for this kind of endeavour – he was mixing it with the journos and pols and various VIP types at the front of the auditorium. Everybody was talking at once, though not to each other, all of them yammering into com systems mounted on their wrists and lapels.

But even so, for this bitty, distracted audience, Malenfant was holding forth about life in space. 'For me the whole course of my life has been dominated by a simple question: *Where is everybody?* Even as a kid I knew that the Earth was just a ball of rock, on the fringe of a nondescript galaxy. I just couldn't believe that there was nobody out *there* looking back at me down *here* . . .' In his sixties, Malenfant was tall, wiry slim, with a bald head shining like a piece of machinery. Close to, he looked what he was, a grounded astronaut, ridiculously fit, tanned deep. 'I lapped up everything I could find on how space is a high frontier, a sky to be mined, a resource for humanity. All that stuff shaped my life. But is that *all* there is to it? Is the sky really nothing more than an empty stage for mankind? But if not, *where are they?* This is called the Fermi Paradox . . .'

He fell silent, gazing at Kate, who had managed to worm her way to the front of the loose pack. He glanced at her name-tag. 'Ms Manzoni. From –?'

'I'm freelancing today.' She forced a smile. She could smell desert dust on him, hot and dry as a sauna.

'And you think there's a story in the Fermi Paradox?'

She shrugged, non-committal. 'I'm more interested in you, Colonel Malenfant.'

He was immediately suspicious, even defensive. 'Just Malenfant.'

'Of all the projects you could have undertaken when you were grounded, why front a stunt like this?'

He shrugged. 'Look, if you want to call this a stunt, fine. But we're extending the envelope here. Today we'll prove that we can touch other worlds. Maybe an astronaut is the right face to head up a groundbreaker project like this.'

'Ex-astronaut.'

His grin faded.

Fishing for an angle, she said, 'Is that why you're here? You were born in 1960, weren't you? So you remember Apollo. But by the time you grew up cheaper and smarter robots had taken over the exploring. Now NASA says that when the International Space Station finally reaches the end of its life, it plans no more manned spaceflight of any sort. Is this laser project a compensation for your wash-out, Malenfant?'

He barked a laugh. 'You know, you aren't as smart as you think you are, Ms Manzoni. It's your brand of personality-oriented cod-psychology bullshit that has brought down –'

'Are you lonely?'

That pulled him up. 'What?'

'The Fermi Paradox is all about loneliness, isn't it? – the loneliness of mankind, orphaned in an empty universe . . . Your wife, Emma, died a decade back. I know you have a son, but you never remarried –'

He glared at her. 'You're full of shit, lady.'

She returned his glare, satisfied she had hit the mark.

But as she prepared her next question, the auditorium crowd took up chanting along with a big softscreen clock: '. . . Twenty! . . . Nineteen! . . . Eighteen! . . .' She looked away, distracted, and Malenfant took the opportunity to move away from her.

She worked her way through the crowd until she could see the big softscreen display at the front of the auditorium. It was a tapestry of more-or-less incomprehensible graphic and digital updates.

She prepared her floating camera drones, and the various pieces of recording technology embedded in her flesh and clothing. The truth was, whatever data came back with those interstellar photons wouldn't matter; today's iconic image would be that pure instant of triumph when that faint echo returned from Alpha A-4, and those graphs and charts leapt into jagged animation. And that, and the accompanying swirl of emotions, would be what she must capture.

But in the midst of her routine she found room for a sliver of wonder. This was after all about reaching out to a second Earth, just as Malenfant had said – maybe it was a stunt, but *what* a stunt . . .

Everybody was growing quiet, all faces turned up to the big softscreen.

The ticking clock moved into the positive.

The shimmering graphs remained flatlined.

There was silence. Then, as nothing continued to happen, a mutter of conversation.

Kate was baffled. *There had been no echo.* How could that be? She knew this was an experiment that would have been accurate to a fraction of a second; there was no possibility of a time error. Either the receiving equipment had somehow failed to work – or else the laser pulse from Earth had gone sailing right through planet Alpha A-4 as if it was an image painted on glass . . .

She peered around frantically, trying to get a first impression of the principals' reaction. She saw the back of Malenfant's head as he stared stolidly at the unresponsive screen, as if willing the displays to change. Veep Della frowned and stroked her chin.

Cornelius Taine was grinning.

Something is very, very wrong here. And you want to know something else?

Kate floated in the dark, freed of gravity and sensation, listening to her own voice.

'Tell me,' he whispered.

It's getting wronger. They tested the whole set-up the day before with a bounce off a deep-space comet a hundred astronomical units out – twice as far as Pluto. I happen to know they repeated the echo test off that same comet a few hours after *the Centauri experiment failed.*

'And they couldn't find the comet.'

You're getting the idea. Michelangelo shouldn't have failed. It couldn't have failed . . .

This was one of her virtual correspondents, an entity (maybe multiple) she knew only as Rodent, his/her/their anonymity protected by layers of encryption and chaff. But the transmission was encoded in her own voice; she liked to imagine it was the other half of herself, dreaming-Kate whispering across her corpus callosum, that bridge between her brain's hemispheres within which was embedded the implant that had dropped her into this virtual world.

But the images that floated before her now, of angular, expensive machinery, had come from no dream.

The laser burst was generated in low Earth orbit by a nuclear fusion pulse. A trillion watts of power compressed into a fraction of a second. They have been building toys like this for decades, at places like Lawrence Livermore. Got a big boost under Gore-Clinton, and even more under Clinton-Clinton . . .

Much had been learned about other worlds, even from Earth,

by techniques like Michelangelo's: the cloud-shrouded surface of Venus had first been studied by radar beams emitted from giant ground-based radio telescopes, for instance. But Alpha A-4 was more than seven *thousand* times as far away as Pluto, the solar system's outermost planet. Michelangelo's vast outreaching was orders of magnitude more difficult than anything attempted before – and in some quarters had been criticized as premature.

Maybe those critics had been proved right. 'So the experiment failed. It happens.'

Kate, the laser worked. Look, they could see the damn pulse as it was fired off into the dark.

'But that's just the first step. You're talking about a shot across four light years, of projecting planetary movements across four years' duration.' The scientists had had to aim their pulse, not at A-4 itself, but at the place A-4 was expected to be by the time the light pulse got there. It had been a speed-of-light pigeon shoot – but a shoot of staggering precision. 'And Alpha Centauri is a triple star; what if the planet's motions were perturbed, or –'

A-4 is so close to its parent that its orbit is as stable as Earth's. Kate, believe me, this is just Newtonian clockwork; the predictions couldn't have gone wrong. Likewise the geometry of the reflection. Once those photons were launched, an echo had to come back home.

'Then maybe the receiving equipment is faulty.'

They were watching for those photons with equipment on Earth, in low Earth orbit, on the Moon, and with the big Trojan-point radio telescope array. Short of the sun going nova, what fault could take down all of that? Kate, Michelangelo had to work. There are inquiries going on at every level from the lab boys to the White House, but they'll all conclude the same damn thing.

In swam an image of Malenfant, justifying himself on some TV show. 'There's nothing wrong with our technology,' he was saying. 'So maybe there is something wrong with the universe . . .'

See?

Kate sighed. 'So what's the story? Obscure space experiment fails in unexplained manner . . . There's no meat in that sandwich.'

Do what you do best. Focus on the people. Go find Malenfant. And ask him about Voyager.

'Voyager – the spacecraft?'

You know, when it fires, that damn laser destroys itself. Makes

*a single cry to the stars, then dies, a billion dollars burned up in
a fraction of a second. Kind of a neat metaphor for our wonderful
military-industrial complex, don't you think?*

She failed to find Malenfant. She did find his son. She cleared her
desk and went to see the son, two days after the failed experiment.

Meanwhile, so far as she could see, the world continued to turn,
people went about their business, and the news was the usual buzz
of politics and personalities – of Earthbound matters like the water
war in the Sahel, the latest Chinese incursion into depopulated
Russia, the Attorney General's continuing string of extra-marital
affairs.

Most people knew about the strange news from Alpha Centauri.
Few seemed to think it mattered. The truth was, for all the mutter-
ings of Rodent and his ilk, she wasn't sure herself. She still sensed
there was a story here, however.

And she was growing a little scared.

Mike Malenfant, aged 30, lived with his wife, Saranne, in a
suburb of Houston called Clear Lake.

He opened the door. 'Oh. Ms Manzoni.'

'Call me Kate . . . Have we met?'

'No.' He grinned at her. 'But Malenfant told me about you, and
what you said to him the night of Michelangelo. Seemed to bug
him more than the failure itself.'

She thought, He calls his dad by his surname? Father-son rivalry?
He didn't look much like his father: rounder, smaller, with dense
black hair he must have inherited from his mother. 'Uh, would
you rather I left?'

'No. My dad is a little 1970s sometimes. I don't have a problem
with what you do. How did you find me? We keep our name out
of the books.'

That wouldn't have stopped her, she thought. But it had been
easier than that. 'I played a hunch. Malenfant used to live here,
with Emma. So I guessed –'

He grinned again. 'You guessed right. Malenfant will be even
more pissed to know he's so predictable.' He took her indoors and
introduced his wife, Saranne: pretty, heavily pregnant, tired-
looking. 'Tea?'

With a camera drone hovering discreetly at her shoulder, Kate
began gently to interview the couple.

Close to the Johnson Space Center, Clear Lake was a place of retro-chic wooden-framed houses backing onto the fractal-edged water. This had long been a favoured domicile of NASA astronauts and their families. When Malenfant's career had taken him away from Houston and NASA, son Mike had happily – so it seemed – taken over the house he had grown up in, with its battered rowboat still tied up at the back.

Some of what Mike had to say – about the life of a soft-muscled, intellectual boy growing up as the son of America's favourite maverick astronaut – was illuminating, and might make a useful colour piece some day. So Kate wasn't being entirely dishonest. But her main objective, of course, was to keep them talking until Malenfant showed up – as he surely would, since she'd sent a provocative note to his message service to say she was coming.

Mike hadn't followed his father's career path. He had become a virtual character designer, moderately successful in his own right. Now, with his business-partner wife expecting their first child, this was maybe a peak time of his life. But even so he didn't seem to resent the unspoken and obvious truth that Kate was here because he was Malenfant's son, not for himself alone.

One thing that was immediately nailed home in her awareness was how much Mike – and, it seemed, Malenfant himself – missed Emma: Mike's mother, Malenfant's wife, taken away by cancer before she was forty. She wondered how much of a difference it might have made to everybody's lives if Emma had survived.

As the low-afternoon sun started to glint off the stretch of lake out back, the old man arrived.

He launched into her as soon as he walked in the door. 'Ms Manzoni, the great pap-peddler. You aren't welcome here. This is my son's home, and I have a job to do. So why don't you take your drones and your implants and shove them up –'

'As far as the implants are concerned,' Kate said dryly, 'somebody already did that for me.'

That got a laugh out of Mike, and the mood softened a little. But Malenfant kept up his glare. 'What do you want, Manzoni?'

'Tell me about *Voyager*,' she said.

Mike and Saranne looked quizzical. Malenfant looked away.

Aha, she thought.

'*Voyager*,' she said to Mike and Saranne. 'Two space probes designed to explore the outer planets, launched in the 1970s. Now they are floating out of the solar system. About a decade ago they crossed the heliopause – the place where the star winds blow, the boundary of interstellar space – right, Malenfant? But the *Voyagers* are still working, even now, and the big radio telescopes can still pick up their feeble signals . . . A heroic story, in its way.'

Mike shrugged. 'So, a history lesson. And?'

'And now something's happened to them. That's all I know.'

Malenfant was stony-faced, arms folded.

For a moment it looked like developing into an impasse. But then, to Kate's surprise, Saranne stepped forward, hands resting on her belly. 'Maybe you should tell her what she wants to know, Malenfant.'

It was as if Malenfant was suddenly aware she was there. 'Why?'

'There's a lot of buzz about your experiment.' Saranne was dark, her eyes startling blue. 'There's something strange going on, isn't there? Don't you think we've a right to know about it?'

Malenfant softened. 'Saranne – it's not so easy. Sometimes there is no use asking questions, because there are no meaningful answers.'

Kate frowned. 'And sometimes there are answers, but there's nothing to be done – is that it, Malenfant? Don't tell the children the truth, for fear of frightening them –'

His anger returned. 'This has nothing the hell to do with you.'

Saranne said, 'Come on, Malenfant. If she's found out something, so will everybody else soon enough. This isn't 1960.'

He barked a bitter laugh.

'*Voyager*,' Kate prompted.

'*Voyager*. Okay. Yesterday the Deep Space Network lost contact with the spacecraft. Both *Voyagers* 1 and 2. Within a couple of hours.'

Mike said, 'Is that so significant? They were creaky old relics. They were going to fade out sometime.'

Malenfant eyed his son. 'Both together? After so long? How likely is that? And anyhow we had a handle on how much power they had left. It shouldn't have happened.'

Kate said, 'Was this after the comet, or before?'

Mike said, 'What comet?'

'The one that went missing when your father's laser tried to echo-sound it.'

Malenfant frowned. Evidently he hadn't expected her to know

about that either. 'After,' he said. 'After the comet.'

Kate tried to put it together in her head. A series of anomalies, then: that missing planet of Alpha Centauri, a comet out in the dark, the lonely *Voyagers*. All evaporating.

Each event a little closer to the sun.

Something is coming this way, she thought. Like footprints in the dew.

A softscreen chimed; Mike left the room to answer it.

Malenfant kept up his glare. 'Come on, Manzoni. Forget *Voyager*. What do you really want here?'

Kate glanced at Malenfant and Saranne, and took another flyer. 'What's the source of the tension between you two?'

Malenfant snapped, 'Don't answer.'

But Saranne said evenly, 'It's this.' She stroked her bump. 'Baby Michael.' She watched Malenfant's uncomfortable reaction. 'See? He's not even happy with the fact that we know Michael's sex, that we named him before his birth.'

'You know it's not that,' Malenfant growled.

Kate guessed, 'Has the child been enhanced?'

'Nothing outrageous,' Saranne said quickly. 'Anti-ageing treatments: telomerase, thymus and pineal-gland adjustments. In the womb he's been farmed for stem cells and organ clones. And we chose a few regenerative options: regrowing fingers, toes and spinal column . . .'

'He'll be able to hibernate,' Malenfant said, his tone dangerously even. 'Like a goddamn bear. And he might live forever. Nobody knows.'

'He's going to grow up in a dangerous world. He needs all the help he can get.'

Malenfant said, 'He's your kid. You can do what you like.'

'He's your grandson. I wish I had your blessing.' But her tone was cool; Kate saw she was winning this battle.

Malenfant turned on Kate. 'How about your family, Ms Manzoni?'

She shrugged. 'My parents split when I was a kid. I haven't seen my father since. My mother –'

'Another broken home. Jesus.'

'It's not a big deal, Malenfant. I was the *last* in my high school class to go through a parental divorce.' She smiled at Saranne, who smiled back.

But Malenfant, visibly unhappy, was lashing out at Kate, where he couldn't at Saranne. 'What kind of way to live is that? It's as if we're all crazy.'

Saranne said carefully, 'Malenfant has a certain amount of difficulty with the modern world.'

Kate said, 'Malenfant, I don't believe you're such a sour old man. You ought to be happy for Saranne and Mike.'

Saranne said, 'And I sure have the right to do the best for my kid, Malenfant.'

'Yes. Yes, you do,' he said. 'And the responsibility. God knows I admire you for that. But can't you see that if *everyone* does what's best for themselves alone, we're all going to hell in a handbasket? What kind of world will it be where the rich can buy immortality, while the poor continue to starve as fast as they breed?'

Kate thought she understood. 'You always look to the big picture, Malenfant. The Fermi Paradox, the destiny of mankind. Right? But most people don't think like that. Most people focus the way Saranne is focused, on whatever is best for their kids. What else can we do?'

'Take a look around. We're living in the world that kind of thinking has created.'

She forced a smile. 'We'll muddle through.'

'If we get the chance,' Malenfant said coldly.

Mike came back into the room, looking stunned. 'That was the Vice President. There's a helicopter on the way from Ellington Air Force Base. For you, Malenfant.'

Malenfant said, 'I'll be damned.'

Saranne looked scared. 'The Vice President?'

Kate frowned. 'Malenfant, don't you think you should find out what's going on before you get to Washington?' She walked to a wall and slapped it, opening up its comms facilities. 'Maybe you ought to ask Cornelius Taine.'

'Ask him what?'

She thought quickly, wondering where those footsteps would next fall. What was the furthest planet from the sun? . . . 'Pluto. Ask him about Pluto.'

Malenfant evidently didn't enjoy being told what to do by the likes of Kate Manzoni. But he punched in ident codes, and began to interact with a small patch of the wall.

Kate and the others waited; it wasn't a moment for small talk. Kate strained to hear the sounds of the chopper.

At length Malenfant straightened up. Before him, embedded in the smart wall, was an image of a planet: blue, streaked with white cloud.

Kate's heart thumped. 'Earth?'

He shook his head. 'And not Pluto either. This is a live image of Neptune. Almost as far out as Pluto. A strange blue world, blue as Earth, on the edge of interstellar space . . .'

Saranne said uneasily, 'What's wrong with it?'

'Not Neptune itself. Triton, its moon. Look.' He pointed to a blurred patch of light, close to Neptune's ghostly limb. When he tapped the wall, the patch moved, quite suddenly. Another tap, another move. Kate couldn't see any pattern to the moves, as if the moon was no longer following a regular orbit.

'I don't understand,' she said.

'Triton has started to . . . flicker. It hops around its orbit – or adopts another orbit entirely – or sometimes it vanishes, or is replaced by a ring system.' He scratched his bald pate. 'According to Cornelius, Triton was an oddity – circling Neptune backwards – probably created in some ancient collision event.'

'Even odder now,' Mike said dryly.

'Cornelius says that all these images – the multiple moons, the rings – are all *possibilities*, alternate outcomes of how that ancient collision might have come about. As if other realities are folding down into our own.' He searched their faces, seeking understanding.

Mike said, 'Malenfant, what has this to do with your laser shot?'

Malenfant spread his hands. 'Mike, I talk big, but we humans are pretty insignificant in the bigger scheme of things. Out there in the dark, somebody is playing pool with a moon. How can we have affected *that*?'

Kate took a breath. *Neptune*: a long way away, out in the dark, where the planets are cloudy spheres, and the sun's light is weak and rectilinear. But out there, she thought, something strange is stirring: something with awesome powers indeed, beyond human comprehension.

And it's coming this way. Whatever *it* is. She shuddered, and suppressed the urge to cross herself.

Saranne asked, 'Are the stars still shining?'

It struck Kate as an odd, naive question, but Malenfant seemed touched. 'Yes,' he said gently. 'Yes, the stars are still shining.'

Kate heard the flap of chopper blades. On impulse she snapped, 'Malenfant – take me with you.'

He laughed and turned away.

Mike said, 'Maybe you should do it, Malenfant. I have the feeling she's smarter than you. Somebody needs to be thinking when you meet the Vice President.'

Malenfant turned to Kate. 'Quite a story you're building up here, Manzoni.'

If, she thought, I ever get to file it.

Outside, the noise of the descending chopper mounted. The reddening evening light dappled on the water of the lake, as it had always done, as if the strange lights in the sky were of no more import than a bad dream.

The limo pulled away. Malenfant, in his Navy uniform, was tweaking his cuffs. A blank-faced young soldier waited at his arm, ready to escort them into the building.

The Vice President's official residence was a rambling brick mansion on a broad green lawn, set at the corner of 34th Street and Massachusetts Avenue. Kate, who wasn't as accustomed to Washington as she liked to pretend, thought it looked oddly friendly, like a small-town museum, rather than a major centre of federal power.

Beyond the security fence city life went on as usual, a stream of Smart-driven traffic washing with oily precision along the street, tourists and office workers drifting along the sidewalk, speaking into the air to remote contacts.

Malenfant said, 'You wouldn't think the damn sky was about to fall, would you?'

'Everybody knows as much as we do,' she said. 'Nothing stays secret. So how come there isn't –'

'Panic buying?' he grinned. 'Rutting in the streets? Running for the hills? Because we don't get it, Manzoni. Look in your heart. *You* don't believe it, do you? Not deep down. We're not programmed to look further than the other guy's nose.'

Unexpectedly the young soldier spoke up. '"This is the way I think the world will end – with general giggling by all the witty heads, who think it is a joke."' They looked at him, surprised. 'Kierkegaard. Sorry, sir. If you're ready, will you follow me?'

When they reached Maura Della's office, Cornelius Taine was

already there, sitting bolt uptight on one of the overstuffed armchairs, already talking.

'Past speculation on artificial realities provides us with clues as to our likely response to finding ourselves in a "planetarium". You may remember movies in which the protagonist is the unwitting star of a TV show or movie, who invariably tries to escape. But the idea that the world around us may not be real reaches back to Plato, who wondered if what we see resembles the flickering shadows on a cave wall. And the notion of *creating* deceptive artificial environments dates back at least as far as Descartes, who in the seventeenth century speculated on the philosophical implications of a sense-manipulating "demon" – effectively a pre-technological virtual-reality generator . . .'

Della, listening, waved Malenfant and Kate to seats. Kate selected an expensive-looking upright that creaked under her weight.

The office was large and spacious. The furniture was stuffed leather, the big desk polished mahogany, the wallpaper and carpets lush. But Maura Della had stamped her personality on the room; on every wall were cycling softscreen images of the surfaces of Mars and Io, the gloomy oceans of Europa, a deep-space image of a galaxy field.

Malenfant leaned forward. '*Planetarium?* What the hell are you talking about, Cornelius?'

Cornelius regarded him coolly. 'The logic is compelling, Malenfant. Your own logic: the Fermi Paradox, which you claim has driven your life. The Paradox defies our intuition, as well as philosophical principles such as the assumption of mediocrity, that it is only on our own apparently commonplace world that mind has evolved. The Paradox is surely telling us that something is fundamentally wrong with our view of the universe, and our place in it.'

Malenfant prompted, 'And so . . .'

'And so, perhaps the reason that the universe does not appear to make sense is that *what we see around us is artificial.*'

Malenfant let his mouth drop open.

Kate sat as still as she could, unsure how to react.

They were both looking at the Vice President, waiting for her lead.

Della sighed. 'I know how this sounds. But Cornelius is here at my invitation, Malenfant. Look, I have plenty of people explaining the *rational* possibilities to me. Perhaps we're in the middle of some huge solar storm, for instance, which is disrupting communications. Perhaps the solar system has wandered into a knot of interstellar gas, or even dark matter, which is refracting or diffusing electromagnetic radiation, including your laser beam –'

'None of which hangs together,' Kate guessed.

Della frowned at her. Malenfant quickly introduced Kate as a personal aide.

Della said, 'Okay. You're right. Nobody has come up with anything that works. It isn't just a question of some new anomaly; we have a situation for which, as far as I understand it, no explanation within our physical law is *even possible* . . . But here is Cornelius, with a proposal that is frankly outrageous –'

'But an outrageous problem requires outrageous proposals,' Cornelius said, his smile cold.

Malenfant said, 'Just tell me what you're talking about, Cornelius.'

Cornelius went on, 'Think about it. What if we have been placed in some form of "planetarium", perhaps generated using an advanced virtual reality technology, designed to give us the illusion of an empty universe – while beyond the walls with their painted stars, the shining lights of extraterrestrial civilizations glow unseen?'

'Which would resolve Fermi,' Malenfant said. 'They're there, but they are hiding.'

'Which would resolve Fermi, yes.'

'And now the planetarium's, uh, projector is breaking down. Hence A-4, Neptune and the rest. Is that what you're saying?'

'Exactly.'

Kate thought it over. 'That's what the Fermi experts call a zoo hypothesis.'

Cornelius looked impressed. 'So it is.'

'It belongs in a zoo,' Malenfant said. 'For one thing it's paranoid. It's classic circular logic: you could never disprove it. We could never detect we were in a planetarium because it's *designed* not to be detected. Right?'

'Malenfant, the fact that a hypothesis is paranoid doesn't make it wrong.'

Della said, 'Let me see if I understand you, Cornelius. You're suggesting that not everything we see is real. *How* much of everything?'

Cornelius shrugged. 'There are several possible answers. It depends on how far the boundary of the artificial "reality" is set from the human consciousness. The crudest design would be like a traditional planetarium, in which we – our bodies – and the objects we touch are real, while the sky is a fake dome.'

Malenfant nodded. 'So the stars and galaxies are simulated by a great shell surrounding the solar system.'

'But,' said Kate, 'it would surely take a lot to convince us. Photons of starlight are real entities that interact with our instruments and eyes.'

Malenfant said, thinking, 'And you'd have to simulate not just photons but such exotica as cosmic rays and neutrinos. You're talking about some impressive engineering.'

Cornelius waved a hand, as if impatient with their ill-informed speculation. 'These are details. If the controllers anticipate our technological progress, perhaps even now they are readying the gravity-wave generators . . .'

'And what,' asked Della, 'if the boundary is closer in than that?'

Cornelius said, 'There are various possibilities. Perhaps we humans are real, but some – or all – of the objects we see around us are generated as simulations, tangible enough to interact with our senses.'

'Holograms,' Kate said. 'We are surrounded by holograms.'

'Yes. But with solidity. Taste, smell . . .'

Malenfant frowned. 'That's kind of a brute-force way of doing it. You'd have to form actual material objects, all out of some kind of controlling rays. How? Think of the energy required, the control, the heat . . . And you'd have to load them with a large amount of information, of which only a fraction would actually interact with *us* to do the fooling.'

Della said, 'And would these hologram objects be evanescent – like the images on a TV screen? In that case they would need continual refreshing – yes?'

Again Cornelius seemed impatient; this is a man not used to being questioned, Kate saw. 'It is straightforward to think of more *efficient* design strategies. For example, allowing objects once created to exist as quasi-autonomous entities within the environment, only loosely coupled to the controlling mechanism. This would obviate the need, for example, to reproduce continually the substance at the centre of the Earth, with which we never interact directly. But any such compromise is a step back from perfection.

With sufficient investment, you see, the controllers would have *full control* of the maintained environment.'

Della said, 'What would that mean?'

Cornelius shrugged. 'The controllers could make objects appear or disappear at will. The whole Earth, if necessary. For example.'

There was a brief silence.

Della got out of her chair and faced the window. She flexed her hands, and pressed her fingertips against the sunlit desk top, as if testing its reality. 'You know, I find it hard to believe we're having this conversation. Anything else?'

Cornelius said, 'A final possibility is that *even our bodies are simulated*, so that the boundary of reality is drawn around our very consciousness. We can already think of crude ways of doing this.' He nodded at Kate. 'For example, the fashionable implants in the corpus callosum that allow the direct downloading of virtual-reality sensations into the consciousness.'

'If that was so,' said Della, 'how could we ever tell?'

Cornelius shook his head. 'If the simulation was good enough, we could not. And there would be nothing we could do about it. But I don't think we are in that situation.'

'How do you know?'

'*Because the simulation is going wrong.* Alpha A-4, the evaporation of the Oort Cloud, Neptune, the vanishing of Saturn's rings . . .'

Kate hadn't heard about Saturn; she found room for a brief, and surprising, stab of regret.

'I think,' said Cornelius, 'that we should assume we are in a planetarium of the second type I listed. We are "real". But not everything around us is genuine.'

Della turned and leaned on her desk, her knuckles white. 'Cornelius, whatever the cause, this wave of anomalies is working its way towards us. There is going to be panic; you can bet on that.'

Cornelius frowned. 'Not until the anomalies are visible in our own sky. Most of us have remarkably limited imaginations. The advance of the anomaly wave is actually quite well understood. Its progression is logarithmic; it is slowing as it approaches the sun. We can predict to the hour when effects will become visible to Earth's population.' His cool gaze met the Vice President's. 'That is, we can predict when the panicking will begin.'

Kate asked, 'How long?'

'Five more days. The precise numbers have been posted.' He

smiled, cold, analytical. 'You have time to prepare, madam Vice President. And if it is cloudy, Armageddon will no doubt be postponed by a few hours.'

Della glowered at him. 'You're a damn cold fish, Cornelius. If you're right – what do you suggest we do?'

'Do?' The question seemed to puzzle him. 'Why – rejoice. Rejoice that the façade is cracking, that the truth will soon be revealed.'

A phone chimed, startling them all. Malenfant looked abstractedly into the air while an insect voice buzzed in his ear.

He turned to Kate. 'It's Saranne. She's gone into labour.'

The meeting broke up. Kate followed Malenfant out of the room, frustrated she hadn't gotten to ask the most important questions of all:

What controllers?

And, what do they want?

Her own voice wafted out of the dark.

You know who's really taking a bath over this? The astrologers. Those planets swimming around the sky are turning their fancy predictions into mush. And if this is the end of the world, how come none of them saw it coming? . . .

It was the fourth day after the Alpha echo had failed to return. Three days left, if Cornelius was right, until . . .

Until what?

'Don't talk about astrology,' she whispered. 'Tell me about reality.'

. . . Okay. Why do we believe that the universe is real? Starting with Bishop Berkeley, the solipsists have wondered if the apparently external world is contained within the observer's imagination – just as this virtual abyss we share is contained within the more limited imagination of a bank of computers.

'I don't see how you could disprove that.'

Right. But when Boswell asked Dr Johnson about the impossibility of refuting Berkeley's theory, Johnson kicked a large rock and said, 'I refute it thus.' What Johnson meant was that when the rock 'kicked back' at his foot, he either had to formulate a theory of physical law which explained the existence and behaviour of the rock – or else assume that his imagination was itself a complex, autonomous universe containing laws which precisely simulated the existence of the rock – which would therefore, imagination plus rock, be a more complex system. You see? If we're in a planetarium there must be some vast hidden mechanism that controls everything we see. It's simpler to assume that what looks real is real.

'Occam's razor.'

Sure. But Occam's razor is a guide, not a law of physics . . . And turn it around. What if the universe is a simulation? Then we can use Dr Johnson's criterion to figure out what is required of the controllers.

'I don't understand.'

The model universe must have a lot of industrial-strength properties. For instance it must be consistent. Right? In principle, anybody anywhere could perform a scientific experiment of the finest detail on any sample of the universe and its contents, and find the fabric of reality yielding consistent results. The rocks have always got to 'kick back' in the same way, no matter where and how we kick them. So you have to build your cage that way. Expensive, right?

And the environment has to be self-contained: no explanations of anything inside should ever require the captives to postulate an outside. Kate, I bet if you had been born in this darkness you could figure out there has to be something beyond. How could your consciousness have emerged from this formless mush?

And so on. The technical challenge of achieving such a deep and consistent simulation should not be underestimated – and nor should the cost . . . Oh. It just reached Jupiter. Wow, what a spectacle. You want to see?

Her field of view filled up abruptly with fragmentary images, bits of cloud fractally laced, stained salmon pink.

She turned away, and the images disappeared.

Strange thought, isn't it? What if Cornelius is right? Here you are in one virtual reality, which is in turn contained within another. Layers of nested unreality, Kate . . .

Kate felt a sudden revulsion. 'Wake up, wake up.'

For long minutes she immersed herself in gritty reality: the pine scent that came from the open window of her bedroom, the song of the birds, the slow tick of the old-fashioned clock in the wall.

Reality?

On impulse, she closed her eyes. 'Wake up. Wake up.'

The clock continued to tick, the birds to sing.

*   *   *

Civil defence programmes were activated, Cold War bunkers reopened, food stocks laid down. Various space probes were hastily launched to meet the advancing anomaly. There was even an extraordinary crash programme to send an astronaut team to orbit the Moon, now seen as the last line of defence between Earth and sky.

Kate knew the government had to be seen doing something; that was what governments were there for.

But she knew it was all futile, and in its own way damaging. Though reassuring talking heads from the President on down tried to tell people to keep calm – and, more importantly, to keep showing up at work – there was growing disruption from the preparations themselves, if not from the strange lights in the sky, still invisible to the naked eye.

Of course it all got worse when Cornelius's countdown timetable became widely known.

She did a little digging into the history of Cornelius Taine.

He had been an academic mathematician. She hadn't even recognized the terms his peers used to describe Cornelius's achievements – evidently they covered games of strategy, economic analysis, computer architecture, the shape of the universe, the distribution of prime numbers – anyhow he had been on his way, it seemed, to becoming one of the most influential minds of his generation.

But his gift seemed non-rational: he would leap to a new vision, somehow knowing its rightness instinctively, and construct laborious proofs later. Cornelius had remained solitary: he attracted awe, envy, resentment.

As he approached thirty he drove himself through a couple of years of feverish brilliance. Maybe this was because the well of mathematical genius traditionally dries up at around that age. Or maybe there was a darker explanation. It wasn't unknown for creativity to derive from a depressive or schizoid personality. And creative capacities could be used in a defensive way, to fend off mental illness.

Maybe Cornelius was working hard in order to stay sane. If he was, it didn't seem to have worked.

The anecdotes of Cornelius's breakdown were fragmentary. On his last day at Princeton they found him in the canteen, slamming his head against a wall, over and over.

After that Cornelius had disappeared for two years. Emma's data miners had been unable to trace how he spent that time.

When he re-emerged, it was to become a founding board member of a consultancy called Eschatology, Inc.

She took this to Malenfant. 'Don't you get it? Here's a guy who sees patterns in the universe nobody else can make out – a guy who went through a breakdown, driven crazy by the numbers in his head – a guy who now believes he can predict the end of humanity. If he came up to you in the street, what would you think of what he was muttering?'

'I hear what you say,' he said. 'But –'

'But what?'

'*What if it's true?* Whether Cornelius is insane or not, what if he's right? What then?' His eyes were alive, excited.

'He's gone to ground, you know,' she said.

'We have to find him.'

It took two more precious days.

They tracked Cornelius to New York. He agreed to meet them at the head offices of Eschatology, Inc.

Kate wasn't sure what she had expected. Maybe a trailer home in Nevada, the walls coated with tabloid newspaper cuttings, the interior crammed with cameras and listening gear.

But this office, here in the heart of Manhattan, was none of that.

Malenfant was glaring at Cornelius. 'You know, I have the feeling you've played me for a patsy through this whole damn thing. You've always known more than me, been one step ahead, used me to front your projects without telling me the full logic –'

Cornelius laughed at him, with a chilling arrogance. He barely sees us as human beings at all, Kate realized. He said, 'Sore pride, Malenfant? Is that really what's most important to you? We really are just frightened chimpanzees, bewildered by the lights in the sky –'

'You arrogant asshole.'

Kate looked around the small, oak-panelled conference room. The three of them sat at a polished table big enough for twelve, with small inlaid softscreens. There was a smell of polished leather and clean carpets: impeccable taste, corporate lushness, anonymity. The only real sign of unusual wealth and power, in fact, was the enviable view – from a sealed, tinted window – of Central Park. She saw people strolling, children playing on the glowing green grass, the floating sparks of police drones everywhere.

The essentially ordinariness made it all the more scary, of course – today being a day when, she had learned, Mars had gone, vanishing into a blurring wave of alternate possibilities, volcanoes and water-carved canyons and life traces and all.

Kate said, 'Malenfant's essentially right, isn't he? On some level you anticipated all this.'

'How can you know that?'

'I saw you smile. At JPL.'

Cornelius nodded. 'You see? Simple observation, Malenfant. This girl really is brighter than you are.'

'Get to the point, Cornelius.'

Cornelius sighed, a touch theatrically. 'You know, the facts are there, staring everybody in the face. The *logic* is there. It's just that most people are unwilling to think it through.

'Take seriously for one minute the possibility that we are living in a planetarium, some kind of virtual-reality projection. What must it cost our invisible controllers to run? We are an inquisitive species, Malenfant. At any moment we are liable to test anything and everything to destruction. To maintain their illusion, the controllers would surely require that their simulation of every object should be *perfect* – that is, undistinguishable from the real thing by any conceivable physical test.'

'No copy is perfect,' Malenfant said briskly. 'Quantum physics. Uncertainty. All that stuff.'

'In fact your intuition is wrong,' Cornelius said. 'Quantum considerations actually show that a perfect simulation *is* possible – but it is energy-hungry.

'You see, there is a limit to the amount of information which may be contained within a given volume. This limit is called the Bekenstein Bound.' Equations scrolled across the table surface before Kate; she let them glide past her eyes. 'The Bound is essentially a manifestation of the Heisenberg Uncertainty Principle, a reflection of the fundamental "graininess" of our reality. Because of the existence of the Bound, every physical object is a finite state machine – that is, it only requires a finite number of bits to replicate its every possible condition. Therefore a *perfect* simulation of any physical object can be made – perfect, meaning undistinguishable from the real thing by any conceivable physical test.'

Kate said uneasily, 'Anything can be replicated?'

Cornelius smiled. 'Including you, Kate. But perfect simulations are expensive. The bigger they are, the more energy they burn. And *that* is the chink in the controllers' armour.'

'It is?'

'As human civilization has progressed, successively larger portions of reality have come within our reach. And the extent of the universe which must be simulated to high quality likewise increases: the walls around reality must be drawn successively back. Before 1969, for example, a crude mock-up of the Moon satisfying only a remote visual inspection might have sufficed; but since 1969, we can be sure that the painted Moon had to be replaced with a rocky equivalent. You see?' He winked at Kate. 'A conspiracy theorist might point to the very different quality of the Moon's far side to its Earth-visible near side – mocked up in a hurry, perhaps?'

'Oh, bullshit, Cornelius,' Malenfant said tiredly.

Kate said, 'You actually have numbers for all this?'

Malenfant grunted. 'Numbers, yeah. The mathematics of paranoia.'

Cornelius, unperturbed, tapped at his desktop surface, and a succession of images, maps with overlays and graphs, flickered over its surface. 'We can estimate the resources required to run a perfect planetarium of any given size. It's just a question of quantum mechanics and thermodynamics.' He flicked a smile. 'Graduate physics. Two equations.

'Look here. For much of its pre-agricultural history humanity consisted of small roaming bands with little knowledge, save for tentative trading links, beyond a disc on the Earth's surface with radius of a few kilometres. To generate planetariums on such a scale would require no more than a few per cent of the energy available to a planetary-scale civilization: *we* could probably do it.

'But by the time you have to fool a cohesive culture covering a hundred kilometres – that's a lot smaller than the Roman Empire, say – the capabilities of that planetary-level civilization would be exceeded.

'The bigger the planetarium, the harder it gets. We can characterize our modern globe-spanning civilization by the radius of Earth and a depth corresponding to our deepest mines. To generate a planetarium on such a scale would exceed even the capability of a civilization able to master the energy output of a single star.

'A future human culture capable of direct exploration of the centre of the Earth, and able to reach comets twice as far away as Pluto, would exhaust the resources of a galaxy.

'And if we reach the stars, we would test the resources of any conceivable planetarium . . .'

Kate was bewildered by the escalation of number and concept. 'We would?'

'Imagine a human colonization disc of radius a hundred light years, embedded in the greater disc of the Galaxy. To simulate every scrap of mass in there would exceed in energy requirements the resources of the entire visible universe. So after that point, any simulation *must* be less than perfect – and its existence prone to our detection. The lies must end, sooner or later. But, of course, we might not have to wait that long.'

'Wait for what?'

'To crash the computer.' He grinned, cold; on some level, she saw, this was all a game to him, the whole universe as an intellectual puzzle. 'Perhaps we can overstretch their capacity to assemble increasing resources. Rushing the fence might be the way: we could send human explorers out to far distances in all directions as rapidly as possible, pushing back the walls around an expanding shell of space. But advanced robot spacecraft, equipped with powerful sensors, might achieve the same result . . .'

'Ah,' said Kate. 'Or maybe even active but ground-based measures. Like laser echoing. And *that's* why you pushed Project Michelangelo.'

Malenfant leaned forward. 'Cornelius – *what have you done?*'

Cornelius bowed his head. 'By the logic of Fermi, I was led to the conclusion that our universe is, in whole or in part, a thing of painted walls and duck blinds. I wanted to challenge those who hide from us. The laser pulse to Centauri – a sudden scale expansion of direct contact by a factor of thousands – was the most dramatic way I could think of to drive the controllers' processing costs through the roof. And it must have caught them by surprise – our technology is barely able enough to handle such a feat – those critics were right, Malenfant, when they criticized the project for being premature. But they did not see my true purpose.'

Kate said slowly, 'I can't believe your arrogance. What gave you the *right* –'

'To bring the sky crashing down?' His nostrils flared. 'What gave *them* the right to put us in a playpen in the first place? If we are being contained and deceived, we are in a relationship of unequals. If our controllers exist, let them show themselves and justify their actions. *That* was my purpose – to force them out into the open. And imagine what we might see! *The fire-folk sitting in the air! / The bright boroughs, the circle-citadels there! . . .* Do you know Gerard Manley Hopkins?'

Malenfant shook his head. 'You were right, Kate. The guy is crazy.'

Cornelius studied them both. 'To practical matters. When the anomalies are visible to all, disorder among the foolish herds will follow. Soon flights will be grounded, the freeways jammed. If you wish to leave –'

Malenfant touched Kate's hand. 'Where is home for you?'

She shrugged. 'I have an apartment in LA. I don't even know where my parents are. Either of them.'

'It's not a time to be alone. Go be with your mom.'

'No.' She was shuddering. Her involvement in all this had long passed that of a journalist attached to a story; now she was just another human being, staring bewildered at the approaching hurricane – but here she was at the eye of the storm, and something about Malenfant's strength reassured her. 'Let me stay. Please.'

He nodded brusquely, avoiding her eyes. 'Cornelius, if you have nowhere else to go –'

Kate said, 'How long?'

Cornelius shrugged. 'The math is chancy. Twenty-four hours at best.'

It feels like half the population of the human race has downloaded.

'Into what?'

Into anything they can find. Some folk are trying to create self-sentient copies of themselves, existing entirely within the data nets. The ultimate bunker, right?

'I thought that is illegal.'

So what do you think the data cops are going to do about it today?

'Anyhow it's futile. A copy wouldn't be *you.*'

You tell me. There are philosophical principles about the identity of indiscernibles: if a copy really is identical right down to the quantum level, then it has to be the original . . . Something like that. Anyhow I doubt it's going to be achieved in the time left.

'I'm surprised we aren't running out of capacity.'

There have been a few crashes. But as ends of the world go, this is an odd one, Kate. Even now it's still just a bunch of funny lights in the sky. The sun is shining, the water supply is flowing, the power is on.

And, you know, in a way it's an exciting time; inside here, anyhow. There's a kind of huge technological explosion, more innovation in the last few hours than in a decade.

'I think I should go now. I have people I'm meant to be with, physically I mean –'

Damn right you should go.

'What?'

More room for me, sister.

She felt affronted. 'What use is huddling here? This isn't a nuclear war. It's not even an asteroid strike. Rodent, there might be *nothing left* – no processors to maintain your electronic nirvana.'

So I'll take my chance. And anyhow there's the possibility of accelerated perception: you know, four subjective hours in the tank for one spent outside. There are rumours the Chinese have got a way to drive that ratio up to infinity – making this final day last forever – hackers are swarming like locusts over the Chinese sites. And that's where I'm headed. Get out of here. There won't be room for everybody.

'Rodent –'

Wake up, wake up.

Kate, with Malenfant and Cornelius, stood on Mike's porch. Inside the house, the baby was crying.

And in the murky Houston sky, new Moons and Earths burst like silent fireworks, glowing blue or red or yellow, each lit by the light of its own out-of-view sun.

There were small Earths, wizened worlds that reminded her of Mars, with huge continents of glowering red rock. But some of them were huge, monster planets drowned in oceans that stretched from pole to pole. The Moons were different too. The smallest were just bare grey rock like Luna, but the largest were almost Earth-like, showing thick air and ice and the glint of ocean. There were even Earths with pairs of Moons, Kate saw, or triplets. One ice-bound Earth was surrounded by a glowing ring system, like Saturn's.

Kate found it hard not to flinch; it was like being under a hail of gaudy cannonballs, as the alternate planets flickered in and out of existence in eerie, precise silence.

It was just seven days since the failed echo from Centauri.

'I wonder what's become of our astronauts,' Malenfant growled. 'Poor bastards.'

'A great primordial collision shaped Earth and Moon,' Cornelius murmured. 'Everything about Earth and Moon – their axial tilt, composition, atmosphere, length of day, even Earth's orbit around the sun – was determined by the impact. But it might have turned out differently. Small, chance changes in the geometry of the collision would have made a large difference in the outcome. Lots of possible realities, budding off from that key, apocalyptic moment . . .'

Malenfant said, 'So what are we looking at? Computer simulations from the great planetarium?'

'Phase space.' Cornelius seemed coldly excited. 'The phase space of a system is the set of all conceivable states of that system. We're glimpsing phase space.'

Malenfant said, 'Is this what we were being protected *from*? This – disorderliness?'

'Maybe. As we evolved to awareness we found ourselves in a clean, logical universe, a puzzle box that might have been designed to help us figure out the underlying laws of nature, and so develop our intelligence. But it was always a mystery why the universe should be comprehensible to our small brains at all. Maybe we now know why: *the whole thing was a fake*, a training ground for our infant species. Now we have crashed the simulator.'

'But,' said Kate, 'we aren't yet ready for the real thing.'

'Evidently not. Perhaps we should have trusted the controllers. They must be technologically superior. Perhaps we should assume they are morally superior also.'

'A little late to think of that now,' Malenfant said bitterly.

No traffic moved on the street. Everybody had gone home, or anyhow found a place to hunker down, until –

Well, until what, Kate? As she had followed this gruesome step-by-step process from the beginning, she had studiously avoided thinking about its eventual outcome: when the wave of unreality, or whatever the hell it was, came washing at last over Earth, over *her*. It was unimaginable – even more so than her own death. At least after her death she wouldn't know about it; would even that be true after *this*?

Now there were firebursts in the sky. Human fire.

'Nukes,' Malenfant said softly. 'We're fighting back, by God.

Well, what else is there to do but try? God bless America.'

Saranne snapped, 'Come back in and close the damn door.'

The three of them filed meekly inside. Saranne, clutching her baby, stalked around the house's big living room, pulling curtains, as if that would shut it all out. But Kate didn't blame her; it was an understandable human impulse.

Malenfant threw a light switch. It didn't work.

Mike came in from the kitchen. 'No water, no power.' He shrugged. 'I guess that's it.' He moved around the room, setting candles on tables and the fire hearth; their glow was oddly comforting. The living room was littered with pails of water, cans of food. It was as if they were laying up for a snowstorm, Kate thought.

Malenfant said, 'What about the softscreens?'

Mike said, 'Last time I looked, all there was to see was a loop of the President's last message. The one about playing with your children, not letting them be afraid. Try again if you want.'

Nobody had the heart.

The light that flickered around the edges of the curtains seemed to be growing more gaudy.

'Kind of quiet,' Mike said. 'Without the traffic noise –'

The ground shuddered, like a quake, like a carpet being yanked from under them.

Saranne clutched her baby, laden with its useless immortality, and turned on Cornelius. 'All this from your damn-fool stunt. Why couldn't you leave well enough alone? We were fine as we were, without all *this*. You had no right – no right . . .'

'Hush.' Malenfant moved quickly to her, and put an arm around her shuddering shoulders. 'It's okay, honey.' He drew her to the centre of the room and sat with her and the infant on the carpet. He beckoned to the others. 'We should hold onto each other.'

Mike seized on this eagerly. 'Yes. Maybe what you touch stays real – you think?'

They sat in a loose ring. Kate found herself between Malenfant and Saranne. Saranne's hand was moist, Malenfant's as dry as a bone: that astronaut training, she supposed.

'Seven days,' Malenfant said. 'Seven days to unmake the world. Kind of Biblical.'

'A pleasing symmetry,' Cornelius said. His voice cracked.

The candles blew out, all at once. The light beyond the curtains was growing brighter, shifting quickly, slithering like oil.

The baby stopped crying.

'Hold my hand, Malenfant,' Kate whispered.

'It's okay –'

'Just hold my hand.'

She felt a deep, sharp stab of regret. Not just for herself, but for mankind. She couldn't believe this was the end of humanity: you wouldn't exterminate the occupants of a zoo as punishment for poking a hole in the fence.

But this was surely the end of the world she had known. The play was over, the actors removing their make-up, the stage set collapsing – and human history was ending.

I guess we'll never know how we would have turned out, she thought.

Now the peculiar daylight shone *through* the fabric of the walls, as if they were wearing thin.

'Oh, shit,' Mike said. He reached for Saranne.

Cornelius folded over on himself, rocking, thumb in mouth.

Malenfant said, 'What's wrong? Isn't this what you wanted? . . .'

The wall dissolved. Pale, disorderly light spilled over them.

Kate watched the baby's face. His new eyes huge, Michael seemed to be smiling.

DREAMS (II)

THE TWELFTH ALBUM

In the bowels of a ship that would never sail again – mourning our friend Sick Note – Lightoller and I sat cross-legged on the carpet of a disused Turkish Bath, and listened to John Lennon.

'Fooking hell,' said Lightoller. 'That's "Give Me Some Truth". It was on the *Imagine* album. But –'

'But what?'

Lightoller, he says now, knew there was something different about the cut from the first chord. It might even be true. That's Lightoller for you.

'Typical Lennon,' he said moodily. 'He goes whole bars on a single note, a single fooking chord. Manoeuvring around the harmonies like a crab. But –'

'But *what?*'

'Where's the fooking echo? Lennon solo always drowned his vocals. This is clean and hoarse. Sounds more like a George Martin production.'

Not very interested, I was staring at the ceiling. Gilded beams in crimson.

We never knew how Sick Note had managed to blag himself quarters on the ship itself, let alone the Turkish Bath.

It was a whole set of rooms, with a mosaic floor, blue-green tiled walls, stanchions enclosed in carved teak. Queen Victoria's nightmare if she'd been goosed by Rudolph Valentino. As Lightoller said, Sick Note must have been the best fooking porter in this whole floating fooking hotel.

'Of course,' Lightoller was saying, 'it's plausible they'd have used this. Lennon offered it as a Beatles song during the *Let It Be* sessions in Feb '69. It was the way they worked. They were trying out songs that finished up on *Let It Be* and *Abbey Road*, even their solo albums, as far back as early 1968 –'

'*Who* would have used the song for *what?*'

'The Beatles. On their next album. The twelfth.'

Compared to Lightoller, and Sick Note, I'm a dilettante. But I'm enough of a Fabs fan to spot the problem with that.

I said, 'The Beatles released eleven LPs, from *Please Please Me* through *Let It Be*.'

'You're counting UK releases,' said Lightoller.

'Of course.'

'And you don't include, for instance, the *Yellow Submarine* album which was mostly a George Martin movie score, or the *Magical Mystery Tour* album they released in the US, or the EPs –'

'Naturally not. So there was no twelfth Beatle album.'

'Not in this fooking world,' said Lightoller mysteriously.

John sang on, raw and powerful.

Oddly enough, Lightoller and I had been talking about other worlds even before we found the album, in Sick Note's abandoned quarters, deep inside the old ship.

You have to picture the scene.

I suppose you'd call it a wake: twenty, thirty blokes of indeterminate age standing around in the Cafe Parisien on B Deck – loaned by the floating hotel's owners for the occasion, all tumbling trellises and ivy pots and wicker chairs – drinking beer and wine we'd brought ourselves, and looking unsuccessfully for tortilla chips.

'Morgan Robertson,' Lightoller had said around a mouthful of Monster Munches.

'Who?'

'Novelist. 1890s. Writes about a fooking big Atlantic liner, bigger than anything built before. Loads it with rich and complacent people, and wrecks it one cold April night on an iceberg. Called his ship the *Titan* –'

'Spooky,' I said dryly.

'In another world –'

'Yeah.'

Lightoller is full of crap like that, and not shy about sharing it.

But I welcomed Lightoller's bullshit, for once; we were, after all, just distracting ourselves from the fact that Sick Note was gone. What else are words for, at a time like that?

Bored, morbid, a little drunk, we had wandered off, through the ship, in search of Sick Note.

We had come through the foyer on A Deck, with its huge glass dome, the oak panelling, the balustrades with their wrought-iron scroll work, the gigantic wall clock with its two bronze nymphs. All faded and much scarred by restoration, of course. Like the ship. Like the city outside which we could glimpse through the windows: the shops and maritime museums of Albert Dock to which the ship was forevermore bolted, and the Liverpool water-front beyond, all of it under a suitably grey sky.

I said something about it being as if they'd towed the Adelphi Hotel into Liverpool Bay. Lightoller made a ribald remark about Sick Note and the nymphs.

We had walked on, down the grand stairway from the boat deck, along the corridor where the valets and maids of the first-class passengers used to stay, past the second-class library and the third-class lounge, down the broad stairs towards steerage.

The second track was, of all things, 'It Don't Come Easy'.

'Ringo,' I said.

'Yeah. Solo single in April '71.'

I strained to listen. I couldn't tell if it was different. Was the production a little sharper?

'Every Night', the next track, was Paul: just McCartney being McCartney, pretty much as he recorded it on his first solo album.

'Sentimental pap,' I said.

Lightoller frowned. 'Listen to it. The way he manages the shift from minor to major –'

'Oldest trick in the book.'

'McCartney could make the sun come out, just by his fooking chromatic structure.'

'I'll take your word for it.'

'And it's another track they tried out for *Let It Be*. And –'

'What?'

'I think there are extra lyrics.'

'*Extra?*'

The next track was quiet: Harrison's 'All Things Must Pass'.

Lightoller said sourly, 'Another *Let It Be* demo. But they were still keeping George in his place. First track he's had.'

The playing was simple and exquisite, little more than solo voice with acoustic guitar, closer to the demo George had made of the song in his Beatle days than his finished solo-album version.

I didn't recognize the next song, a Lennon track. But it got Lightoller jumping up and down.

'It's "Child of Nature",' he kept saying. 'Fooking hell. They tried it out for the *White Album*. But Lennon held it back and released it on *Imagine* after the split –'

Now I recognized it. It was 'Jealous Guy'. With different lyrics.

'Fooking hell,' said Lightoller. 'This has only appeared on a bootleg before. And besides, this is no demo. It's a finished fooking production. *Listen* to it.'

That's Lightoller for you. Excitable.

We had reached the alleyway on E Deck that Sick Note had always called Scottie Road. You could tell this was meant for steerage and crew: no carpet, low ceilings, naked light bulbs, plain white walls.

We worked our way towards the bow, where Sick Note had lived the last years of his life.

'Sick Note would never go down to the engine rooms,' Lightoller reminisced.

'"Reciprocating engines",' I said, imitating Sick Note. '"A revolutionary low-pressure turbine. Twenty-nine boilers."'

'Yeah. All nailed down and painted in primary colours to show the kiddies how a steam ship used to work. Not that they care.'

'No,' I said. 'But Sick Note did. He said it was humiliating to gut a working boat like that.'

'That was Sick Note.'

Away from Scottie Road the ship was a labyrinth of rooms and corridors and ducts.

'I never could figure out my way around here,' I said.

Lightoller laughed. 'Even Sick Note used to get lost. Especially after he'd had a few with the boys up in the Smoking Room. Do you remember that time he swore –'

'He found a rip in the hull?'

'Yeah. In a post room somewhere below. A rip, as if the boat had collided with something. And he looked out –'

Sick Note had found Liverpool flattened. Like the Blitz but worse, he said. Mounds of rubble. Like the surface of the Moon.

'. . . And he saw a sky glowing full of shooting stars,' Lightoller said.

It was one of Sick Note's favourite drunken anecdotes.

'Of course,' said Lightoller, 'this old scow probably wouldn't have survived any sort of collision. The hull plates are made of brittle steel. And it was just too fooking big; it would have shaken itself to pieces as soon as a few rivets were popped –'

Lightoller can be an anorak sometimes. But he used to be an engineer, like me.

Correction. He is an engineer, like me.

At last, on F Deck, we found the Turkish Bath.

Sick Note had made this place his own: a few sticks of furniture, the walls lined with books, posters from rock concerts and Hammer horror movies and long-forgotten 1960s avant-garde book stores plastered over the crimson ceiling. I found what looked like a complete run of the *International Times*. There was even a kitchen of sorts, equipped with antiques: a Hoover Keymatic washing machine and a Philco Marketer fridge-freezer and a General Electric cooker. Sick Note always did have an uncanny supply of artefacts from the 70s, or late 60s anyhow, in miraculously good condition, that the rest of us used to envy. But he'd never reveal his source.

And there were records here too: vinyl LPs, not CDs (of course), leaning up against each other all the way around the edge of the floor like toppling dominoes; the stack even curved a little to get around the corners. The odd thing was, if you looked all the way around the room, you couldn't see how they were being supported – or rather, they were all supporting each other. It was a record stack designed by Escher.

Lightoller bent to look at the albums. 'Alphabetized.'

'Of course.' That was Sick Note.

'Let's find the Beatles. B for Beatles . . .' He grunted, sounding a little surprised. He pulled out an album with a jet-black sleeve. 'Look at this fooking thing.' He handed it to me.

The cover was elementally simple: just a black field, with a single word rendered in a white typewriter font in the lower left-hand corner.

God.

Just that, the word, and a full stop.

Nothing else. No image. Not even an artist name on the cover. Nothing on the spine or the back of the sleeve; no artist photos or track listings, or even a copyright mark or acknowledgement paragraph.

The record slid into my hand inside a plain black-paper inner sleeve. And when I tried to pull out the record itself – reaching inside to rest my fingers on the centre label – the sleeve static-clung to the vinyl, as if unwilling to let it go.

The vinyl was standard-issue oil black. The label was just the famous Apple logo – skin-side up on what was presumably Side One, the crisp white inner flesh on Side Two. Still no track listing – in fact, not even a title.

I held the album by its rim. I turned it this way and that; the tracks shone in the light.

Sometimes I forget how tactile the experience of owning an album used to be.

'Look at that fooking thing,' breathed Lightoller. 'A couple of scratches at the rim. Otherwise perfect.'

'Yeah.' An album that had been played, but cared for. That was Sick Note for you.

We exchanged glances.

Lightoller lifted up the glass cover of Sick Note's deck, and I lifted on the album, settling it over the spindle delicately. Lightoller powered up the deck. It was a Quad stack Sick Note had been working on piece by piece since 1983. No CD player, of course.

When the needle touched the vinyl there was a moment of sharp crackle, then hissing expectancy.

The music came crashing out.

And that was how we found ourselves listening to a puzzlingly different John Lennon.

Side One's last track was the big song McCartney used to close *Ram*: 'Back Seat of My Car'.

'Another song they tried for *Let It Be*,' Lightoller said. 'And –'

'Shut up a minute,' I said.

'. . . What?'

'*Listen* to that.'

In place of the multi-track of his own and Linda's voices that McCartney had plastered over his solo version, the song was laced with exquisite three-part harmonies.

Beatle harmonies.

'Lightoller,' I said. 'I'm starting to feel scared.'

Lightoller let the stylus run off, reverently.

I got up from the carpeted floor and walked around the room. There were framed photos and news clippings here, showing scenes from the ship's long history.

I couldn't mistake the pounding piano and drum beat that started Side Two.

'"Instant Karma",' I said.

'A single for Lennon in February 1970.'

'In our world.'

'Great fooking opener.'

Then came a Harrison song, a wistful, slight thing called 'Isn't It A Pity'.

Lightoller nodded. 'Another one they tried out in early 1969, but never used. It finished up on George's first solo album –'

The next track was 'Junk', a short instrumental McCartney wrote when they were staying with the Maharishi in India. It sounded like the theme of a TV show about vets. But it was sweet and sad.

We just listened for a while.

With the gentle guitars playing, it was as if Sick Note was still there, in this cloud of possessions, the very air probably still full of a dusty haze of him.

. . . Here was the ship in dry dock in Belfast after her maiden voyage, with that famous big near-miss scar down her starboard flank. Here she was as a troop carrier in 1915, painted with gaudy geometric shapes that were supposed to fool German submarines. Here was a clipping about how she'd evaded a U-boat torpedo, and how she'd come about and rammed the damn thing.

'"Old Reliable",' I said. 'That was what Sick Note used to call her. The nickname given her by the troops she transported.'

'He loved this old tub, in his way,' said Lightoller.

'And he did love his Fabs.'

That was Sick Note for you.

The fourth track was 'Wah Wah', another Harrison song, a glittering, heavy-handed rocker with crystal-sharp three-part harmony.

Lightoller nodded. 'Harrison wrote this when he stormed out during the *Let It Be* sessions. He kept it back for his solo album –'

'In our world.'

'Yeah. I guess he brought it back to the group, in the *God* world . . .' Lightoller was sounding morbid. 'But there was no fooking twelfth album, was there? This must be a fake. Or an import, or a compilation, or a bootleg. Once Allen Klein and Yoko got involved they were all too busy suing each other's fooking arses off.'

I picked up the album sleeve. For a possession of Sick Note's, it was surprisingly grubby. Specked with some kind of ash. I felt obscurely disturbed by Lightoller's loss of faith in his own bull-shit. 'But all the Allen Klein stuff started in the spring of '69. Even after all that, they made another album together.'

'*Abbey Road*.' Lightoller nodded, and I thought the spark was back in his eyes. 'Yeah. They might have hung around for one more try. But something would have had to be different.'

I kept roaming the room.

More clippings, of how White Star had merged with Cunard in 1934, and the old ship lost out to newer, faster, safer vessels. She was almost sold for scrap – but then was put to work as a cargo scow in the southern Atlantic – and then, after Michael Heseltine parachuted into Merseyside after the 1981 riots, she was bought up and bolted to the dock, here at Liverpool, and refitted as a hotel, the centre of what Heseltine hoped would become the regen-eration of the city. Fat chance.

'So,' I said, 'your theory is that this album comes from an alter-nate world where somebody shot Allen Klein.'

Lightoller shrugged. 'It might have been something bigger.'

'Like what?'

'I don't know. Like nuclear fooking war.'

'Nuclear war?'

'Sure. If the world was going to fooking hell, it would have touched everybody's lives, even before the Big One dropped. For the Beatles, it just kept them in the studio together a while longer.'

'Their contribution to world peace,' I said sourly.

'They used to think like that,' he said defensively. 'What was that story of Sick Note's? He found some way out the back of the boat –'

I tried to remember. 'Liverpool was rubble.'

The surface of the Moon. But Sick Note might have found some cellars, where things had survived – GE cookers and Philco fridges and Beatle albums – sheltered from the fire storms, preserved since 1971.

I felt scared again.

'We're running out of LP,' said Lightoller.

'So what?'

'So there are a lot of great tracks not here,' he said. 'Like Lennon's "Love". Harrison's "My Sweet Lord" and "What Is Life". "Imagine", for fook's sake.'

'They must have been issuing singles.'

'You're right.' I could hear the pain in Lightoller's voice. 'And we'll never get to hear them.'

'But if we found the other world . . .'

We were silent for a while, just listening.

Lightoller said softly, 'What if we couldn't find our way back?'

I shrugged. 'Sick Note did.'

He eyed me. 'Are you sure?'

Neither of us tried it.

The fifth track was 'God', in which Lennon, at great and obsessive length, discarded his childish idols, including Jesus, Elvis, Dylan, even the Beatles.

'Oh,' said Lightoller. 'There's the compromise. What McCartney agreed, to keep Lennon on board.'

'That and not doing "Teddy Boy".'

'At least Lennon didn't push for "Mother".'

I tried to focus on the music. The production didn't sound to me much different from the way I'd heard it on the *Plastic Ono Band* album.

But some unruly piece of my brain wasn't thinking about the Beatles.

Sick Note had said he saw shooting stars, everywhere, over ruined Liverpool. *Oh.*

'Comets,' I said.

Lightoller said, 'Comets?'

'Not nuclear war. Comets. That's it. If a comet hit the Earth, debris would be thrown up out of the atmosphere. Molten blobs of rock. They would re-enter the atmosphere as –'

'A skyful of shooting stars.'

'Yes. They would reach low orbit, keep falling for years. The *air* would burn. Nitrous oxides, acid rain – the global temperatures would be raised all to hell.'

'So in some alternate world a comet landed on Yoko, and the Beatles never broke up.' Lightoller laughed at me. 'Only a true Beatles fan would lay waste to the fooking Earth to get a new album.'

'I don't think this is funny, Lightoller.'

'God' wound to its leaden close. The stylus hissed on the spiralling intertrack, and Lightoller and I watched it. I knew what he was thinking, because I was thinking exactly the same.

This would be the ultimate track – the twelfth track on the twelfth album.

The last new Beatles song we would ever hear.

Because, of course, by now we both believed.

It was recognizable from the first, faded-in, descending piano chords. But then the vocals opened – and it was Lennon.

'It's "Maybe I'm Amazed",' I said, awed. 'McCartney's greatest post-Beatles song –'

'Just listen to it,' said Lightoller. 'He gave it to Lennon. *Listen to it.*'

It didn't sound like the version from our world, which McCartney, battered and bruised from the break-up, recorded in his kitchen.

Lennon's raw, majestic voice wrenched at the melody, while McCartney's melodic bass, Starr's powerful drumming, and Harrison's wailing guitar drove through the song's complex, compulsive chromatic structure. And then a long coda opened up, underpinned by clean, thrusting brass, obviously scored by George Martin.

At last the coda wound down to a final, almost whispered lament by Lennon, a final descending chord sequence, a last trickle of piano notes, as if the song itself couldn't bear to finish.

The stylus hissed briefly, reached the run-off groove, and lifted.

Lightoller and I just sat there, stunned.

Then the magic faded, and I got an unwelcome dose of reality: a sense of place, where we were and what we had become: two slightly sad, slightly overweight, forty-ish guys mourning the passing of a friend, and another little part of our own youth.

Lightoller put the album back in its sleeve, and slotted it carefully into its place.

We found our way outside, to the dock.

The old ship's stern towered over us. It was late by then, and the ship blazed with light from its big promenade decks and the long rows of portholes. Up top, I could see the four big funnels and the lacework of masts and rigging. People were crossing the permanent gangways that had been bolted to the side of the ship, like leashes to make sure she never shook loose again.

'She's an old relic,' said Lightoller. 'Just like Sick Note.'

'Yeah.'

'All fooking bullshit, of course,' he said.

'Other worlds?'

'Yeah.'

It was starting to rain, and I felt depressed, sour, mildly hung over. I looked up at the stern and saw how the post-Heseltine paint job had weathered. Even the lettering was running. You could still make out the registration, LIVERPOOL, but the ship's name was obscured, the I's and T's and the N streaking down over the hull, the A and C just blurred.

We turned our backs and started the walk to the bus stop.

Lightoller and I don't talk about it much.

I'd like to have heard those singles, though.

AFTERWORD

A reference to Dante's 4-dimensional geometry, mentioned in 'Dante Dreams', can be found in 'Dante and the 3-sphere', Mark Peterson, *American Journal of Physics* vol. 47, pp 1031–35, 1979.

'Martian Autumn' is dedicated to Colin Pillinger and the *Beagle 2* team. The *Beagle*, riding ESA's *Mars Express* spaceprobe, is scheduled for launch in June 2003, and should land on Mars at Christmas that year.

'Sun God' is based on a splinter of fact. Earth and Moon swim together through a sea of objects called NEOs: near-Earth objects, or Earth-crossing asteroids, with orbits similar to Earth's. Some are rocky, some metallic, others are rich in organics. Some NEOs have orbits which seem too close to Earth's for coincidence. A small, dim NEO called 1991JW, discovered at Palomar Observatory, tracks the Earth so closely that it has been suggested it may be a Saturn V third stage, abandoned after delivering its Apollo to the Moon, lost and rediscovered decades later. The story is a pendant to my novel *Titan*.

Of the stories set in the multiple universes of the Manifold, 'Sheena 5' is set in a closely related variant cosmos to that of my novel *Time*; 'Huddle' and 'The Fubar Suit' are pendants to *Space*; and 'Grey Earth' is a pendant to *Origin*. 'Refugium' and 'Touching Centauri' are each set in their own parallel universes within the Manifold. The ideas in 'Touching Centauri' are further explored in 'The Planetarium Hypothesis: A Resolution of the Fermi Paradox,' *Journal of the British Interplanetary Society*, vol 54 nos. 5/6, May/June 2001.

'Tracks' derives from an interview I conducted with Apollo 16 astronaut Charles Duke in July 1999, the thirtieth anniversary of

Apollo 11's first lunar landing. The story is based on a vivid dream Duke had before his only spaceflight.

'Marginalia' is a pendant to my novel *Voyage*. 'The Gravity Mine' is a pendant to my novel *Time*.

I was honoured to win the British Science Fiction Association Award for best short story in 1998 for 'War Birds'. 'Moon-Calf' won the Analog Magazine Analytical Laboratory Award for best short story of 1999, while 'Sheena 5' won the same award for 2000, and won second place in the Theodore Sturgeon Memorial Award for best short fiction of 2000. 'Huddle' won the Locus Award for Best Novelette for 2000. 'The Gravity Mine' was a Hugo nominee for best short story of 2000.

Stephen Baxter
Great Missenden, UK
December 2001

ACKNOWLEDGEMENTS

'Moon-Calf', first published in *Analog*, July–August 1998.
'Open Loops', first published in *Skylife*, ed. Gregory Benford and George Zebrowski, April 2000.
'Glass Earth, Inc.', first published in *Future Histories*, ed. Stephen McClelland, 1997.
'Poyekhali 3201', first published in *Decalog 5*, ed. Paul Leonard and Jim Mortimer, September 1997.
'Dante Dreams', first published in *Asimov's*, August 1998.
'War Birds', first published in *Interzone* 126, December 1997.
'Sun-Drenched', first published in *Bending the Landscape*, ed. Stephen Pagel and Nicola Griffith, June 1998.
'Martian Autumn', first published in *Mars Probes*, ed. Mike Ashley, 2002.
'Sun God', first published in *Interzone* 120, June 1997.
'Sun-Cloud', first published in *Starlight 3*, ed. Patrick Nielsen Hayden, 2001.
'Sheena 5', first published in *Analog*, May 2000.
'The Fubar Suit', first published in *Interzone* 123, September 1997.
'Grey Earth', first published in *Asimov's* December 2001.
'Huddle', first published in *Magazine of Fantasy and Science Fiction*, May 1999.
'Refugium', first published in *Mammoth Book of Science Fiction*, ed. Mike Ashley, 2002.
'Lost Continent', first published in *Interzone* 164, February 2001.
'Tracks', first published in *Interzone* 169, July 2001.
'Lines of Longitude', first published in *Dark of the Night*, ed. Stephen Jones, November 1997.
'Barrier', first published in *Interzone* 133, June 1998 (as 'The Barrier').
'Marginalia', first published in *Interzone* 143, May 1999.

'The We Who Sing', first published in *Microcosms*, ed. Gregory Benford, 2002.
'The Gravity Mine', first published in *Asimov's*, April 2000.
'Spindrift', first published in *Asimov's*, March 1999.
'Touching Centauri', first published in *Asimov's* June 2002.
'The Twelfth Album', first published in *Interzone* 130, April 1998.